MW01441899

MARIUS-ADRIAN

THE MOUNTAIN OF DRAGONS

Second Book of
THE SONG OF THE LAST SUNSET

ISBN: 9798340737342

Table of Contents

Names

I punched the willow in front of me, then turned furiously towards Aella.

"I want names!" I roared.

"No," she calmly replied, completely unimpressed by my fury.

The serenity in her cold eyes, burning like two ice globes, and the monotony on her ash-colored face ignited a wildfire of frustration within me. She walked past me and sat on the edge of the small lake, looking at the billions of sparkling dots scattered across the dark canvas of the sky.

"It's a quiet night," she whispered, her voice barely audible above the soft breeze. "I love the silence, don't you?"

"I love honesty," I told her, kneeling in front of her. "I want you to tell me the names of every man who dishonored you. Now!"

For a few heartbeats, she remained silent, her gaze fixed on the tranquil surface of the lake. Then, without a glance in my direction, she uttered a single word.

"No."

We stood at the foot of Gherbonat, a mountain from the Redat chain, in the northernmost reaches of Derahia. Beyond the lake's edge lay a gaping depression where the village of Bragovik nestled. The hundred warriors who accompanied me, members of my clan, were hidden deep in the forest. For a while, it was a relief to escape their annoying company and to have some peaceful time with the woman I loved, but things quickly deteriorated.

Before Aella was captured by my twin brother, Larion, and brought to Romir, she was the servant of Garen the Black, the former leader of the clan that was now under my rule. She was subjected to his will through a magic ring, bound to it seven hundred years ago by my ancestress, Arika Grayfang. Garen used her exceptionally powerful magic to mask his bloody attacks on the lands of Derahia, and to slip away unscathed whenever our soldiers closed in on his trail.

That night, Aella confessed to me that Garen used to abuse her often, and because of the ring, she was forced to endure it. And not just him, but his close friends too. It hurt that I wasn't there for her when she needed me most, and I knew I couldn't heal her scars, but that wouldn't stop me from killing all those who caused them. To the last one.

"Why?!" I thundered.

"Because you can't go into camp and kill your own people. The others will lose their trust in you, and now is not the time for that."

I halted my tongue for a few seconds, weighing. "I don't care. What, are you going to let them get away with it?"

At that time, I was twenty-one years old. I was young, reckless, impulsive, and used to consider myself invincible, and all the precarious situations I had escaped alive in recent months had only reinforced my beliefs.

She stroked my hair with a sad smile. "For now."

I clenched my jaw, pulling away from her touch. "Tell me who it was? Yorric?"

"No. Anyway, what you would do to them would be child's play compared to what I will do. Revenge, like any delicacy, must be served at the right moment to be fully savored."

I lifted my brows. "When?"

"When I consider."

"Of course! How in the Burning Hells didn't I think of that?"

She remained silent, drawing her knees up to her chest and wrapping her arms around herself, steadfastly avoiding my eyes. A gentle breeze whistled through the trees, rippling the starry reflection on the lake's mirror. I realized that the bitterness in my voice saddened her, but I was too stubborn to back down.

"I want a name, Aella," I insisted, trying to temper my voice.

"Fine, so be it," she conceded. "I will tell you *one* name, and you are free to take his life. After you're done, I will tell you others."

"You could have done that from the beginning, damn it."

She hesitated for a long while, looking thoughtful and indecisive over the calm waters, and for a few moments, I started to wonder if I really wanted to know. It was clear she didn't want to tell me, it was clear she felt compelled. She took a deep breath and turned to me.

"Larion," she said apathetically, her shimmering eyes pinning me.

"You're lying!" I burst out furiously, grabbing her arm.

"Not at all. You can ask him when you get the chance."

"Larion wouldn't do that."

"Let go of my arm," she told me, and the words sounded more like a warning than a request.

"When?"

"On the way to Romir, after he captured me. Let go of my arm, Darion!"

I didn't do it. I was frozen, and all the interactions with Larion since Aella's arrival at the palace played through my mind. I remembered his strange behavior in her presence and the guilty looks he threw her way. Several times it seemed he wanted to tell me something, but he would change his mind at the last moment, and I was too caught up in my own troubles to press the issue. "*On the way back...*" he began when he handed me the ring, but abruptly stopped, promising to tell me another time. "*I'm sorry for other things too,*" he murmured to Aella on the day we took Melchior's life, his gaze heavy with shame as it remained fixed on the ground. It all made sense. *The scoundrel! The bastard! The piece of shit!*

I could feel a slight vibration around me, a sign that Aella was using the ether, and my fingers unclenched from her forearm. I was lifted into the air and thrown like a stone into the frozen lake.

"What the hell is wrong with you?!" I yelled after I managed to surface.

"You were too heated," she yelled back, her voice raised to mask the gentle lapping sound of the small waves. With a slight frown, she absently caressed her arm. "You needed to cool down."

"I regret giving you the ring!"

The calm had melted from her gaze, replaced by fury. She grinned angrily through clenched teeth, and her long, pointed ears peeking through strands of obsidian hair lay back, just like a cat ready to pounce. The air vibrated again, and a giant invisible hand grabbed me, yanking me from the water and throwing me further toward the center of the lake. After I surfaced again, I saw Aella's silhouette swiftly disappearing into the dense shadows of the forest.

I swam to shore and crawled onto the muddy, slippery grass, then let myself fall on my back, catching my breath.

"Larion, you bastard. Just wait until I get my hands on you," I whispered.

I remember shaking with fury. The hatred for my own brother delicately intertwined with the longing I still felt since leaving Romir. There is no greater pain than having to hate the people you loved. "*One day, brother,*" I said to myself.

I took a deep breath.

Aella was right, the night was quiet, silent, dead. The only sound I could hear was the faint song of the waves stretching onto the shore, pushed by the mountain's breath.

"You deserved it," I heard Kayra's voice coming from behind me.

"On that we both agree," I said, quickly getting up and turning towards her.

I hadn't felt safe enough to stand with my unprotected back at her ever since she aimed her drawn bow at me. All our recent interactions were short and tense, ending more or less with her growling some insults at me. She had followed us on the night we escaped execution and saw the carnage we left on that field. She reproached me, not just once, that some of the soldiers we killed didn't even want to fight, but just to escape with their lives. I can't say for sure whether she was right or not, because in the chaos of battle, it was hard to tell if those who crossed my path wanted to kill me or not.

"Mentioning the ring was unwise of you, knowing how much suffering it caused her. A folly, like everything you've been doing lately, on the other hand."

"Did you come all this way just to tell me how stupid I am?"

Mathias materialized from the blue and faded shadows that the night light wove, spider-webbed among the trunks of the trees. "Yenna told us about the lake, and we came to see it too," he said in a clear voice. "We didn't know we'd run into you here."

Mathias was a Shadow Walker, a man who had crossed the threshold of death, but had been brought back to the world of the living from the Realm of Eternal Night, also known as Evernight. Initially, he was under the control of a necromancer, but his freedom was restored with the latter's death. He looked just like a human being, tall and pale with hair black as a raven's feather. His eyes, however, were completely dark; two black voids gaping on his face.

"The water is cold, I just checked," I joked. He smiled. Kayra rolled her eyes, then sat next to me.

"Are you still determined to send your people away?" Mathias asked me, leaning over and running his hand over the stones on the shore.

"Yes, tomorrow morning, I'll choose someone to lead them in my absence. We can't enter Bragovik with a hundred armed individuals. However, I'll keep Yenna and Kaldur."

"I'll keep them," Kayra repeated. "You talk as if they're animals."

"We'll need someone who knows the mountain paths even a little. The road to Yermoleth won't be an easy or short one," I replied, ignoring her stung.

"Would releasing the Daughters of the Night be a wise thing?" Mathias pondered aloud.

He stood up, holding a slightly flat-shaped stone between his fingers. After gazing thoughtfully at the forest, he spun, sending the stone skimming across the lake, where it bounced several times off the water's surface before sinking.

For a while, we remained silent, watching the ripples that originated from each point where the pebble crushed the lake's starry reflections. Waves clashed against each other, giving birth to more waves. Just like our choices do.

"Do you think it wouldn't be?" I asked cautiously.

The Shadow Walker didn't answer. He bent down, feeling the shore again. Kayra studied me in silence, waiting for my actual response. Mathias hurled another stone, disturbing once again the peace that the lake had barely reclaimed.

"I would have their rings. They would be under my control," I told them. "I wouldn't allow them to harm others."

"As strange as it sounds, I believe you," Kayra said. "I know that if the rings end up with you, you will keep them under control. But will Aella let you take the rings?"

"Why wouldn't she?" I asked her with feigned indifference, trying to pretend that this thought hadn't crossed my mind at all in recent days. I shivered, feeling the night's coolness kissing my damp body.

"Aella likes to hold the reins, as far as I can see, and whoever has the girls will be able to control everything," the archer told me. "As I said, it was foolish to tell her you regret giving her the ring... the real folly, however, was that you gave it to her in the first place."

"I spoke in anger," I snapped. "I don't regret giving her the ring, for Heaven's sake. I trust her."

She snorted with anger. "You just got blown into the middle of the lake like a..."

"What Kayra means to say," Mathias interjected, "is that the Daughters of the Night would be a formidable weapon in the wrong hands."

"In anyone's hands," Kayra corrected, standing up.

"I don't intend to use them as a sword, but as a shield," I assured her. "And I bet my life that Aella won't either. I need the peace they would offer, nothing more."

"As you say," she muttered uncertainly. "I'm going for a walk around the lake."

"I'll follow you in a few moments," Mathias told her.

She nodded, then started along the shore with almost inaudible steps. Mathias watched her silently, and the corners of his pale lips lifted in a crocked smile.

"She's beautiful, isn't she?"

"She is," I agreed. Kayra was tall, with a body fit enough for shooting a bow, even a longbow perhaps, and hair as red as the sun before sunset, long enough to reach her slim waist.

"Finding someone to love you to death is a blessing, but finding someone to love you even beyond, is a miracle."

"Agreed."

"Have I ever told you how I died?"

"No, I'm sure I'd remember. People I talk to don't often tell me about how they died."

He laughed, sending another stone skimming over the water before it plunged into the depths.

"We had a fight right before. I told her I didn't want to see her again and left. It wasn't long before I ran into the necromancer and his army of the dead. She was the only thing on my mind as I was fading away. I thought about how our last memory could have been a beautiful one, if not for a meaningless argument."

I was immediately overwhelmed with guilt and regretted my hasty reaction earlier.

"I should go to Aella," I said.

"And I should follow Kayra. I wish you a good night."

"And to you."

The way back to camp was longer than I remembered, and more than once, I felt lost among the eerie trees. Those moments of solitude gave me a chance to reflect on the past four months and how fate, or perhaps the gods, had determined my life. I was so far from home and the path I needed to take would lead me even further away. Besides, I felt a mocking hatred for my brother creeping into my life; perhaps the same my ancestors felt for theirs. Would I end up killing him; would he end up killing me?

"No!" I growled. Not us. I hated him for what he had done to Aella, and I'll probably beat him unconscious the next time we meet, but nothing more. I decided that in a few years, when the waters had calmed and the wounds had healed, I would visit him. If they would ever heal.

"*Time heals all wounds,*" I told myself.

King Alfred was determined to take my life. I didn't hate him for it; in fact, I respected him because I had killed his son, and it was his duty to avenge his death. He would arrive in the Redat mountains in a few weeks, leading a huge army. According to Yenna, the clan people wouldn't be able to withstand the invasion, lacking unity, experience, and equipment. They wouldn't be able to fight against the Frevians. They would run, hide, or die. I didn't plan to fight them either. I wasn't too worried they could find us, for the mountain range was absolutely vast, stretching from east to west over more than one hundred fifty kilometers. Yet, I wasn't going to underestimate him.

The guild of wizards spread across Miria, the Circle, had sent its most powerful assassins after us, and unlike Alfred, they were a more immediate threat. On the night we escaped from Romir, the wizard master Kolan lost his life, as did his apprentice Lars and possibly the other apprentice, Erik. In response, the Tower of Fire had set its hounds on us. I didn't know how many or where they were, but what I did know was that they were getting closer.

A branch snapped under my foot, making me startle and curse angrily. Instinctively, my hand flew to the hilt of the sword at my waist as I squinted, scanning the dark forest. Although the moon hung above, the tangled claws of the trees blocked its light like a veil. I quickened my pace. Eyes that didn't exist watched me from everywhere, the soft breeze whispering against my neck like a breath. Maybe it was the assassins, or maybe it was all in my head... or maybe it was something worse.

Only when I heard the voices of my people and saw the light of torches flickering through the trees did I realize how tightly I was gripping the sword in my hand. I breathed a sigh of relief as the playful light of the campfires welcomed me. I left the darkness behind.

Merwin was sitting among several young women, skillfully manipulating the flames before them to take on all sorts of shapes. The girls were thoroughly amused by the young wizard's tricks.

"Make a crow! Can you make a crow?" one of the girls requested. When the wizard raised his eyebrows in amusement, the girl, thinking she had mispronounced the word in the common tongue, began to imitate the sound of a crow.

"I'm not sure it's possible," he sighed.

As soon as he finished speaking, he raised his hands, and the flames rose from the campfire, shaping themselves into the form of a bird in flight. The young girl burst into laughter, throwing her head back and clapping her hands. Merwin had blended well among the mountain people; much better than I had.

"*Az'fielumra*," I heard Yenna's voice as she cut my path.

"*Az'falandra*," I replied.

She eyed me in silence for a few moments, probably noticing my wet clothes, then began, "I went near Bragovik."

"I went for a swim," I replied, faintly amused.

"The village is fortified. They've built a wooden wall as tall as a man, placed sharp stakes in front of the wall, and guards beyond it. A few houses outside were burned. It's likely they were attacked by another clan in the recent days. It won't be easy to raid them, but with the Black Queen's powers..."

"We will not raid them," I interrupted, giving her a stern look.

"But..."

"You told me that we have animals and our own crops. Why, in the name of all that you hold holy, would we want to steal from others?"

"We have enough to survive, chief, but not nearly enough to feast. This is our way."

I crossed my arms and shot her the ugliest scowl I could muster. "It was your way. Whoever disagrees should come and tell me personally. When we want to feast, we will work harder, not steal."

"I understand."

"Who do you think is most capable of leading the people in my absence?"

"Are you leaving?"

"Yes. You and Kaldur will accompany me. We will be gone for a few weeks, or months."

"You honor us. May I ask where we are going?"

"We're looking for someone who lives in these mountains."

"An ally?"

"That remains to be seen."

I didn't know if Yermoleth was an ally or not. Not even Aella could say for sure, as the last time she met him was seven hundred years ago. But we needed to reach Shartat, the Mountain of Dragons, because that's where the key to the dungeon of the Daughters of the Night was last seen. Yermoleth could help us.

"Do you know these mountains?"

"I know them like the back of my hand; you've made the right decision choosing me."

"Back to my first question."

"I would suggest Yorric, but I know you're not entirely fond of him."

Yorric was one of the closest friends of Iorval, the former clan leader, and he harbored a deep hatred towards me for his death. Twice in the past week, he had defied my orders, and I warned him that if he disobeyed a third time, his head would roll. That threat subdued him for the moment, but his hatred remained like a smoldering fire, waiting to flare up.

"The only people I trust from here are too green to lead."

"In that case, Eldric."

"I was thinking of him too," I confessed. "I'll announce him tomorrow at dawn. Have you seen Aella?"

"She went deeper into the forest," she told me, nodding towards the silhouette of a dead oak tree in the distance, shielded from the bold light of the flames.

I tipped my head and walked in the direction she indicated. Regihold's booming laughter stormed through the camp, as he watched Eldric nearly lose his balance after swinging at air with Spear, his massive war hammer. The weapon was indeed a spear attached to a block of stone. Its real name was Dawnbringer, and it belonged to a prophecy from Verdavir, speaking of a legendary warrior named Ezerekai, who would one day pull it from the stone. Unable to unleash the weapon, Regihold didn't wait for that warrior to arrive; he chipped away at the stone until it took the square shape of a hammer's weight. The spear's tip protruded from the other side of the weight, gleaming oddly under the firelight.

For a while, I stood still, pondering whether I should approach Eldric now or wait to make the announcement before all the camp tomorrow. I couldn't say I trusted him enough to lead my people in my stead, as we had barely exchanged a few words, but he seemed like a level-headed man, and besides, I trusted the others even less. Ultimately, I decided to wait. That was a task for tomorrow.

I left the campfire's light and plunged into the darkness where Aella awaited me. Her luminous blue eyes pierced the night's heart, tracking my every step. She sat stiff with her legs tucked under her, choosing not to react in any way as I approached. I sat beside her, watching the dozens of fires burning below, glimmering among the night-shrouded woods. There was something soothing about it.

"They produce too much light," I said to her, taking her hand and bringing it to my lips.

"I've masked them," she replied listlessly. "No one would see them unless they come very close."

"I know. I almost got lost because of it."

She didn't respond, withdrawing her hand. Only then did I notice Lyra, sleeping beside her, wrapped in a thick woolen blanket. The little girl, just nine years old, had clung to Aella since the day we met. I reached out to cover her better, but Aella slapped my hand away, then ran her fingers across the girl's cheek. A smile appeared on her face; one I'd often seen on mothers watching their children. The smile vanished when she turned to me.

"You're clumsy, you'll wake her."

"Waking Lyra is no easy task," I laughed.

"You'll catch a cold, change your clothes!" she replied, throwing me a leather bag in which I had a change of clothes.

"I'm sorry."

A tear ran down her cheek, and she tilted her head back, taking a deep breath. Furiously, she wiped away the tears.

"Change your clothes," she hissed.

I obeyed, dressing in silence, recalling the words I said. The ring had been a yoke of slavery, and I had told her I wanted to keep her bound.

"I shouldn't have said that," I whispered, sitting next to her again and wrapping my arms around her.

She kept her face blank and her mouth shoot, then pushed me away and freed herself from the embrace, then lay down with her head on a folded blanket. I placed my hand on her thigh, tracing the fine line of her body with my fingertips, moving up her back and back down her leg.

I struggled to stay awake, but not after long I fell asleep. That night, I had one of the most vivid dreams of the past weeks.

Aella was looking at me with tearful, exhausted eyes, forcing a smile. She cupped my face in her hands and bent my head, planting a kiss on my forehead.

"It's the only way," she said quietly.

"No!" I snarled. "We must resist! We have to try."

The wind blew cold around us, and the moon shone in the clear sky with a light as strong as daylight's, but much paler. We were high above the clouds, on the flat top of a massive pyramid. Cyclopean towers stood out like blackened, dead fingers amidst the sea of clouds below, reaching out as if to grasp the stars. Who could build something like that?

There was something else there. Something that radiated pure evil, filling my heart with the deepest dread. Only once in my life had I felt something like it.

Yohr'Sherrat.

"I love you!" Aella muttered, kissing me one last time. She turned, stepping towards a perfectly round hole in the floor's center.

I tried to run after her, but something, I couldn't see what, grabbed me. "We must stop!" I cried, but whatever was carrying me leaped from the top, flying above the clouds. I was tucked into a giant hand, looking through the crack between two reddish-scaled fingers at the swarm of shadows that were darting from underneath, flying in our wake. Aella, just a faint shadow barely visible in the distance, fell into the gaping pit, then a bright light emerged from within, illuminating the entire sky. I heard a boom as the entire structure collapsed through the cloud carpet. The evil floating in the air evaporated.

"Aella!" I screamed with all my strength, feeling my heart shatter just like that black stone pyramid.

I woke up with her standing over me, shaking my shoulders, her eyes full of worry. I wanted to speak, but my words choked in my throat.

"Is everything alright?" I heard Regihold's deep voice nearby. Merwin and Yenna were behind him.

"It was just a nightmare," Aella told them.

My cheeks probably burned with embarrassment. I looked up at them, trying to appear calm despite the rapid breaths that made it seem like I had been running for hours. Merwin sighed in relief, and Yenna sheathed her short swords.

For a few moments, we all remained in awkward silence, then Aella spoke, "Dawn is still far. We should get back to sleep."

"Good idea," Regihold agreed, throwing his hammer over his shoulder. Yenna wished me a peaceful night, and Merwin nodded goodbye.

"What did you eat to grow so big?" I heard Yenna's voice as she walked away with Regihold.

"Oh! What hasn't he eaten?" Merwin replied, and Regihold gave him a friendly slap on the shoulder.

Lyra looked at me half-asleep.

"Just a nightmare," I assured her.

She smiled, stifling a yawn, then closed back her eyes.

There were no stars left in the sky.

"I'm sorry," I murmured to Aella.

"Me too," she said, laying her head on my shoulder. "Me too."

Secrets

Excerpt from Elena's journal, dated the twenty-ninth day of the sixth month, Iura, in the year six hundred twenty-three after the Conversion:

... This morning was unusually cold. A messenger from my father came with the first rays of dawn. I saw him from the window, entering the palace courtyard, shivering under his thin cloak, the hood pulled over his eyes.

Master Radagrim arrived shortly thereafter, his usual foolish smile in tow, to inform us that my father had already led his army across the Derahia's border. Larion, who had just been awakened by the old wizard's persistent knocking, scowled at the tidings but held back any comment or threat he might have considered, instead inclining his head in resignation.

"Should I go out to meet my father-in-law, then?" he asked me.

"There's no need," I replied in the most polite tone I could muster at that early hour.

He clicked his lips. "Oh, but it would be proper."

I knew where this conversation was heading, so I chose not to respond. The news that the Frevian army is going to cross his lands had irked him from the moment he heard them, and the fact that my father hadn't even asked for permission, simply announcing his intentions, was the last straw.

"I should summon my bannermen and confront him; that's the proper course of action. A response in kind!"

"That wouldn't be wise, sire," Radagrim interjected cautiously.

"Thanks for the advice," the king muttered. "You are dismissed."

"Queen Lenore will accompany him," the old man added quickly.

"Mother?!" I exclaimed.

"Are you asking me?" Larion snapped.

"Did she mention the reason for her visit?" I asked, ignoring my betrothed.

"It wasn't mentioned in the letter. Probably because of recent events..."

"Thank you," I interrupted him. "Please leave us."

"Very well!" he said, smiling broadly.

"I'll come to you in an hour or two," the king told him before the wizard could leave. "We have important matters to discuss… in private."

"I'll be waiting," the old man replied, then bowed and left.

Larion started rummaging through the closet, flipping through the neatly arranged clothes and leaving a mess behind. I noticed he didn't mind making a mess in the room, knowing I would be the one to clean up after him. I'll have to teach him to clean up his own mess soon.

"In private," I repeated.

"That's what I said, yes."

"Alright, then so be it."

He dressed in silence, his face frowned in a sneer. I felt more than once he was about to say something but didn't. I didn't push it. I sat on the bed with my hands pinned between my thighs and started going over what I had to do that day. Sneak out unnoticed again, find the girl, bring her to the palace... keep her safe. Or did Larion know? It seemed impossible; I had made sure not to be followed. Should I tell him about Jane? Not yet.

Mother will soon arrive in Romir—another unsettling thought, one more variable I had to keep in mind. She likes to spread her webs wherever she goes, skilled at making others play along with her tune, and often, her webs overshadow mine. "*Two vipers,*" Dad used to call us whenever we argued, which was often.

I needed to push that thought aside; today, there was no room for such worries. My focus was on Jane; getting to her before my father's assassins could. I was caught in a game of *commanders and generals* against him, and I had no intention of losing.

Larion flinched, cursing. He lunged towards the wardrobe and flung its doors open with a swift movement, then began to rummage through the clothes.

"Where the hell are you?" he growled, his voice barely a whisper.

"What are you looking for?" I asked, exasperated.

"That voice," he barely whispered, then spun to face me, "You wouldn't understand!"

He slammed the doors shut, murmuring something for himself.

"Will you have these fits often?" I asked.

He stormed out of the room without saying another word to me. For a long time, I stared at the door that slammed shut behind him, trying to understand what made him suddenly so cold. I tended to believe it was my father's fault. After the Night of the Blood Moon, things had started to go well between us. We were there for each other, soothing our pain and bandaging the wounds caused by his brother and the Black Queen, but something shifted in him. Have I done something?

I had lost hope that Darion would be captured by those from Derahia, especially since my betrothed had significantly reduced the number of soldiers hunting him, after learning about the army gathering in Frevia. It was foolish of my father to come with so many soldiers, because if Larion decided to declare war, he would have the Circle on his side, being the one *invaded.* Even if Father's intentions were not to invade Derahia, it wouldn't matter at all. But Larion would not declare war on us, would he?

I smiled when I realized I was holding my hand over my stomach, without breathing, hoping to feel some movement. I had been doing this a lot lately, although I knew it would be at least another two or three months before our son would start to kick. Our *son*. I took the Black Queen's words for granted; she said it would be a boy, and being such a powerful witch, she probably will be right. His name will be Rorik.

I ate a few pieces of lemon cake, then dressed and sat next to the window, careful not to miss the call to prayer. For a few moments, I began to wonder if it had already passed. It didn't take long for the bells of the Great Temple to ring, followed shortly by smaller ones scattered throughout the city, and this, for the first time since I can remember, brought a smile to my lips, albeit accompanied by a gnawing sensation in my stomach.

I went down to the Great Hall, and for some reason I couldn't understand, I felt very confident that this time, I would succeed in finding Jane. She disappeared shortly after Rorik's death, probably out of fear of my father. Maybe mine too. I hadn't had much opportunity to converse with her, and from our brief, monotonous, and formal exchanges, I'm unsure of the impression I left on her, but I'm certain she doesn't regard me as a friend. Neither do I see her as one, but she carries my brother's child in her womb, and her safety has become my personal problem. Rorik loved her. He died with her handkerchief tied around his arm.

Damn you, Darion!

"Princess Elena, it's a delightful day, don't you think?" Beatrice greeted me the moment she saw me descending into the hall.

"It is," I replied, smiling at her. "Perfect for a walk. Would you like to come?"

"Of course."

We had such a formal conversation for appearances every time we pretended to run into each other accidentally in certain parts of the palace. Though she serves as my maid, judging by the elegance of her attire, most would mistake her for a lady of Frevian descent. I knew how to take care of my girls.

We had hardly started walking when a girl of about twelve crossed our path, smiling timidly at us, seemingly gathering the courage to ask something. It took me a few moments to recognize her. She had the same blue eyes, the same golden hair, the same timid smile, and the same rosy, plump cheeks with high cheekbones. She was the spitting image of her older sister, Arlieth.

"Princess Elena," she greeted me, inclining her head. "Have you seen the King by any chance?"

"He might be in Radagrim's tower, but I'm not sure," I replied. "Aethelwit, right?"

She nodded happily, pleased that I knew her name.

"Then I'll wait here. I don't like getting close of that old decrepit tower."

"How are you feeling, Aethelwit?"

"Good, thank you!"

Like her sister, she was a bad liar.

"I haven't had the chance to say this yet, but I'm very sorry for your loss. Arlieth was also a dear friend of mine."

She nodded again, pressing her lips together, a small red line across her now pale face.

"How is your family doing?" I continued.

"Father is gone all day searching for Dari..." she began but suddenly fell silent, unsure whether to utter Darion's name or not. My betrothed quickly lost his temper when someone did. " Father is always out of town, hunting," she resumed, "and Mother refuses to leave her room since Arlieth died. She keeps saying we should return to Blackstone, but we never do. Larion promised he would go with me to her grave, to bring her flowers. "

The glossy shimmering of tears appeared in her eyes, but she quickly blinked them away.

"What flowers will you be taking her?" I asked, mustering a smile.

"Roses and tulips. She always told me that she couldn't decide which she liked more, so we'll bring... we'll bring..."

Her voice broke, and her chin started to tremble uncontrollably as tears streamed down her cheeks. I hugged her tight, then gently pushed her towards the exit.

Damn you, Darion!

Beatrice let out a loud, shuddering sigh. She looked at me curiously over Aethelwit's head, probably wanting to know what we would do with her next, because we needed to get to Oswin as soon as possible. I raised my shoulders askance, beginning to wonder if it would be a good idea to take her with us. Probably not. Certainly not.

"Please forgive my outburst," she apologized as soon as we stepped onto the trodden ground of the palace courtyard, trying to compose herself.

"You have nothing to apologize for," I responded, embracing her again. "You've been through a lot. If you can't find Larion, we'll go with you to Arlieth when we return, in a few hours."

"Thank you," she murmured and departed a few steps before halting. "Do you think we'll have justice?" she asked in a low voice. "For Arlieth, for the king, and for your brother."

"We will," I replied, trying to sound confident, though I harbored the same doubts. "Evil cannot go unpunished. They will find Darion."

"I was talking about the Black Queen," the girl said, "not about Darion. She was the source of evil. She twisted his mind. If it wasn't for her, none of this would have happened."

"Sooner or later, she will answer for her crimes," Beatrice assured her with a kind smile.

We said our goodbyes and watched her return to the palace with small, uncertain steps. I hadn't realized it until then, but Aethelwit was right. Aella had gotten under the prince's skin from the first nights she was brought here, increasingly inserting herself into his life and pushing others out. Darion was a man, that making him inherently foolish, and Aella was as beautiful as she was cunning, controlling his every move. She did a better job with him than I could do with Larion.

"Poor thing," said Bea, brushing a strand of black hair from her face.

"Aella will die," I said smiling.

"I hope so."

"But before that, she will suffer. A lot."

She widened her eyes, raising her thin eyebrows, then smiled, either loving the cruelty in my gaze or being relieved that it wasn't directed at her.

The halberdiers at the gates bowed their heads as we passed by. Bea winked at one of them, making him straighten his back and puff out his chest. Some men are so predictable. Why couldn't Larion be like them?

"Maybe she's already dead?" Beatrice suggested.

"You're very optimistic today."

"Speaking of optimistic, have you talked to Julia?" she asked later, somewhat cautiously.

I hesitated. "No. Does she want to talk to me?"

"She's going back to Frevia, with the rest."

I laughed. Julia was leaving too. I didn't know whether I should be angry or sad, but I couldn't feel anything. Almost all the maids from my personal suite had chosen to return to Frevia in recent weeks. Some missed their homes; others were afraid of my new home. I couldn't blame them, nor did I intend to persuade them to stay. I've known some for years, others only for a few months, but the only one I ever considered a close friend was Beatrice.

"Are you leaving too?"

It was her turn to laugh.

"Leave where? I like it here. Besides, I have no one in Frevia. Or anywhere else for that matter, you know that. I only have you."

"My home is your home," I told her.

She cast me a sidelong glance, grinning. "Of course." Despite her chuckles, she couldn't conceal the sadness in her eyes. "Do you think we'll find Jane at that inn?"

"*I fear not,*" I almost said, but I bit my lip, reminding myself that negative thoughts would serve no purpose. "I hope so. It's the best lead we've had."

"She's probably a scaredy-cat. We'll need to be careful with her, or she'll get meow and run away. And, you know how fast cats run when they're afraid."

"Wait until you see how fast I can run. Anyway, she did well to hide. My father is an unpredictable man, and without Rorik, he wouldn't hesitate to raise his hand against her. He fears the child in her womb. If it's a boy, he could claim the throne when he comes of age."

"Can I say something? Something that might upset you."

I rolled my eyes, gasping, because I knew what she was going to say. Even so, I nodded, "Say."

She tucked her head between her shoulders. "Isn't your father right? A bastard on the throne of Frevia doesn't sound too good."

"I won't let anyone kill my brother's child," I responded sharply, ignoring the reason in her words. In what kind of world do we live, that our conscience is shaped to consider the murder of a child reasonable? A cursed one, no doubt.

"And what will you do if he is a boy and claims the right to throne when he comes of age?"

"I'll see then. Maybe I'll have his tongue and hands cut off, so he can't claim anything."

"A clever idea," she mocked me, then laughed nervously. "I should write a book with all your clever ideas, like when you thought that a fresh haircut would make Jane fonder of you. I should call it 'The Elenistic Innovations.'"

"No need, I have it all in my diary. Speaking of the child, until he comes of age, I'll have time to think of a better plan. For now, let's find her and bring her to the palace. I'll hire her to work for me, and if you agree, she'll be your roommate."

She wrinkled her nose and snorted, ready to refuse, but before she could speak, I added, "I'll get you a larger room, with two beds, more light... more wardrobes. My mother is coming to Romir, and I'm too scared to leave Jane alone."

"Fine," Beatrice sighed. "I'll take care of her, as long as she doesn't snore. As for your mother, I don't know what to say."

"I'm not thrilled at the thought either."

"I'll take your word for it. You did have your quarrels in Montrias."

My mother and I have never been the best of friends. Not even friends. We tolerated each other, but that was how far the string stretched. She was always much fonder to Rorik than to me, and since Melchior appeared, she's completely forgotten I exist. Not that I cared. She is a very cunning woman, very clever, but I'm not going to let anyone, not even her, harm Jane or her unborn child.

"Is it moving?" Beatrice asked, noticing my hand over my stomach.

"Not yet. But when it does, I'm not going to miss it. Jane should be in her fifth or sixth month by now. It's probably kicking already."

"A terrifying thought," she pondered out loud.

"What?"

"To have something alive inside you, moving. Uh, I never want to be a mother."

"What will you do if your husband wants a child?"

"Who says I'll have a husband? I have you, that's enough for me."

"As you say."

Before long, we arrived at Lady Vera's house on Acacia Street. Only today did I notice that the street probably got its name from the multitude of acacia trees planted on both sides of the road. It reminded me a lot of the roads back home, filled with trees and tall houses with elegant patterns embedded in the stone walls. The red tile roofs indicated the status of the people living there; wealthy people, merchants, perhaps even knights from well-known families or lords.

Oswin was waiting for us on the stone stairs before the threshold, idly playing with a small knife. He looked at us with the same bored, uninterested expression he usually adopted when Beatrice was around.

"You didn't hurry at all. Where have you been wandering?"

"A little respect, boy, you're speaking to a princess, not your mother," Bea scolded him.

"I'm sorry. Where have you been wandering, Princess?" he asked, bowing deeply.

"Got anything better to do?" I asked him.

"Not until the King returns. After that, I'll leave with him on Darion's trail. I hope we find Jane by then."

"With a bit of luck, we'll find her today."

Lady Vera, cheerful as always, was waiting inside with cakes and berry tea. Due to constant nausea, I only accepted the tea, and even that with some reluctance. I don't feel very comfortable accepting any drink from an old lady who has vision problems and who, among other things, sells poisons. For Vera, the fact that we were both born on the piece of land our ancestors decided to call

Frevia meant a lot. I don't know how Oswin found her, but the old lady was more than happy to help us.

"You are very beautiful today, Queen Elena."

She always called me that, and I would smile and compliment her in turn. Today I complimented her green dress with puffy sleeves, more suited for grand events than for receiving guests. She always called me *Queen*, and I absolutely loved how it sounded, though I tried not to show it. I stopped telling her I wasn't yet a queen, because it seemed not to matter to her.

"Can I offer you anything else, my queen?"

"No, thank you very much, Vera. You're already doing plenty for us."

"The cakes were truly delicious," Beatrice added as well, resting her hands flat on the table.

We went up to the room where Vera had stored all the clothes we wore when we went out and didn't want to be recognized. Oswin followed and leaned against the wall opposite the door, waiting. Once again, I wondered what was he hiding behind his perpetually scowling and bored expression. He had a reason for staying in Romir, instead of returning to Frevia, but he refused to share it with me.

Once again, I found myself staring at the odd tapestry on the wall of that room. It depicted a bizarre landscape, half of it a scorched realm, covered with black clouds and dead trees with twisted trunks and claw-like branches, over which the head of a blood-red lion presided. The other half showed a field covered in greenery and blooming trees, with the sun shining above the clouds like cotton. In that corner stood the head of a black lion.

Beatrice nodded towards the door, giving me a playful wink.

"I can't undo your corset," she said loud enough for Oswin to hear from outside. "I think the lace is knotted."

I rolled my eyes. "Are you sure?" I asked, playing along.

"Very sure, and I think mine is stuck too. Maybe we should call Oswin to help?"

"But you're naked," I replied, bringing a hand to my mouth in an attempt to suppress my laughter.

"Don't worry, he doesn't seem to like women."

I heard Oswin snort loudly from the other side of the door, then stomp down the stairs. We both burst into laughter.

"You like to tease him, don't you?" I asked, shaking my head.

"Absolutely! He's always so grumpy and easy to tease. I wish I could have seen his face."

"He's in love with you," I said.

"I know, and that makes everything even more delicious."

"He's not a bad-looking boy, though."

"That's how it is with these lords. They'd bed you but wouldn't marry you because you're not noble and daddy would scold them. Not all are like Darion."

I was shocked and gave her a reproachful look, but she just shrugged nonchalantly and turned back to the cupboard, pulling out a pair of brown trousers that clung to the leg. We dressed in silence. Like the last time, we chose simple brown woolen clothes, hoping not to stand out on the streets. I tied my hair in a simple bun at the top of my head, leaving only a few strands loose.

"I'm sorry," she said when my hand fell on the door handle.

"You have nothing to apologize for."

"Darion is a bastard who deserves to die, no doubt about that. In fact, I swear I wish it. But at least he didn't abandon Aella after using her, as most at court would."

"You're right there," I admitted.

In the living room, Oswin listened intently to Vera's explanations about why it was advisable to mix black viper venom with ground poppy root to make it harder to detect during autopsies. I couldn't help but wonder why Oswin was suddenly interested in poisons, but I was quickly distracted by Beatrice's grin, which soon turned into a muffled laugh.

The lord stood up, thanking Vera for her hospitality and explanations, then left ahead without a word to us, making Beatrice laugh even harder. He waited outside, fully covered in his black cloak.

"Where to?" he asked.

"Aren't you feeling hot under that cloak?" Beatrice asked, raising her eyebrow.

"She was seen at the Flying Rat inn," I replied. "I heard it's not too far from here."

"I know where it is," said Oswin. "Follow me."

We walked with our heads down, hoping that no one on the crowded streets of Romir would recognize us, although it was unlikely. Especially since Beatrice's large bottom, very visible through the tight trousers, attracted all eyes, just like honey attracts flies.

I decided that tonight I would tell Larion about Jane, maybe even ask for his help if we couldn't find her. I knew he would find out eventually, and I thought it better if he heard it from me. Of course, he already knew, but I would only find out a few hours later.

The inn was a stone building that rose three stories high, with a winged rat painted above the door. The name of the inn was written in golden letters on the solid wooden door. Using a pest as the image of your business wasn't exactly a good strategy, but nevertheless, there were quite a few people inside for such an early hour. The innkeeper, a thin and fat man with an aggressive face, waited for us behind the counter, polishing a mug large enough to be used as a bucket. He smiled, revealing a mouth full of rotten teeth. Beatrice scoffed at the strong smell of alcohol and took a step back. Oswin scanned the room uneasily.

"Welcome! What can I get for you? A room, food?" the man asked, speaking with a strange, foreign accent that I'm pretty sure I hadn't heard before.

"Information," I replied, returning his smile.

"That might be more expensive than both, miss."

"We're looking for a girl," I said, lowering my voice. "About the same height as me, with light, almost white hair, green eyes. Have you seen her?"

"Why are you looking for her?"

"It's none of your business," Oswin scoffed. "Have you seen her or not?"

"The girl is family," I told him. "She made a mistake and ran away from home; we're just trying to bring her back."

"And why did you come to look for her here?"

"Other information, for which we paid good money, sent us here," I answered.

"Well, I'll be!" he exclaimed, leaning over the counter, and scrutinizing me closely. "I know many girls who look like you described."

"How many of them are staying here?" I asked, and he shrugged.

"None," he answered after a while. "You paid for nothing. Whoever sent you to me was making a fool of you."

I placed a gold coin on the counter. "Are you sure?" His eyes glittered as he reached for the coin, but I pulled it back before he could grab it.

"Come with me," he said, heading through a door behind the counter.

We followed without question, and the only one of us who was thinking clearly, Beatrice, stuck close to me and whispered, "I don't think this is a good idea."

"Why?"

"Why?" she repeated, nervously, taking a sharp breath. "I hope Oswin knows how to use that sword."

We followed him through a dark, narrow, and dusty hallway with no windows, which ended in a series of steps leading down to the basement. I felt the cakes I had eaten that morning rising in my throat and swallowed hard. The innkeeper descended into the cellar, and, after exchanging suspicious glances with Beatrice we followed like stupid mice, unknowingly walking into the trap.

The wooden steps creaked terribly under our weight, and the stale, thin air below only intensified my nausea. The cellar was spacious, dimly lit by the sickly rays seeping through a pair of tiny windows near the ceiling, half-covered by brittle shelves laden with bottles of various shapes and sizes. A few barrels were lined up in a corner, emitting a strong smell of sauerkraut, and several shelves crammed with boxes of all kinds of vegetables were stuck to the walls on either side of the door.

Everything was in disarray. Nothing was aligned. Burning Hells, it was chaos, and my mind craved for order. I blinked several times, trying to suppress the ringing in my ears and the pressing sensation of my stomach twisting.

Beatrice screamed when a fat rat jumped over her foot, which made Oswin chuckle. The innkeeper just raised his shoulders in a shrug.

"It's called the Flying Rat for a reason," he joked. "Now come on, tell me, what business do you have with Jane?"

A wave of warmth and calm enveloped my body, and for a few moments, I believed that the last two weeks of searching were finally about to bear fruit.

"We're friends," I told him. "She ran away from home, and we want to bring her back."

"How much are you willing to pay?"

"It depends," I said quickly, as Oswin seemed to be losing his patience. "If you bring her to us, a lot. If you tell us exactly where we can find her, decently. If you give us a rough idea of her whereabouts, a few silvers."

"Stay here," he grinned. "I'll go bring her to you."

He hurried off, and before we could react, he slammed the door shut behind him. Oswin dashed towards the door, but the metallic click of the lock echoed before he could reach it. We were trapped, locked inside.

"Oswin began to yank at the door violently, but despite its weathered appearance and trembling joints, it refused to yield.

"We're locked in!" Oswin bellowed.

I turned to Beatrice, who was pale, her eyes shining with tears. Oswin kicked the door, causing it to shudder wildly, then cursed, seeing it was to no avail.

"What are we going to do?" Bea asked, her voice barely a whisper.

"Stay calm, you won't get hurt," I told her.

"How can you be calm, Elena? He's going to kill us!"

"Nothing bad will happen," I assured her, as Oswin kicked the door again. Still nothing.

I had a lot of experience to mask my feelings, I tried so hard to be able to appear something that I was not in front of others, and I'm glad I did. If Beatrice saw the hand of fear that gripped me, she would become even more frightened, and we didn't have time for that; we needed to think. But how to think when nothing was as it should be?

Everything was disordered!

Oswin threw his full weight against the door once more, but it remained resolutely sealed.

"Conserve your energy," I told him calmly. "We might need it."

Bea gasped, trembling. "Need it for what, Elena?" When I didn't respond, she pressed closer to me, her voice urgent, "Are we going to fight? I don't know how to fight, Elena."

Oswin nodded grimly, stepping back and drawing his sword from its sheath. Beatrice whimpered like a frightened child at the sight of the weapon.

"Give me the knife from your back," I told him.

"Heavens!" Bea uttered as she saw me reaching for the knife. "Azerad, please protect us!"

"You don't need Azerad," I said impatiently. "I'll protect you. You won't get hurt."

"Fine. I believe you! Really, I do! But what does he want from us? Heavens, there's a rat here!" Bea spoke so quickly that her voice turned hoarse, drawing in a deep breath before preparing for another round.

"Calm down!" I hissed. "The rat is more scared of you than you are of it, and soon, that will be the case for that innkeeper."

"You won't get hurt, none of you will," Oswin promised. His tense posture reminded me a lot of Prince Darion.

"Footsteps," I said, pulling my friend behind me. Oswin positioned himself between me and the door, ready to fight.

Bea widened her eyes. "There are several," she whimpered.

"Stay behind," Oswin said.

"Only attack if necessary," I ordered him.

He remained motionless, not taking his eyes off the door, almost as if he hadn't heard me. I remember Rorik telling me that Oswin fought against Darion and won, so he must be a pretty skilled swordsman. Few people can boast about beating the rebel prince in a duel.

We heard the key turning in the lock, then the door slammed against the wall, causing some of the shelves to tremble, as four men armed with long knives entered. The innkeeper followed them, closing the door behind him. He glanced at Oswin's sword, then leaned back against the door. His accomplices exchanged tense looks. The fool probably didn't realize Oswin was carrying a sword under his cloak, so his men had come only with knives. Even so, it was four men against one.

"How about you give me the coin," the innkeeper suggested, "and maybe I'll let leave with your lives. Anyway, so much money would only weigh you down in your quest."

"Don't come any closer!" Oswin shouted at one of the four, who took a step towards us.

"You will tell us everything you know about Jane," I said, stepping out from behind Oswin, "you won't get a single copper, and maybe, just maybe, you'll get out of this unharmed. That's the final offer."

Laughter erupted from him, echoed shortly by three of his henchmen. Only three. The fourth, a tall, skinny man with red hair who appeared to be about thirty years old, studied me thoughtfully.

"This one's spirited," the innkeeper sneered to the others. "Maybe we'll keep her for a while."

A torrent of laughter engulfed them again, but the red-haired man remained unaffected, his face locked in a pensive expression. He regarded me silently, with visible shock that intensified with each passing moment. He understood the danger of death they were in. He was beginning to realize who I was.

"You're keeping me for yourselves?" I asked, raising an eyebrow, and stepping completely in front of Oswin. He lowered his sword and muttered something under his breath but didn't try to stop me. He was ready to intervene at any moment. "Castrate him!" I ordered the men in front of me. "Or you will all lose your manhood."

"Big words," our captor growled, pushing himself from the door and advancing toward me.

The redhead swiftly intervened, stepping in front and striking him in the head with the handle of his dagger, sending him crashing to the ground.

"My apologies, Princess Elena. I didn't recognize you at first," the man said, turning to face his bewildered colleagues.

Everyone backed off as if scorched, as I edged closer to the innkeeper. I wanted nothing more than to plunge my fingers into his terror filled eyes and to burst them out like grape berries.

"Where is Jane?" I asked calmly. The cold calm can sometimes be scarier than an outburst of fury.

"Please forgive me, Princess!" the man cried, throwing himself at my feet, his face planted on the ground.

"You were asked a question," one of the four men growled, kicking him with his boot.

They were furious, and understandably so. Although they were just a group of thugs the man whimpering at my feet probably paid, they seemed to fully understand the grave situation they were in.

"She left a few nights ago. She ran out of money to pay for her room, and I threw her out. But I swear I did her no harm. She had a friend, Meredith Grey, who visited her quite often. I heard them talking a few times; the girl lives near the Colorful Square. That's all I know!"

"I believe you," I smiled at him, and for a moment, it seemed his fear dissipated. "You wanted to rob and rape me," I then reminded him.

"No, no, no! I wouldn't have done that. I just wanted to scare you. I'm not a violent man. I've never hurt anyone, believe me."

I pulled out four gold coins and handed them to the redhead. The man hesitantly accepted them.

"If you manage to find this Meredith Grey's house in the Colorful Market, I will give you two more each. I'm sure the innkeeper will give you all the details. Right?"

"Yes, rats eat me if no. I will do everything in my power to help you, I promise."

"Thank you! I hope you're a man of your word."

"I am," he said. "When I give my word, I intend to keep it, no matter what."

"And so will I. As I said earlier, not all of you can leave here with your privates intact," the innkeeper wailed, causing Beatrice to gasp again, covering her mouth. I turned to the men waiting behind him. "Either you or him."

"Hold him!" one of them said, and two others had already thrown themselves at him, pinning him to the ground like a pig, ready to be sacrificed.

"Please, no! Forgive me, Princess Elena," he begged.

"You brought this on yourself," the redhead growled.

"Let's go," Beatrice urged me, grabbing my arm.

I chuckled. "No, I want to watch."

They pulled down his trousers as he struggled, crying, but he wasn't strong enough to escape.

"Enough," I intervened. "I just wanted to scare him. We're all friends here, right?"

The innkeeper nodded spasmodically, a crooked smile on his tear-streaked face. We ascended the stairs, with Oswin and Beatrice trailing behind me, leaving the fat man to sob in the basement, trousers around his ankles.

Beatrice clung to me like a frightened kitten. Once we were outside, I approached the one with red hair, named Jackard. "Tomorrow morning, after the bells of the worship temples ring, I will descend in front of the palace. Bring me news about Meredith's location."

"Do you feel better?" Oswin asked Beatrice as soon as we got onto the street.

"I don't want to hear another word about it," she warned him, walking ahead.

He shook his head, mumbling a "women," before turning to me. "For a moment, I thought you were going to let them castrate him."

I sighed, escaping a giggle. "For a moment, I thought so too. And my mother says I'm heartless."

We returned to Vera's house and changed back into our usual clothes, then Beatrice and I headed back to the palace. Oswin chose to stay, probably continuing his discussion about poisons.

I couldn't remember ever seeing Beatrice so shattered. She had barely spoken a word the entire way back, responding to my questions with forced politeness. I feared she was going to tell me she would return to Frevia, for which I would have blamed only myself. After all, it was because of my misjudgment that we ended up in that basement. Later, however, she admitted she was just ashamed of how she reacted in the face of danger and the fact that she hid behind me. I wasn't upset about that. Beatrice had been my friend, companion, and lover for a very long time.

She stayed in my room until the sun began to hide behind the faded clouds in the west. Before she left, she was again cheerful, bouncy, and jokey as if the gloom outside had covered the sins of that day.

Larion wasn't in the room. He had been absent all day. I rearranged the clothes in his wardrobe, then sat at the desk and began to jot down all the events that had transpired. I was almost finished when my betrothed returned, completely ignoring me, and began to dress in his nightclothes.

"I'm glad to see you, my dear," I started after a while, pushing the journal aside.

"What do you want?" he barked, pulling his nightshirt over his head.

I snapped, tossing my palms flat on the table. "What do I want? To know what's gotten into you! You've been acting like you've lost your mind for a few days now. You pretend I don't exist."

"I don't care whether you exist or not. I have enough on my mind, and probably in my head, to worry about arguing with you. Especially after talking with Radagrim."

"Maybe I should leave. It seems you're bothered by my presence in the same room as you."

He clicked his tongue. "You know where the door is, or do you want me to show you?"

"Jerk!" I burst out.

"Keep making noise," he told me. "I sleep better with noise around."

As strange as it sounded, it was true. In recent days, he had often asked me to recount memories before falling asleep. Often, he didn't even seem interested in what I had to say. He just wanted to avoid silence. He didn't like silence.

"Better tell me what you talked about with Radagrim," I requested.

"I can't."

"Then keep your secrets!"

"As you keep yours. For almost two weeks, you've been sneaking out of the palace with Beatrice and Kharstlan's boy. Why? Actually, no! I don't care why. Get laid with whoever you want, wherever you want."

"But I..." I began after I managed to recover from the shock, but he interrupted me. He was angry, likely waiting for a long time to unleash it all on me.

"If you know that baby isn't mine, you'd better leave the city now, while you still have your head on your shoulders!" he yelled at me.

I jumped up from the table, causing the chair to crash with a muffled sound onto the rugged floor. "How dare you?!" I was determined to knock some sense into him, but he grabbed my hand before I could slap him.

Leaning in slowly towards me, he whispered, "I'm not going to raise Oswin's child, or the cook's, or the stable boy's, or the unwashed redhead's with whom you came out of The Flying Rat today. Is it clear?"

"You are following me," I said tersely.

I sneered furiously and struck him across the face with my free hand. He cursed, then pushed me towards the door while I struggled in vain to resist. Finally, he shoved me out, slamming the door behind me. Fortunately, the hallway was empty. I straightened the hem of my dress and, summoning all the strength and self-control I could muster, walked to Beatrice's room, maintaining a composed and calm demeanor. In my mind, I replayed his words over and over, cursing myself for not disclosing Jane from the start. I knew these outings were risky, but I hadn't realized just how damning it all appeared from an outsider's perspective.

When I saw that Jane's room door was locked, I felt despair slowly taking over. I couldn't hold back my tears anymore. I knocked several times, but no response came from inside.

"Beatrice?" I whispered.

"Coming!" her voice joyfully answered. She opened the door and peeked out. "I thought you were Oswin. He sometimes drops by in the evening with a desire for conversation or company. He usually gives up quickly after realizing he's not invited in."

She immediately noticed the trembling of my chin, which I could no longer conceal, and stepped aside, signaling me to come in. I entered with large, rapid strides and threw myself onto the bed, burying my head beneath a pillow. I didn't utter a word; I simply cried. She hugged me, pressing her cheek against my back in a comforting embrace.

After a while, I dozed off but was awakened by the creaking of the wooden floor. Beatrice was tiptoeing around, trying in vain not to make noise. Usually, I'm a very deep sleeper, according to Larion, but this time, worries kept me partially awake. I turned to her and watched as she tried to quietly open the window. The window hinges refused to keep the silence, whining like a cat stepped on its tail.

"May the rats gnaw on you!" Bea cursed in a whisper, then turned to me. "Sorry, I didn't mean to wake you, but this heat is unbearable. I had to open the window."

"Larion kicked me out," I told her.

She stiffened her back. "Did you two argue again?"

"Yes. This time it was worse than before."

"What happened?"

"He called me a whore." Beatrice's eyes widened. "Not to my face," I added quickly. "He knows I've been sneaking out with you and Oswin, and he thinks we're doing it to have sex in secret."

She snarled. "With Oswin, ih!"

"He believes I'm sleeping with half the kingdom. In fact, he even made a list. Oswin, the stable boy, the cook, Jackard, and who knows who else. He's the only man I've ever slept with, damn it. Now he says he's not sure if the child is his."

I placed my hands protectively over my stomach, wondering if my son could feel my anger and distress. He couldn't, he was too small.

"I can't believe it!" Bea burst out, stomping her foot on the floor.

"Don't worry, I'll return the favor. Just wait and see! I'll make him apologize on his knees."

Beatrice smiled, leaning her head back with a contentedly sigh, as a cool breeze filled the room, billowing her nightshirt.

"Will you tell him about Jane?" she asked after a while.

"Only when he tells me what he's hiding. He's acting so damn strange. Often, he flinches, then signals me to be quiet and starts looking around the room like a madman. It's as if he hears voices. This morning, he started rummaging through the wardrobe. I think he's losing his mind."

"Azerad forbid! How long has this been happening?"

"He always reacts as if he hears voices. At least since I met him. But I can't exactly call myself completely sane either," I said, glaring at the glasses on the table.

She followed my gaze, then kneeled and aligned them. She knew she had done a good job when she heard me sigh with relief.

"Two madmen," I continued. "What better people to rule a kingdom?"

She laughed. "Do you really think he hears voices?"

"I don't know. I wish he would be more open with me. Anyway, I'm going to him to get my journal. I can't sleep and I still have a lot to write in it, a lot happened today."

"Do you want me to come with you?"

"No need. If he apologizes on his knees, I'll stay there. If not, I'll come back here. Don't lock the door, Oswin surely won't come anymore."

I tried my best to smooth out the wrinkles in my dress before leaving, in case I encountered someone, but I might as well have walked naked, for I didn't see a soul on my way to the king's room. In a world without consequences, I might even try it. Not even a guard was on duty. Anyone could have entered the royal chamber to assassinate him. Even me. I'll have to raise this issue sometime. It felt like I had only dozed off for a few moments, but seeing the palace empty, I realized at least a couple of hours had passed.

The king's door was unlocked. I pushed it open gently, stepped inside, and saw Larion asleep on the bed. I silently picked up the journal from the table. Clenching my jaw as I looked at the chaotically arranged books, I couldn't help myself and quickly fix the mess before turning back for the exit.

Larion twitched, likely caught in the throes of another nightmare. Ever since I met him, he regularly had nightmares, and each time, he was able to perfectly recall what he dreamt. He told me they all started the night he returned from the north, with the Black Queen as his prisoner.

"Bhalphomet! What have you made me do!?" he yelled, full of anger.

His body convulsed, as though caught in an invisible vice, struggling for breath. The journal slipped from my grasp, hitting the floor with a resounding thud as I rushed to his side. He snarled like a wild animal, the anguish etched into every line of his face. Without hesitation, I seized his shoulders, shaking him with urgency.

"Larion, wake up!"

"No!" he said, grabbing my hands. Tears leaked from his tightly closed eyelids, and his teeth gritted from the force with which he clenched them.

"Elena!" he screamed, filled with terror.

"You're having a nightmare! Larion, you're scaring me, wake up!"

He stopped trembling. His pale lips, a straight line across his face, slowly twisting into a forced, wide smile. He began to laugh, tears still streaming from his closed eyes. I saw his body jolt in the darkness, rising suddenly, nearly knocking me over. Yet, his grin remained fixed, his head swiveling precisely in my direction, though his eyes remained shut tight.

I waited a few moments, hoping he would come back to himself, but it was in vain, so I slapped him across the face how hard I could. The smile disappeared. He opened his eyes.

"Are you well?" I asked, frightened.

He wrapped his arms around me and slowly pulled me over him, breathing heavily. He seemed to be fighting to control his tears.

"I'm sorry," he said with a voice laden with pain. "I'm an idiot, I shouldn't have said all those things."

For a fleeting moment, I wanted to make him apologize on his knees, as I had promised I would do, but the horror and remorse in his voice made me change my mind. Whatever he dreamt, it tormented him to the core of his being.

"Me too," I said, laying my head on his shoulder. "Me too."

Chakar

Excerpt from Saya's journal, dated the twenty-ninth day of the sixth month, Iura, in the year six hundred twenty-three after the Conversion:

...This morning, just like yesterday and the day before, we spun in circles, making no progress at all.

"We're close," Wolf insisted with a stern voice. "Just like us, they've been wandering these woods for days. Their scent lingers thick in the air."

"That's good," Sparrow said.

"There are others with him," Wolf added. "Many have passed through these paths, and most scents are equally lost."

"So, they have company now," Sparrow concluded. Or asked. I couldn't tell because her accent made every sentence sound like a question.

"I can't say for sure, but I tend to believe they are. They're probably clan people. King Larion said these mountains are full of wildlings organized in tribes."

"That's what he said," Lady Sparrow repeated, dismounting.

I pulled on the reins to stop the horse, then jumped down from the saddle and stretched my legs, filled with gratitude for the short break. I had been riding since sunrise, and my back, ass, and neck ached terribly. Parzival dismounted too, cast a curious glance at me out of the corner of his eyes, then tied his horse to the trunk of a tree. I passed by him and tied my horse in the same spot, then sat down on the green grass at the edge of the path.

The path that crossed the slope we were on now was wide enough for me not to be afraid to doze off for a few moments, until Sparrow and Wolf decided which way we would continue. In the last few days, we had only ridden on winding and narrow paths, and usually, along these serpentine roads there were gaping holes that threatened to swallow you up at the slightest distraction. Falling asleep in the saddle and waking up falling dozens of meters into a chasm was not something I was in a hurry to experience anytime soon. Parzival sat down next to me, then stretched out on his back with his hands under his head. I mirrored his posture, looking towards the treetops that blocked the sky.

"Rest up," Wolf said. "I'll go scout the area to see if I can find anything concrete."

I tucked my head between my shoulders, fearing Lady Sparrow's response, but to my great surprise and relief, she nodded. "Take care of yourself!" she urged him.

He leaned over from the saddle and kissed her, then pinched her bottom, making her jump in place. She huffed, then looked in our direction. Both of us quickly turned our heads towards the treetops, pretending we hadn't seen anything. Wolf laughed, and Sparrow spat out a few words in the strange language spoken on the Storm Islands, which sounded as if someone had taken a bunch of sharp sounds and mixed them at will.

The wizard assassin urged his steed forward, swiftly vanishing up the narrowing path that ascended the slope. Sparrow's laughter bubbled forth sounding melodious and childish, like any word spoken from those thin lips.

I was glad to see their human side, no matter how rarely they were willing to display it. Their steel discipline and always severe and sharp gazes, never tired, often made me wonder if they were truly human. But in certain moments when they thought no one was watching, or they were too tired to care, I could see her husband stealing a kiss from her, or I could hear her whispering something to him in a sweet voice that brought a wide smile to his face. The fact that any display of affection between members of a couple is completely forbidden when others are present is one of the few things I still remember from what I read about the Storm Islands. Probably this information remained deeply engraved in my mind because of the way I was raised, as in the Coral Islands you could almost walk naked down the street, and no one would care. If they were on one extreme, we were on the other. Although the two of them had left Tokero over fifteen years ago, they continued to adhere to that authoritarian way of life with rigorous strictness.

Sparrow sat down next to us, letting her hair loose, which now fell straight over her shoulders. She had a strange way of sitting, with her legs tucked under her, back straight, and hands on her knees.

"It's a blessing to be able to rest our feet, isn't it?"

"*Why don't you let us do it more often, then?*" I wanted to say, but I also harbored aspirations of being promoted to the rank of witch in the relatively near future. "It is, Lady Sparrow," I replied, swallowing my words.

"Derahia is a beautiful country. It's a pity we catch it on the verge of war," she continued.

"War?" Parzival wondered. "Truly, Lady Sparrow, it's more of a very costly hunt than a war. The reaction of the king of Frevia was completely exaggerated; to gather the army for such a thing."

The woman ignited in mocking laughter before fixing us with a gaze of refined superiority. I surmised that her demeanor wasn't intended to be unkind but rather an inherent aspect of her character. "You don't see the world as it really is—you see the rose bulb, but not the thorns. These mountains are vast; King Alfred won't find them easily. Perhaps he won't find them at all."

"Well, even if they're not found, what does it matter? There are only two of them. No matter how powerful this *Black Queen* is, what could she do on her own?"

Sparrow clicked her tongue before clasping her palms on her knees. Her black eyes, like two beads, shifted onto me. "Saya, what do you think?"

"About whether the country is on the verge of war or not?" I reiterated, buying myself more time to think. She nodded. "I agree with Parzival that, for the moment, there is no serious danger of war."

"Go on."

"The prince's name was on the lips of people in all the villages we've passed through so far. I heard people talking about him at the tavern in the last village where we resupplied. I heard people talking about him on the way to the botanist from whom we bought red maracrin two days ago. Even the children running through the fields with sticks whispered his name as they played."

"People spoke his name with fear, not idolizing him," Parzival pointed out.

"Some people," Sparrow emphasized. "Do you think everyone in the entire country loved the late king? He had both enemies and friends, and Darion, too, has enemies and friends. He will eventually find supporters, don't doubt it. Even if not enough to conquer Romir, probably enough to wage a prolonged war. Right now, he's just a smoldering coal, but if you don't throw water over it, it will start a fire."

"I'm sure the sleep potions I made are enough to extinguish them both," Parzival joked. "Especially now that we mixed all the best ingredients."

I turned my gaze to Lady Sparrow's mare, grazing peacefully in the shade of the tree to which she was tethered. In the leather pouch of the saddle were three potions made by Parzival, so potent that their mere scent would be enough to make you fall asleep. Or at least, that's what he guaranteed. The assassin insisted that the potions remain with her after my colleague fell asleep while riding and hit his head on a branch, falling off his horse. If we ran out of potions, we would need to gather all the herbs again, which would divert us significantly from our path.

"Do you think it works?" I asked.

He raised his eyebrows and pursed his lips, visibly offended. "I made it, didn't I?"

"But you haven't tested it."

"Are you volunteering to test it?" he sneered.

I smiled because that's exactly where I wanted the conversation to go. I desperately needed rest, but I always found it very difficult to fall asleep. The fear of not being able to sleep always kept me awake.

"With pleasure. Lady Sparrow, may I?"

Sparrow raised her eyebrows in surprise, then fell silent in thought, her petite face wrinkling as she muttered something inaudible. I couldn't help but marvel at her every time I looked at her, recalling the fierce battle between her and Wolf and the remarkable speed with which her seemingly frail frame could move. Though she was the same height as me, I could never match her agility or precision.

"You can try," she concluded, with a hint of uncertainty lingering in her voice. "If you sleep too much, I'll tie you to the saddle and carry you like that until you wake up."

I stood up, feeling the fatigue weighing me down, teasing me like an annoying lover. I took one of the potions from the saddlebag and held it up to my eyes. A purple, slightly viscous liquid hit the glass walls of the container with every movement of my hand. Both Sparrow and Parzival watched me attentively, with anticipation and tension.

I removed the cork cap from the vial, which came off with a wet, muffled sound, and immediately a strong, sweet smell spread all around us. It didn't smell like anything familiar, but it was pleasant. "*How long should it last?*" I wanted to ask, but all I managed to get out were some tired squeaks. I started to laugh, but even my laughter sounded strange.

"I think I made it stron... stronger... than necessary," Parzival said, blinking frequently.

"Quickly put the cap back on and set it down," Sparrow ordered me, then pulled a wooden flute, resembling a sparrow, from an inner pocket of her very large tunic.

She began to blow into the peculiar flute, and the sounds that emerged from the other end sounded like the song of a sparrow. Other birds responded to her trill, and suddenly the whole forest was engulfed in Sparrow's song. She stopped playing the flute and looked at me with a wide smile.

I put the cap back on the potion, and the muffled sound produced by the cork made me burst into uncontrollable laughter. I left the potion on the grass and noticed that even Parzival was laughing in tears. Lady Sparrow began to chuckle, resting her head in her hands. Shortly after, my chest and throat started to burn from laughter, but no matter how hard I tried, I couldn't stop. A caterpillar crawled on the green ground beneath my feet. The last thing I can remember before falling asleep is that I was about to tell the caterpillar how fat it was.

I woke up feeling terribly rested, thank the heavens, with the warm light of the evening sun caressing my hair. It didn't take long for me to remember everything that had transpired. I tried to sit up, only to realize that I was enveloped in my sleeping bag. The trees seemed much more scattered than where I had fallen asleep, and the ground much less steep. I emerged from the bag and saw Sparrow, standing about twenty paces away from me, in the arms of her husband. When she saw me, she rose from him, straightening her back, then nodded for me to approach.

I was sure we weren't in the same area where I had fallen asleep. It was still a forest, of course, but the whole landscape was very different from before. Sparrow's gaze was neutral, and Wolf's slightly amused. I saw Parzival sleeping on his side, drool dripping onto the patchy emerald carpet.

"I hope you've rested enough," she began. I could almost taste the warning from her words.

"I'm very sorry," I said quickly.

"At least we know Parzival's potion is effective," Wolf laughed, and Sparrow elbowed him in the ribs.

"I realized it affected you as well only when you started laughing, Mrs Sparrow," I quickly uttered.

"When I found you, she was still laughing like a mongoose," Wolf told me, pinching her cheek.

Her jaw tightened. "Wake Parzival up, I have a task for you two."

I complied, without asking questions, as she seemed extremely upset, just like a sulky child caught doing something wrong.

Waking up Parzival wasn't easy at all. Even without the effect of the potion, my colleague sleeps very heavily. A few days ago, he slept while riding through a storm that almost knocked me off my horse, and he woke up surprised, not understanding why he was wet.

Now, he only woke up only after the fourth slap, looking at me in surprise.

"Why are you in my room, Saya?" he asked, blinking a few times, and wiping away his drool. Then he pushed me aside, crawling out of the bag like a worm. Like a caterpillar.

"We have work to do," I told him.

He shook his head, then asked, "Work? You mean you and me? Sounds good."

"You and her, yes," the assassin witch said in a steely voice, making him jump to his feet. "Follow me!" She led us about fifteen meters downhill from where my sleeping bag was.

At the edge of a narrow path, in the not very tall grass, lay two corpses.

"Eww! Shells and crabs!" I exclaimed, stepping back as soon as I saw them.

They were two men. One was tall and athletic, didn't seem older than thirty, and the other, quite chubby, seemed barely over forty. Both had their throats slit, and the chubby one had a deep cut on his belly, with his guts covered in insects, lying on the ground.

"Hells!" Parzival exclaimed, covering his mouth with a handkerchief he pulled out of the inner pocket of his tunic.

"Neither one nor the other," said Sparrow. "Two corpses."

"Darion?" I asked, voicing the first thought that crossed my mind.

"Possibly," Wolf added, who was now beside us. "*How did he get here without me hearing his steps?*" I wondered. "Possibly not. You see, the cuts are much finer than those on the bodies examined in Romir. He might have gotten hold of a better sword. I found this place just before I heard Sparrow's flute. After returning to you, I loaded you all on horses and brought you here. Darion was here a few days ago, or weeks. Same with Aella. They haven't gotten far; I can smell them. We might catch up to them in a day or two."

Finally! This journey has lasted longer than I would have liked. I was very excited to be chosen as a member of the expedition, but I didn't expect the situation to become so uncomfortable and exhausting. I smiled, remembering my tiny room in the Tower of Fire, the books piled under the bed, the smell of dust I kept swearing to swipe the next day, and even the annoying professors. Maybe we were even going to make another stop in Romir after we manage to capture them. Then I realized with a hint of fear that we hadn't captured them yet.

"They need to be buried," Sparrow said, looking at the two of us, and Wolf placed a shovel with a short handle in Parzival's hands.

"You mean by us?" I asked, surprised.

"I mean by you," she nodded.

"But... why? They're already dead, what does it matter? If the dead sleep, leave them be, that's what we say."

"And we say: respect the dead," Sparrow followed in a reproachful tone.

"They finished a race we're still running," added Wolf softly.

"Correct," Parzival conceded. "You mentioned Darion was here, sir?"

"Indeed. They climbed this path and encountered another group of about eighty people descending from the top. Maybe a hundred. They stopped here. These two were killed, then they ascended the slope, descending on the eastern side. They left the corpses in the open field, prey to animals and insects," he added with disgust.

"At least they don't let the local fauna starve," I joked, instantly silenced by the severe stares of the two assassins.

"Perhaps they were taken prisoners by the savages," Parzival suggested.

"I doubt it," Wolf replied. "If the clan people came down from the mountains, they probably came down with a purpose. Their encounter with Darion either turned them back or sent them in another direction. We still don't know what happened, but our fugitives are among them."

Parzival raised his shoulders. "If they're accompanied by a hundred people, I suspect capturing them alive is out of the question."

Wolf and Sparrow exchanged a quick glance, then Sparrow responded. "As you've seen, your potions are quite potent. We'll throw all three bottles into their midst, and they'll fall asleep like babies. Most of them, if not all. Depending on the situation, we either capture Darion, or both."

"If we only catch the prince, we'll take him to Blackstone and wait there for Aella," Wolf informed us.

"Blackstone?" Parzival inquired.

Sparrow's angry gaze made him quickly regret his question. "Young Enarius, I gave you some maps to study while we were in Romir," the woman scolded. "Did you read them?"

"Of course," Parzival replied tensely.

"Of course," she repeated, frowning. "Then you know what Blackstone is, don't you?"

"Of course."

"Go on," she urged, flicking her hand impatiently.

"Uh... a black rock?" he guessed.

"Are you asking or telling?"

"I'm telling you, of course."

"Do you have bees buzzing in your head?" the woman snapped at him.

"Blackstone is a fortress a little further east from here," Wolf told us. "If we manage to capture at least Darion, we can use him to set a trap for the Black Queen, right there."

"That's if she comes after him," I said.

"She will come," Sparrow assured. "She didn't go through all that trouble to keep him alive just to let him die now. But if not, we'll wait for Darion to be executed, then we'll go after Aella."

"Do you think he'll be executed?" I asked, recalling the promise I made to the King: to try and bring his brother back alive.

"Because of him, if not by his hand, the heiress of Blackstone died," Mr. Wolf replied. "I think the people there are very angry with him. In their fury, they may not even wait for the King's arrival to pass judgment."

"Many lives have been taken by these two!" I exclaimed with shock.

"Come on now," urged Sparrow. "I believe you have work to do, don't you?"

The two assassins turned their backs on us, leaving.

Parzival bent down, grabbing one of the corpses by the long-stiffened legs that crunched as he pulled. He gestured for me to take hold of the hands, but I stood frozen for a moment, trying to figure out if he was serious.

"You truly have bees buzzing in your head if you think I'll lay my hands on two carcasses," I exclaimed.

"I'm not heaving them onto my shoulders. Especially not this one with its guts hanging out. We can't bury them here; the ground is too hard. I see a river further downstream, perhaps that's a good spot."

"We are wizards, for Azerad's sake!"

I stepped into the ether, feeling the power of the swirling river flowing around me, connecting everything, covering everything. It was violent that day, furious, but I commanded it to obey me, and it listened. I loved to control it and to be controlled by it, to feel it envelop me in a warm embrace. I sensed a vibration coming from Parzival, a series of waves with a unique pattern, caused by the magic flowing through his body. The signature of a wizard. Sparrow and Wolf have one too, as does anyone who can touch the ether. Except Aella, if what that aspiring wizard at Romir's court said was true. That thought, like any thought related to the strange couple, was terrifying.

I lifted both corpses into the air using the power of the ether, and from the fatter one, some remains fell, which made me first curse, then glance panicked over my shoulder, hoping that our two tutors hadn't heard me. Parzival stepped a few paces to the side with a squint, as the bodies floated past him. Seeing them now, any trace of the happiness I had felt earlier at the thought that we were finally getting closer to the fugitives, was extinguished. I swallowed hard.

"Are you well?" Parzival asked, coming over to me. He held his small shovel over his shoulder in a manner that indicated he had done this before.

"I don't like corpses," I replied. "They're unnatural."

"What else is more natural than death?" he asked, furrowing his brows in the middle. "Haven't you seen dead people before?"

"I've seen a few thousand, but I don't remember anymore."

His nostrils flared. "A few thousand, really?"

"Yes. I was five when Mount Veruviud erupted. The victims were in the tens of thousands."

"I remember reading about that. I'm sorry to hear it. Did you live nearby?"

"Right under it, from what my aunt told me."

"I'm glad you're here now," he said, then blushed, looking away.

"I believe you. Without me, you would have had to carry them on your back." He began to laugh as I gestured towards the two carcasses.

We walked for a while as the sun descended lower and lower, its golden rays turning orange, and later red. I looked south, thinking of Romir and for a few moments even of Princess Elena. I smiled, remembering our last interaction, then saddened at the thought that Darion had killed her brother.

"Do you think it was Darion?" I asked, nodding towards the corpses.

"Who cares about Darion, he's just a man. A fireball and he's dead. It's the Black Queen I fear," he replied.

"Elena told me we shouldn't underestimate him either. She said he's very dangerous."

"Did she tell you that during her private visit?" he asked, and a grin spread across his face.

I couldn't stop my surprised gasp. "How do you know?"

"The walls were very thin, and you two were very noisy," he laughed.

"Shells and crabs!" I squealed. "The room was between yours and theirs."

"Only shells... no crabs," he joked, and we both burst into laughter.

I stifled a muffled laugh, tinged with hysteria at the mere thought of it. "Do you think Sparrow and Wolf heard me?"

"I'm sure even Radagrim, with his *keen* hearing, would have heard your moans."

"Let's never mention it again," I told him.

"I'll keep it locked away in my head, I promise."

"Seriously, Parzi, I wouldn't want the whole Circle to find out."

"But what a story it would be! At first, I thought it couldn't possibly be Princess Elena herself—probably just another girl with a similar voice. Then I saw the looks you two were giving each other all morning. I won't tell anyone, I promise. I'll take the secret to my grave."

"I don't know why I don't believe you."

"Because you don't know me," he said casually. "Perhaps you would have had the chance to get to know me better if you hadn't always been so busy whenever I invited you to Etherveil, for meals."

"Maybe when we return to the Circle, I'll have more free time."

He frowned. "Maybe I'll be busy."

"I don't think you will be," I said, throwing him a teasing smile. He suddenly looked away.

He stopped after a few steps, bending down and pushing the tip of the shovel into the ground. I almost started laughing thinking about the absurdity of the situation. I was looking for a place to bury two corpses on the northern border of Derahia, alongside Parzival Enarius, known in the Circle for his bootlegged potions. We were accompanied by the most skilled assassins in the world, and just a few days ago, I slept with the future queen of the country.

"What's the matter? Do you feel like digging?" he asked, perhaps assuming I found amusement in observing his digging technique.

"No. Just that, life is..."

"Unnatural?" he suggested.

"Unnatural," I agreed with a smile.

It took Parzival quite a while to finish digging the grave. I offered to help him several times, but fortunately, his male pride prevented him from accepting help from me, a mere, fragile woman. The sun was setting faster behind the peaks, and the shadows stretched towards the east, reclaiming the territory they had lost at dawn. I loved the night, but it also frightened me.

"I think we're done," he concluded, crawling out of the one-meter-deep hole.

"In another life, you would have been a gravedigger," I told him.

"Thank you! Impressive, isn't it?"

"I didn't say you were a good one," I said as I submerged again into the ether, lifting the corpses.

He laughed, shaking his head resignedly. "It's quite impressive, you know?"

"My humor?"

"The way you bend the waves. You carried both bodies here and you didn't even seem tired. I can barely lift two stones."

"But you can do other things too, I only know this. I once tried to cast a fireball and ended up singeing my eyebrows."

"I remember," he said with a hint of a smile. "But still, I haven't encountered anyone who can do what you do with such ease."

I laid the bodies in the grave, trying to appear as indifferent as possible, although I was ecstatic every time someone complimented my magic. Parzival began to fill the pit, which didn't take long. When he finished, he stumbled to the edge of the stream and plunged his hands into the icy water. I cast one last glance at the grave and shuddered at the thought that one day, I would be the one lying in it. I was sure I wouldn't depart to the marble palaces of the erthals, as the Zerevists preach, nor to Hakulamathera, as the Fyrgon worshippers claim, but underground, in the cold and eternal darkness, in the abode of the dead.

Parzival came beside me, waving his hands and spreading cold droplets of water everywhere. This time, I carried Mr. Wolf's shovel.

We dragged our feet along the winding path, which became narrower or wider in certain places. From the cold ocean of moonlight in the sky, only a few drops managed to penetrate the dense web of branches. Parzival repeatedly insisted on igniting a light globe to guide our way ahead, but I declined each time. I didn't want the light to attract any of the barbarians who made their living in those regions. Or worse... Darion.

When we finally made it back, Wolf was asleep, buried in his sleeping bag. Sparrow sat with her back against a tree, a few meters from her husband. She contemplated with a strange and complete focus the peculiar bird-shaped flute that mimicked the song of a sparrow, which she had used to call her husband earlier. She showed no sign of having heard us, but I had no doubt she knew we were there.

"Tonight we'll set up camp," she said after a while, without lifting her eyes from the flute. "We won't travel at night anymore, only during the day. We're close, and we don't want to risk running into them. Our understanding of Aella and her abilities remains inadequate for the time being."

Parzival smiled contentedly, wished us a good night, and eagerly dove into his sleeping bag. It seemed unreal how little time passed from the moment he wrapped himself until he started snoring. I settled down next to the assassin, knowing I couldn't possibly fall asleep, given that I had barely woken up a few hours ago.

Knowing that Lady Sparrow wasn't very talkative, I took out my journal, squinted my eyes and began jotting down everything that had happened. It was a blessing to have the leisure to take notes. When I grow old... no, if I grow old, it will be nice to read.

"If you want to sleep, Mrs., I can keep watch," I offered to Sparrow.

"I couldn't sleep," she said, lifting her head and looking at me for the first time since we returned. "How are you feeling, Saya?"

I placed the quill back in the inkwell, trying not to appear surprised by her question. She looked at me with her black, almond-shaped eyes. Her ebony hair accentuated the whiteness of her skin, typical of those from the Storm Isles.

"*I'm dying a little more every day and would sell my soul for a bed,*" I wanted to say. Instead, I replied, "Tired, but otherwise fine."

"You don't seem very convinced."

"I'm a bit troubled, it's true. It's the first time I hunt... people."

"For me, it's the first time hunting a nartingal, but it seems there's a beginning for everything, is it not. Perhaps you'll enjoy it, and you'll join the Black Brotherhood. We'll need more wizards, especially after Wolf and I leave."

"You're leaving?" I asked, surprised.

She turned to her husband and smiled. "'Leaving' might be a bit of a misnomer here, child. We were never truly part of them, but rather more like hired specialists, if you will. We were primarily assisting them, but we weren't meant to be here permanently," she said. "Sixteen years ago, we agreed to retire after two hundred eighteen successful missions."

"A very specific number," I commented.

"It is a precise figure because it is tied to a debt and an oath that needed to be resolved. The full story is rather intricate, but the essence is that our last mission fell short. We tracked down Sihad and took out several of Aethelred's acolytes, but the man himself slipped through our grasp. I managed to pluck his eye just before he escaped through a pal'ether."

She frowned, as if the memory left a sour taste. She tucked her flute into the inner pocket of her coat and glanced back at her sleeping husband.

"My husband and the Council of the Fire Tower thought the mission was a success, given our accomplishments. But how can it be deemed a success when Aethelred got away? This mission must be a true success. It's imperative."

"Your departure will leave a big void," I told her. It was the plain truth; I wasn't trying to flatter her.

"You and Parzival would make a good team. With your combined talents, you could achieve a lot."

"I'll think about it," I replied, though in reality, I had nothing to think about.

The answer was obvious. Living on the road and putting my life in danger daily wasn't as appealing as the life of a royal witch. For reasons understandable to me, but probably not to the assassin. She shrugged.

We remained in silence for quite some time, during which I simply struggled to wrote, because of the darkness, and daydreamed about the future that might await me in the coming years. Life in Romir.

I drifted from one thought to another, and it didn't take long for the worries of the days ahead to catch up with me. When I glanced at Sparrow, I saw that she was looking at me too.

"On the Storm Islands, people don't worship any god," she began, without me saying anything. "We believe in *chakar*. An impersonal force that rewards those who do good and punishes those who do evil. And today, you have done good."

"Have we done enough good?" I asked.

She nodded, visibly convinced, as if she held all the secrets of empirical ways of measuring the *chakar*.

"The more good we offer to the world, the more good we will receive in return. But right now, it doesn't even matter because Darion has already done too much harm. Soon, he will get what he deserves."

Bragovik

In the morning of the day we descended into Bragovik, Aella wore her human form, the one I fell in love with. It had become somewhat unfamiliar to me. She listened quietly, without any reaction, as I told her about the dream from the previous night. She seemed calm, but she always seemed calm. Often, I found myself intensely studying her face as I spoke, seeking the faintest shadow of concern, the subtlest sign of an ill omen veiled beneath her serenity. But there was nothing. Nothing I could perceive, at least. Her undisturbed gaze was my sanctuary, the place I always sought refuge.

I, however, was troubled, knowing there was a real possibility that the things I dreamed of could come true, just as they had in the past.

"Just a nightmare, probably," she concluded when I finished.

"Do you think so?"

"What could we possibly seek in one of the cities of the First Gods?" she asked in a low voice.

It was a valid question; one I hoped never to find the answer to. I feared those strange creatures, those deities imprisoned in their own temples where they were once worshipped. The mere mention of their names would draw their fiery eyes upon you. Fortunately, during that time, I only knew one, and in my heart, I had a foolish sense of tranquility, born from the thought that I would never have to deal with them again, because, after all, Aella was right. What could we possibly seek there?

"You're right," I laughed. "We're not mad."

She nodded, then raised her hand, and the air above her outstretched palm began to burn. I jumped back in alarm, grabbing my sword. She chuckled. The flames had turned into a continuous beam of red light that decreased in length and intensity, becoming glassy. The liquid fire thickened, and in just a few moments, in front of Aella, only a beautiful crystal mirror remained.

"Next time, let me know before you do that," I requested. She turned to me, pinched my cheek lightly, but said nothing. With a graceful motion, she began to straighten her disheveled hair in front of the magical, floating mirror.

The first cool rays of the sun traced yellow lines across the clear sky, signaling to my people that it was almost time to pack up the camp and resume our journey. Today, I was going to reveal to them that I would be absent in the coming weeks, during which Eldric would take on my role and responsibilities.

Despite everything that had happened until then and despite the uncertain future, full of obstacles, in that strange moment of peace and quiet, seemingly detached from the events of the last month, I was happy. I leaned towards her, kissing her forehead, then let out a long sigh, resting my head on her shoulder. She remained still, her reflection looking at me from the mirror. Seeing my smile, she smiled back.

"I'm trying to tidy up my hair a bit," she said. "A comb would be useful."

"We'll buy one in Bragovik," I told her.

"I don't like the idea of staying too long in that village. It's too close to Blackstone."

"We'll stay until the blacksmith manages to plate the handle of my sword. It's the only village with a blacksmith in this region. Plus, I want to sleep in a real bed again... at least for one night."

She didn't respond. After a while, the mirror went out, melting in the morning, and she turned to me. She undid the hair that I had tied into a knot behind my head, then began to braid a few thin braids, similar to those worn by people in my clan.

I saw Kayra and Mathias returning from the forest, walking shoulder to shoulder through the camp. Everyone hurriedly moved out of their way, as they all feared the Shadow Walker. At that time, I didn't pay much attention to this, thinking that their reaction to seeing the man with the empty eyes, who appeared out of nowhere and disappeared just as suddenly, was completely normal. Especially since the mountaineers were particularly superstitious. But the reason they feared him was much more severe, rooted behind the mountain range, in the city beyond the golden grassland. In Rhal'Ellieh, the city of Yohr'Sherrat.

A group of young men, some carrying battle axes, others swords attached to their belts, ran up the slope towards us. They stopped a few steps away, bowing hastily. The one called Kaldur began to speak.

"*Az'fielumra*, Master Darion! Are you coming to train with us?"

I smiled, and he smiled back excitedly. Kaldur was a warrior; I knew that from the first night I saw him, when he came to bring me a rabbit he had just hunted. He was muscular, with thick and powerful arms. His chestnut hair reached his waist, tied in iron rings, and the shadow of a mustache adorned his face, which he stroked proudly whenever he wanted to seem lost in thought. I had seen him watching me train, alone or with Regihold, and one morning he gathered the courage to come and ask if he could join. He had potential. He was like a rough stone, still had much to learn, but I was sure I could polish him. In the last few days, we had practiced sword fighting every morning, and he always came accompanied by others. More and more every time. Without realizing it, I was preparing my army.

"*Az'falandra*, Kaldur! Not this morning. Train without me. You already know the moves, you just need to practice them."

He nodded somewhat disappointedly, then left with the others.

Later, I saw Regihold and Yenna climbing towards the camp together. They both seemed in good spirits, and Yenna was eyeing the giant with every step they took.

"I think Yenna has found her fourth husband," Aella suggested with a smile. She said this because Yenna had been married before. Three times.

"It certainly seems so," I replied.

"Regihold will have to get a ring," she said.

"A ring?"

Aella raised her thin, black eyebrows, her surprise evident at my lack of knowledge, which to her seemed obvious. "Yes. If a man wants to marry a woman, he must kneel before her and offer her a ring. If the woman accepts it, then they can get married."

"What silly traditions these people have," I chuckled.

"Your people, you mean?" she replied with a slight frown.

In Romir, things were much simpler when it came to engagement. The man or the father of the man had to go to the father of the girl, or even to the girl herself if her father was no longer alive, and make the request known. A small fee was paid, *the price of the bride*, which was usually a few silvers or a few gold coins, then a date was set for both to appear at the temple for the official ceremony.

"My people," I corrected myself.

"To me, it seems like a beautiful custom," she said.

"Perhaps."

With the corner of my eye, I caught Aella clenching her fists and pursing her lips. She rose from beside me, seating herself a few steps higher on that slope.

"*What have I done now?*" I remember wondering, surprised by her sudden anger, which, to my immature twenty-one-year-old mind, seemed like a true mystery.

"*Az'fielumra*!" greeted Yenna, who came beside me.

"*Az'falandra*!" I responded. "Could you gather the people? I have an announcement to make."

She nodded and, spinning on her heel, began to move around the camp, directing everyone toward me, like a skilled sheepdog gathering the sheep around the shepherd. I stood up as the lines of people began to thicken. I scanned them all, pausing for a moment on the hostile gaze of Yorric. I winked at him, grinning, eagerly waiting for the slightest reason to kill him. He didn't give me one. He was a dangerous man, an instigator whose head didn't sit quite right on his shoulders.

"I will have to leave the clan for a few weeks!" I shouted.

I waited until the whispers ceased, during which the Black Queen came with small steps behind me. I noticed that, like me, she was studying Yorric. The man unsuccessfully tried to meet her gaze, then muttered something under his breath and lowered his head.

"You were saying something, Yorric?" I snarled.

"Nothing, Master Darion," he responded half-mouthed.

"A large army is heading towards us even as we speak. They are coming from the south and will probably arrive here in a few weeks. There are too many of them and too well-equipped for us to fight."

Some were worried, some were angry, and some looked at me with obvious doubt. Yorric fell into the last category.

"We need allies, and I know where to find them," I continued. "Yenna and Kaldur will accompany me, and Eldric will lead the clan until I return."

No one made a sound. They watched me in silence, occasionally exchanging confused looks between them, laden with distrust. I could hear some people translating my message for others that did not understand the common tongue. Eldric nodded, looking left and right, probably searching for hostile faces.

"If that's what you ask of me, I will become your blood brother, *fradezs sehyar*," Eldric said, stroking his long, yellow beard.

"That's what I ask," I replied.

I drew my sword from its sheath, then placed my left hand over the edge, halfway between the hilt and the tip. Pressing down, I ran my palm to the end of the blade, trying not to flinch as the cold steel bit into my flesh. Red tears now streamed along the edge, dripping into the grass. A few days before, Aella had taught me the entire ritual of choosing a blood brother, *fradezs sehyar*. Eldric was to become my right hand and advisor, and in the event of my death, the leader of the clan. He also placed his hand over the blade of my sword, following my example.

"From this day forth, our blood is bound," I said.

"I swear to fight and die for you," he promised.

"And I swear there will always be a place for you at my table and under my roof."

Kaldur, who was to accompany me to Yermoleth, let out a sharp cry, beginning to clap, and soon everyone around us followed suit. Even Lyra was hopping and chirping, probably without understanding why. I embraced Eldric, as tradition dictated, and his tired but somewhat cheerful gaze reminded me greatly of my late father, King Harold.

"Watch out for Yorric," I whispered as I held him.

"He's our enemy, brother," Eldric whispered back, nodding grimly.

I parted ways with the warriors of my clan that afternoon, but I promised myself I would return to them. I called all the young men who had trained with me in recent days and told them that I counted on them to keep order for Eldric. They respected me and looked up to me as a warrior, and I needed them. I didn't know how long I would be gone, but if Yorric came to believe that I had died, he would try to take over the people. He feared me, but not Eldric. I didn't kill him that day, although I had a feeling he would cause trouble. I spared him, and that was one of the biggest mistakes of my life.

I left accompanied by Aella, Kayra, Lyra, Merwin, Regihold, Yenna, and Kaldur. Mathias wasn't with us, but I had no doubt he was following us from Beyond. He was always close to Kayra, like a shadow. Above, the sky was clear and blue, but I could see the leaden clouds creeping closer through the peaks rising like trees to the north. A storm was coming, but it was still far off, and I wasn't worried it would catch us before we reached Bragovik.

After a while, Aella took hold of my left hand, in which I still felt the cut pulsating with every heartbeat. A brief vibration, followed by a barely perceptible wave of warmth, and the pain subsided. She didn't even glance at me, continuing to walk silently at my left, occasionally tugging at her oversized pants. The thought of being healed by someone through the ether would have terrified me to death just a few months ago, but now I found myself utterly indifferent to it.

Lyra slipped between us. She had been doing that a lot lately. She seemed to enjoy our company, and we loved her lively presence. Aella never hesitated to join in her games, whether it meant spending hours chasing after her to pick pinecones or searching for stones with certain shapes, or even weaving flower wreaths. I wondered if those who uttered the name of the Black Queen with voices full of fear would change their minds if they saw her weaving a flower crown alongside the little girl.

Yenna led our unusual procession, accompanied by Regihold, while the rest of us followed at a leisurely pace. We passed by the lake where my dear Aella had thrown me just a day before, then descended through a rocky valley, strewn with weeds and saplings.

The last stretch of road took us through a forest that seemed to envelop the village. We stopped a few hundred meters from Bragovik. The trees around had been cut down, leaving an expansive patch of open ground between the village and the forest, to prevent invaders from approaching unseen.

The storm from the north was advancing.

"That's the village," Yenna told me. "They have a blacksmith there, as I said. Although, from what I see, he might be very busy because of the attacks."

"That's where my weapons were repaired," Kaldur also said.

"They repair weapons for mountain people?" I asked in surprise.

He displayed a queer grin as his eyes meet Yenna's. "We send those among us who resemble them more in speech and appearance. Like Yenna, for example."

"I don't resemble them," the woman huffed. "I know their way of speaking well enough not to raise suspicion, boy."

"And even if they suspect you're not from Derahia, money is money, it doesn't matter where it comes from," said Merwin.

"That policy doesn't seem to have served them very well," Kayra spoke up with a grimace. "To give weapons to enemies."

The village was enveloped by a nearly two-meter-tall defensive wall made of tree trunks driven vertically into the ground, tightly bound together. Wooden sharp stakes were surrounding the gate, their tips pointing towards the forest, and the charred skeletons of half-collapsed houses lay desolate outside the wall. The village was far to the north, situated right on the border of the kingdom, and the people likely faced waves of barbarians very often. They adapted. At first, I thought it was a miracle that the village was still there, but it was actually just the strong will of the people to protect their homes and families.

"We weren't their enemies," said Kaldur. "Not us. We never attacked them, not even during Garen's time. The village is swarming with archers, and they're always on guard. It's not worth the risk."

"The wall is new," remarked Yenna, "they probably built it in the last month. And those burned houses are new too."

"Means they've been attacked recently," concluded Kaldur.

"The people on the walls are on high alert," said Mathias, who appeared out of nowhere beside us, causing Kaldur to take a step back. Yenna grabbed Regihold's arm, but released it immediately, assuming a chaste demeanor. They were afraid of Mathias.

"Enemies are probably still nearby," Kayra remarked.

"In that case, it'd be a good idea to leave the forest," Merwin chuckled nervously, scanning the surroundings.

"Are we in danger?" Lyra asked.

"No," Aella hurried to assure her, but even she turned her head when a fallen branch cracked just a few steps behind us, probably due to an animal stepping on it. "But Merwin's right, we shouldn't waste any more time."

Aella enveloped us in a magical veil, cloaking us from view. We decided it was best to stay hidden until we entered, and from there, try to avoid as many curious looks as possible. As I would soon find out, everyone already knew about me and Aella. Lyra's eyes widened in amazement when she saw us disappear.

Inside the veil, everything looked the same; if I couldn't feel the magical vibration of the ether, I wouldn't even have known. The Black Queen pulled me closer to her, as the magical shield covered a fairly small area.

"Impressive!" exclaimed Merwin. "Terrifying, but impressive without a doubt. I can barely feel a ripple of ether. Almost hard to believe."

"Now I see you!" giggled Lyra after skipping inside the veil. "Now I don't see you!" she said, jumping back.

Kayra grabbed her hand and pulled her towards the village, followed by Yenna and Regihold, then me and Aella, and finally Kaldur and Merwin. The latter two walked slower and kept some distance from me and Aella, trying not to step beyond the ether curtain and become invisible. That would probably cause us trouble.

Above the gates was a wooden platform where two men stood, looking in our direction. Both of them took an arrow from their quivers, fitting them into their longbows. I remember scowling at the sight, as the longbow was a cursed weapon, capable in certain cases of piercing even a steel breastplate. But few were strong enough to draw its string. As we approached, I could see them better and realized that both wore chainmail shirts under their loose, billowy blouses. They seemed prepared for war.

One of them, tall and broad, with a beard that reached his chest, raised his hand in the air, signaling us to stop. He was around thirty years old and judging by the width of his back and the thickness of his arms, he seemed capable of using the weapon he held.

"What brings you to Bragovik?" he shouted. I smiled at the sound of his northern accent, similar to Yenna's.

Kayra took a careful step and said, "the storm is approaching, and we're looking for shelter. A place to spend the night."

The man raised his gaze to the clouds that had already swallowed the peak of the mountain we had left behind, and pursed his lips. He exchanged a few brief glances with the man on his right, short and stocky, but with arms thick enough to crush skulls. He had black, curly hair, reaching just above his shoulders.

"You have a bow," observed the redhead. "Do you know how to use it?"

"You put the arrow on the string and shoot," Kayra said indifferently.

"Just make sure you put it with the right end, otherwise you'll cut the string," the redhead jested. The other began to laugh, slapping his belly with his free hand.

Kayra smiled politely at them, then took out her bow, preparing an arrow. The two men widened their eyes, stifling their laughter. Aella frowned.

"Kayra... it's not necessary," Merwin whispered to her, forcing a smile.

"Shoot here," the red-haired one said, seeing that the archer was eager to demonstrate her skill. He struck the wooden wall, which stood chest-high and served as a palisade, with the bow's end.

The guards took a few steps to the right, reaching the edge of the platform, then leaned in to be more covered by the wooden barricade. It was a hard-to-miss shot, but still, in the mocking glances of the two, I could see they were hoping for the woman to fail so they could continue laughing.

"Don't rush," the taller one said, "we wouldn't want you to miss, it's a small target."

He, of course, was joking, as the defensive wall was a meter and a half high and three meters long. In terms of thickness, it was thin, but enough to stop arrows sent by attackers towards the defenders.

Kayra drew her bow, aiming towards the palisade, then stopped. It was as if she was listening to the wind. To my surprise and the amusement of the guards, the archer pointed the arrow at the sky, then shot. The two men raised their eyes, watching the projectile become smaller and thinner until it was lost against the backdrop of the sky. They burst into laughter. One of them took out two bronze helmets.

"You missed," the stout one said, after putting his helmet on.

"I hope your arrow doesn't pierce any heads on its way down," the other added with a hint of seriousness in his voice. Kayra just shrugged, putting her bow back over her shoulder.

"Now, will you let us in?" she asked.

"You can come in," the redhead conceded. "Because you made us laugh. But there is a fee: ten pieces of copper per person. The village was full of strangers until a few days ago."

"Full of strangers?" Merwin asked. "How come? It doesn't seem like a very welcoming destination. No offense."

"There are many who hunt for Prince Darion and his witch," the black-haired one said.

I noticed Yenna flinched, and even Kaldur tensed his back. That's when I realized they didn't know I was a prince.

"We benefited from it," the other said. "More people to help us defend against the mountain folk. Not that we're not capable on our own, as you can see. And, of course, it's a pleasure to have some pleasant faces around here, because enough... ahhh, Hells!"

Both jumped back like frightened cats, nearly tumbling off the platform when Kayra's arrow pierced the edge of the palisade, barely a few centimeters thick. Even I startled, more taken aback by their sudden cry than by the arrow itself. Wide-eyed, they both stared first at the arrow, then at the bowwoman.

"You signaled me to shoot there, didn't you?"

"Open the gates," the one with red hair muttered, looking over his shoulder at the gatekeepers, then nodded in Kayra's direction, taking off his helmet. "Good shot!"

The wide wooden gates were pulled aside, revealing a plethora of sharp stakes pointing towards the entrance.

If the gates were to give way, invaders would have to make their way through the stakes, under a constant rain of arrows. Several carts were waiting nearby, covered with damp hides, likely to be pushed in front of any breach that might occur in the wall. More such carts were strewn throughout the village.

Regihold paid the entrance fee for the entire group.

A few young men, stationed in front of the gate, silently studied us, and more than once I had the feeling that their gaze would stop on me and Aella. At one point, Merwin got too close to us, and my blood ran cold, expecting him to step into the veil and disappear from the sight of the guards. But thank the gods, he didn't.

Bragovik was a large village, numbering almost a thousand people. I saw many wearing leather armor or chainmail, and almost everyone carried a sword or an axe at their belt. Even the women. It's no wonder they resisted the savages for so long. Clan people preferred fights they could win easily and without losses, fights against those who couldn't defend themselves. Many among them were thieves, few were warriors.

"We shouldn't linger here for too long," Aella whispered to me. "The ones hunting us might return."

I nodded gravely, looking at the people who roamed the streets, searching for potential enemies. Streets perhaps is an inappropriate term, as the houses were scattered everywhere, without any order, and the beaten path wound through them. On the roofs of some houses, especially those closer to the wall, were scattered wet animal hides, to prevent them from catching fire if attackers threw torches. A mound of earth stretched along the wall to allow those inside to easily see beyond. It would have been easy for them to skewer invaders, but it wouldn't have been as easy from the outside. The wall had breaches, but these narrow openings were guarded by spearmen, with a multitude of stakes aimed at them.

The defense of that village was impeccable, and it would have been difficult to conquer without losses, even by a large and well-trained army. However, everything around indicated that the recent attacks were quite intense. Probably the invaders were numerous enough to afford to attack such a defense.

They also had a temple of worship, but the roof was burnt, and the walls were charred. Probably that building was the target during the initial attack. It made sense, as the priests cherished their artifacts of shining metals, which they considered holy, and their ceremonial robes made of fine materials.

The inn was quite large and stood out from the other buildings, being the only one, except for the temple, that had an upper floor. A sign hung above the door, swaying in the wind, signaling the impending storm. "Inn," was written on it. You didn't need catchy names if your inn was the only one in the area.

The place was empty. Initially, even the innkeeper was absent, so we sat at the tables scattered around the room and waited quietly. Aella lifted the barrier around us, then covered her eyes using the clock borrowed from Kayra. I wasn't worried about being recognized, as I didn't look like a prince at all; rather, I resembled the wildlings hiding in the mountains. But Aella's bright eyes would undoubtedly give her away. Legends spread like wildfire across the entire country and beyond, tales of the bright-eyed witch who decimated armies. 'Army'—that was the term on everyone's lips.

The main hall of the inn was dotted with round tables and high-backed chairs. A few lanterns, now extinguished, hung from the walls and beams traversing the room. The place seemed well maintained, to my surprise.

Before long, the innkeeper appeared. A cheerful and lively old man, who apologized ten times for making us wait.

"You're very lucky," he told us after we paid for four rooms. "If you had come just two days earlier, you wouldn't have found anything available. A lot of people have been around lately, as many as blades of grass, searching for that rebel prince. There's a pretty price on his head, they say."

"Why do you think we're here, if not to catch that stinking rat?" Merwin asked with a deep grin.

"Rats are all those from Romir. How many times have we asked for their help, and all they did was send us a handful of soldiers who did nothing but eat our food and drink our beer, then left? The same goes for those from Blackstone."

"Seems like you're doing quite well without them," Kayra observed.

"We manage. What else can we do? I'll tell you what: to die! That's what's left for us to do. It wouldn't hurt if that prince would come to hack them. Maybe that would change things around here! I heard his lady slaughter a few hundred."

I let out a loud gasp, but kept my mouth shut.

"Oh, but don't listen to Grandpa!" a young woman shouted from behind a small door that opened at the back of the inn. "He's been saying nothing but nonsense lately. We, like everyone else, are on the King's side and hope from the bottom of our hearts that..."

"Who's everyone else?" interrupted the innkeeper. "You name me ten people in this village who are on the King's side, and I'll go drink milk from the pig's teat right now. You find me ten people who wouldn't side with that Darion if war broke out!"

"You've said enough, father," said a man around forty who entered through the same door the girl had come from earlier.

"But I spoke the truth," the old man defended himself, as his son grabbed him by the shoulders and gently pushed him towards the exit.

"Please, excuse my grandfather," the young woman said again.

She had blue eyes and blonde hair, her face incredibly similar to Arlieth's. I swallowed hard.

"People seem to believe that a rebellion has begun," I observed.

"Well, hasn't it?" the girl asked. "Rumors have it that Prince Darion is roaming the kingdom, gathering his loyal men to attack the capital."

I remember being furious beyond measure. I didn't want the crown, I never did. The girl in front of me probably noticed my anger as she quickly averted her gaze.

"We've already paid for four rooms," Merwin said hurriedly.

"Of course," the girl replied, taking four pairs of keys from behind the counter.

"Rebellion, you hear?" I muttered, turning to Aella after the girl left ahead.

She silently weighted me with a solemn air, then shrugged. I wanted to ask her what she was thinking, but I didn't expect to get an answer, so I just started walking ahead.

All four rooms were upstairs. I shared a room with Aella, Kayra with Mathias, Regihold with Yenna, and Kaldur slept with Merwin and Lyra in the largest of the rooms.

From outside, we could hear the wind roaming the now empty streets of Bragovik, roaring like a furious lion. Lightnings streaked through the dark clouds, giving birth to thunders that made the wooden-framed old windows tremble.

"I'm glad we found a room," Aella said as soon as I locked the door behind. "I wouldn't want to be outside in such weather."

"Can you believe those people think I've started a rebellion?" I asked, unable to shake the girl's words from my mind.

"The girl resembled Arlieth remarkably," she told me.

"Changing the subject."

"Does it matter what they believe? If what the innkeeper said is true, it means some people would support you in case of war."

"War..." I repeated. "High Heavens! I'm not seeking war."

"Sometimes peace can only be achieved through war."

She stretched out on the bed, leaving me to frown at the storm raging outside. I sat down beside her. Wisps of smoke, carrying with them a tempting smell from the kitchen below, crept into the room through the poorly fitted floorboards.

"I'll stay a few minutes on the bed until the storm passes," I told her, not wanting to talk about wars anymore. "Then I'll go to the blacksmith."

Aella rested her head on my chest. I kissed her on the forehead, absentmindedly stroking her hair. I didn't realize how tired I was until I lay down in bed. I closed my eyes for a few moments, and when I reopened them, the storm had already passed, and the faint rays of the sunset were casting a reddish hue on the wall. I had probably slept for a few good hours.

Aella still slept in my arms. I unsuccessfully tried to slip out without waking her, then took my sword, which I left leaning against the wall. Aella smiled at me with half-closed eyes before turning away to go back to sleep.

"*There will be no war,*" I lied to myself as I left the room.

Jane

Excerpt from Elena's journal, dated the thirtieth day of the sixth month, Iura, in the year six hundred twenty-three after the Conversion:

The grimace filled with terror from my betrothed, during last night's nightmare, kept involuntarily appearing in my mind as I struggled with the sleep that refused to come. It was just like one of those moments when I read the same paragraph from a book several times, trying to see the message the author hidden among the lines. I knew there was a message, I knew it was there, and I knew I couldn't understand it yet, and that drove me crazy. It was as if I could feel the scream filled with horror and remorse, echoing through the walls of his dark chamber.

"*Bhalphomet! What have you made me do?*"

"*What did you dream, you idiot? What scared you so much?*" I wondered, looking at him sleeping. I held him tight, feeling overwhelmed by a strong desire to protect him. My anger from the previous day faded into the shadows stretching like dark canvases over the tall walls.

I frowned, remembering the brutal way he pushed me out, and slapped him across the face. He continued to sleep undisturbed. It was to be an arranged marriage, but certainly not one I regretted, as I had grown very fond of this northern king. We were both broken, and the wounds inflicted by Darion were still deep and fresh, but it was much easier to recover together.

When I finally managed to fall asleep, the bells of the worship temples began to ring loudly throughout the city. I had to meet that Jackard, whom I paid to find the woman named Meredith Grey, who lived in the Colorful Square and whom I hoped could lead us to Jane.

I rose reluctantly and glanced down at Larion, who was still peacefully asleep, undisturbed by the exasperating bells. I smiled warmly at him before giving him a strong whack on the head with the pillow.

"What?" he asked, looking around confused. "What's happening?"

"Wake up," I said. "We've got stuff to do. I hope you don't have any court meetings or other nonsense because I plan on dragging you along all day."

"Why?" he asked, still confused.

"Just to show you I'm not sleeping with anyone. Not with Oswin, not with the stable boy, not with the cook!" I hissed, smacking his head with the pillow after each person mentioned. "Get up and get dressed!"

He opened his mouth, likely about to apologize, but I silenced him with another blow of my fluffy weapon. He let out a defeated sigh, begrudgingly got up, and muttered something to himself. He dressed quickly and had to wait for me for a long time while I fixed my hair and hid my dark circles. He didn't like waiting at all. He paced restlessly from one wall to another, asking me every thirty seconds, "Is it taking much longer?"

"Probably," I always replied.

He would scowl, and I would smile, tilting my head to the side and biting my lower lip, pretending to be intimidated by his restlessness.

"Can you at least tell me what we're doing?" he asked at some point.

"Do you remember on the day of the tournament... when Rorik opened the competition and won?" I asked.

He nodded, then turned to me, assuming a serious expression. I didn't enjoy talking about that day, and he knew it.

"The girl to whom he gave a rose immediately after winning was named Jane. She was a maid in Montrias, and at the same time, his secret love. I realized this when I noticed she went to clean his room too often and stayed longer than necessary. Dad didn't approve of their relationship, but he didn't interfere as long as he didn't get her pregnant. Of course, Rorik, being an *idiot* like any other *idiot*, got her pregnant."

I emphasized the word *idiot* and looked at him meaningfully. He smiled gently, lowering his gaze to my barely noticeable bump.

"Dad lost his mind," I continued, "but he couldn't do anything to Jane. Not as long as my brother took care of her."

"Poor thing," Larion murmured, understanding where I was going with this.

"Exactly!" I said coldly, trying to detach myself from the sharpness of the words. "Now Jane is pregnant and alone in a foreign country, in a foreign city. I'm sure she doesn't trust me, but I want to take care of her, whether she likes it or not. She's out there somewhere, I just need to find her."

"Then we'll find her and bring her to the palace. And if that drives my dear father-in-law mad, even better."

I shook my head, laughing. "You're unbelievable."

I took one last look in the mirror, ensuring everything looked flawless, then placed it onto the table, making sure to align the tail perfectly parallel to the edge of the table, just as it should be.

"Finished," I declared triumphantly.

"Praise Azerad!"

We descended together. Beatrice was already waiting for us in the Great Hall, wearing a dress snug on her chest, abdomen, and thighs, the same shade of blue as mine. She raised her eyebrows when she saw Larion, then bowed her head obediently.

"Beatrice, always a pleasure to see you," Larion said half-heartedly. "I suppose you'll be joining us wherever we go."

"Likewise, King Larion. I won't be accompanying you; it is you who will be accompanying us, isn't it, Princess? Don't worry, it's no trouble, you're welcome to come."

Larion chuckled, trying for a moment to come up with a retort, but eventually gave up.

"Princess Elena," she greeted me, then leaned in and whispered in my ear, "The one who makes the kings kneel."

I giggled, and she smiled like a child when promised something. Without a doubt, she'll ask for details later, then be disappointed when I confess that I gave in and forgave him without making him do anything. For now. Larion looked at me curiously, probably wondering what Bea whispered to me, but he didn't bother to ask. We walked out of the palace arm in arm, with Bea to my right.

Jackard was chatting with Oswin in the shade of a house in the square by the north gates of the palace. They both frowned when they noticed Larion walking alongside me. Jackard straightened and stared at his feet, unwilling to meet the king's eyes.

"Long live King Larion," he muttered. Larion simply nodded, casting a cold glance in his direction.

After Oswin and Larion shook hands, I took the lead. "What did you find out about Meredith Grey?"

"She's a servant at Lord Gravens' villa. I tried to talk to her, but the guards at the door wouldn't let me in. I could have told them I was sent by Princess Elena herself, but I wasn't sure if it was appropriate."

"I don't see why not. Anyway, take us there," I requested.

I didn't know what to think about all this. I felt my betrothed had many questions, but he held back, not wanting to show in front of the others that he had no idea why we were there. A heavy atmosphere hung over us, undoubtedly caused by the presence of the King in our group. Oswin wasn't as talkative anymore, and even Beatrice seemed to have lost her desire to tease him, which didn't happen often.

Jackard led us through the city until we reached a narrow street that ran parallel to the Colorful Square, lined with tall houses of one or two stories. The roofs were tiled in various shades of blue, seemingly in tune with the nearby market.

The red-haired man stopped, nodding toward the building across from us. It was certainly the largest on the street, both in length and height. It rose three stories high, with intricate patterns resembling waves carved into the tall walls, up to the balconies adorned with flowers. Two guards, wielding long spears and chainmail armor, stood in front of the stairs leading to the massive wooden gates.

"Here," said Jackard. "But those two aren't very talkative."

"That's exactly why we brought the King," Bea said, patting Larion on the shoulder. "Unlike others, he can enter wherever he pleases, whenever he pleases," she added, looking insistently at Oswin.

Larion laughed, understanding the hidden meaning behind Beatrice's words. I chuckled too, remembering the bewildered look on my future husband's face when, on my first night in Romir, I entered his room with Beatrice and began undressing. He was confused and didn't manage to say much, but he didn't object either. Bea was my gift to him, and in return, he left me pregnant. Oswin didn't flinch, probably preferring to pretend he didn't understand.

"Remind me again," Larion said. "Who are we looking for?"

"Meredith Grey," Oswin replied. "She could lead us to Jane."

"Of course," my betrothed said, piercing me with his gaze.

"There won't be a need anymore," Bea said quietly, looking over my shoulder.

I followed the direction she was looking and saw Jane coming from the end of the street. She was accompanied by another woman, whom I could only assume was Meredith. Meredith seemed to be around twenty years old, slightly plump but beautiful, with a cherubic face and tiny dimples in her rosy cheeks.

"Is that her?" Larion asked.

"Mhm," Bea nodded.

Jane looked exactly as I remembered her, perhaps just a little more drawn. She wore a plain dark brown dress, made of coarse material with a frayed and shabby appearance, under which I could clearly see the outline of her belly. Her silver hair, so strange, so unique, seemed to glow in the summer sun. I almost couldn't believe I was seeing her. I had been searching for her for so many days that I had begun to get used to it, and although I hoped to find her, deep down I doubted I would succeed. They were approaching us directly, completely unaware of our presence.

The street wasn't very crowded, but the girls were deeply engrossed in their lively conversation. Without thinking, I placed the promised gold in Jackard's hand, then hurried towards Jane. Larion followed in my footsteps.

"... and I had to lift the bucket because he was afraid," Jane chuckled. "Such a big man scared of such small creatures."

Meredith laughed, covering her mouth with the palm of her hand, but there was a hint of sadness in her laughter, perhaps sensing the bitterness Jane was trying to cover with happy memories; the tears hidden behind the laughter. No doubt they were talking about Rorik and his fear of spiders. I smiled too, recalling his expression when he saw one crawling across the table while conversing with Lord Fairslarr. He didn't display his fear in front of others, but his eyes kept darting towards the tiny creature inching closer to him. I sat beside, and with a subtle movement, I sent the spider to weave webs in the marble palaces of the erthals. When I talked to him later, he pretended not to have noticed it at all.

Jane's eyes landed on me. She flinched and halted abruptly, visibly torn between attempting to flee, or staying put. The color drained from her already pale cheeks as she tightly gripped Meredith's dress sleeve.

"I don't harm anyone..." she whispered so softly that I could barely hear her voice.

I approached and hugged her tightly before she could make a move to flee. My high-heeled shoes wouldn't be of much use if I had to chase after her, and I preferred not to start my day running barefoot through the city after a pregnant woman. She hugged me back, but I could feel the rapid beating of her heart. Beatrice was right, she was just like a frightened kitten, and it fell upon me the daunting task of showing her that I was her friend.

"I've been so worried about you," I whispered. "How are you feeling? How's the pregnancy?"

"Alright," she replied, pulling away from the embrace and locking eyes with me. "I'm fine. It's probably a girl, that's what several women have told me. Midwifes, women who know their stuff."

"Whatever it may be..."

"And I'll leave Romir. I don't even know where. Somewhere far away, and I promise you won't hear from us again..."

"You don't have to leave," Larion chimed in. "Elena has been searching for you for weeks because she feared for your safety. Both she and I are willing to do whatever it takes to keep you and the child safe."

She shielded her belly with her hands over and took a step back.

"The child is a girl," she insisted with a trembling voice. "Please, just let me go and I promise I won't..."

"Let's go somewhere away from prying eyes and talk," I suggested, noticing people casting curious glances at us from windows.

She seemed poised to shove me aside and run. Perhaps she would have even tried if not for Larion. "Where should we go?" she asked in one breath.

"Wherever you feel safest," I responded, smiling warmly at her.

She nodded, then turned to Meredith askance. "I can't accompany you," Meredith answered her unspoken question. "You'll be safe, Jane, if the King himself promised it, then it will be so."

There was something in her undertone that suggested she was trying to convince herself as much as she was trying to convince Jane. Jane probably hadn't said very nice things about me. In Montrias, I mostly treated her with indifference. I wasn't looking to befriend her or sleep with her; in other words, I didn't care. When I saw Rorik making eyes at her, I thought that in a few weeks, I would find her sobbing in the hallway after he discarded her, as he had done many times before with other maids. But weeks turned into months, and months into years, and she was still there. There were moments when Rorik argued with Father because of her, and I was afraid he would leave the palace, just like Father's uncle, King Arthur, had run away with the maid who stole his heart. Ellie was her name, Grandma used to say.

"Thank you for everything," Jane said.

"You're welcome," Meredith replied. "I can't wait to see you again. Take care, Jane." She bowed her head in front of us and then hurried into the villa. She didn't seem very calm seeing that we *kidnapped* Jane, but she probably understood she couldn't do anything.

"I'll leave you now," Oswin said. "I don't think you need my help anymore."

"You make it sound as if we did," Beatrice retorted with a mischievous smile. He shrugged.

"Thank you so much, Oswin," I said. "Honestly. You've been a great help."

"It was my pleasure." He nodded and left, but not before throwing one last hostile glance at Beatrice, who smirked playfully, winking at him.

"Which way should we go?" I asked Jane.

"We can go to the inn where I'm staying."

She started walking ahead, and I had to hurry to catch up with her. Larion and Beatrice followed close behind, probably to give the girl the space she needed. I relied on my betrothed to catch her if she tried to escape.

"I'd be pleased if you came with us to the palace," I said to her without beating around the bush, after a long period of walking in silence. She understood that I wasn't politely asking her to come with us, but directly ordering, so she simply complied. Of course, her agreement echoed the enthusiasm of a lamb about to be led to slaughter, but at least it was a start.

She led us to an inn in the east of the city, a simple building, somewhat humble, perhaps even invisible to wealthier travelers who happened to be looking for a room in the city. But a good option for those with lighter pockets, as Jane.

Above the door was written in white paint: "*The Sleeping Giant Inn.*"

Jane entered first, and the innkeeper greeted her with a wide smile, which disappeared completely when he saw Larion. He widened his eyes in astonishment, staring at him as if he had seen a ghost. He seemed scared, but also relieved, and there was something in his expression that indicated he was about to run and embrace him. But he quickly regained composure. He made a bow, demonstrating the proper respect for the King, before inquiring about how he could be of service to us. I told him that we were here to wait for Jane, who would be leaving with us. Then, he insisted and insisted on bringing us something to drink until all three of us relented and accepted at least a cup of coffee.

"Darion used to eat here," Larion told me after the innkeeper left the counter. "That's why he reacted like that. The old fool thought I was him. He almost hugged me."

After spending the first day in Romir, Prince Darion left the impression of being a bit foolish, reckless, and easily manipulated. The gossips circulating about him among the nobles were nothing short of delicious. He made enemies among many high-ranking individuals, creating rows of enemies he probably didn't even know about. But the truth was, he had many friends among the soldiers and common people. People who loved him. He became known as a prince who was on the side of the common man. Was he planning a rebellion back then? How long had he been trying to plant this image in people's minds? He wore his mask so well that he even fooled me. Are we in danger?

"Why the hell didn't I see any guards in the palace last night?" I burst out.

Larion and Beatrice exchanged quick glances, both taken aback by my outburst. "It must have been the guard shift," Larion suggested casually.

I thudded my fingers against the tabletop, one at a time, while my gaze never left his eyes. "And do you find that normal?" I challenged. "I'm going to talk to the captain."

"I'll handle it," he assured me.

"You better. And know that I didn't see any patrols on the streets either. What are those people guarding? What are they paid for? If we were attacked..."

"Attacked by whom?" Beatrice interrupted, confused.

I shrugged, choosing not to voice my thoughts. Maybe I'm just exaggerating. "*May Azerad make it so!*"

Shortly after, the innkeeper brought a tray of honey cakes, three cups of coffee, and one filled with sugar. I was hungry, and the enticing smell of the cakes combined with the steaming coffee in front of me brought a wide smile to my face. Jane appeared shortly after, wearing a rucksack of patched leather on her back. She had a defeated and resigned glare.

"Miss Jane, shall I bring you a coffee too?" the innkeeper asked, leaning over the counter to hear her better.

"No, Tom, thank you so much! Coffee doesn't sit well with my stomach. You've already done so much for me, thank you," Jane replied.

"I did what anyone who declares themselves zerevit would do."

Despite Tom's refusals, Larion left some silver coins on the counter before we left, as Jane had stayed at his inn without paying anything. It was noon when we arrived back at the palace, and my betrothed had spoken with some maids about the new room I had promised to Beatrice; the one she would share with Jane. We decided not to disturb her for the rest of the day, as she didn't seem very pleased to see me, although she tried not to show it. When Larion was around, she seemed completely terrified, but that was not surprising, given that he bore the face of the man who had ruined her life.

When we returned to our room, I collapsed on the bed, trying to convince myself that I wasn't dreaming. That I had finally brought Jane to the palace, where she was safe. At least that was something I could do for Rorik; to care for his child, to give him a home, a future, and the love he would have given him.

Larion, who was with me in the room, looked at me with a smile, then sat on top of me and began to kiss my neck.

"Now, in broad daylight?" I asked hurriedly.

"Mhm," he grunted.

"No, no, no! First, you tell me what you talked about with Radagrim. You said you would tell me."

"After we finish."

"Now, Larion," I insisted, pushing him off me.

"High Heavens! You're impossible," he muttered.

I sat on his chest, feeling his still-rapid heartbeat. He placed his hand on my exposed thigh, skillfully moving up to my hip and back, under the fine fabric of my dress, sending shivers through my whole body. He was completely absent as he did this.

"I promised the old man that I would take this secret with me to the grave. It is very important, Elena, very important, not to tell anyone. Not even Beatrice. Not even me, let no one hear us."

"My lips are sealed."

"Radagrim believes that Aella is not a human being," he told me, then paused, waiting for my reaction.

I was astonished, of course, but I didn't react. For a moment, I expected to feel his chest trembling because of laughter. He didn't laugh, he was serious.

"You said she had horns and silver skin," I recalled. "Is that what it's about, isn't it?"

"Yes. The wizard says there are some writings that talk about a species of intelligent creatures, very similar to humans, very skilled in the secrets of magic. Nartingals, he said they were called They looked exactly as I described Aella to you but were able to take on human forms. Yet even when they pretended to be human, they couldn't hide their glowing eyes. You've seen them too, Elena."

"Nartingals," I repeated. "Do you think Darion knew?"

"He definitely knew. I have no doubt."

"Horns and silver skin," I whispered. "Larion, are you sure?"

"Do you think I'm crazy?" he grumbled arrogantly. "Even I couldn't believe it, but I know what I saw," he continued in a gentler tone.

"Are we safe?" I asked, sitting up to see his face. Half of his face glowed under the weight of the rays projected through the window, while the other half was shrouded in the room's shadow.

"Yes," he replied promptly. "Either Alfred will kill them, or the Circle's assassins."

"Do you really believe that?" I asked cautiously.

"Yes. Everything will be fine."

He was right. Things were going to end well, as they should.

Then... why am I so afraid?

Blue Night

The ground was muddy, and the air damp, but to my great relief, I saw only a few clusters of villagers around, who showed no interest in us. The storm had brought in the cold, which nipped me through the thick fabric of Regihold's cloak. I walked alongside Merwin in the direction indicated by the innkeeper, towards the edge of the village, where the forge was located. Above, dark heavy clouds spun, laden with rain, but to the west, the sky was clear, enveloped in a reddish aura from the setting sun.

Merwin tightened his lips every time he slipped in the mud, flailing his arms wildly to maintain his balance, then letting out a colorful curse that drew the attention of the villagers. Attention that we didn't need.

"Temper your mouth! We're trying to go unnoticed," I whispered.

"My apologies. These boots aren't made for this muck, neither am I. I swear, in the South even the mud is more civilized than what you have here, the air less biting, and the water more..."

"Wet?"

"Mock me all you want, but it's true. Not to mention the storms. Quite unpleasant; the wind roared like a lioness in heat. I thought it would sweep the inn away."

"I slept through the whole thing," I said indifferently. "It was a good sleep."

A thunderclap echoing from beyond the northern peaks darkened the wizard's face, and his lips formed a curse that was probably aimed at the gods.

"Speaking of storms," said the wizard, "do you think your lady could teach me to throw lightning bolts from the sky?"

I flinched, remembering the Night of the Blood Moon and the dozens of corpses left behind by Aella's storm. "Ask her."

"Surely she'd be more inclined to respond if you asked. I've tried initiating conversations with her a few times, but she's not very talkative with me."

"She's not talkative with anyone. And she usually doesn't answer questions if she thinks you already know the answer. She can be complicated sometimes, but you get used to it... eventually."

"Then I'll ask her directly."

"What do you mean, teach you?" I asked after a while. "How do you learn these things?"

I never quite understood how wizards wielded ether, although I asked for explanations several times and was eager to listen. I couldn't understand, not being able to touch magic like they could. It would be easier to describe colors to a blind man. Merwin fell silent for a few moments.

"Imagine you're in a river," he began. "Depending on how you move your hand, or in this case, your mind, you can make waves. Some bigger, some smaller, some more complex, others more... well, simple. You can make waves that crash into waves and give rise to other waves. The more ether you can absorb, the more waves you make. But to make complex waves, brute strength isn't enough, you have to learn how to draw them. The storm caused by your beloved is the result of incredibly complex and large waves. I'm sure I can draw enough ether to summon at least a lightning bolt from the sky, but I need guidance to weave the waves. I don't know any spell that originates from somewhere else, other than myself. I didn't even know it was possible."

"So, it all comes down to flailing your hands and imagining you're making waves?"

"No!" he exclaimed, shaking his head from side to side. "You have to feel them, command them. It isn't even necessary to use your hands."

He extended his index finger, and a flame sparked, dancing above it.

"You're drawing attention," I said calmly, scanning the surroundings.

None of the few people around showed any sign of noticing. That, or perhaps due to the strangers who had visited them in recent days, they had ceased to pay attention to small things, like a flame hovering above the hand of a wizard.

"Inevitable," he chuckled, making the small fire disappear.

The blacksmith shop, located on the terrace of the blacksmith's house, couldn't compare at all to the one in Romir, but it seemed to have everything necessary for that profession. I found the blacksmith bent over the forge; his face red from the heat. I cleared my throat to announce our presence. He raised his head, adopting a hostile expression, then using the tongs, he grabbed the reddish edge of a blade above the forge and plunged it into a trough of water. The steel hissed, sending clouds of steam into the air. He had long blond hair, with the tips blacked, probably because he had gotten too close to the flames and singed them.

"Nice work," I said, gesturing toward the blade in the trough.

"What do you want?" he grumbled. "We don't serve strangers anymore, so move along. And we have enough on our plate as it is."

"The handle of my sword is old and rusty, just needs replacing, or at least covering. It shouldn't take long," I said, tapping my coin pouch.

"Money is good when there's peace. But now there's war, and we need swords. They'll keep us alive, not money."

"My good sir, without money, how do you buy the necessities for the forge?" Merwin asked.

"The mountain is nearby, are you blind? Azerad provides us with everything we need, we just have to not be too lazy and gather its gifts. Now, don't waste any more of my time!"

I turned to leave, aware that if I stayed any longer, I'd punch him. I wasn't used to being refused or treated with superiority, but it was something I had to get used to. I wasn't a prince anymore. An old man came out of the blacksmith's house and turned his attention toward us. Like a magnet, his eyes fell upon my sword.

"Where did you get that sword?" he asked with hostility.

"It was a gift."

"Gift my ass, damn thief! I should call the guards."

"It'll be the last thing you do," I assured him with an icy voice, glancing at him and then at the blacksmith.

"Let's all calm down," Merwin intervened soothingly.

"What did you do to the one who carried it?" the old man asked.

"He gave it to me," I insisted.

He slapped his hand across the wall, then said, "You lie!"

"His name is Arthur, and he lives in a shack with his wife, Ellie. He is my friend."

The man's face brightened, but I could still see disbelief in his tired eyes.

"I still don't believe you, lad. Arthur wouldn't have given up his weapon. Unless..." he trailed off, studying me intensely. "Erwin, what did the prince from Romir look like? The one that the scums from Blackstone kept looking for. That Darion?"

My blood froze in my veins, and my hand descended to the hilt of the sword. I was undecided about what to do, for I found myself in a village full of armed men, with archers waiting on the rooftops of houses, eager to shoot at something. Only then did I realize how foolish the idea was to come to Bragovik.

"Like him," said Erwin the blacksmith, taking a step back, realizing who he had before him. He grabbed his hammer, which lay leaning against the forge, and his thick arms tensed. He was ready for a fight.

I was ready to draw my sword when Merwin began to laugh.

"Darion you say. And who am I, the woman he ran away with?"

Erwin smiled, but I did not. I couldn't remain calm while the blacksmith held his hammer and was just a few steps away from me. I didn't know what his intentions were.

"We're also looking for Grayfang. Why do you think we came all the way here, to this Azerad forsaken place? No offense," the wizard spoke.

"We were told he fled north," I said, reluctantly prying my hand from the weapon.

"I don't care if you are Darion or not," Erwin said. "Romir doesn't help us, and neither does Blackstone; so it's not my concern." He set his hammer down and reached out his hand. "Let me see that sword."

I hesitated, and the old man took a few steps closer, continuing to stare at me. Eventually, I gave him my sword, thinking that Merwin would kill him if he tried anything. The blacksmith pulled it halfway from its sheath and whistled.

"It's beautiful, isn't it?" the old man asked.

"The best I've seen," the blacksmith acknowledged.

"Just a piece of iron," Merwin commented, shrugging.

"Iron?!" the old man burst out. "It's the highest quality steel, you fool! For many years, I've tried to reproduce it, but the secrets of forging such a weapon have long been lost. And as for you," he said, looking at me, "my pigs are better liars. You reminded him of himself, that's why he gave you the sword."

I nodded. "That's what he told me too; that he was a warrior, like me."

"And like you, prince, he was a nobleman. Arthur Tarrygold of Frevia."

"He chuckled at the sight of my widened eyes. Even Erwin started to laugh, while Merwin appeared puzzled by the entire scene.

Arthur Tarrygold was once the king of Frevia, but he fled the palace, relinquishing the crown, with his beloved, a woman of humble birth. He took with him only the legendary family sword, the Heart of Dawn, which now, through a simple twist of fate, or perhaps a game of destiny, came to me. I remember that in the early days when I was on the run with Aella, I recalled the story of King Arthur and felt so much that I was living it.

"The Heart of Dawn," concluded the blacksmith. "It's a pride for me to have held it in my hands. And it will be a pride to repair its handle, Prince Darion."

I nodded. "I'm not Darion, but thank you."

"And we would be grateful if you wouldn't spread such rumors," Merwin spoke. "The last thing we need is to wake up chased through the streets with swords and knives. Ah... and axes, let's not forget about axes."

"The people here don't care about the problems of those in the south even as much as dirt under their nails," Erwin said. "And they don't care about us either. If they did, they would have sent aid."

"I'm surprised that the mountain folk have the courage to attack such a large and well-defended village," I said. "From what I've heard, their clans rarely reach a thousand, and even more rarely do they have the necessary equipment for serious combat."

"The Blood Wolves, that's what they call themselves," the blacksmith told us, spitting out the name like a curse. "There are quite a few of them. Maybe a thousand, maybe more. The village may be large, but we only have about three or four hundred men able to fight, of which three-quarters are useless. Damn it, one stabbed his own feet twice!"

"Over a thousand," I repeated in surprise. "High Heavens! And did you inform Romir about this?"

"Your brother sent a handful of soldiers who did nothing. They just sat and drank while we fought under the scorching heat to fortify the place, then they said the barbarians probably killed each other. The scums left, and the next night we were attacked. Others came from Blackstone, but only to ask about you, not to defend us."

"They all shit on us," the old man spat.

"There will come a time when justice will be served," I declared.

I hated the injustice done to them and wished I could help, but I needed to reach Yermoleth and then the Mountain of Dragons. We had to free the Daughters of the Night; too much depended on it. But I vowed that I would return, I swore that I would come back to help them.

"It will come," the blacksmith agreed. "But only if Darion wins the War of Lions. That's the only way things will change in the kingdom."

He was talking about the dream of my ancestor, the prophetess Arika. She transformed Aella and the other girls into Daughters of the Night, using a spell created by Yermoleth himself. She prophesied that one day, two brothers from my family, the Grayfang family, would start a war that would shake the entire kingdom. Some believed it had already happened, as all generations of twins in the family ended up killing each other. Others believed it would never happen, and others believed it was happening right then.

"There is no war," I assured.

"That's what we believe, at least," Merwin chimed in.

"I'll repair the handle for you," the blacksmith finally said. "Come tomorrow evening to pick it up."

I sighed. "Tomorrow evening?"

"This is the Heart of Dawn. The work must be impeccable."

I nodded, looking at the weapon one last time before leaving. It wasn't easy for me to part with it, especially now that I knew what it was. On the way back, my thoughts revisited the elder monarch, residing in his humble dwelling alongside his consort, and I vowed to myself that I would make a visit to his abode once more. At that time, I made many promises that I didn't know if I could keep.

"Do you think we're in danger?" Merwin asked in a low voice.

"I don't know. I tend to think not, but we should still be on guard."

"You were so annoyed, you almost hit both the blacksmith and the old man. Be calmer."

"I was calm," I responded dryly.

"Like a bull stung in the rear. So, what about the sword?"

"It belonged to the old king of Frevia, Arthur Tarrygold. He fled the palace about fifty years ago with a maid, Ellie, with whom he still lives a few hours from Romir. He took the legendary sword of the family with him when he left, and a few weeks ago, he gave it to me. He didn't reveal his identity, and I didn't figure it out."

"Destiny seems to be on your side, my friend," he said with a quiet voice.

"Destiny?"

His right hand draped across my shoulders as he spoke, his voice unnecessarily loud. "Destiny, fate, Azerad, Deoa, the gods. My friend, I'm talking about that force, whether personal or impersonal, that governs it all. The Absolute, if you may."

"I don't believe in all that. Destiny is malleable."

"Your prophetic dreams are malleable," the wizard told me. "Because you see the paths you *can* or *cannot* take, but destiny is the path you *will* take and that is unchangeable. Everything is decided and everything has a purpose. That's my belief, supported by at least five scholars that I know of."

"Maybe," I shrugged. Not because I was considering his idea, but because at that moment, I didn't care about philosophy, theories, or any other triviality that distracted us from our purpose.

Darkness already enveloped the village. More and more men with chainmail shirts and helmets were circling the wall, occasionally glancing beyond, into the blackness outside. Weak waves of light, undulating and flickering, emerged through the windows of some houses, lighting our way. The lights were also lit in the temple, and a soothing song poured forth from within, ascending to the heavens, where the worshipers hoped their god would listen. Merwin looked at, then signaled with his head in the direction of the building. Although initially I was prepared to refuse, I changed my mind and nodded. I wasn't very attracted to Azerad because I had no certainty whether he existed or not, but even I felt the need for the comforting embrace that place bestowed upon you.

The hall was quite small for such a large village. The ceiling had a hole above the altar, and the walls were still black in places. The remaining portion of the wall depicted erthals wielding fiery swords and clad in clean-colored garments, while Azerad was likely portrayed on the now-missing section of the ceiling. It seemed that he had fallen, leaving the villagers in nobody's care, I thought with a sneer.

To my surprise, the temple was crowded with people, mostly women and children, with the occasional men scattered here and there. Three young women stood in front of the altar, one of whom I recognized as the innkeeper's niece. The resemblance to Arlieth was striking, and for a moment, I wondered about the chances of the girl being one of Lord Lanre's bastards. The girls sang a ballad to Herradiel, the erthal of war, also known as Azerad's Fury, seeking his help and blessing.

Despite the small size of the hall, the candles and lamps placed everywhere were not enough to dispel all the shadows, leaving the corners of the room shrouded in darkness. The pure voices of the girls picked up pace, the notes fell heavier, and the verses passed more rapidly. Their trill was accompanied by the wind whistling through the hole. The song quickly became a call to arms; the stern expressions on the men's faces indicated they were ready to answer that call, prepared to give their lives to defend their homes and families.

The song gradually faded, the notes diminishing in intensity until they completely died out, but the echo of their voices still lingered in my mind.

"Beautiful," Merwin whispered.

The three glanced over the room, then the one resembling Arlieth stepped forward, cleared her throat, and began to sing. I recognized the song before the first verse ended. It was a love song, filled with assurances and declarations that everything would be resolved. It was called "*Blue Night*." Arlieth sang it to me on the morning Aella and I were supposed to leave, on that day when nothing was right, when nothing was resolved. Arlieth's voice sounded better, but the girl wasn't a bad singer either. Arlieth could have had all of this at the temple in Romir if she hadn't taken an arrow in my place.

My foolish prince.

"If there really is a god, as you say, and that god has decided everything... I'll find him and shove destiny up his ass," I muttered, then turned towards the exit.

"If there truly exists one, I hope he's a forgiving one," Merwin chuckled, following me.

Cold tears began to fall from the high sky as soon as I stepped outside. It would probably rain on those in the temple too, through the hole in the ceiling. "*That's how much Azerad cares about you,*" I thought. I tried to push out of my mind the memory of that last morning with Arlieth, before my life fell apart. I've treated her so unfairly since Aella was brought to Romir, and for that, I hate myself even now, in my old age.

We arrived back at the inn, where the old innkeeper was polishing a glass, talking to a man about thirty years old, clad in chainmail, who had both a sword and a round wooden shield with iron margin. A few people were seated at tables, discussing in low voices, so as not to drown out the silence outside. They wanted to hear when they would be attacked.

"Can you tell everyone that we should talk tomorrow morning?" I asked Merwin before parting ways with him, at the entrance to my room.

He nodded. "Are you well?" he inquired.

I hesitated, asking myself the same question. "Yes," I lied.

"Your face says otherwise. Ever since you heard that song..."

"It brought back some memories."

"Unpleasant ones?"

"I don't know," I responded, turning away from him.

I heard the joyful laughter of Lyra even before I entered. She sat with her back to Aella, who was braiding her blond hair. Kayra and Yenna sat on the floor, their feet crossed beneath them. Silence fell as they noticed me.

"We, ladies, hold court," the young one informed me in a formal tone.

"Forgive me, Your Highness. Had I known, I would not have disturbed you," I replied with a deep bow, and she began to laugh.

"Have you repaired the sword?" Aella asked, smiling.

"It will be ready by tomorrow. I'm off to have a beer, so I won't bother you anymore."

For a few moments, I lingered in the narrow corridor, watching the rain beat against the window, undecided whether to invite the others with me, or not. I decided not to, desiring solitude, if only for a brief respite. I descended once more into the hall and seated myself at the most secluded table, nestled in the darkest corner, pondering whether this choice would shield me from stares or draw even more attention.

I requested a beer from the innkeeper and surveyed the surroundings. None seemed interested in me, they surely had their own problems to deal with. I saw the old man's niece entering, covered from head to toe in a thick cloak, which she handed to him. He passed her the tankard and gestured toward me. The girl huffed angrily, making a furious little stomp, then came quickly to my table.

She handed the tankard, then assessed me for a few moments in a completely unsubtle manner. Even the slender, slightly arched brows reminded me of Arlieth. She slipped into the chair beside me, smoothing the hem of her dress as she sat.

"There's talk around the village that you are Prince Darion," she said directly, in a low voice.

I smiled, then took a long sip. "Of course there's talk. I know where this rumor started: from the talkative blacksmith, no doubt. I told him not to spread such words."

"I saw you at the temple," she said afterward. "You stayed very briefly, then left just as I began to sing." Since I didn't respond, she continued, "Didn't you like the song?"

"I did. It just reminded me of someone," I said.

She blinked a few times. "Someone dear, I hope."

"Very dear. You resemble her in many ways. Lady Arlieth of Blackstone."

"Oh," she muttered, suddenly saddened. "I heard she died about three weeks ago. Maybe a month."

"That's true," I replied with a heavy heart, feeling the weight of her death pressing upon me again.

Both she and my father passed away that day.

"I heard that... Prince Darion was to blame. Is it true?"

She examined me closely, waiting to see how I would react. I didn't react; I was numb.

"Darion would never harm her," I assured her. "He would have given his life for her."

"I understand..."

"But that night the gods decided otherwise. She jumped in front of an arrow that was meant to... to hit me."

In those moments, I wondered why I was telling this stranger all of this. I didn't know if it was prudent to confess who I was. Something about that somewhat familiar look prompted me to bare my soul to her.

"I'm sorry," she said in a voice so low it could have been the whisper of the wind from outside, then placed her hand over mine.

Tears filled my eyes. If I had known she was going to be hit, I could have warned her before she reached me. If I had known, I would have told her from the beginning to avoid the mist and run into the forest. If I had known all of this was going to happen, I wouldn't have accepted Rorik's duel invitation. If I had checked the sword when I received it, I could have stopped the fight before it started. If I had known that Melchior was going to attack, I could have avoided the attack and thus stopped the chain of events that led to the Night of the Blood Moon. If I had taken Aella's ring from Larion the moment I found out about it... So many things I could have done differently, so many things I could have done better.

"Me too," I said, trying to bury all my regrets in the drink from that tankard.

I took another long sip.

"I'm glad you're here, and as my grandfather said earlier: you have our support. Will you help us get rid of the wildlings?" she asked.

"I'll try," I replied. I was telling the truth, though I had no idea how I could help.

"The people here hoped that the current king would care more about us than the previous one, but obviously that wasn't the case. But about you, rumors say you're different."

"Different?" I asked, my full attention still fixed over her hand, that was covering mine.

"It's said that you dressed in simple clothes and spent time with common people, that you acted different from the nobles at court. A friend of the common folk."

"I suppose it's true," I said. "I never categorized people as simple or noble. I treated with respect those who deserved it, whether lords or farmers."

"You would make a good king," she said.

"I don't want to be king."

She puffed. "Why is it that those like you don't desire the crown, while those who have it don't deserve it?"

"I'm not fit to rule," I responded flatly.

"I don't believe we could find anyone more suitable," she whispered.

Her cold fingers tightened around mine. She stared at me intently, leaning slowly towards me, and for a moment I felt like in those days long ago when I sat next to Arlieth at the most secluded table we could find in the Great Hall, stealing quick kisses when we thought no one was looking. The urge to relive those moments was so overwhelming that for a moment I almost responded to the invitation of those slightly parted lips. I longed to kiss Arlieth again, to lose myself in her blue eyes and listen to her gossip for hours on end. But she wasn't Arlieth.

"If that's how it's decided, I'll become king whether I want to or not," I said in an askance manner.

"Yes," she replied, pausing far too close to my face. So close that I could feel her breath caressing my lips.

My eyes traced the shadows cast by the delicate outline of her slightly parted lips over her small chin, as I leaned to her.

"You drink beer without me. Is that how good of a friend you are?" I heard Regihold's voice just as our lips almost touched.

He approached us with loud stomps, accompanied by Merwin and Kaldur. The girl abruptly drew her head back and withdrew her hand from mine, then rose.

"Would you like anything else?" she asked.

"Four more mugs," I told her.

"Three," corrected Merwin, "and a glass of sweet red wine, if you please."

The girl bowed, then left, but not before casting me one last fleeting glance, her cheeks burning red. The three of them sat, and both Merwin and Regihold flashed me the most mischievous grins they could muster. Kaldur seemed neither surprised nor shocked, as mountain men often took multiple wives.

"You're quite the charmer," Merwin whispered across the table, leaning in.

"I'll teach you someday," I promised him.

I stayed until late and lost count of the beers. Even Merwin reluctantly accepted a mug, which he wrestled with for several hours. Throughout the night, I saw that young woman, Arlieth's double, whose name I didn't even know, smiling at me from behind the counter. After each glass I emptied, her smile became more provocative, and the invitation it conveyed became harder to refuse. But Aella was waiting for me in the room, and I was hers.

As I stumbled up the stairs to my room, the inn was already empty. Kaldur and Merwin were more sober, and only because of them did Regihold and I manage to climb the spinning stairs without incidents.

I don't have many memories from the rest of that night, but I vividly remember the headache I felt in the morning. Aella was awake and smiling at me knowingly, and beside her, with wide-open eyes staring at the ceiling, was Lyra. She had slept with us because she didn't like sleeping with the two. Kaldur was snoring, and Merwin was talking in his sleep, and the girl seemed to think they were somehow communicating.

I asked Aella to soothe my headache, but she insisted that Lyra do it, who, reluctantly, agreed. She wasn't entirely confident in her powers and always preferred not to use them unless necessary. Like when she had to heal me from Sihad's wounds or destroy the idol of Yohr'Sherrat in which I was trapped. But the little one managed to ease my pain effortlessly, and later she woke Regihold from his hangover. Kayra didn't seem very happy that Aella made her drink from the Great River, but she didn't object much.

It was past noon when we all crowded into Merwin and Kaldur's room, which, although the largest, was not made to accommodate so many people. But I didn't mind; in fact, in a way, it amused me. I started by apologizing to Yenna and Kaldur for not telling them I was a fugitive prince, but neither of them seemed bothered by it.

"It wasn't our concern," Yenna told me. "Wherever you came from or whatever title you had, you killed Iorval and we have to follow you. That's what our path demands, and if we don't respect our ways, then we are nothing but animals."

Aella repeated our plan. She had roughly indicated to Yenna the location of Yermoleth's house, and both the woman and Kaldur had agreed it would take at least a week to get there. Maybe more. That mountain, according to the two, was called *Shaitahar Canair*, the

Demon's Fang. The people of the clans avoided it, sometimes even detouring several kilometers on difficult trails just to not get close. A powerful creature lived there, a demon, friend to trolls and other monsters of their kind. And not just any trolls, they insisted, but talking, intelligent beasts, akin to humans.

"No doubt it's Yermoleth," spoke Aella.

"The Demon's Fang," Merwin repeated. "Sounds like a very welcoming place, perfect for a visit."

"Now would be the time to decide if you truly wish to proceed or not. Once we venture into the mountains, there may be no turning back," I cautioned.

I enjoyed their company, but I didn't want to put them in any danger. Lyra pouted as soon as she heard my suggestion, not wanting to depart from me and Aella. By then, she had become incredibly dear to me.

"If my little friend here, Lyra, says the voices in her mind told us to follow you, then I'll follow you," declared Merwin, starting to laugh.

"Regihold?" I asked.

The giant pondered, a process that usually took quite some time. He stroked his recently trimmed beard thoughtfully, then his gaze fell upon Yenna, who gave him a timid smile, brightening his face.

"Of course I won't back down!"

I turned to the archer. "Kayra?"

She looked at me silently for a few moments, then nodded with a serious air.

"Mathias?"

"Where she goes, I go," answered the man who stood in the corner of the room, his back against the wall.

"Then we leave at dawn tomorrow," I declared.

"You forgot to ask someone," scolded Aella, then her bright gaze fell upon the little one. "Lyra?"

The girl smiled, happy to be noticed. "I'll accompany you! That's what Deoa asked of me."

"Yermoleth is a friend to you?" asked the Shadow Walker.

"I'm not sure. But I tend to believe he will help us. The last time I saw him, seven hundred years ago, he told me that one day I would return to him to ask for his help."

Mathias nodded, but he didn't seem convinced at all. People change from day to day. The child of the night towards which we were heading was certainly very different from the one Aella had met seven hundred years ago. To some extent, I shared the uncertainty, yet this option appeared to be the best among our limited choices. The alternative was to head straight to Shartat and hope that the dragons living there wouldn't discover us.

"What kind of help do you hope to obtain?" asked Kayra, her voice sharp and cold as the iron tips of her arrows.

"Anything is welcome," replied Aella in her formal, cold tone. "Even simple information."

"Simple information," Kayra repeated, frowning.

"It would be more than what we already have," I interjected. "The Daughters of the Night are sealed in Shartat, and the place is teeming with dragons. I wouldn't want to go there completely clueless. But if anyone has any other ideas, I'd like to hear them. It's not a solid plan, I admit, but it's the only one we have."

"It seems you burn differently when you know more," laughed Merwin.

"It's not a solid plan," Mathias agreed, ignoring the wizard. "But I would really like to meet Yermoleth. A child of the night born like that."

Aella hadn't always been a daughter of the night. Seven hundred years ago, she was just a human living beyond the Redat Mountains. Arika, the queen of Romir, had prophetic dreams about the return of the First Gods and realized that the present-day wizards wouldn't be able to stand against them. She searched the world far and wide for many years, looking for a solution to the problem that consumed her like a disease. One day, her path led her north, to Yermoleth. He taught Arika's wizards the spell for creating other nartingals.

The spell was not very ethical, and Arika would never have been able to use it in Romir without starting a revolt. No sane wizard would willingly go through such a thing, to such pain and torment, but Arika had a lot of power and a desperate desire that drove her forward. Power and madness.

She marched north, beyond the Redat Mountains, into the world that then, as now, was considered uncivilized. No one cared what happened to the people there, because they did not conform to the southern way of life. She killed thousands. Anyone who crossed her path, died. She spared only those who could reach the Great River; those as Aella. She, and nine others survived the transformation, but hundreds died in terrible agony.

"Then you are narrow-minded, Shadow Walker," Yenna hissed, her hand clenching around Regihold's large forearm. "I don't like that we're heading towards the demon, but I'm forced to follow you."

"You're not forced to do anything," I said. "Kaldur, do you think you can lead us there?"

"Yes, Master Darion."

"You can turn back, Yenna."

"I will come. Kaldur is unripe; he couldn't even lead you to the door of the room," the woman said.

Kaldur smirked maliciously but didn't respond.

A day ago, Kaldur and Yenna had bought us clothes and cloaks. Better clothes, made of black leather, suitable for the strong winds we would encounter on the mountain ridges on our way to Yermoleth. Tonight, I was supposed to go to the blacksmith to get my Heart of Dawn back, and tomorrow morning, we were going to leave Bragovik.

Things seemed to be somewhat favorable for us. I prayed to the gods that this day would end well and that we could leave without unfortunate events. But I prayed in vain, for destiny had already prepared my path and the gods had decided that tomorrow the earth would run red with blood.

Lion's Fangs

Excerpt from Saya's journal, dated the first day of the seventh month, Iureia, in the year six hundred twenty-three after the Conversion:

The sickly and pale rays stretched through the tattered gray clouds, as if laboring to pierce the damp air. The atmosphere was oppressive, and nature itself terribly still, almost dead. Occasionally, we could hear the murmurs of the trees when a weak gust of wind descended from the mountain heights. The memory of yesterday's storm still lingered in the air, and the foreboding of a new one could be seen in the clouds forming to the north.

The winds yesterday were so strong they nearly blew me off my horse.

"We have nowhere to shelter, and no reason to stay here!" Sparrow shouted, her voice barely cutting through the roar of the storm.

She was right. The lightning stretched like skeletal hands, ready to seize the treetops above us. We couldn't shelter beneath them, and certainly couldn't approach the rocky walls too closely, for fear of the boulders hurled down by the winds.

The storm ceased a few hours before sunset, but the rain returned before long. This time it was gentler, but cold and relentless. The sunrise found me with chattering teeth, soaked to the bone. I also worried for the journal I kept wrapped in leather in my horse's saddlebag. I wouldn't have liked to lose all my writings from the past month.

Sparrow rode ahead, followed by Parzival and finally me. The trail we were on was narrow, and more than once we had to dismount and lead the horses by their reins when the path became too tight and perilous. Wolf had gone on reconnaissance before sunrise. He kept saying that we were very close and that our targets were accompanied by a large group of people.

A day earlier, Sparrow had asked Parzival to reduce the effect of one of the potions. They were too strong and impossible to use if the situation required a more delicate approach. Now, according to Parzival, you had to keep your nose pressed to the mouth of the bottle of diluted liquor to feel its effect.

"Can you teach me how to make such potions?" I asked, pulling my horse closer to his as the path began to widen.

"No," he replied without taking his eyes off the road.

I puffed, scowling at him. "And why not, may I ask?"

"Why do you want to know?"

"It's something I could use. If you didn't hibernate like a bear every night, you'd see I suffer from insomnia."

"It's not just about using the right herbs," he said, adopting an air of erudition. "The fire you use to boil it is important too; the fire born from ether. You can poison yourself if you use too much magic."

I wrinkled my nose, gasping. "You can't poison yourself from those plants, even I know that much. Do you really think I'm that dumb?"

"You can make poison out of anything, if you know how. You can make it even if you don't know how, and that scares me about you."

"You're such a..."

"Apprentices, a little quiet please!" Mrs. Sparrow requested.

I shot one final ugly look at Parzival before cutting him off, passing between him and Sparrow. The assassin woman held her shoulders raised, her back straight. Was she even breathing? The two of them were always on high alert, always ready, but this morning something seemed terribly different.

We stopped in a clearing to change our wet clothes, then continued on our way. It was past noon when we found Wolf, who was waiting for us at the edge of a lake, gazing thoughtfully towards the nearby valley.

"I found them," he said as soon as we managed to get in hearing range.

I could feel a pit forming in my stomach, and my heart began to beat faster. I observed Parzival, mounted to my right, pulling tighter on the bridle of his horse, his face growing serious.

"They've diverged from their traveling companions, yet they're still not alone. Though still escorted, their retinue now numbers, I'd say, less than ten."

"Encouraging," I murmured sarcastically.

Not quietly enough, as both Wolf and Sparrow turned to me at once. Wolf seemed amused by my comment, but his wife looked at me as if I had made her drink seawater.

Crabs and shells.

"Tell me, Saya, isn't ten smaller than a hundred?" Sparrow asked.

"It is, Mrs. Sparrow."

"How many times?"

"Ten times," I replied as quickly as I could.

"And aren't you glad we have to face ten times fewer enemies?"

"I am, Mrs. Sparrow."

"They're in a village at the foot of the mountain," said Wolf. "I haven't seen them, but I've circled the village enough times to realize they went in there and haven't come out. The village is quite large. It has a protective wall and a few archers. They probably have trouble with the wild clans living in these mountains."

"How do we proceed?" Parzival wanted to know.

"We must consult first," Sparrow said. "Let's scout the settlement."

Wolf led us along the edge of the lake, under the tangled branches overhead, and then down the green slopes of that valley. The trees swayed slowly in the wind flowing from the north like rivers, pushing us forward, closer to Darion.

"Are you feeling alright?" Parzival asked, riding his horse alongside mine.

"Yes," I replied. "I can't wait for it to be over, to capture them and go home."

Home. The Tower of Fire wasn't my home, but it was the closest thing to it I ever had. If I had become a witch in Romir, would that old, gloomy city have become home to me?

"Wolf and Sparrow will take care of Aella, I have no doubt," he whispered.

"Probably, but let's not forget about Darion," I cautioned.

"Darion," he scoffed. "He's harmless. He can't do anything to you because he can't wield the ether."

"You're right," I agreed. It is foolish to fear a simple man.

We stopped at the edge of the forest, not far from the village. It indeed had a defensive wall made of logs, with a few gaps here and there. The villagers had cut down trees and cleared vegetation around the settlement to ensure a better view of the surroundings. We could see some faces peeking out for brief moments over the wall. They didn't even realize they were being watched. Others lay stretched out on straw roofs, with bows nearby.

"I see holes in the wall," said Parzival. "Maybe we can sneak inside."

"Why sneak in when we could just walk through the door?" I asked him.

"We don't know how welcoming they'll be, and we don't know if they're loyal to Darion or not."

"You're right."

"We can't sneak through the gaps," Wolf told us, frowning at the wall. "They left those spots empty to lure enemies there. Those portions are probably better guarded than the entire wall."

"What if the defenders fall asleep on duty?" Parzival asked, smiling.

"In broad daylight, others would see them falling," said Sparrow. "We'll go in, but we'll do it after nightfall. What's the next step, Parzival?"

Parzival frowned, wanting to show how seriously he took his role. For a few moments, he didn't respond, trying to give the impression that he was lost in thoughts, although I was sure he had everything planned already.

"If the village has an inn, we'll probably find them there. We can also stay there ourselves and then follow them. We'll see what they do..."

"Have you not paid attention to anything we've discussed in the past few days?" Sparrow asked sharply. "Do you have bees in your head? Didn't you hear that..."

"What Sparrow means to say," interrupted Wolf, casting a disapproving glance at his wife, "is that we know far too little about Aella and her affinity to magic. If we get too close, we risk her noticing our magical signature."

"You're right, sir" said Parzival.

"Saya, do you have a plan?" Wolf wanted to know.

"No," I replied hastily.

I did have a plan. I was thinking of using the ether to ignite the roofs of a few houses. People would likely gather to extinguish the flames, and then we could throw a concentrated potion to put them all to sleep. If Aella and Darion were there, I could have pulled them out. But I chose to remain silent. I didn't want Sparrow to tell me that I had bees in my head.

"Of course you don't," complained Sparrow. "Oh, these youths. Were we like that at their age?"

"At their age," repeated Wolf with a smile, his face lighting up. "When we sneaked into the attic..."

"Shh," hissed Sparrow, blushing. "Let's get back to the plans!"

The sudden blush brought a smile to my lips and made me wonder what Wolf would have said if Sparrow had allowed him. A ray of sunlight managed to sneak through the gray clouds and make its way through the branches of the green roof, casting itself over Sparrow's face. Her black eyes sparkled, and the blush on her cheeks was accentuated by the paleness of her skin, which seemed to glow under that gentle radiance.

"We're not in a hurry," said Wolf, still smiling. "If no opportunity arises, we can wait until they come out. Why willingly enter the cage?"

"*Especially with the lion there,*" I mused silently, thinking again about that prince.

"And if an opportunity arises, we'll take it," added Sparrow.

So we waited, gazing at the last clean clouds that seemed like smoke, rushing across the sky as if fleeing from the storm, just like yesterday. It was cold for a summer day, and the desolate atmosphere only accentuated my dreadful unease, the gaping void that grew larger with each passing hour.

For a good part of the day, I sat on the roots of a tree protruding from the ground like giant serpents. The village was still. No one entered, no one left. Time seemed to freeze. Even the stormy clouds clung to the high peaks, refusing to descend into the valley.

"Are you feeling alright?" Parzival asked, sitting down to my right.

"Mhm," I replied. "Why do you keep asking me that?"

"You seem quite stressed."

"I'm fine, just lost in thoughts. Sweet of you to notice."

A smile crept onto his lips as he lowered his head, attempting to conceal it. "I'm more concerned about the storm behind us than those two. It seems to be moving in a different direction now, though."

"Where did Sparrow and Wolf go?" I asked, looking around.

"They left to check the perimeter of the village. They want to make sure once again that Darion is still there and to search for possible escape routes in case we enter tonight. At this point, I'm not even worried if he's fled the village already, for we're close and we'll catch him soon, then it will all be over."

I could feel a hint of sadness in his words, like a shadow spreading quickly over his chubby face.

"You don't seem happy," I noticed.

He shrugged. "We'll return to the Circle, and things will go back to normal."

"Yes. You sound like you don't want that?"

He opened his mouth and drew in a deep breath, as if about to say something, then changed his mind. He nodded, stood up, then left. There was something he wasn't telling me.

When Sparrow and Wolf returned, the last rays of light had already vanished behind the mountains to the northwest, leaving us at the mercy of the dark clouds swirling like a vortex. Sparrow was smiling, but something about the way she walked unsettled me. They approached almost noiselessly, and the only reason I noticed them was because I was looking directly in the direction they were coming from.

"There are people hidden among the trees to the south," Wolf said.

"Darion's rebels?" Parzival asked.

"Unlikely," the assassin-wizard replied.

Sparrow added, "Not everything revolves around them."

"They're probably wildlings," Wolf continued. "I haven't heard anyone in their group speak the common tongue; the language they speak is rough and unrefined. I counted seven hundred."

"Seven hundred?!" I exclaimed. "They'll attack the village!"

"Probably," Sparrow said almost indifferently. "And our targets are there. As you can imagine, or I hope you can," she continued, looking at me and Parzival, "if Aella is killed by them, we won't be able to take her alive to the Circle."

"*Of course we can imagine!*" I thought, pursing my lips.

"Which, wouldn't be so bad, because we've been told that if it's too dangerous to capture her in..." Wolf tried to say, but stopped and quickly lowered his head when his wife shot him a venomous look.

"Stay focused!" Sparrow urged us. "This attack might be the opportunity we've been looking for."

We all nodded at once, like three recruits responding to their superior's command.

"However, we won't take any risks," Wolf added sternly, and his wife nodded in agreement.

"I see movement!" Sparrow whispered. "Shadows among the trees, emerging from the forest."

Silence fell upon us. We all moved closer, trying to peer into the now dense darkness between us and the village. I could make out several silhouettes leaving the trees line, but it wasn't until the first lightning bolt erupted in the distance that I could see how many there were. Most wore leather armor, others chainmail or scales, and all were armed with swords, axes, spears, or bows.

The villagers had spotted them too, because shortly after, we could hear commotion coming from there. A few lit torches were thrown over the wall, illuminating the field outside, and people with bows and spears gathered to meet the attackers. Probably behind the nearly two-meter-high wall was a raised earthen mound, giving the defenders a chance to strike at the invaders without too much difficulty.

The clan stopped in front of the village. Above the gates, perched on a wooden platform, stood a few tall men armed with longbows.

"Take one more step, and we shoot!" one of the defenders shouted.

A savage took a few steps forward, his hands wide open, to show that he wasn't afraid. Another lightning bolt tore through the sky, illuminating the horrifying scene unfolding before us. The man was tall, broad-shouldered, and bald, with a long beard. I couldn't make out his facial features well because of the distance.

"If shoot, I'll catch you and stick arrow up your ass, then make you eat!" he yelled, and this sparked waves of mocking laughter among his men.

"This doesn't look good," Parzival said slowly.

"They will resist," Wolf told us.

"We are four wizards; maybe we can help them," I suggested.

"Maybe," Sparrow said thoughtfully. "But it's not our concern; we are here for Darion and the Black Queen."

I gasped. "Not our concern? I thought the Circle's role..."

"The tone, Saya!" the assassin woman warned me. "You'd do well to remember, because I won't repeat it again."

"I'm sorry..."

"I won't tolerate disrespect."

I hung my head like a beaten dog.

"I am Thorgard, master of the Blood Wolves!" the man shouted, drawing his sword from its sheath. "And I have come with a proposition!"

"Speak, then," the archer on the wall replied.

"One hundred swords, one hundred axes, twenty chainmail shirts, fifty metal helmets, one hundred sheep, thirty cows, and twenty young women, fit to bear children. That's the demand of us! In exchange, we spare lives of you!"

The archer prepared to respond, but something behind the wall caught his attention. He began to speak with someone inside.

"They won't actually give them women, will they?" I asked.

"I think they're negotiating," Parzival whispered with feigned indifference.

Then, to my great surprise and that of everyone around, the village gates opened. A small crack, through which a timid beam of light spilled onto the covered ground. A man emerged from inside, and the door closed behind him, leaving him alone against the entire army.

He strode forward with determination, his silhouette resembling a dark shadow against the backdrop.

"What is he doing?" Parzival muttered.

"Aella!" whispered Sparrow.

Then I saw her. She stood on the high platform where the archers were. Although her face was human, I could see her eyes shining even from that distance, defying the darkness of the night. The Black Queen herself.

Another flash of lightning. I shuddered as I saw the face of the man standing, without a hint of fear in his gaze, before Thorgard. It was Prince Darion. Even from afar, the resemblance to Larion was striking. Yet, something about him seemed terribly different, untamed, and dark.

"I am Darion Grayfang, master of the Dancing Shadows! *Tagur'zavaj*!"

"Are you hurry to die?" Thorgard asked with amusement.

"Accept my challenge, coward!" the prince thundered, followed by a roar from the sky, shaking the earth.

"You will beg for mercy!" Thorgard shouted. "I accept!"

Darion drew his sword just in time to parry a violent strike aimed at his head.

The leader of the Blood Wolves threw himself with all his might at the prince, delivering blow after blow. The man was fast, and Darion mostly stayed on the defensive, blocking attacks frequently and striking rarely, with slow, almost lazy strikes.

"The fight is already concluded," Sparrow remarked, and Wolf nodded grimly.

"Anyway, we only need to take Aella alive," Parzival said.

He, like me, saw the same thing: that Darion was losing.

"You really have bees in your head," Sparrow hissed. "Can't you see how fluent the prince is?"

"He's just playing with the barbarian," explained Wolf.

He was right. After another parry, the prince's sword darted like a viper towards the man's right leg. It struck him above the knee, making him fell sideways, cursing in his own language. Darion regarded him thoughtfully, with the same curiosity a lion shows when toying with a limping antelope. Thorgard scrambled to his feet, leaning heavily on his left leg, attempting one final attack. Too slow. With an incredibly fast swinging cut, Darion beheaded him.

I gasped, bringing my hands to my mouth as Thorgard's body collapsed lifelessly to the ground. His head now lay at the feet of the killer, who looked at it for a moment before kicking it with his boot, sending it rolling at the Blood Wolfes.

"I was promised a real fight! I'm still waiting!" Darion yelled.

He took a step in their direction, but they all drew back. The people on the walls began to cheer, shouting his name.

"*Premet ie'zav!*" the mountain people began to chant, bowing to him.

"*Mar pramet ieor'varamnlia!*" the prince uttered.

Then, without any fear, as if they were not his enemies, he walked into their midst. They spoke in low voices, and I couldn't make out what they were saying, but from the tone, it seemed like the prince was scolding them. All of this was happening under the watchful eye of the Black Queen.

"What the hell just happened?" Parzival asked.

"He challenged the clan leader to a fight, killed him, and took over the clan," said Wolf.

"Seems like he's done this before," I remarked.

"He's gathering an army," Sparrow grimaced. "What do you say, Parzival, still think Derahia isn't on the brink of war?"

"No, Lady Sparrow. And the people in the village are chanting the traitor's name like a fuc… like a prayer. The King needs to hear about this."

"He will," assured Sparrow.

After a while, the savages retreated into the woods, and Darion returned to the village, where he was welcomed as a hero. Perhaps he was a hero. Undoubtedly, many lives would have been lost if he hadn't intervened. Word would spread, and tales of the prince who stood in harm's way to save his people would be told. He would gain even more supporters.

Crabs and shells!

"We'll enter the village tonight," declared Sparrow. "They'll probably let their guard down or reduce their numbers. We can sneak in through a gap in the wall and scout the area. Maybe we can somehow lure the prince or Aella out."

No one objected. I felt it wasn't a good plan. I felt too many things could go wrong, but still, I didn't have the courage to contradict her. We waited for a few hours, watching the dark outline of the clouds retreating from above the settlement. The storm avoided us.

The moon was waning, and the light limited, but even so, we could see heads peering over the wall, fewer and fewer, scouting the area. They had escaped the dogs and abandoned caution, without realizing that now the wolves were at the gates.

We emerged from the cover of the night-shrouded forest when a fleeting cloud covered the moon like a curtain. My heart raced and my stomach twisted as we approached the edge of the village. We pressed our backs against the wooden wall just as the moon's sickle finally cut through the thin veil of the cloud. We moved silently until we reached a gap. It was a place where two stakes were missing, wide enough for us to pass through one by one.

Wolf entered first, followed by Sparrow, and then me. When Parzival tried to pass, Sparrow stopped him and whispered something in his ear. I later found out she had handed him the vial of diluted sleeping potion and instructed him to pour some of the liquid over two cloths, just in case it would be necessary. She told him to wait for us outside.

Many torches were burning within the walls, but due to the multitude of houses built haphazardly everywhere, wherever we went, we stepped into shadows. We silently crept from one house to another. Or at least Wolf and Sparrow were silent; I had the rare and undesired talent to stumble every ten steps. Sparrow turned in my direction and signaled for me to wait against the wall of a house until she and Wolf had a chance to better survey the area. Although I didn't like the idea of being left there alone, I felt compelled to agree, but not before looking at both of them with frightened and pleading eyes.

I can't say how long I waited, but several times I saw people walking around. Some even noticed me, but they didn't seem to care at all.

Then I saw the Black Queen. You couldn't mistake her because of her eyes. She came out of a tall house, probably an inn, accompanied by the prince himself. He was saying something to her, but I was too far away to hear what, and she seemed to be laughing. She turned and pinched his cheek, then he pulled her into his arms, covering her with kisses. For some reason, I smiled. They seemed like ordinary people. Simple people, living a simple life. But my smile faded when the image of that headless man, still lying at the village gates, came back to my mind.

He was a criminal who had killed his own father and probably his betrothed. She was a killer who had murdered dozens of people just a month ago.

Someone else came out of the house. A tall, slender man, with an elegant gait. He came up to them and said a few words, then the prince began to laugh heartedly. The young newcomer spoke to them for a few moments, during which the Black Queen listened in silence, nodding as he finished. She kissed Darion one last time, then went back into the inn.

Left alone, the two of them began to stroll leisurely, coming towards me. I wanted to retreat to the crack in the wall, but chances were that if the others didn't recognize me, neither would these two. Although my hair was dyed in vibrant colors, my head was covered, so I was almost sure I would go unnoticed.

"...already prepared to hurl fireballs into the crowd when I heard Aella's voice in my mind. *Stay put*! Almost made me wet my pants," burst out the man accompanying him.

"It scared the living daylights out of me the first time it happened too," Darion chuckled. "We were being chased by that wizard from Sihad who possessed a bear."

"Speaking of which, you mentioned Aella crossed paths with... you know who. You never told me about that."

"I don't know much more than you do," the prince shrugged. "She just said it happened a few hundred years ago."

"You're not at all..." but his voice abruptly stopped, and to my horror, he turned instantly in my direction.

It was then that I felt his magical signature. He was a wizard! The prince followed his gaze, and when his eyes fell on me, he stirred. I took a few steps back, maintaining eye contact, while he inched closer with uncertainty. He held up his hands like I was a frightened animal, and he was trying to assure me that I was safe. With no intention of waiting to confirm the situation, I turned on my heel and strode briskly in the opposite direction, heading back towards the wall, all the while struggling to contain the urge to break into a run. The two of them trailed behind me at a leisurely pace, showing no signs of urgency. As we moved, the wizard leaned in and whispered something to him, his voice grave.

"Wait!" shouted the prince.

I began to run towards the exit. I didn't dare to turn my head back to them, but even so, I could hear them quickening the pace. I leaped outside, turning towards Parzival, who was leaning against the wall. He stood up as soon as he saw the fear on my face, ready to speak, but no words came out.

When I looked back at the crack, I met the dark eyes of the prince, who was staring at me as if I were a ghost. He didn't seem threatening at all, just surprised. The wizard emerged from behind. Their attention was entirely focused on me, neither of them noticing

Parzival, who stood beside them, holding the cloths soaked with the sleeping potion.

"Saya Starfrost," Darion said with attention, and my blood froze in my veins.

How does he know my name?

I took a step back, and he took a step towards me, raising his hands again to show me he meant no harm.

"I've been wondering when I'd meet you," he continued, seemingly picking each word with great care. "I think I am your friend."

Two shadows slipped out from inside the wall, swift and silent. The prince wanted to say something, but immediately Wolf grabbed him from behind, covering his mouth with the cloth taken from Parzival's hand. The prince's hands clenched over Wolf's arm, but his grip was too strong. I felt the wizard stepping into the ether just before Sparrow applied the same treatment to him.

Darion looked at me one last time before falling limp into Mr. Wolf's arms. Sparrow released the wizard, letting him collapse face down onto the damp ground.

"We got them," she said with satisfaction.

Don't Die in Vain

Excerpt from Saya's journal, dated the second day of the seventh month, Iureia, in the year six hundred twenty-three after the Conversion:

I used the ether to make the two sleeping prisoners levitate behind us until we reached the horses waiting at the edge of the forest. There, Sparrow placed special shackles inscribed with suppressive runes on the wizard, to prevent his access to the Great River. Wolf unfastened the prince's sword and attached it to Sparrow's saddle, who then proceeded to inspect the wizard.

"What a strange pal'ether," she murmured, taking a silver-bladed knife from the wizard's belt. She unfolded its leather sheath and attached it to her own belt on the right side, then placed the knife there. The two katanas were secured on the left side.

Despite my objections, Sparrow decided that I will share the same horse with Darion's friend. He was tied up and placed behind me, propped up against my back, while Darion, also bound with his hands behind his back, ended up on the same horse with Parzival. The assassin witch rode behind us, hand on her weapon, ready to intervene in case the two woke up and tried to overpower us.

Wolf led the column. We rode along the road that skirted the forest, aiming to reach Blackstone long after sunrise. Just before sunset, Sparrow seemed to think. The quickest route would have been to traverse the forest in a straight line, saving more than half a day's ride, but the night was too deep and the tree shadows too dark for someone unfamiliar with the paths.

"He called my name," I uttered with dread.

At first, nobody responded. They were just as shocked as I was.

"I heard," Wolf spoke after a while. "Maybe he has connections in the Circle. Perhaps he knew about us before we found him."

"Unlikely," Sparrow said.

"Then how does he know my name?" I pressed, looking at the man who slept against Parzival's shoulder.

"We'll find out when he wakes up," Wolf assured me. He turned to his wife, looking into her eyes for a few moments, then said, "I'll go ahead, I'm much faster alone. I'll head to Blackstone and ask for an escort to help us cross safely. I'll meet you on the road tomorrow."

"Be careful," Sparrow requested.

"And you. If they try anything, kill them. Without hesitation!"

"Without hesitation," the woman repeated.

Wolf spurred his horse, prowling forward like the venom of a dragonfish, disappearing into the dark road ahead. In just a few moments, it was lost in the night. All I could hear now was the sound of the hooves and my heart pounding so hard it felt like it might leap out of my chest. Though I trusted Sparrow and knew she was just as capable as her husband, Wolf had a much more agreeable personality, and I would have preferred his company anytime.

Something strange lingered in the cool night air, a morbid foreboding that left a bitter taste in my mouth, one that even all my pleasant memories, few as they were, couldn't sweeten. Not even the prospect of a life as a royal witch in Romir. Something weighed heavily upon us.

Fatigue made me see dark shapes out of the corner of my eye, sweeping among the trees, perfectly hiding behind a trunk just as I turned my head. But it was all in my mind. If someone had really been running on our trails, they would have woken up hit in the face with a bolt of ether before I could even feel their presence. I turned my gaze to the serene face of the lethal woman riding behind. Her reassuring smile washed over me, imbuing a sense of calmness that momentarily eased my apprehensions, if only for a fleeting moment.

The wizard, who was leaning against my back with his hands tied behind him, began to move quite a bit. Every time there was a bump on the road and the horse made a sudden movement, his face, resting over my shoulder, would press against mine. The bristling of his freshly shaved beard prickled against my skin. I pushed him back with a slow movement of my head, then held my breath, listening for any change, no matter how small, in his breathing rhythm. But there was none.

When the sun began to climb from behind the eastern peaks, I could see the prince startle. Sparrow approached Parzival cautiously, studying the prisoner intently. He began to squirm, then opened his eyes, slowly lifting his head from my colleague's shoulder. For a moment, the expression on his face was one of confusion. He frowned and directed his eyes straight at me. I swallowed hard, immersing myself in the river of ether as a precaution.

"You're taking me to Blackstone," muttered the prince after tearing his eyes away from mine and surveying his surroundings.

"Romir is too far," Sparrow told him.

The lion turned to Sparrow, watching her for a moment. The assassin held his gaze, displaying a vague smile, sweet as poison, meant to warn him that any wrong move could be his last.

"Blackstone is also too far," he rasped, then cleared his throat. He didn't seem scared at all, as I would have expected him to be upon waking up, but rather defiant in a completely passive way. "And I see you've taken the longer route around the forest. You won't make it in time."

"Do you think so?" Sparrow asked him.

"I'm sure," Darion replied. "My men will cut off your path and butcher you like pigs. Merwin, are you awake?"

"For a few hours now," the wizard answered cheerfully, rising from my shoulder. "My lady, I hope this journey was as enjoyable for you as it was for me."

For a few hours? Did he brush his face against mine on purpose?

Darion laughed.

"Off the horses!" Sparrow demanded.

Merwin immediately descended, nearly losing his balance due to his bound hands, but the prince pretended not to hear, examining the surroundings once more before casting a thoughtful glance at Parzival. He was as tall as my colleague, but his body seemed built for fighting. No doubt he could overpower Parzival. Sparrow placed her hand on the hilt of her sword as a final warning.

"Katana," Darion commented unimpressed. "Even two. Are you from the Storm Islands?"

The assassin stared at him intently, as he jumped off the horse. He landed steadily on his feet, as if he had dismounted with his hands bound many times before. He raised an eyebrow when he saw his sword tied to Lady Sparrow's saddle.

"Did you figured it out by face or by sword?" the assassin wanted to know.

"Both. But I look at the sword first," his response came in an instant.

"Wise. We can continue the conversation as we go. Move to the front and quicken your pace. If you stop, I will kill you. If you try to flee, I will kill you. If I think you're better off dead..." She paused, looking at Darion interrogatively.

"You will kill us?"

"Very well! Now, let's move! "

The two prisoners exchanged a final glance before moving ahead. Sparrow positioned herself between me and Parzival, her eyes fixed firmly on the prince's neck. A swift and well-placed strike, and our journey to Blackstone would come to an end.

"They're wizards," Merwin told him. "All three of them. Probably sent by the Circle."

"Wizards with swords," Darion marveled.

"I'm just as surprised as you are."

"Indeed, we are the ones sent by the Circle," declared Sparrow.

"Why didn't you kill me?" the prince wondered.

"Your fate is not in our hands. The king will decide what to do with you once we reach Blackstone."

"You won't make it in time. You're still far away, as I can see, and it's already morning. Do yourselves a favor and let me go. What's the point of dying?"

Sparrow opened her mouth to respond, but it was Merwin who spoke first.

"And if you let him go, maybe you'll release me too. That is, if any of you don't intend to keep me for personal purposes," he added, winking at me.

Unintentionally, I laughed, which brought a smug smile to his face. Parzival grimaced at him, but he didn't seem to notice, his gaze focused solely on me.

"Let us worry about that," Sparrow said to Darion.

"As you wish," Darion responded, shrugging. He looked at us in a manner that suggested we were the ones captured, not him. "But I warned you. Your blood won't be on my hands."

"You have enough blood on your hands already," the assassin cut him off.

"I won't argue with that. I did what was necessary to survive, like everyone else. I'm sure your swords have tasted blood in the past, and I'm sure they will taste it again if your life is in danger and circumstances demand it."

Sparrow clicked her tongue derisively. "You killed your father," she accused with a sneer.

"When I shot the arrow that took his life, I didn't know it was him," said the prince, tightening his jaw. "It was dark. I only saw the shadow of a man running with a sword in hand towards... my beloved."

"Would it have made a difference if you knew it was him? Would you have let the Daughter of the Night die?"

Darion's eyes flickered into hers. "Daughter of the Night?" he repeated the words as a question. "You seem to know quite a lot, from what I see."

"I asked you something else."

He shrugged again, a sad expression settling on his face. "It's a simple question," Sparrow added.

"The answer is far from simple."

"Then let's talk about someone else. Rorik."

"Rorik was part of Sihad, I'm sure you've heard of them, given that your assassins failed to deal with them."

"Oh," I exclaimed, widening my eyes in surprise, and raising my eyebrows.

I turned to Sparrow, whose expression was blank, devoid of any reaction. The thought that a prince might ally with a group of sorcerers who were declared enemies of the Circle was terribly unsettling for me. But not for the assassin. Or if it was, she knew how to hide it. She nodded.

"I wasn't thinking about Rorik, but I'm not surprised at all. After all, Queen Lenore invited Melchior to the palace."

"Queen Lenore?" now it was the prince's turn to be surprised. "That wouldn't surprise me. So far, I've only met one decent Tarrygold."

"And I only met one Grayfang. And here I speak of your brother," Sparrow interjected.

"I'm not a good man, but neither is Larion. Returning to Sihad, you probably didn't know they worshipped one of the First Gods."

Sparrow froze. She locked eyes with me, then very slow turned her head towards the prince, as if her neck was stiffened.

"I suspected as much," she muttered in a whisper. "After all, they stole a few idols, along with other pal'ethers."

"What are the First Gods?" I asked, abruptly feeling the cold grasp of the morning chill.

"Ha!" Merwin burst out. "Didn't I tell you their Circle is useless? They don't even teach this much."

"You'll learn when it's time to learn," Sparrow reproached me. "Some knowledge is only meant for those who can bear its burden. Apprentices are not allowed to know of such great evil."

"You've outlawed knowledge," growled the wizard. "And such knowledge... stupidity is beyond limits. The Maker is rolling in his grave!"

He was probably talking about Belvick the Maker, the founder of the Circle.

"The minds of the young are weak and easily influenced," said Sparrow. "The temptation is great, the power sweet, and the promises bright. Many would be drawn to them like flies to... Many would be drawn to them. We keep such secrets to protect them. That makes me wonder: how you know of the First Gods?"

The prince's gaze seemed to pierce through us. "I entered in the world of one of them and pierced his throat," replied Darion, his cold voice only intensifying the chill.

"You're either mad or just a liar!" Sparrow spat.

The prince ignored her jab, smiled mischievously, then continued, "I can describe him in great detail. The shadow stretching over the entire world, the eyes from which flames flowed, the tentacles large enough to shatter a castle. I can tell you how he tempted me, the visions he unveiled, the hatred and malice that made the stars themselves to flicker. They would be vague explanations, but I think you know as well as I do that, thank the Heavens, there are no words in this world to describe him. I can tell you his name."

"Don't you dare!" she screamed.

Merwin says, "Darion, don't..."

The words spoken by the prince were heavy with terror, I could feel it, and now fear reigned over us. I was afraid too, although I couldn't understand why, or what was the creature he talked about. Tentacles large enough to shatter a castle. I shuddered.

"If you make the same statements when we get to Blackstone, maybe..." Sparrow begun.

"We won't make it to Blackstone!" the prince shouted, making me startle in fear. Even Merwin and Parzival were taken aback by Darion's sudden fury, but Sparrow didn't flinch. The prince lowered his voice and continued, "Tell me, witch, do you still think I did wrong by killing Rorik?"

The woman didn't respond for a few moments, staring blankly, completely absent.

"What I believe is irrelevant," she said after a while. "But let's move on. Arlieth, your betrothed."

Darion hesitated. I could see his arms tensing, and his back straightening. Even the rhythm of his breathing quickened.

"I didn't kill her," he said heavily.

"Kolan?"

The prince scoffed disdainfully. "You don't know the whole story, yet you accuse so easily."

"You have more excuses than honor."

"Honor," he repeated, spitting out the word as if it were poisoned. "I've lost things more precious than honor."

After that, Darion didn't utter another word. He walked alongside Merwin, while we rode behind them. We traveled like that for several hours. Sparrow asked him a few more questions to which she received no response. Several times, the prince's eyes darted towards his sword, which was tied to Sparrow's saddle, but her stern gaze prompted him to look away.

I watched him eagerly, barely managing to restrain myself from asking how he knew my name. Perhaps Sparrow wouldn't appreciate me interrogating the prisoner without her approval.

"Are you feeling well?" Parzival whispered to me, almost pressing his horse against mine.

"Do you think the Black Queen will ambush us?" I asked directly, without trying to conceal my unease.

"Who cares? Wolf will be here soon. I don't think we need to worry."

"I just want to get back and eat a fish pie in the town square."

"Fish pie?" he laughed. "That doesn't sound good even if you put them in the same sentence, let alone on the same plate."

"It's not that bad," I laughed.

"It sounds dreadful, but I'm willing to make this sacrifice for you, my fair lady," Merwin interjected, turning his head to look at me.

"Eyes forward!" Sparrow warned him.

"I should put something in his mouth," Parzival mumbled.

"Try," the prince challenged him sharply.

"You've got a big mouth," Parzival said, deepening his voice.

Darion stopped. "Why don't you come closer and tell me that?"

Parzival yanked the bridle, a smug smile curling on the prince's feral face. His unkempt braids and slightly overgrown beard lent him an air akin to the wildlings.

"Don't stoop to his level," I urged Parzival.

"Darion, wouldn't it be better to..." Merwin attempted to advise him.

"If he comes closer, I'll kill him," Darion cut him off, his voice unnervingly calm. "I'm fed up to the brim with these pursuers."

Parzival was red with anger, but he restrained himself, nodding slightly towards me.

"Keep moving!" Sparrow demanded. "That was the last warning. Next time, I strike. Patricide, know that no one cares whether you live or die, and as for you, wizard, even less. Move!"

Darion turned and set off, closely followed by Merwin. The time for pretenses and banter was over; now the prince was showing his true face. I could feel his almost palpable fury boiling within him, like a volcano ready to erupt. The wizard, on the other hand, seemed calm. He was young and arrogant, too playful, intentionally exuding an air of foolishness, but I doubted he was foolish. He seemed harmless, and such people are often the most dangerous. His eyes often drifted towards his silver knife at Sparrow's belt. A pal'ether, she called it. A pal'ether for what?

The path ahead of us widened and became more well-trodden, fragmenting into several roads that wound through the green hills at the foot of the mountains, flowing like rivers southward. The few white clouds in the otherwise clear sky, like wisps of smoke, watched over us from above.

It was midday when I saw Mr. Wolf emerging from behind the hill ahead. He was closely followed by dozens... no, hundreds of mounted men. Three hundred. Not even half of what the rebel prince had recruited the night before, in front of that village. That's not including the traitors chanting his name from within the village. But unlike the prince's men, these were well-equipped and all of them wore chainmail or scales, with helmets and swords or maces. I didn't know much about conventional battles, but the satisfied smile on Sparrow's face told me everything I needed to know. We had the advantage.

"More meat for the butcher's table," the prince muttered with sadness.

Although he didn't seem impressed at all, his wizard, Merwin, visibly paled. Black flags, bearing a white sun surrounded by six stars, were mounted on long poles, and held by the men at the rear of the Blackstone column.

Wolf tugged at the reins, halting in front of us, then quickly jumped off the horse and hurried towards his wife, without even casting a glance at the prisoners. Sparrow dismounted gracefully and with controlled movements, then approached her husband with small steps. She was about to say something, but Wolf hugged her tightly, kissing her forehead. He whispered something to her; she giggled. Both Parzival and I watched them with mouths agape.

A young, short man, with blond hair tied in a knot at the back of his head, dressed in a long chainmail shirt, leaped off his horse and ran towards Darion. All I could see in his eyes was anger. The prince straightened his back, pulling his shoulders back and pinned him with his gaze.

"You don't want to do this, Cedric," he growled as the soldiers began to gather around us.

The young man, Cedric, launched a gloved fist toward the prince's face. Darion swiftly dodged, leaning to one side, then countered by headbutting him in the mouth, causing Cedric to stagger back, nearly losing his balance. Cedric growled in frustration like a rabid dog, before retaliating with a powerful strike that sent the prince tumbling to the ground. Wolf moved to intervene, but his wife raised a hand, signaling for him to hold his position.

"You killed my cousin, you murderous dung-eater!" Cedric shouted.

Darion leaned on his back, and pulling his legs to the chest, he succeeded in crossing his shackled hands in front of his body. Lunging at Cedric, he seized him and pulled him to the ground. The prince knelt on his chest and struck him with the iron edge of the handcuffs across his face. Sparrow lowered her hand, and Wolf, receiving permission to act, attacked Darion. It only took a moment for Darion to be brought down, with the assassin atop him and a knife under his chin.

"Do it!" the prince grinned.

Wolf turned to his wife, who, with a discreet gesture, signaled him to hold back.

"You're not lucky," Wolf said to Darion. "But wait a little longer."

Cedric jumped to his feet, filled with hatred, drawing his sword.

"Lanre will put your head on a spike if you don't let Darion alive for him," warned a rider who watched the scene somewhat amused.

"Give me that!" Cedric shouted, sheathing his sword back and gesturing towards the man's spear.

The man handed it over, albeit reluctantly. All the soldiers watched in silence. Cedric turned the spear around, gripping it near the tip.

"Get off him!" he ordered Wolf.

"It's not a good idea," the assassin cautioned.

"Boy, put the spear down before you hurt someone," Sparrow urged.

"With all due respect, woman, but don't meddle in matters that don't concern you. Keep your nose in your own pot."

Wolf rose from Darion and reached Cedric in two strides, snatching the weapon from his hand with a swift motion and plunging it into the ground.

"I advise you to treat my wife with respect!" growled the man. Cedric nodded, mouthing a "*sorry*" from his lips.

However, Cedric did not yield. He grabbed the spear with both hands and pulled it from the ground, almost falling backward as the spear came loose. He turned the weapon and grasped it again near the tip, then spoke to Sparrow in a gentler tone, "I won't kill him, Miss. I'll just beat him until he loses consciousness."

Merwin looked around alarmed, searching for help. Parzival smiled. Cedric struck, but the prince rolled to the side just before the spear's shaft hit the ground. Darion got up, then took a blow to the ribs, followed by another to the leg.

"Back off, Cedric!" he spat.

But Cedric didn't listen, striking one more time. The spear's tail descended vertically, aimed for his head. This time, Darion used the chain of the handcuffs to block the blow, then grabbed the weapon. I widened my eyes in horror as, with a swift movement, the spearhead flew from Cedric's hands, impaling his throat.

He collapsed backward, mumbling something unintelligible, as blood streamed through the hands clenched around the wound. A soldier came from behind, grabbing Darion and knocking him to the ground, while others pulled the spear from his clenched fist. They began to strike him with fists and feet. Merwin tried to intervene, but Sparrow seized him to the ground, whispering something in his ear. Parzival looked at Cedric, who was convulsing on the beaten path, then jumped off his horse and ran through the lines of riders surrounding us to the roadside, where he knelt down and began to vomit.

Cedric twitched one last time before his body remained motionless, hands still clenched around his throat, eyes wide open. I always believe someone's eyes will close by themselves as the person dies. Finally, Wolf managed to calm the furious soldiers, and surprisingly, the prince was still alive, rising on his own and brushing the dust off his clothes. His nose and mouth were bloodied, and he was likely covered in bruises, but still breathing.

"Are you also a wizard?" Darion asked, spitting blood at Mr. Wolf's feet.

He ignored him and, grabbing the chain linking the handcuffs, pulled him for the edge of the road, where he pushed him into the shade of a tree. The prince tried to stand tall, to show no sign of weakness, but I could see him making great efforts not to limp. Sparrow gestured for the wizard to follow Darion. He complied.

"What happens now?" I asked her. "Shouldn't we hurry to Blackstone?"

"Yes, indeed, and we will hurry. However, first and foremost, we need to make sure that no one murders the murderer until we arrive. Also, we need to find some scouts and dispatch them into the forest to preempt any potential ambush. We will leave soon. Dismount and stretch your legs."

I listened to her, but like a cat whose curiosity overrides reason, I headed towards the prisoners. A few soldiers stood nearby, with bows and crossbows, joking and laughing loudly, completely insensitive to the death of the young man. For a few moments, the image of him drowning in his own blood came back to my mind. I shook it away.

"You shouldn't have killed him," I said directly, stopping in front of them.

Both looked up at me at once. The monkey-like grin that the wizard had worn throughout the day was gone; now he was worried. Darion didn't look very well either, and the traces of the earlier beating were becoming more visible. His left eye was beginning to bruise, and droplets of blood were streaming from his right nostril.

"He shouldn't have hit me," the prince said calmly. "I gave him several chances to back off, but he refused. He gained courage because he saw me tied up. I also gave you plenty of chances to release me."

"Do you realize they'll kill you for this?" I asked, struggling to meet his gaze.

"They would have killed me anyway." He examined me in silence for a few moments, then smiled. "Come on, ask," he urged.

My fingers clenched into a fist, feeling annoyed by his smirk. Still, I asked, "How do you know my name?"

"I dreamed about you."

"Is this another inappropriate joke?"

Merwin laughed. "There are no inappropriate jokes, Saya, only overly sensitive audiences. As for Darion and jokes: this guy is more serious than... I don't even have a comparison."

"I can see the future, in dreams," the prince said, ignoring his friend. "And I dreamed about you too."

"Of course," I replied, trying to make my skepticism as visible as possible.

"You asked and I answered," he said with a shrug.

"Now you're a prophet too, it seems. You have infiltrators in the Circle, don't you?"

"You think I knew you were on my trail, but still chose to chase after you?" he asked, wiping the blood from his mouth. "I only came because I believed you could be a potential ally."

He smiled when he saw traces of disbelief appearing on my face. Disbelief in myself, because he was right. I sat down in the grass with my legs crossed beneath me, in the same manner I saw Sparrow and Wolf sitting.

"So, tell me, how did you dream of me?"

"It was a symbolic dream. You were using ether to make boulders fly around, and Merwin was trying to reach you."

"That would be me," the wizard chimed in.

I blinked a few times. "Is that all?"

"That's all I dreamed about you, but I could feel your name. Saya Starfrost."

I didn't answer. I was too shocked to speak.

"Take heed of my words, we won't make it to Blackstone, and these soldiers won't stop Aella. The Night of the Blood Moon will happen again, and this time will be much worse. Leave while you still can. Don't die in vain."

"Nice of you to worry about me, but I am more than capable of taking care of myself. Your situation should..."

"Saya," he cut in, pausing for a long moment, and pursing his lips into a straight line. "You nearly sat on a venomous snake."

I followed his glance to the black serpent coiled a few meters away from me, hidden among the tall grass strands, then jumped to my feet, screaming. "How on earth did that get there?!"

They both burst into a dumb male laugh, soon joined by the soldiers guarding them. Sparrow rushed over, stopping beside me, then noticed the serpent.

"Apologies," I mumbled.

"Black viper," said Darion. "Highly venomous."

Sparrow drew one of her katanas, and with a swift motion, she severed the raised head of the snake, then pushed the weapon back into its sheath. The soldiers ceased her grumbling as they saw the swinging cut.

"You know the local creepers," she remarked.

"I like to know what can kill me."

"Interesting creature, the black viper. Did you know that the females tend to devour the males when they are no longer useful?"

"They're also good at killing sparrows," the prince retorted.

I thought Sparrow would get angry, but instead she chuckled. I got up and turned back, sulking.

Not long after, we left. Darion and Merwin were surrounded by a handful of soldiers with spears and swords, but even so, Sparrow and Wolf were always nearby. Parzival and I walked further back. I felt very uncomfortable because of the fleeting glances some of the soldiers were throwing at me. Parzival noticed too. He rode with his chest puffed out and a furrowed brow. I smiled warmly at him every time he turned to me. He was really a good friend.

We were on a wide road carved into the not-so-steep edge of a hill when the scouts came fleeing from the forests. Their horses were very fast. They ran swiftly along the slopes, leaping over the bushes at the edge of the forest.

"Savages!" shouted the closest one, stopping abruptly.

My blood ran cold, and a huge pit formed in my stomach. I turned to Darion, noticing that he was looking at me too.

The scouts informed us that at least five hundred wildlings, if not more, were heading towards us from the direction of the forest. In the northern part, the hill rose gradually a few tens of meters, and on its crest was the forest. In the south, the hill descended, not very steeply, stopping at a river with currents too rapid to be crossed.

The men dismounted, forming a wall of shields facing towards the forest, their backs against the river. Darion had been right; Aella was coming to save him.

From the trees on the hill's ridge, savages began to flow, stopping at about thirty meters from us. My throat felt dry as if I hadn't drunk water for days, and my stomach twisted. Our soldiers shouted orders; some were confused, trying to position themselves as best as possible in the wall, others angry, but most were scared. We were outnumbered, but looking at the wall forming before us, I found courage. An incomplete wall, which instead of forming a straight line, undulated, with places where people were too far apart and places where they were too crowded. The enemies were undisciplined; we could win.

"Everything will be fine," Parzival whispered to me, his face pale.

"Thank you," I smiled, letting out a sigh that made me shiver.

We approached the group guarding Darion, standing behind the wall. As sorcerers, we were to strike from a distance, hurling stones and fireballs. I could easily break their shield wall when needed, picking up the enemies and throwing them like stones in the currents below.

I glanced over the wildling's rows, searching for the Black Queen, but I couldn't see her anywhere. That wasn't a good sign.

No one was riding at that moment, with the horses nervously neighing behind the wall. It's said that animals sense the approach of death and fear it. The air vibrated around us, and a sudden sensation of fear gripped my heart, a thought likely whispered by Aella. The horses went mad, rearing and running in all directions, trampling over the people in the shield wall. In just mere seconds, our line shattered like a very fragile statue of glass.

"Reform the wall, hold your positions!" Wolf shouted, but the horses ran among them, breaking up the formation even more.

The clan folk had abandoned the formation they had struggled to maintain, now running with their weapons held above their heads, shouting at the top of their lungs like wild beasts.

"Something's not right! Where's the Black Queen?!" I cried with a trembling voice.

Parzival shrugged, completely pale.

The ether trembled again. A wave of magic came from behind us, passing through my body and making my soul leap with fear, almost leaving my body. I turned my head, and almost screamed when I saw at least a hundred warriors appearing out of nowhere between us and the river.

And the Black Queen was among them.

She was indeed a nartingal, with ashen skin and horns above her head. It has suddenly become clearer that we had no chance of victory. Our shield wall was gone, and the horses trampled everything, knocking down the soldiers. Above all, we were surrounded. A sphere of fire manifested in Parzival's hand. He pushed me aside, stepping towards Darion. He wanted to kill him; we couldn't let them take him alive.

"*She's utterly ruthless,*" I recalled Elena's words.

A crystal beam, shining pale like a cluster of stars, struck Parzival in the face, and droplets of blood sprayed onto my clothes and face. In an instant, the lifeless body collapsed with a thud. It all happened so quickly that he probably didn't even know he was dead. I was too shocked to scream, to cry, or to run, just like a deer suddenly facing the hunter.

A soldier had the same idea as Parzival—to kill Darion before the rescuers could reach him. The prince's eyes flickered into mine, his lips forming the word '*run*'. A man simply appeared behind the approaching soldier, as if he had teleported there. He was pale and tall, dressed in black leather clothes and wearing a cloak of the same color. His eyes, if that was an appropriate term, were completely black and empty. He pierced the soldier with his sword before the latter could strike the prince. The other men who were supposed to guard him had already fled, trying to escape to the east or west, but the savages coming from the north had already blocked the roads. We were trapped. Darion vanished into his men's ranks, followed by that strange man, and only then did I realize that I had done nothing to stop him.

Hell broke loose.

A large, fat man, carrying a huge battle axe already stained with blood, set his eyes on me, and grinned greedily. I reached out towards the Great River, but every time I tried to step into it, I felt the swift currents of the ether pulling me out. I was too scared to connect to magic. A young man wearing scaled armor leapt in front of me, dodging a blow from the savage, then with one swift movement pierced his stomach. The barbarian continued to fight, striking the soldier with the axe's handle several times on the head, but the soldier finally managed to bring him down. He struck him with the sword over the head until his face ceased to look human. The young man turned to me, his eyes full of fear, and several streaks of blood ran down his forehead.

"You're a witch!" he screamed. "Do something, help..."

A spear thrown from somewhere struck him in the back of the head, piercing his skull and coming out through his open mouth. The trembling eyes of the man lowered to the steel tip protruding from his open mouth. He whimpered, then looked into my eyes; tears began to trickle down his cheeks. He begged me wordlessly for help, or perhaps for a quick death—I couldn't discern—but all I could do was turn my back and sink deeper among the Blackstone soldiers, trapped like in an enclave.

Few remained in formation, fighting, because most, faced with imminent death, scrambled to get as far away in the center of that mass of people as possible. If you fell, you were trampled. If you stopped, you risked getting too close to the wildlings swirling around us, stabbing and slashing mercilessly. To keep swimming further away from the edge of that circle, tightening like a noose, was the only thing left to do.

I reached out once more to the ether, but no matter how hard I tried, I couldn't grasp it. I couldn't remain calm long enough to manipulate the waves of magic. I saw a group of soldiers counting almost thirty, making their way through Darion's warriors, towards the forest.

Wolf and Sparrow were there. Anyone who managed to pass through the soldiers was cut down by them.

Wolf deftly sidestepped the swing of an axe, then delivered a precise blow to the attacker's leg, bringing him down like a tree under a woodsman's hatchet. With a swift motion, he slit the throat of another enemy, then slashed the face of the fallen one. Sparrow unleashed a flurry of rapid attacks on a foe hiding behind a shield. It didn't take long to breach his defense, painting a red line along his cheek. Wolf sent a burst of fire that exploded with a loud boom, causing some of the attackers to jump back, then plunged into their ranks, delivering death in all directions.

Several ether spheres shining like white crystals fell upon the mass of fleeing combatants, triggering explosions and agonizing cries, mowing down entire groups of soldiers. Undoubtedly, the magic of the Black Queen. I lost sight of them as they escaped over the crest of the hill.

Everyone around me was screaming, begging for mercy, or crying, so I did the only thing left to do: I followed their example. The air was filled with the stench of blood, sweat, and urine, and because of the bodies multiplying with every passing moment, it became increasingly difficult to breathe.

"Hit them in the head!" someone with a strong Nordic accent shouted. "Don't ruin the armor!"

I couldn't breathe anymore. I struggled in vain to push aside those crowded around me. Some were impaled by spears, pierced by arrows, or slashed by hurled axes, dying but having no place to fall. The dead remained standing among the living, but in that growing hell of wounded and dying, it was hard to discern who was who. Then, I lost my balance and somehow, I had enough space to sink into the sea of bodies. In moments, I was on my side, covering my head with my hands, struggling to contain my choking sobs. All I could see around me was a forest of legs, with corpses scattered here and there.

I saw a daisy, defiantly standing between the crushed blades of grass. It had miraculously survived the hundreds of feet that had trampled everything around it. All I could do was follow its example, that is, to stay down, pretending to be dead, and hope that no one would stab to check. I was stepped on several times, on my feet, or my torso, once even on my head, but I didn't make a sound.

I wouldn't know how long I stayed there, but eventually, the screams died down, replaced by bursts of laughter and words thrown around, sometimes in their native language, sometimes in the common tongue. They stripped the dead of their armor. There were others still pretending to be dead. I could hear their sudden screams when they were discovered and killed. How long would it be until my turn came? How much will it hurt? Will it end quickly?

My heart stopped when I heard a pair of footsteps stopping beside me. Someone leaned over, then placed two fingers on my neck to check my pulse. I almost whimpered in fear, realizing that my hands were trembling again.

"Dead?" shouted someone with a rough voice.

"Mhm," murmured the man above me. His voice resembled that of the prince.

I felt him slipping his hands under my limp body and lifting me. I could barely resist the temptation to open my eyes, and every time I tried to step into the ether, I was thrown back out.

Before long, the noises diminished in intensity, and the sunlight I could see through the thin curtains of my eyelids, dimmed. We entered the forest. Whoever was carrying me set me down carefully.

"Saya, it's me, Darion."

I didn't respond. I felt a hand touching my chest.

"I can feel your heartbeat. I know you're alive."

I opened my eyes to meet the stern face of the prince, crouched next to me. His face and clothes were stained with blood, probably not his own, and his sword was strapped to his waist again. All his earlier wounds had disappeared. I wanted to beg him to let me live, but when I opened my mouth, all that came out was an almost mute sound.

"You've escaped safely," he told me, "but I doubt you'll ever have such luck again. You've used up your luck for a lifetime. Go west in a straight line until you reach the edge of the forest, and then head south from there. Eventually, you'll find a village, and the villagers will help you reach Romir. Do you understand? Saya, I'm talking to you, do you understand?"

"Yes," I half-mouthed.

"You've escaped with your life, make the most of it. Don't come back. Don't die in vain."

After saying these words, he friendly patted me on the shoulder, which made me flinch, then stood up and walked away in the opposite direction.

I jumped to my feet as well, and began to run among the trees, heading in the same direction as the sun. Soon, the voices faded behind, swallowed by the distance. All I could hear was my heavy breathing and the somewhat soothing song of the leaves in the summer breeze. It was as if the forest itself was trying to calm me, but hadn't it seen the massacre that had just taken place right at its edge?

Because of my tear-blurred vision, I stumbled over the protruding roots of a tree, crashing forcefully onto the hard ground. I didn't get up. I curled and started to cry. I was defeated, exhausted, and fear had numbed all my senses, instead of sharpening them.

I would have stayed there sobbing until I fell asleep if I hadn't seen Sparrow running in my direction. I got to my feet, and the crying and trembling became uncontrollable. The assassin hugged me tightly.

"It's over now," she said, but her voice was full of concern. "Are you hurt?"

"No. I'm fine. But Parzival is dead," I said, then started crying even harder.

"I looked for you, but there were too many crowded together. I couldn't find you."

I believed her. I was sure she had tried to find us, but with Parzival dead and me being particularly short and surrounded by tall men, I was practically invisible.

"I think Aella killed him," I said amidst sobs. "She smashed his head... completely."

The woman tightened her grip, sighing.

"I still have his blood-stained clothes. How did this happen?"

Wolf came running from behind a tree, closely followed by eight men in armor, a small remnant of the soldiers from Blackstone. There was sadness and horror in their gazes, the pride and calm they had just a few hours ago had disappeared, as if it had never existed. Even Wolf had a thick bandage over his left arm, and like Sparrow's clothes, his were also red with blood. They had probably killed a lot of enemies.

"She somehow managed to cover a hundred men and mask the ether waves," Wolf said. "I've never heard of such a thing. They surrounded us. Our men were inexperienced, and we didn't manage to organize ourselves quickly enough to block the charges from both sides."

"Especially since some of the *proud* warriors who were supposed to help us fled before the battle even began!" spat Sparrow, releasing me from her embrace and turning to the men behind Mr. Wolf.

No one dared to respond or contradict her.

"I'm very sorry about Parzival," Wolf told me. "I've found your horse, but mine and Sparrow's are still missing. The communication artifact is in my saddlebag, which we'll need to inform the Circle and Romir about what happened."

"What do we do next?" I asked, wiping away my tears.

"First, we find the horse," Sparrow began, "then we find those two again and kill them without hesitation."

"Alone, or shall we wait for help from the Circle?" I asked.

"We don't need help," she said firmly. "There's no point in wasting so much time."

"Lord Lanre will be more than happy to offer you men to assist in the search," one of the soldiers said.

Sparrow eyed him with an unfriendly stare. "We don't have time to take care of them. We would have been better off if you hadn't come at all; you only slowed us down, and when the time to fight was at hand, you ran away like scared rabbits in front of a hound!"

"Some ran," the man said calmly, "others stayed and fought. We did everything we could."

"All you did was give weapons, armor, and horses to the enemy," the assassin woman spat. "I'm going to try to find my horse, if they haven't taken it already. The sleep elixirs were in his saddlebag."

I followed Wolf into the depths of the forest's labyrinth, where about twenty soldiers awaited, scanning the surroundings with alert and horrified looks. Some were so gravely wounded that I doubted they would survive much longer. One man had a hole in his left cheek, revealing a mouth red with blood; another had a very wide gash on his leg, and the blood coagulating there was black; undoubtedly, it was infected.

I tried to avert my gaze from them, but wherever I looked, I saw wounded soldiers. Wolf led me past a boulder the size of a large house to my horse, which was waiting tied to the trunk of a tree. I pressed my forehead against the sturdy head of the steed, immediately feeling the tears welling up again. I hadn't given him a name, because it would have hurt even more when I had to let him go. I simply called him, *Horse.*

I reached for the bag attached to Horse's saddle and pulled out my journal to make sure it was still intact. As soon as I opened it, a sheet slipped out, dancing in the air and gently settling on the grassy carpet. A young redhead nearby picked it up and, limping towards me, handed it over. He smiled shyly. I didn't have the strength to smile back. I held the sheet in front of my eyes and began to read silently.

"*The ingredients and preparation method for the sleep potion. Follow it exactly, Saya!!! And yes, exactly means exactly...*"

Although he had initially refused to reveal the recipe for the elixir, he had written it on a small page from his notebook and slipped it into my journal. At the bottom of the sheet, in small writing, was the following warning:

"*If you put too much ground indirro bulb and too few velera petals, you risk creating a very powerful aphrodisiac. If that happens, come to me immediately.*"

I started laughing loudly, slipping the sheet back into the journal, but my laughter quickly turned into wailing.

"Are you all right?" the young man asked, taking a step in my direction.

At that moment, I unleashed my power, throwing myself once again into the river of ether. The current pushed me towards the shore, trying to pull me away, but my rage roared louder. I overpowered it, drawing in more magic than ever before, as my eyes settled on the huge boulder on the opposite side of the camp. I reached out my hand and focused all my fury and power on it, covering it with magical waves. It began to tremble, and the men leaning against it hastily stood up, running in the opposite direction.

"Saya, what are you doing? Let go!" Wolf shouted.

I saw his jaw dropping in amazement as the rock detached from the ground, starting to levitate. The young man, who had been eager to talk just moments ago, now stepped back, his face etched with fear—fear of me. The fear that grips the common mind when confronted with something far greater than itself. I leaned down and slammed my palm into the green earth beneath, and the boulder plunged back with speed, causing the surrounding forest to tremble under my power. Some men started to scream, others prayed, and others were too tired or injured to react.

Wolf reached me in a few steps, but I was already on my feet, and my fury made the giant rock rise again. "Enough, Saya! This is too much power; it will consume you!" he growled.

I gathered the ether waves tightly around the boulder like invisible tendrils. Then, screaming at the top of my lungs, I smashed it into the green face of the ground, picturing Aella where it struck. This time it cracked with a powerful noise that reverberated among the trees like harrowing whispers. It split into two large pieces and several smaller stones.

But I wasn't done; I still had power left, and I wanted to see what my limit was. Aella's face was still on my mind, gray and horned—a true demon. I wove ether around each boulder simultaneously and lifted them all at once. Wolf grabbed my outstretched hand, looking at me with... was it fear?

"This won't bring him back. This won't bring anyone back," he whispered with pity. "If you don't learn to control your hatred, the hatred will control you."

I collapsed to my knees, and the rocks fell with me, sending booming echoes through the entire forest. My chest burned as the invisible hands of the Great River seemed reluctant to let me go. It wanted me to drink more. I wanted the same, but I resisted, stepping away. It felt like stepping away from life itself.

"I will kill the Black Queen," I yelled through gritted teeth. "I swear!"

Time for Forgiveness

Excerpt from Elena's journal, dated the second day of the seventh month, Iureia, in the year six hundred twenty-three after the Conversion:

Jane looked hesitantly at the steaming bowl of soup in front of her, hoping that perhaps a long enough hesitation would spare her from the inevitable fate that awaited. I cleared my throat loudly to remind her that I was still there and that I was beginning to lose my patience. She took the spoon and dipped it into the bowl of soup with the slowest possible movements, then raised her gaze, watching me sit at the other end of the table with my arms crossed.

"But I'm not hungry, Princess," Jane whimpered.

I pulled the bowl towards me and took a sip right in front of her, then pushed it back, spilling some in the process. Beatrice, standing behind her, made colossal efforts not to burst into laughter at the exasperation painted all over my face.

"See? It's not poisoned," I assured her, exhaling sharply. "Nor is it made with rotten meat or boiled—nothing to scorch your rosy little tongue."

Jane nodded, then glanced back and forth between me and the bowl. "But still, I'm not hungry..."

"That's enough!" I exclaimed, smashing the table with my palms, and rising. "Either you eat willingly, or I'll force it down your throat! Your choice."

"I would suggest you eat willingly," Beatrice said with a malicious smile. "But the second option sounds amusing too. In fact, you know what? Don't eat!"

I growled at her, which made her burst into laughter like a drunken jester. Jane sighed. With no choice left, she leaned over the bowl and began to sip in silence. It reminded me of the times when I was a child and the handmaiden, Egwene, forced all sorts of vegetables down my throat, showing no mercy for my tears. But Jane wasn't seven years old! She hadn't eaten anything since we brought her to the palace, choosing to spend all her time locked in her room, pretending to sleep. Not even Beatrice, who slept in the adjacent bed, managed to get a word out of her.

"After you finish, you'll come with us for a walk in the palace's garden, willingly or not. When we finish that, we'll have lunch, and you'll taste every single dish on the table, and may Azerad have mercy on your soul if you refuse! Do you understand?" I demanded.

"Yes, Princess," she replied defeatedly.

"Very well. I'll fatten you up like a piglet."

"And when we deem you fat enough..." Beatrice began, her mischievous grin never wavering. She let out a shriek, mimicking the sound of a knife slicing through the air.

"Refrain yourself!" I shouted at her.

"I'll refrain, I promise," she said, biting her lip. "I'm sorry, mother, if I was too mean to my little sister. Will you forgive me?" When she saw that I didn't respond, she continued, "You should thank us; we're preparing you for motherhood. Jane plays the role of the shy little girl, and I play the role of the... naughty one."

I sighed, massaging my temples. Jane glanced at my belly but made no comment. I hadn't told her I was pregnant yet, but this might open the door to her more talkative side.

"I'm just at the beginning," I told Jane, "but maybe you can tell me what to expect next."

"I'd be happy to," she nodded.

Those were the first words she uttered without being forced to. We were making progress. Snail-paced progress, but progress nonetheless.

After Jane finished her meal and, willingly or not, put on one of Beatrice's dresses, the three of us headed to the royal garden. As usual, she was very reserved, and the forced smile she wore whenever greeted by someone made it seem like she was there against her will. Which was probably true, but the fresh air and sunlight did her good, so I intended to take her for a walk at least three times a week.

Except when Dad arrives. I know the scum wouldn't miss the chance to get rid of her. The girl was carrying Rorik's illegitimate child; as for me, I got pregnant before marriage. "*You're both a disgrace to the Tarrygold name,*" he told us the morning before the tournament. Those were the last words he spoke to my brother, and now that memory pains him deeply.

The royal garden is one of the few places in Romir that I love. It's a feast for the eyes—an immense floral labyrinth even larger than the palace itself, adorned with flowers of all kinds and colors, brought from every corner of the world. Dacryean roses with their deep, blue or velvety petals, vibrant red climbing blossoms from the distant land of Verdavir cascading over trellises, endless rows of tulips in every imaginable hue, their delicate heads nodding in the breeze. Fragrant lavender stretches out in gentle waves, mingling with the bright bursts of golden marigolds and the soft pastels of peonies. Exotic orchids, with their intricate patterns, peek out from beneath lush ferns, while towering sunflowers turn their faces towards the sky, basking in the sunlight. The air is filled with the heady scent of jasmine and honeysuckle, intertwining to create an intoxicating aroma.

Even Jane couldn't help but let out a hesitant smile at the sight of an arbor covered in climbing roses. She was thin and pale. We had to tighten her dress quite a bit at the chest, because she was missing Beatrice's ample bust. Still, Jane had a unique beauty. It wasn't hard for me to understand what Rorik saw in her.

"How do you find it?" I asked her.

For a moment, she seemed confused, as if she didn't understand the nature of my question, then she jolted. "The garden? Beautiful."

"Liar, liar, eyes on fire," Beatrice interjected, shaking her head from side to side. I cleared my throat.

"But I do like it!" Jane hurried to respond. "It's just that... Rorik brought me here the day before..."

A glint appeared in her eyes, reflecting the grief and anger that made her dig her nails into the palm of her hand. If she had encountered Darion at that moment, she would have surely gouged out his eyes before he could do anything. Bea nodded towards one of the benches nearby, hidden between two decorative columns covered with blue Dacryean roses. Jane was trying hard to maintain a serene face; just like me, but the pain in her soul, vividly visible in her stare, and the mention of my brother brought tears to my eyes as well.

Damn you, Darion!

"How was that day?" I asked after we all settled down. "The one before the tournament."

She didn't say anything. She wanted to respond, but she was already on that verge between the fragile calm she barely maintained and the crying fit that would have awaited if she uttered a single word.

She was too burdened to speak, so I began, "He was different that day, like a completely different person. I had a quarrel with Larion—Bea, you probably remember—and the last thing I wanted to see or hear was Rorik. He came to me that evening, asking to talk privately, which was unusual because he never did that. He usually spoke his mind openly, no matter who overheard. I told him to leave, insisting I had no time for his nonsense, but he refused to go and kept pressing me to listen. I remember he seemed almost frightened. I thought something might have happened to Dad, or Mom… or, even worse, to my cat from Montrias."

Jane smiled, and Beatrice let out a chuckle. I hadn't realized just how much I missed my cats.

"What did he tell you?" Jane wanted to know.

"That he loves me," I replied, almost in shock. A part of my mind had locked away that memory, and until now, I barely paid it any attention. "He told me he loves me and not to forget it. He hadn't said that since we were kids, so many years ago that… oh. I didn't respond. I could have told him I loved him too, or said so many things. If only I had known it would be my last chance..."

The words were swallowed by the torrent of tears I couldn't shed—not there, in front of the people wandering around. Jane hugged me, pressing her cheek against my shoulder and crying silently.

"He told me that tomorrow he will challenge Darion to a demonstrative duel during the tournament," I recalled aloud, after managing to regain my composure. "It seemed odd, but it wouldn't be the first oddity he's done, and I knew he despised the Prince, so I didn't question him further. In the end, he asked me to promise that I will take care of you if anything happens to him. I told him I didn't know what he drunk, but I'd like to try it too."

Beatrice and I started to laugh, and even Jane smiled shyly, then wiped the tears from her eyes. When she pulled away from the hug, she looked at me for the first time as if I weren't trying to eat her.

"He told me that if he ever leaves, to come to you because you would take care of me. I asked him what he meant; leave where? But he just told me not to worry. May Azerad forbid, it's as if he knew he would die, but he couldn't have known, could he?"

"No," I replied, feeling a void forming in my stomach. "He couldn't."

"But it seems so," whispered Beatrice under her breath.

"But he couldn't! I repeated.

"On the day of the tournament, he rode to you and gave you a rose, in front of everyone," Beatrice added. "Don't get me wrong, it's clear he loved you, but even he knew he would have trouble with the king after the tournament."

"And are you implying that he knew Darion was going to be a slippery snake and use a real sword, and still chose to do it?" I asked sharply. Beatrice shrugged.

"The monsters that did this to us are still free," Jane spat out, full of hatred.

"For now," I assured her. "They won't be able to run forever. One day, they'll make a mistake and meet their end. Everything will be resolved in time, you'll see. We'll be avenged, and the world will be a safer place."

Jane nodded, almost dreamily, slowly turning her gaze toward the statues planted not far from us, arranged in a circle, all facing a common point. Once, according to my future husband's words, special channels were dug behind them, and climbing roses covered their stone dresses to give a certain life to the dead stone. Over time, those channels were covered, leaving the stones with the monotonous, lifeless gray of stone—solitary and sad. Exactly as they should be.

"Rorik used to laugh at those statues," Jane told me, subtly nodding toward them. "He found it amusing that whoever sculpted them gave them little horns."

"The artist had a sense of humor," Beatrice remarked. "Or perhaps those girls were truly mischievous."

Jane smiled, but my thoughts suddenly drifted to Aella and the words of my betrothed. A *nartingal*, he called her. Those statues, worn down by the scythe of years, made me wonder if Romir has a history with those sorts of creatures.

Only Romir? Many years ago, I learned from the wizard master Grifellgor about a statue dating back to the time of Belvick the Maker, found in the basement of the Circle's first building. The statue of a nymph—a woman with horns and sharp ears. On the pedestal beneath her was inscribed: "*Dear friend, I will never forget you.*" The master rambled for hours about the symbolism behind it, but what if there was no symbolism? What if the woman was depicted with horns not as a symbol of royalty, but because she actually had horns?

We stayed there until lunchtime. Jane seemed to regain some color in her cheeks and became more talkative, looking surprised when too many words escaped her, like a kitten discovering it could meow. She told us how she had opposed coming to Derahia several times but eventually gave in to my brother's insistence, who feared leaving her alone in Montrias with our mother. I hadn't told her yet that Mother was riding to Romir as we speak; it was probably the last thing she needed to hear.

Jane, like me, noticed the same changes in my brother's behavior that I had seen, and all of it started when mother brought that cursed wizard, Melchior, to the palace. The only good thing Aella had ever done in her entire life was to kill him. According to her, Rorik had begun to shout at her very often or lose his temper, apparently for no reason. He seemed scared or worried, and sometimes, strange things happened around him.

"What kind of strange things?" I intervened.

She hesitated. "I'm not sure if it's appropriate to say, especially since I might have imagined it all."

"Now I'm intrigued," I chuckled.

"Me too," said Beatrice, leaning in with raised brows. Her eyes flicked between Jane and me, then back to Jane. "You two look strangely alike. Burning rotten mice, I can't believe I didn't notice it until now."

After exchanging a quick glance with Jane and wondering how Bea could so swiftly shift from one topic to another, I said, "Whatever you have to say about Rorik, it will mean a lot to me. Good or bad."

Her pale cheeks turned white. She barely found the courage to part her lips and speak. "One night, a few days before leaving for Romir, I sneaked into his room to surprise him. It was foolish of me, I realize now, but we had grown so close, and I truly believed there were no secrets between us. I... I wanted to wait for him, hidden under the covers, and..."

"Naked?" Beatrice interjected with a smirk on her lips.

Jane blushed and lowered her eyes.

"It's not relevant, Bea," I scolded her. "Please continue."

"Yes, naked," said Jane, displaying a shy smile that made both of us laugh. "I sat on the bed, covered myself well, and waited."

She shuddered, then swallowed hard, stopping her speech until a group of ladies passed by us, paying us no mind as they discussed probably mundane topics. I thought our discussion was also somewhat mundane, completely unprepared for what Jane was about to reveal.

"As soon as I heard him enter the room," she continued, "I realized something was wrong. He slammed the door and was breathing heavily, as if he were scared—no, horrified. He was horrified. Suddenly, I was too afraid to let him know I was there, and he didn't notice me. He paced back and forth from one wall to another, talking to himself, whispering strange things, rehearsing a speech."

"Heavens," exclaimed Beatrice. "And all this time you were there, under the covers?"

She nodded, her chin trembling. "I was fully covered, and he was so distracted by whatever he was about to do that he didn't even notice my shape under the blanket. He sat on the floor and began to whisper, then started speaking louder and louder."

"What was he saying?" I asked, feeling goosebumps forming on my skin.

"It seemed like he was praying. The air suddenly froze, and even though I was covered, I could barely control my shivering. Whether it was cold or fear, I couldn't tell then, and I still can't now. I lifted the edge of the blanket and watched him prostrate himself. The silence around us… I had never experienced such silence before. It was as if there was nothing anywhere—no one in our room, outside it, not even a single soul left in the entire world! Then he said, 'I've returned with news, Mighty Lord.'"

"I never considered him a religious person," said Beatrice, adjusting her position on the bench.

"He wasn't," I affirmed. "He was quite repulsed by the idea of religion in general."

"If he was praying, he wasn't praying to Azerad," Jane shuddered.

"But to whom?" I raised my brows.

"I don't want to talk about it anymore; I shouldn't have even mentioned it. I was tired, I don't know what I heard."

I looked at her, frowning. She clasped her hands in her lap, trying in vain to hide her trembling.

"Jane, if it's about my brother, I'd like to know. Please."

She sighed, but nodded approvingly. I waited eagerly, holding my breath, but she remained silent.

"If you want to tell her alone, I can leave," offered Beatrice.

"It's not necessary," Jane hurried to say. "I'll tell you if you really want to know." She shifted, then looked me in the eyes, her gaze making me clench my jaw. "Immediately after, I heard Rorik say, 'The expedition has returned, but, as expected, they didn't find the city.'"

"What expedition?" I asked, and she shook her head.

"I don't know, but after he said that... Azerad protect me!"

She almost screamed the last part. I looked around, surveying the imposing garden to ensure no one was nearby, and the place felt emptier and more desolate than ever. Everything suddenly appeared less colorful, as if all its nuances had been drained by the sun's almost cold rays. She held her breath, on the verge of tears. When her eyes met mine again, the purest expression of terror I had ever seen was carved over her face.

"Something answered him," she said in a voice as low as a moan.

"Something?" I asked, clenching my teeth.

"There was something with us, something evil, something unholy. It wasn't Azerad, it couldn't be."

"Are you sure no one else entered the room with him?" Beatrice asked, with a hint of amusement in her voice. Despite the tone she tried to display, she seemed frightened.

Jane mechanically nodded, then placed her hands over her stomach. "I'm sure. I didn't tell anyone else about this. Rorik left immediately after, and he didn't even know I was there. I dressed as quickly as I could and ran away. I didn't care if anyone else was in the hallway and saw me; I just wanted to get out." Her eyes flickered in horror. "That thing, whatever it was, didn't leave. I couldn't see it, but it was still there, watching me from the darkness, and I swear... I swear when I was about to leave, it called me. It said '*Mary.*'"

"Mary?" I repeated.

"Yes. My mother wanted to name me that, but my father disagreed, so they named me Jane. My grandmother used to tell me that my mother always called me Mary Jane whenever my father wasn't home. But no one else knew that."

"Azerad forbid!" Beatrice murmured.

We all remained silent, watching the shadow slowly spreading over the garden like a droplet of blood in the cold water. A dense cloud covered the sun. My body was paralyzed with fear and too many thoughts raced through my mind in those moments. I pushed them all aside and took a deep breath, adopting a casual demeanor.

"Regardless of what it was, my brother took the secret with him to the grave," I uttered, and both Beatrice and Jane nodded at the same time, almost relieved that we were ending the discussion. "I think it's time for us to have lunch."

We walked in a profound quiet toward the Great Hall, none of us feeling inclined to speak any longer. Beatrice looked at me questioningly, raising her eyebrows, and in response, I shrugged. As ridiculous and insane as Jane's story sounded, for some reason, I believed her. Perhaps it was the authenticity of fear that accompanied every word that left her lips, or the sincerity in those eyes perpetually drowned in tears, but I was almost certain she was telling the truth.

Surely, Melchior's cursed hand was involved.

Jane returned to her old self, pale and tense, although this time I could understand her fear and even shared it. When we stepped inside, the Great Hall was almost empty. Unusual for that time of day. A few ladies were scattered around the tables, speaking in low voices, but besides them, there was no one else.

"Have we arrived too early?" Beatrice frowned.

"I don't think so."

I went to one of the tables, glancing at the courtesans who stopped whispering as I approached. Leaning in, I aligned a misplaced fork parallel to the rest of the unused utensils, then scanned the group, recognizing one of the young women as Lara Veleront. The only reason I knew her name was that her brother, Toader, had been one of Darion's very close friends. After his and Aella's escape, I had a few people follow Toader to ensure he didn't cause any trouble—I had someone keeping an eye on all his close friends. Now, I even have a spy stationed at Tom Alver's inn. For a while, I knew everything everyone from Veleront family was doing.

I smiled at her.

"Princess Elena," Lara greeted me, bowing her head.

"Lara," I replied, following her example. "Do you know where everyone is?"

"All the men are in the throne room, for the war council."

"What war council?"

The first thing that crossed my mind was my father and the Frevian army now marching towards Romir. I feared the situation escalated and now Larion is preparing an armed response.

"All I know is that there was a major battle near Blackstone, and Darion and his men won."

My mouth went dry "Darion and his men won a battle?"

"Yes. He's gathering an army of barbarians in the North. He probably has a few thousand, or even hundreds of thousands."

"Hundreds of thousands?" I snapped. "Do you even understand what that number means? Never mind. Thank you."

I instantly regretted snapping at her, realizing it was a clear sign of weakness. Jane and Beatrice had also heard the conversation, their faces reflecting concern as they stared at me. I approached them, feeling dizzy, with my heart pounding in my throat. Darion's name, along with words like "war" and "invasion," was being whispered around the tables, tossed like venomous arrows by weak-minded girls who would believe even the silliest of rumors.

"Wait for me in my room," I told the girls. "I'll go see what's *truly* going on. There's no need to worry just yet."

"You don't seem worried at all," Jane observed.

"That's because I'm not. I'll come to you with news after I find out *exactly* what happened."

With that, I turned on my heels and headed toward the throne room, feeling the dizziness and nausea intensify with each step, overwhelming me with every breath. I was terrified, but I didn't intend to show it, especially to Jane and Beatrice, who were particularly frightened. Despite Bea often being mean to Jane, I sensed that Jane was the stronger of the two.

As I walked to the throne room, my mind fixated on two things: the growing number of people Darion had managed to gather, and my betrothed's foolishness in underestimating the threat from the start. Had Blackstone already fallen? How much territory had we lost?

The more I thought about it, the more absurd the idea of an invasion of Derahia became. He couldn't amass a force large enough to pose a threat to us, not in such a short time, not with Lanre's men and the Circle's assassins on his trail.

I paused for a moment in front of the bronze doors, the lions sculpted on each of them glaring menacingly, baring their fangs in a silent warning to stay out. And rightfully so—it probably wasn't a good idea to barge into a war council. The guards standing watch glanced at me with confusion, unsure whether to stop me. I pressed my lips together and pushed one of the doors aside, stepping in with perhaps too much impudence.

At first, no one paid me any attention, but it didn't take long for Larion's gaze to fall upon me and for the room to fall silent. He sat on his high throne, and several chairs were brought into the room for the other participants. There were thirty-two men, probably all the important nobles present in Romir at the time. I smiled, making a deep bow, and the only one who smiled back at me was the Grand Master Radagrim Emberflame.

"My dear, we're in the midst of a war council," Larion told me with a sigh.

"I know, and I apologize for arriving so late, but it seems that the messengers sent to inform me got lost along the way."

One of the lords, fat and bald, dressed in boldly vivid violet silks, cleared his throat, smirking with a false politeness before speaking. "Princess, with all due respect, but a war council is not a suitable place for a woman."

I studied him from head to toe. On the chest of his robe was embroidered a coat of arms representing two roses with their stems spiraling around each other. I didn't know him, but I was sure I had seen him a few times in the palace, so he was probably just one of the minor lords from Derahia whom I hadn't deemed worthy of learning his name or his coat of arms. Or to show respect.

"Then perhaps you should leave the room, my lord" I replied with a smile, as the entire room burst into laughter.

Larion gestured towards one of the empty seats.

"As the most important member of the assembly has only just arrived," he began, looking at me amused, his remark eliciting laughter, "I suppose I must repeat myself. Master Radagrim was contacted by Wolf and Sparrow, the assassins sent to track Darion down. They managed to capture him and obtained an escort of soldiers from Blackstone to take him to trial. Lord Lanre was away with the bulk of his troops, but the citadel was able to spare three hundred well-equipped soldiers for the mission. However, they were attacked on the way by a horde of savages led by the Black Queen herself. There were around seven hundreds of them, and they managed to surround the soldiers, winning the fight with minimal losses. Over three-quarters of those from Blackstone perished, and one apprentice as well. The traitor escaped."

"Saya?" I asked in one breath.

"No," said Master Radagrim. "Parzival Enarius, killed by the Black Queen's magic."

I breathed a slight sigh of relief, perhaps showing more than I should have in that place.

"And now," Larion said, "we are faced with the likelihood of Blackstone being besieged. In addition to this, according to the report of the two assassins, a village in the north called Bragovik is full of sympathizers of my brother. Before you arrived, we were discussing how we should act against those traitors. Several lords advised me to send troops there and burn the village to the ground, to serve as an example to others considering joining this rebellion of his. However, Master Radagrim advised me to wait, saying that a military act against my people would be a hasty decision. My dear, what would you advise me to do?"

Some in the room chuckled, but others looked at me with visible interest, awaiting my response. Larion probably realized it would be exceedingly difficult for me to keep my mouth shut, so he asked me to speak before I did so on my own.

"Master Radagrim is partially right. It wouldn't be wise to strike against *our* own people. We would extinguish the fire in Bragovik, but undoubtedly such an act would spark others throughout the entire kingdom. Yet, waiting wouldn't be advisable either, as we would allow the flames to spread. My proposal is to send informants to that village and to all major cities in Derahia. Loyal individuals everywhere, who will infiltrate the ranks of the traitors and gather as many names as possible. Names and addresses. When we deem that we have enough information and the time is at hand, we strike. Everywhere, at the same time."

A grave silence fell over everyone. One of the nobles, tall, with twirled mustaches, whom I recognized as Lord Janos of Branford, laughed briefly, then looked around for support, searching for other amused faces, but no one smiled, so he cleared his throat, adopting a serious expression.

"This is a good plan," Larion concluded.

Radagrim said, "My King, I would advise against it. Killing thousands, perhaps tens of thousands of people across the entire country is a desperate and unnecessary measure. Darion has only a few hundred wildlings and a few bored villagers who would bury their heads in the sand at the first whiff of battle. This is certainly not an army. The victory against those from Blackstone was due to the Queen Black's trickery, who hid a hundred soldiers using ether, thus allowing a surprise attack from behind, rather than due to the superiority of Darion's troops."

"Master Radagrim," I began, "the entire plan is based on avoiding bloodshed for as long as possible. With their names and addresses, we will only strike if the situation demands it and if there is no other way. It would be advisable to assassinate the leaders of the rebellion as quickly as possible, before our hand is forced, namely Darion and Aella. But if we fail and they manage to gather enough warriors for an invasion, I will prefer to reduce the number of their allies in the country as much as possible before we end up fighting on two fronts."

"This is a good plan," someone else chimed in. I immediately recognized him as Lord Alfric Grayfang, Larion's uncle. "May Azerad help us avoid shedding the blood of our own people, but if they choose to rebel, we will have no choice. They will either die on the battlefield, with weapons in their hands, after having already killed loyal men, or in their own homes, before they could do any harm to us."

"It seems I did well to allow my betrothed to stay," Larion concluded, and other nobles nodded in approval with foolish grins on their faces. They probably still didn't take me seriously, and that was fine. I wanted it that way—I'm just a naive girl, don't mind me. "Tonight, I will send a garrison of seven hundred spearmen and three hundred archers to Blackstone. They need archers the most; that's the easier way to fight a witch."

"And the Circle will send ten wizards to Derahia, each specialized in battle magic. When the rebels venture out of the mountains again, they'll be met with an appropriate response."

"What are you talking about, old man?" a nobleman asked provocatively. "If we wait for them to come out, we're just giving them the opportunity to gather more people. Sometimes you must smoke out the den if you want the fox to come out. We need to join King Alfred and attack the Redat Mountains."

"That might be contraindicated," the old man said in a conciliatory tone.

"And why would that be *contaminated*?" the nobleman asked, still angry.

"Because you, Lord Janos, don't know Darion." The one speaking this time was Alfric, his tone as cold and hard as steel.

"I know him well enough to know that he's just an arrogant upstart who's barely come of age, Lord Alfric," Janos defended himself.

"Just as I am?" Larion wanted to know. "We're the same age, after all."

"No, my King! Your Majesty, you are different, as if you weren't even related."

"And yet, we're twins," Larion pointed out.

I know my partner well enough to be aware that he hates flattery and is disgusted by flatterers. He looked at Janos with a stern smile, as if ready to say something more, but remained silent.

"He was underestimated once on the Night of the Blood Moon," Alfric continued. "Forty died. He was underestimated a second time, today, in the Battle Near Blackstone. Over two hundred died. When will we learn from our mistakes, Lord Janos?"

"What I have learned from mistakes is that we must kill him before he brings war to our lands."

"In that case, you have learned nothing. At the age of nine, when other children were reading fairy tales and ballads, Darion was already studying the writings of the greatest strategists who ever lived. By twelve, he was easily outsmarting both me and my late brother in *commanders and generals*. Perhaps the boy is not a diplomat and doesn't have social graces, we all know that, but on the battlefield, I assure you, he is a formidable opponent. Do you think that if we go after him in the mountains, he will come out to face us? He will flee and hide, continuing to prepare until he decides it's time to fight, and when he decides that, Lord Janos, you do not want to be on his territory."

"Uncle is right," Larion agreed. "It's foolish to send troops into the wilderness without knowing where to find him. It's a waste of time and resources. We must wait and, in turn, prepare ourselves. Personally, I don't believe he will attack Blackstone. Probably if he hadn't been captured, he wouldn't have even brought his troops into the open, and one day we would have found ourselves with uprisings spreading throughout the kingdom and tens of thousands of savages descending from the mountains."

Tens of thousands of savages.

"We probably won't come to that," Radagrim said. "Because our wizards told me they will kill them soon."

"The same wizards who captured Darion, then lost him?" someone in the room asked.

With his ever-present foolish grin and ignoring the jab, Radagrim replied, "Indeed."

"If they captured him once, it means they could have killed him," I said. "They didn't, hoping to bring him alive to trial, but I'm sure they won't do that a second time."

"That's correct!" exclaimed Radagrim, raising a finger in the air.

Things were already settled, so it didn't take long for the entire assembly to be adjourned. A new council was scheduled in two weeks, one that would include all the important lords in the country, and possibly my father as well. I hoped to leave arm in arm with Larion, but the bootlickers reached him before I could, engaging in endless discussions, so with his permission, I returned to our room.

Jane and Beatrice were waiting for me on a bench in the hallway, not far from the door. They stood up as soon as they saw me, not even trying to hide their irritating eagerness to question me. I gestured toward the door, and they followed obediently, like well-behaved children.

"There is no war," I told them as soon as the door closed behind us.

Jane breathed a sigh of relief, tucking a strand of hair away from her face, but Beatrice looked at me slightly skeptically. She had spent enough time with me to know I was a very good liar.

"Don't believe me?" I asked with a sly smile.

"Not even a little. That happened at Blackstone?"

I told them almost everything, leaving out the possible invasion of Derahia by the mountain people. I wasn't sure if Beatrice fully believed me, but Jane seemed satisfied with my assurances.

"But if Darion descends into Derahia," Beatrice began, "I want you to promise that we'll return to Frevia. We don't have to suffer in their stupid war. Damn men and damn their wars."

"Maybe it would be better," Jane said, then widened her eyes and quickly added, "Princess."

Darion killed my brother, so it would be my war too, I wanted to say, but I held my tongue. Instead, I said, "If Darion manages to gather enough troops to attack us, they'll probably kill each other before setting foot on our land. They're not called savages for no reason."

By the time Larion reached the room, it was late. Beatrice and Jane were long gone, and the moon had taken her brighter brother's place in the sky. I wondered if I was the moon in my family's sky. With Rorik dead and no other heirs, the throne would come to me, a woman. Perhaps Derahia and Frevia could merge into a single country. Heavens, I had never thought of that before.

It was clear that my betrothed was worried, but he did his best to smile nonetheless, his weary features almost trembling in the attempt to hold up that smile. He sat beside me on the bed, kissing my belly, then my lips.

"Are you feeling alright?" I asked him.

"Yes."

His fingers had begun to roam around my neck, slowly descending between my breasts and stopping at my abdomen. I could feel his hand trembling. He rose to his knees, facing me with his back hunched and his shoulders slumped, as if he was about to collapse under the weight he carried. The weight he refused to share. The flickering flames of the oil lamps hanging on the walls cast dark shadows on his severe and furrowed face. I stood up as well, taking his hand in mine.

"No," he then said. "I'm not feeling well at all."

"Tell me what's on your mind."

"He's my brother, Elena," he said in a whispered voice. "I know you hate him... I hate him too, but he's still my brother, and I know him. Believe me, this isn't him. That cursed demon is to blame. She twisted his mind ever since she arrived here. While she was locked up, she would lure him to her dungeon and destroy him piece by piece, only to rebuild him to her liking. She deserves to die, not Darion, he's just a fool caught in her snares."

"Oh, my dear, if they capture him again and you choose to spare him, it will only cause more strife. The nobles won't accept it, nor will my father. Probably not even your uncle would agree."

"What about you? Will you accept it?" he asked, searching my eyes for any hint of sympathy.

I hesitated, my voice catching in my throat. He looked at me intensely and fearfully, and for a few moments, it seemed like he regretted asking the question. I didn't know what answer to give him because the truth is, Darion's death is akin to a sweet dream for me.

He let out a loud sigh. "I'm sorry, I shouldn't have asked you that."

I remembered the story Jane told me, about the ritual Rorik performed in his room and the creature he was talking to. *What the hell have you gotten yourself into, you dummy?* Maybe Larion was right, maybe like my brother, Darion wasn't evil either, and Aella had had the same effect on him that Melchior had had on Rorik.

A chill ran down my spine as I thought of Rorik alone in his chambers, whispering to that demon. If Melchior twisted his mind and led him down a dark path, then perhaps Darion was just another victim of fate. My anger wavered, replaced by a pang of sadness. How many lives had this evil ruined? How many more would suffer before it was over?

"If he's captured and brought to Romir, I wouldn't oppose him staying alive, imprisoned somewhere," I replied with a heavy heart.

"Thank you," he said gratefully, forcing a smile.

"But it doesn't matter what I do, because the others won't agree, you know that, don't you?"

"I know, but he's my brother. Maybe I can make it work out."

"You can't make it work out. Not after everything he's done, believe me. The time for forgiveness is long gone."

He shrugged in resignation, then closed his eyes and took a deep breath.

"Maybe. We'll see. As Azerad wills it."

"As Azerad wills it," I repeated, kissing him on the forehead.

The Black Lions

The Battle Near Blackstone—another stain on my name, more straws thrown onto the smoldering fire of anger already burning in the hearts of those in Romir. Aella had won that battle, and the mountain folk had shown no mercy to the surrounded soldiers. They killed every last one of them, leaving no survivors. Many had tried to feign death, hoping to deceive the violent fate my warriors were so eager to deliver. That would have been Saya's fate too if I hadn't pulled her from that battlefield, releasing her into the woods. Looking back, it's hard for me to understand why I did that, attributing it all to that last shred of humanity still clinging in my heart after witnessing the massacre. Perhaps it was destiny, or perhaps the gods themselves had intervened, for that act would almost cost me my life in the weeks to come—and save it in ways I could never have foreseen.

Aella had seen. Nothing escaped her. She was waiting for me at the edge of the forest, wearing the serene face of the daughter of the night, silently weighing me, as she always did. Her expressionless face seemed like the most complex of masks. When I got close enough, she pulled my face to hers, capturing me in a long kiss. Ever since I managed to slip behind my men's ranks with Mathias, she had stuck to me like glue.

"You let her go," she said after breaking the kiss, looking at me without showing any emotion or betraying any thoughts. "Why?"

I shrugged, and she nodded, as if that answer was all she had hoped to find out. "She didn't fight," I told her as we descended towards the road strewn with corpses. My men were still collecting equipment from the fallen. "I saw her a few times, caught in the heap, crying. If she has even half the mind of a bird, this day should send her fleeing back to the Circle."

She didn't respond, scanning the battlefield as if trying to see something that eluded us.

"The other two escaped, though," I told her. "I would have liked them to die; they seemed dangerous."

"The sword-wielding wizards?"

I approved with a motion of my head. "Mhm. I overheard their apprentices talking. They called them Wolf and Sparrow."

She turned her head, her shining eyes locking with mine. After a prolonged moment of silently pondering the information, she smiled and gently squeezed my cheek. "We'll get rid of them next time."

On the day she first appeared to me as a daughter of the night, I told her about a nightmare where we were chased by a wolf and a sparrow. Neither of us managed to decipher it then, to understand the symbolism behind it, but now it was clear. It was a warning related to the two wizard-assassins. If they were going to keep coming after us, we had to get them out of the way, and soon.

They knew about Aella and were determined to capture her alive. After that day, I was certain that the next time we met, they wouldn't make the same mistakes—they would come to kill. I remembered how effortlessly that man had thrown me to the ground and held a dagger beneath my chin. I had never seen anyone move with such fluidity.

"Take whatever you can and let's go!" I shouted to the sea of people ahead. I turned to Aella and said, "More from Blackstone will come soon, and we don't want to be caught off guard."

"Regihold is waiting with fifty men in the forest. If they attack again, we'll encircle and slaughter them just like the first time."

"I don't want any more people to die."

Her eyes flickered into mine. "After this day, it's inevitable. More will come."

I knew she was right. She always was. Alfred and his army were probably already in Derahia, and although I planned to hide from him, I feared that in one way or another I would be forced to fight. There was no turning back, not anymore.

The sun shone brightly, the summer's heat mingling with the stench of death and the odor of blood that had soaked into the earth.

I left Aella's side, but she followed silently like a shadow, her fear that I might be abducted the moment she blinked keeping her close. Kayra and Mathias were resting in the shade of a tree on the hilltop. Mathias seemed to be speaking to her in a soothing tone, but the archer grumbled something with her forehead creased in anger. They both stopped talking when they noticed me approaching. Kayra frowned conspicuously. The Shadow Walker regarded me with his dark, vacant eyes, his expression as inscrutable as ever.

"You're injured," I remarked, noticing a visible wound on the man with the empty eyes' shoulder. Instead of blood, a greenish vapor oozed from the wound, dissipating into the air.

"A poorly placed spear thrust. Sometimes it's worth accepting a hit if it means taking a life in return."

I nodded, unaware that those words would save my life just days later.

"I would heal you," Aella said, "but I don't think it's possible. I could try."

"Worry not, daughter of the night. It's not the first wound I've suffered; I've had worse. It will heal on its own in a few hours, maybe less."

"I owe you my life. Thank you for coming after me," I said sincerely. "Especially you, Kayra. I know how much..."

"Forget the empty words and don't get captured next time!" she cut me off.

"Much blood has been shed," the Shadow Walker said, looking at his partner with sadness.

Spending so much time around Kayra, Mathias had begun to adopt her views on violence. In a perfect world, Kayra might have been right, but such a world can never exist as long as its inhabitants have free will. And without free will, would it even be perfect?

Kayra bore deep scars from her past, wounds so profound that she was willing to unleash her arrows at anyone who shed blood needlessly. Ever since the Night of the Blood Moon, she had developed a sudden, growing hatred for Aella and me. The more time she spent around us, the more she began to doubt not only us but also herself and *Deoa*, for asking them to protect us.

I shrugged with little sensitivity. "And tears and piss—that's what battles are made of. There's nothing you can do; some live, some die." She parted her lips, her teeth bared in a silent growl. I continued, "But I'll tell you again: you still have time. Turn back. If you come after me, you'll only stain your hands with more blood."

"I would give a hand to have any choice to depart from you, but if Deoa told Lyra to keep an eye on you, our fates are bound," she spat. "Those people surrendered! You could have spared them, but you chose to stand by and watch as they were massacred." I had rarely seen such visible disgust on anyone's face.

"Spare them for what?" I retorted. "To give them the chance to regroup and attack again? To waste the lives of my men because I'm too weak to do what must be done? I'm not willing to take that risk; the enemies you spare today will stab you tomorrow."

"*And yet, you saved that girl's life,*" Aella whispered in my mind.

"This is your war," Mathias said. He turned to Kayra and added, "It is his war."

"*Az'fielumra*, Master Darion!" a voice came from behind. "We've taken what was to be taken: weapons, armor, and horses. This has been the richest loot in years, and we've lost only twenty men."

The voice belonged to Collvan, an influential member of my new clan, the Blood Wolves. He was tall and lean, with short-cropped hair and a black beard that reached his chest and was braided at the tip. In many ways, he reminded me of Eldric, my blood brother from the Dancing Shadows, who was tasked with leading the people in my absence.

I nodded. "Very well. Gather the men; we retreat to the mountains."

"Master, may I suggest something?"

"Speak."

"This road leads to a city and a fortress that the people of the valley call Blackstone. If your wife could hide us, I'm sure we could raid it without any problems."

Kayra snorted, looking angrily at the man, while Mathias made no gesture. Aella smiled at me, probably because she was referred to as 'my wife.' Collvan dared not raise his eyes to her. No one in this clan had the courage to even approach her, for this was the first time they had seen a child of the night.

"Not today, Collvan. Today we have fought enough and gathered enough. But there may come a time when we must fight again. When that day comes, we will not fight on their land, for they will come to ours."

I was, of course, speaking about King Alfred of Frevia, who was determined to bring his troops into the Redat Mountains to find me.

"I understand," he replied, though I was sure all he understood was that my tone allowed no further discussion.

Regihold soon arrived as well, with Lyra on his shoulders and his massive battle hammer in hand. He left the girl in Kayra's care and went to select forty stout men to stay behind with him, holding the rear of the group in case of trouble. The giant seemed full of life. He waved his hammer cheerfully as he surveyed the men scattered before him, and Yenna clung to his arm like a tick, her incessant chatter never faltering. It didn't seem to bother him in the slightest, for he was just as talkative.

I left the main road, guiding my men through the forest along paths known only to us, making every effort to leave as few traces as possible. Those in the rear were tasked with covering our tracks. I knew that even the mountain people couldn't completely conceal their passage in such large numbers, but their tracks were sparse, and the Derahians feared venturing onto the mountain trails. Even when we hunted Garen the Black with Lord Kartag's soldiers two years ago, we avoided the narrow paths and checked meticulously before entering areas where the dense undergrowth could conceal an ambush.

Lanre, in his unbridled fury towards me, would have taken any risk, of that I was certain, so we had to remain vigilant at all times. It wasn't just him; the clans frequently clashed over trivial matters, such as a goat or a chicken going missing overnight. Their promises of loyalty were fragile, which always struck me as peculiar, considering the strong allegiance they showed to their leaders.

The forest swayed, following the contours of the hills it covered like a blanket. In many places, the slope seemed too steep to be passable, but there was always a path, covered with thick grass and layers of fallen leaves, winding down in steps to the base of the hill, among bushes and brambles. The riders took other paths, longer but wider roads suitable for animals, planning to meet us all at the foot of a mountain that night.

"I noticed you were quite smiley when Collvan called you '*my wife*'," I told Aella as we descended a steep slope, following a path among the old, silent trees. She led the group, guiding us along the same path they had taken earlier that day, when they set the ambush for the assassins.

"Was I?" she wondered, trying her best to seem confused.

"Yes."

"Maybe I was," she replied, shrugging with feigned indifference.

I smiled. "Maybe I need to find a ring."

"Darion, a word!" Merwin called out, pushing his way through the narrow path among the line of followers trailing behind me.

"Merwin, we haven't had a chance to talk since the battle," I said.

Aella stepped ahead, making room for the wizard to stand beside me. It was clear she wanted to continue the conversation, and now she probably harbored resentment towards Merwin, although she wouldn't let it show.

"Indeed, we haven't," he said to me. "And what a battle it was, many of theirs perished and few of ours. May all our battles be the same!"

"Tell that to Kayra."

"I'd wake up with an arrow in my rear, and I'm not keen to experience that just yet. I once met a woman who was more than willing to stick things up my—well, never mind. Speaking of the dead, I don't recall seeing the body of that girl with the dyed hair. What was her name... Sarah?"

I cast one quick glance at Aella's back before answering. "The one on whose shoulder you drooled? She survived and fled into the forest."

He smiled, then nodded. For a while, we walked in silence, listening to the cheerful and silent whispers of the men in the column and pondering once again about Wolf and Sparrow. If they caught up to us once, they would surely do it again.

"My knife is still with that woman," Merwin told me. "I hope to retrieve it one day."

"Where did you get it?" Aella asked over her shoulder.

"It's been in my family forever. I'd tell you it's a pal'ether, but I doubt your keen eye has missed such details, am I right?"

I frowned, as I didn't know it was a magical artifact, then shrugged, for I didn't care either way.

"What do you know about it?" Aella replied.

"It helps me focus. It gathers ether and allows me to use it as if I had absorbed it myself. It would be of no use to you, of course, as you don't use the Great River..."

"But it would be to those who have it now."

Merwin nodded gravely. "That's why we need to retrieve it."

"It's unlike any others I've seen," Aella said thoughtfully. "Once we recover it, I'll want to study it more closely."

"What do you mean, unlike any others?" Merwin asked.

Aella didn't respond anymore. The wizard muttered a few words under his breath when he saw he was being met with silence, but he didn't say anything out loud.

"What do you think about Saya?" I asked later.

It took him a while to respond, which was odd because he never missed an opportunity to talk about girls who caught his eye. One possibility was that he didn't like her enough, and another was that he liked her too much.

"She's not bad," he said hurriedly, after realizing the long pause he had taken.

I smirked. "Maybe we'll meet her again."

"Do you think so?" he asked with a hint of hope.

"You are in heat," Aella said, leaning to avoid snagging her horns on an oak branch.

"Now you're in the mood for talking," Merwin muttered with a dry smile. Turning his attention to Aella, he continued, "The eye sees, the heart desires. She's beautiful, pleasant to talk to. It's hard to dislike such a girl, not like that witch they call Sparrow. The kind of woman you better avoid and hope she avoids you too." He fell silent for a moment, then added to himself, "Strange times. I never thought I'd hope for a woman to avoid me."

We reached the foothills of a hill where the path split into several trails, each leading in a different direction. The road that Aella led us on began to widen, and the trees started to grow at more considerable distances from each other, as we were approaching the edge of the forest.

"Be careful not to fall," Aella cautioned me. "We wouldn't want to break that potion."

The potion that the assassins used to put me to sleep. It was in the saddlebag of the same horse where my sword had been hung. We destroyed two of the vials and kept the third, as Aella wisely noted, "You never know when we might need it." Even now, after all this time, I can't help but laugh and feel a pang of guilt over how it was ultimately used.

Not long after, we emerged into a rocky valley that skirted the familiar shape of the mountain from which we descended to Bragovik two days prior. Trees were scarce there, replaced by gray rocks that adorned the desolate landscape. We walked for several hours through that depression, guided by the last rays of the day, until we entered another small forest.

When we reached the site where we were to make camp—a wide clearing nestled against a rocky wall—the sun was slowly setting behind the peaks, and the first stars began to twinkle in the twilight sky. Several hours passed until those who would bring the stolen horses arrived, and just as long until Regihold and those who remained to guard our backs appeared.

That night, I had to intervene three times to stop fights that broke out in the camp because of the spoils captured, and each time I was very close to losing my temper as I listened to them argue in a very ill-spoken common tongue about why the piece of armor belonged to some and not to others. Not all mountain people could speak the common tongue, although many of them understood it to some extent.

When the spirits had calmed down a bit, Aella led me to a river that sprang from the mountain, cutting through the forest to the south. We shed our clothes and plunged into the icy waters, with the thin sickle of the moon faintly shining from the high sky. We sat together in a spot where the currents were gentle, allowing the icy water to reach up to our necks while we remained seated.

"You're so beautiful," I said, still trembling.

"The clans will need to merge," she responded.

I sighed, nodding reluctantly. "Of course, we'll do as you wish."

"It's necessary that if they have a single leader, they should bear a single name," she said.

"Fine."

She frowned, then reached out and caressed my cheek with the tips of her fingers. A gesture to which, at the time, I paid no attention.

"Let's talk about something else," she said.

"I'm just tired," I replied.

"It's been a long day. A lot has happened, and a lot more could have happened. Let's leave our troubles for tomorrow."

"Thank you!"

A faint smile appeared on her serene face, but it widened with each moment she studied me. "You mentioned something today," she began, looking at me meaningfully. "You seemed to suggest that... Collvan gave you a good idea."

After a few moments of silence, during which I tried to figure out what she was referring to, my face lit up in realization.

"Are you talking about when he suggested I use a sling instead of a bow?" I asked, referring to a conversation I had with Collvan on the way back.

She looked at me almost shocked, her mouth hanging open in amazement, as if she couldn't believe what she was hearing. She puffed, then nodded resignedly.

"Yes, it's a good idea!" I said. "A sling, when used properly, can be even more effective than a bow, although it's challenging to achieve precision at long distances. It's also easier to carry. However, for now, I prefer to stick with the bow. I haven't used a sling before, and given today's events, it doesn't seem like the best time to learn. I just need to figure out where to get a bow from."

She nodded again, then leaned forward, submerging herself in the water. When she resurfaced, she glanced around before fixing her shining blue eyes on me.

"Let's head back. Those assassins may not be very far, and I'd prefer not to face them naked."

I grinned. "I could strangle them with my…"

"You spend too much time with Merwin," she snorted, clearly unamused.

The camp was still abuzz with activity, with people clustered in groups, speaking in hushed tones. Most of the conversations were in their native tongue, but now and then, I caught fragments of speech in the common language. Merwin was already sound asleep, with Lyra nestled in Regihold's thick cloak, resting beside him.

That night, the sky remained clear, and I couldn't see any black swath covering the brightness of the stars. We settled where our backpacks awaited us tossed onto the grass. Retrieving our cloaks, we covered ourselves and stretched out on the cold ground.

It didn't take me long to fall asleep, and soon my dream transported me to a garden filled with hedges, roses, and corpses. Dozens of soldiers, their cloaks adorned with the emblem of the Tarrygold royal house, lay lifeless beneath archways draped in clinging roses. Their blood pooled in the shallow irrigation ditches along the stone path that cut through the garden, mirroring the rosy hue of the flowers above.

In front of me, blocking my path, stood a man with his back turned and his head raised towards the sky. Above, the heavens roared with the echoes of a battle ripped from the depths of the Burning Hells, reminiscent of the grisly scenes depicted in the Zerevist temples. The darkness was suffocating, thick clouds completely obscuring the sky and drowning the world in an abyss of shadows. Monstrous, twisted creatures with bat-like wings clashed violently with dragons. Dozens, perhaps hundreds, of dragons soared amidst the chaos, but the shadowy demons outnumbered them by the thousands, their forms barely distinguishable in the gloom.

The man turned to face me. A Shadow Walker.

He wore only a pair of black pants, secured at the waist by a thick leather belt, and a pair of boots. A belt, stained with blood, crossed his chest, securing a sword to his back. His physique was similar to mine, but the sight of the numerous cuts and the copious blood loss left me wondering how he was still standing. His face was bare of hair and marked with scars etched with strange symbols, as though branded into his skin, and his eyes were black. A whisper surfaced from the depths of my mind: The Betrayer of All.

"A bold attempt," he said to me, "but futile. When will you accept your fate?"

I was trying to contain my anger and calm my mind, reminding myself of my goal. It wasn't him I needed to kill; he was just a distraction from my true goal. I lifted my gaze to the sky once again, now observing the vague shape of a colossal mass of tentacles and wings hovering over Montrias, crushing the dragons that dared to oppose it, like insects beneath its weight. She was there too. I could feel her name and the bitter taste that the thought of the imminent confrontation left in my mouth.

Khyalis. We were bound by more than destiny, our connection deeper and more ancient than I could comprehend at that time. As I looked into the future within my dream, I couldn't grasp the full extent of the bond we shared.

I lowered my gaze back to him. "You will not take our hope. As long as there is hope, we will continue to fight."

"Hope," the man spat, drawing the sword over his shoulder. "Nothing more deceiving."

Under my glare, the wounds that crisscrossed his entire body began to close as the edge of his long sword started blazing.

I woke up feeling invigorated, the same calmness that always enveloped me before battle settling over me. I looked up at the fragile light of the stars, trying to figure out what that dream represented. Turning to Aella, I saw that her cold stare was already fixed on me.

"Nightmare?" she asked me in a whisper.

I nodded, then told her in a tone far too calm for the fear I felt in my heart, "I dreamed of the Last Sunset."

She widened her eyes, sitting up abruptly, then leaned closer. "Are you sure?" she asked me in a grave tone.

"No. I don't know."

"Tell me exactly what you dreamt."

Without wasting any more time, I began to recount every detail. When I finished, she fell into silence for a long time.

"I'm going for a walk," she told me. "I need to clear my mind."

"I'll come with you."

She nodded but left without waiting for me.

I shrugged off my cloak, then hurriedly rose, grabbing my sword from the ground and securing it to my belt. I caught up to her in a few steps and took her hand.

"That's what it sounds like," Aella whispered, her voice barely audible. "Lyra said that *Deoa* of her said it would happen, but I didn't dare to believe her words. I need to have a talk with her tomorrow about that creature she calls a god. The more I think about it, the more I fear that it might be one of them."

"Aella..."

"What if she's communicating with one of them while..."

I stopped her, placing both hands on her shoulders and turning her to face me. She closed her eyes and took a deep breath. "Lyra doesn't know anything, except that this *Deoa*, whoever or whatever he may be, has been helpful to them. If you overwhelm her with all sorts of questions, you'll only scare her. You're scaring me right now."

"You're right," she said after a while.

Her ears drooped, lowering in such a way that their sharp tips rested behind her shoulders. I had never seen her so distraught.

I hugged her tightly, holding her close as I pressed a kiss to the crown of her head, nestled between her horns. "No matter what comes, we'll get through it. I promise."

She nodded but kept silent.

"When you mentioned the idea given by Collvan, were you referring to him calling you 'my wife?'"

She nodded again.

"I like how that sounds," I said, brushing a lock of hair aside from her forehead.

"Maybe you can do something about it," she suggested.

"I will."

A timid, forced smile appeared on her furrowed face. "I'll wait."

If my dream truly took place after the Last Sunset... Heavens! What chances did I have against such an enemy? That Shadow Walker, the Betrayer of All, was right; in such a world, hope was merely the faint memory of a memory. That night, the light of the thousands of stars scattered above seemed feeble and insignificant compared to the darkness that surrounded them.

The next morning, I took the necessary steps to have Collvan appointed as my *fradezs sehyar*, blood brother and leader of the clan in my absence. It was a role he and Eldric would have to share. As the Master, I could have as many blood brothers as I deemed necessary, but to avoid potential disputes, I preferred to keep the number as low as possible.

I pulled aside Yenna, Kaldur, Collvan, and six other members of the Blood Wolves, and after nearly an hour of discussions, they all agreed that their village was in a better position than that of the Dancing Shadows in case of an attack. I ordered Kaldur to return to Eldric and inform him that, by my order, all members of the Dancing Shadows would need to relocate with everything they have to the village of the Blood Wolves and establish settlements there, a task which Collvan promised to assist with. Merging the villages was something that had to happen, because since I killed their leaders, they had become my responsibility, and it was easier to mount a defense with everyone in one place.

Kaldur wasn't pleased at all about being sent as a messenger, and neither was I, but I couldn't send Yenna away from Regihold without causing unnecessary drama. The giant had a soul as large as his stature. The village of the Blood Wolves was hidden deep in the heart of the mountains, in a location that would allow them to retreat easily if Alfred's army ventured that far. I reminded them dozens of times to avoid fighting unless absolutely necessary, as they stood little chance against a well-organized army.

It wasn't yet noon when everything was arranged, and I, Aella, Yenna, Kayra, Regihold, Mathias, Merwin, and Lyra were getting ready to part ways with my people and head towards the Demon's Fang.

"Who are we?" Collvan asked, as I checked once more that I had everything I needed in my satchel.

I turned to Aella, raising my eyebrows. "*The Blood Wolves or the Dancing Shadows,*" she responded, talking in my mind.

Without hesitation, as if I had been asked this hundreds of times before and each time I gave the same answer, I said, "The Black Lions."

Collvan smiled friendly at me, then bowed and said, "I like it. Take care of yourself, brother; the place you're heading to is cursed."

"So am I," I replied.

Kaldur also came to bid farewell, displaying a crooked smile in an unsuccessful attempt to hide his disappointment. I pulled him aside, placing a hand on his shoulder. "I'm sending you because you're the most suitable for this task. If I had sent anyone other than you and Yenna, Eldric wouldn't have believed the order came from me, and for such tasks, you're much more capable than Yenna."

This was just a big lie, but a well-placed one, as his face brightened a bit. Kaldur was a better fighter, and I would have preferred to keep him by my side, while Yenna would have certainly been better at delivering my message to Eldric.

"Moreover," I continued, "you have trained the most with me. Find all the fighters eager to learn and make sure they know how to wield the sword and spear. Prepare warriors for me; we might need them soon. Did you see the shield wall of those you fought with yesterday? Teach my people to do the same and organize them. The Black Lions will grow, and they will need capable warriors and leaders."

The last words felt strange, yet they flowed from my mouth before I even realized it. Then, a memory surfaced: I remembered sitting next to Aella on a tall hill covered in yellow grass and fallen rusty leaves. I knew that place; it was barely a day from Romir, north of the city. A large army surrounded us, people spread out in all directions, with banners depicting a Black Lion waving in the cool breeze.

In a heartbeat, the vision faded.

"I will not disappoint you, Master Darion!" he promised, puffing out his chest and straightening his back.

Feeling a shiver run down my spine, I nodded. "I know."

Before we left, Collvan approached and gave me a short hunting bow and a quiver of arrows, which I strapped to my back. We parted ways immediately, circumventing the mountain to the east and then heading north through a vast, untamed wilderness. The dense forests covered the slopes, their thick canopy casting deep shadows over the forest floor. There were no signs of human presence—only the endless stretch of ancient trees, their gnarled branches intertwined like the fingers of forgotten giants.

The paths Yenna led us on were so intricately concealed that it was hard to imagine finding them without her guidance. Often, the trail would vanish without warning, forcing us to push through waist-high grass, scramble over tangled underbrush, and duck beneath low-hanging branches. The wilderness seemed to close in around us, only to reveal the path again a few hundred steps downhill, as if the forest itself were testing our resolve.

At dusk, Kayra spotted a deer, and using ether, Aella managed to calm and lure it towards us. Whatever spell she cast, the animal remained calm as Lyra danced around it joyfully. A faint smile also appeared even on the stern face of the archer as she ran her hand over the deer's neck.

"Can we take him with us?" Lyra asked with innocence.

"We already have Regihold," Merwin responded, beginning to laugh.

Much to the little girl's dismay, Aella released the deer and it turned its back on us, skipping quickly through the trees. Due to the high mountain walls surrounding us, nightfall was coming faster in Redat. We camped at the mouth of a shallow cave found by Yenna in a rocky wall flanking the bank of a river.

"It's probably the den of a bear or a troll," she speculated. "Such caves are rarely uninhabited."

"It's empty now," Aella insisted. "And if the inhabitant returns…"

"Regi will growl at it and scare it off," Lyra suggested, then turned to Aella, flashing her a smile. "Or maybe you can make him friendly, like you did with the deer."

"I can try," Aella replied, smiling back at her.

We made a fire, and Kayra managed to bring down two birds, while Yenna and Regihold came back with wild fruits and fish. We had a hearty meal that night.

The Demon's Fang rose among the mountains to the northeast, tall and sharp, somewhat solitary, piercing through the smoky clouds above. That's where we needed to go, and Yenna estimated the entire journey would take around ten days, barring any bad weather on the ridges we were to cross. Aella believed that after reaching the mountain, we might lose another day or two before finding Yermoleth.

The following days proved to be warm, even scorching, but the breeze from the forests we traversed greatly tempered the heat in the air. I had the opportunity to use the bow gifted to me by Collvan, and Kayra, who agreed to train me, scoffed in disdain every time an arrow missed even by an inch from her designated target.

"You're too much in your head, shoot already!" she would say. "Oh, if only you'd think as much every time."

"I hit a bear charging straight at me right in the eye," I boasted.

"You won't be that lucky twice."

"I wasn't," I admitted. She was always so haughty, but I tried my best not to pay her any mind. "You're very skilled. Where did you learn to shoot so well?"

"In Verdavir. My father was an archer in service to the lord who ruled over our lands, as was his father before him. He wasn't blessed with sons, only daughters, so he taught us all how to shoot, to continue the family tradition."

"How many sisters do you have?"

"You ask too many questions," she frowned.

"Two," Mathias answered, appearing beside me. "Sherav and Rosalind. You might find it hard to believe, but she's the most charismatic of them all."

We all laughed.

In the following days, we climbed and climbed until the trees disappeared around us, leaving only shrubs, and even those became sparse. We had to make more frequent stops because of the sheer slopes we had to navigate. It didn't take long for all of us to collapse from exhaustion, except Aella, who frowned every time she heard us panting. Something had changed in her since the night of that dream. Whether it was because of the dream itself or because I had come so close to death, I couldn't tell.

She took advantage of every stop to teach Merwin how to control the red lightning, but progress was very slow. Merwin had learned to throw small lightning bolts from his arms, and once, he had almost succeeded in forming a sphere of pure ether, like the one Aella had used to kill Kolan on the Night of the Blood Moon, but he still had much to learn before he could make the lightning dance across the sky.

"Years of practice," Aella said.

The winds were strong up there, and the weather very cool, while down in the depressions around the mountains, it was much too warm. Regihold wore his armor most days, whether hot or cold, saying he was so accustomed to it that he would feel weighed down without.

On the tenth morning, the Demon's Fang loomed ahead, stretching up towards the gray clouds that blanketed the sky. We had slowed our pace, aware that our destination was near. After so many days on the road, we could do little more than trudge wearily up the seemingly endless, forested incline.

"Is there any chance Yermoleth might be hostile?" I asked Aella during that afternoon break.

"I don't know," she replied. "I wish I could be sure, but I don't know. It's best to remain cautious until we see how things unfold."

Everyone nodded silently. Yenna drew both her swords from the sheaths strapped to her waist and began sharpening their edges. I retrieved the Heart of Dawn, placing it on my knees and studying it in silence. It was still sharp, still capable of killing, even after decades of lying dormant in its sheath, in the old king's cabin.

The thought of what might await us ahead made us completely forget what was coming from behind. But the assassins hadn't forgotten about us.

Battle in the Mists

Excerpt from Saya's journal, dated the twelfth day of the seventh month, Iureia, in the year six hundred twenty-three after the Conversion:

Eleven days had passed since we narrowly escaped with our lives from the savages' ambush, seven since we were forced to abandon the horses and Horse because of the difficult terrain, and three since Wolf kept insisting that we were close. The day started like any other, with Sparrow mercilessly waking me up by poking me in the ribs with the tip of her shoe and telling me that we needed to have breakfast and tea, then hurry to set off on the road.

Not even the sun had set off on the road!

I nodded in silence, then reluctantly ate the last pieces of fish caught by Wolf a few days ago. He was preparing chamomile tea. Always chamomile tea! This morning, another mountain awaited us that we had to climb, because that's what our fugitives had done.

"Eight," Wolf said more to himself, taking the teapot off the fire.

"One more or one less doesn't make much difference," Sparrow responded, studying the silver-bladed knife she had taken from Merwin.

Some days, Wolf would tell us that, judging by the smell, there were seven of them, while on others, judging by the tracks found, there were eight.

"I think I'm starting to understand," he murmured. "No. But otherwise? Hmm..." He fell into deep thoughts.

"Care to enlighten us?" Sparrow prodded him.

"Sometimes I find seven pairs of tracks, sometimes eight, but I can never sense more than seven distinct individuals. Tell me, what creature has no scent and can vanish completely without leaving a trace?"

Wolf handed her the tea, as she pondered the question for a moment. She frowned, looking at her husband as if he were crazy, then delicately took the cup from his hands.

"Perhaps you're reading the tracks wrong," she suggested.

"I wish it were so. But I fear I'm right."

Their conversation brought an image to my mind, a memory I hadn't given importance to until today, attributing it to the trauma during the battle.

"A soldier tried to kill Darion right after the battle began," I told them abruptly. "And maybe I didn't see it properly, perhaps it was just a vision because of the sun reflecting off all those armors, but... I think I saw a man suddenly appearing beside him. He just appeared out of thin air."

The assassins exchanged a few tense glances, then Wolf asked, "Did you manage to see his face?"

I needed a few moments to gather the courage to respond, because his question, as vague as it was specific, made it obvious that what I had seen was true.

"His eyes seemed completely black."

"Shadow Walker!" Sparrow snarled furiously.

Wolf handed me the teacup with a fluid smoothness. His face was dark and stern, yet at the same time gentle.

"Aella is more cunning than I thought!" she exclaimed, her tone laced with disgust as she spat out the name. "I wouldn't be surprised if Darion is just a fool who sees only what she wants him to see. He claimed Rorik worshipped the First Gods, but if a Shadow Walker serves her, how long until she takes the next step?"

"Perhaps she has already taken it," Wolf suggested, his tone as calm as ever. "Or perhaps she never will. Maybe we're jumping to conclusions. Remember, sometimes it's the narrow and hidden paths that lead to the truth."

Sparrow sighed as if she had been holding her breath for hours, then closed her eyes. When she opened them, all the anger and disgust from moments ago were wiped away, replaced by the same unshakeable calm that appeared on her husband's face.

"*Ai joh*, you're right. Let's ponder what we already know. They have a Shadow Walker. Whatever the reason he accompanies them, it would be best to kill him too."

"But what is it?" I asked after I gathered enough courage to chime in their conversation.

"An abomination," Sparrow replied. "A deceased person pulled back into our world through powerful, forbidden spells, that manage to breach *Shonagary*—the realm of the dead."

"And can it become invisible?"

"It can travel between our world and another that is separated from ours by a veil, but mimics the image of it. When it's Beyond, we can't see it, but it can see us."

I glanced around, alarmed, which made Wolf chuckle softly. His laughter didn't bother me; on the contrary, it was reassuring. It reminded me that I still had much to learn and that my worries might be unfounded.

"We would feel it if it were close," he reassured me.

"A world that looks like ours," I repeated, hardly believing it. "Crabs and shells! Would I also feel when the Shadow Walker approaches?"

He shrugged. "Probably not."

I swallowed hard, letting out a forced chuckle. "Mrs. Sparrow, you mentioned the First Gods again?"

A long silence creeped over us, so deep that I jumped when I heard the wind whistling through the branches. None of them moved.

"The First Gods..." she repeated with genuine caution, turning to her husband with a doubtful glance.

"This is forbidden knowledge," Wolf said. "There could be serious consequences if it were discovered that we shared such secrets with a young aspirant."

I knew I shouldn't press further, but the question escaped me. "Why? That wizard, Merwin, was upset that the Circle 'outlawed knowledge.' Why is discussing these gods so dangerous?"

Sparrow scowled. "There was a time when this knowledge was not restricted. Knowledge means power, Saya, and such power should not be wielded by those who lack the discipline to control it. It is a double-edged sword that often cuts those who hold it."

"One day you will learn, but not now," said Wolf. "You are young, and the burden and temptation that come with it could be too much for you. Sometimes I feel they are too much even for me."

"Although you are *Sihirokhori moro*," Sparrow whispered to herself, barely audible.

The man nodded but said nothing more. I had to repeat that word to myself several times to ensure I wouldn't forget it, as I planned to translate it as soon as I returned to the civilized world.

"I understand," I told them.

I didn't understand, nor did I insist. I wouldn't have received an answer. For a while, I even thought I detected a faint trace of fear, well masked by the visibly forced calmness in Sparrow's voice. But now I'm not so sure, because the two of them don't seem to know how to fear.

I finished my tea, slung my satchel over my back, and set off through the silent, untouched wilderness, with the assassins leading the way. Ever since we began to approach this mountain, the trails and paths had become sparse, and the ones we did find seemed to blend into the untouched landscape, probably made by the animals that lived there. It wasn't long before we found the remnants of another campfire made by our targets, who were becoming increasingly careless with each kilometer traveled, leaving more and more traces.

Perhaps they didn't expect us to still be on their trail, thinking that the massacre eleven days ago had motivated us to turn back. It certainly motivated me, so if they believed that, they were right to a certain extent.

"Eight," said Wolf, surveying the area. "Eight pairs of footsteps. As I've said before, they also have a child with them. They're close, probably less than an hour ahead."

"We'll proceed in silence from now on," said Sparrow, then turned to me to gauge my reaction.

"Of course," I replied as politely as I could.

"And we'll be mindful of where we step, and if we trip again, we won't scream," she insisted.

"Understood."

She was referring again to yesterday, when I stumbled over a cluster of fallen branches. Of course I screamed, I was just startled; did she expect me to bite the ground with a solemn and calm face? That's probably what she would have done.

I was terrified by Aella, and I also wished for her death. For the sake of Parzival and all those fallen on the edge of that forest, for the sake of the wizard Kolan and those fallen on the field in front of Romir. It was the first time in my life that I truly wished for someone's death, that I truly believed it was justified beyond measure.

But what about Darion?

"Darion saved my life," I told them.

They both turned to me in perfect synchrony, their faces blank, waiting for me to elaborate. I recounted how he had taken me in his arms and led me into the woods to shield me from his own people, and as I voiced that event for the first time, I realized how unbelievable it all seemed. As if it had been a dream. Or a nightmare?

"Noble of him. He's atoning for a sin," Sparrow said after I finished recounting. "But it's futile to try turning back after burning the bridge. No good deed can erase his crimes."

"I know," I told them. "But maybe we can capture him alive and take him to Romir."

"You want to capture him alive after what happened last time?" she asked.

"Sparrow is right," Wolf said to me. "The risk is too great, and I'm not willing to take it either. Especially since we lost Parzival's sleep potions along with Sparrow's horse."

I was surprised to find that the possibility of the prince's death saddened me. In recent days, I had often found myself involuntarily remembering his arms, protectively wrapped around as he carried me into the forest. At first, the thought had terrified me, but now it offered a strange sense of protection.

"Perhaps..." I wanted to insist.

"I've made a decision, Saya!" the woman cut me off.

"Understood."

"We'll continue our journey," Wolf declared.

They were swift. Swift, tireless, and incredibly agile, as if their entire lives had been spent climbing such sheer and endless slopes. The forest echoed with the lively song of birds, their melodies reverberating through the cracks in the wall of trees. Not only once did I see a creature, be it a squirrel, hare or fox, studying us with an almost human curiosity. It was as if they hadn't seen humans in those parts before, which could very well be true. Perhaps to them, we were just large, foolish animals wandering where we didn't belong. That's certainly how I felt.

To the north, the forest continued to climb uphill, with gaping chasms opened from place to place, their edges almost concealed by bushes and weeds, ready to ensnare unwary passersby. I almost became one such passerby. I stepped on a boulder that wasn't securely fixed in the hard ground. The stone, tired of occupying the same spot for hundreds of years, rolled under my weight, plunging into the abyss, and I almost followed. My heart stopped in my throat, and my body went numb with fear. Sparrow quickly spun, grabbing and pulling me back onto the path with a single, decisive motion.

"I didn't scream," I blurted out in one breath.

She smiled at me. "Very well. Let's continue."

"Do you need a moment?" Wolf asked, noticing my trembling knees and hands.

I nodded, then staggered a few steps away from the cliff and slumped down at the base of a chestnut tree, hand place over my chest to calm the rabbit-like beatings of my heart. I tried to push the fact that I had almost died out of my mind. Sparrow also dropped her satchel and sat a few steps away, but Wolf remained in the same position, contemplating.

A squirrel appeared on the branch of a tree rising from the abyss where I had nearly fallen. It was likely drawn by our voices.

"The animals on this mountain are strange," I said when I noticed that the assassins were watching it too.

"There are many oddities around here," Wolf agreed. "Something seems unnatural."

"Or too natural," replied Sparrow. "I'd like to know what the Black Queen is searching for on this mountain. At first, I thought she was looking for other clans to join her lover's war, but if she is indeed doing that, she has chosen to go to the only place where there seems to be no sign of humans."

"You two rest your legs," said Wolf. "I'll go see what I can find."

He left his backpack next to us, then bent down, kissing his wife, and continued up the trail.

Aella was a child of the night, a nartingal. During that battle, I've seen her in her real form—demonic, but otherworldly beautiful. Even her death would have been inherently sad if she was indeed the last one of her kind.

How many secrets did she carry? Where did she come from? Where were her parents? What happened to the others of her species? Perhaps she revealed her secrets to the prince, but he too was destined to die.

The death of knowledge was always a sad thing, because unlike the death of a person who continues to live on in the hearts of those who remember, the death of a memory is eternal.

"You seem troubled," Sparrow observed.

Her black eyes, like two beads, peered at me from her beautiful and seemingly wise face. She looked in a way that suggested she held the answer to all the questions troubling me, but something made me hesitate still.

"Probably just tired. Ever since we released the horses, the backpack is weighing me down, and my legs are numb from all the walking," I replied.

She giggled, looking at me from beneath her long, black lashes. Her voice was always sharp like a dagger. "Perhaps we should have left you with the soldiers from Blackstone, let them take you back to Romir. I can see the journey hasn't been easy for you."

"No. I'm glad I came," I lied. "Maybe I can still be of help."

"I don't doubt it. The battle ahead won't be easy, but it must be faced."

"*Of course it won't be easy. There are eight of them and only three of us,*" I thought, but kept this to myself.

Seeking to dispel the awkward silence that often settled between us in the absence of conversation, I asked, "What shall we do about his comrades?"

"The Shadow Walker must be killed, but the others we could spare. Anyway, that depends more on them than it does on us."

I gasped, then said with a perhaps too inappropriate voice, "Wolf mentioned they have a child with them… Mr. Wolf."

"They do, I've seen the tracks myself. We'll do everything in our power to keep the child away from the battle's reach. If possible."

I clenched my jaw, fighting the urge to raise my voice at her. We stood in silence for a while, surrounded by the gentle hum of nature. The woman retrieved the pal'ether confiscated from the wizard and delved into studying it with unwavering focus. This had become a common sight in recent days.

"Have you heard of Belvick the Maker?" she suddenly asked, without tearing her eyes away from the silver dagger.

"Of course," I replied dryly, feeling offended by her question.

"Do you know why he was called 'the Maker'?" she pressed.

"Because he founded the Circle, about a thousand years ago."

She smiled faintly, then shook her head. "No one knows for sure. That's the most plausible and widely accepted theory, but there's also a legend circulating among scholars. It suggests that he managed to create a pal'ether."

I lowered my head, looking at the artifact in her hand with a furrowed brow. In response, she smiled. She handed me the knife and tapped with her finger where the handle met the blade. I had to almost press the knife against my eye to see the tiny letters engraved on the slightly raised portion at the base of the handle.

"Zarya," I read aloud.

"Now turn it over," she requested.

"Belvick!" I exclaimed, reading the inscription on the other side. "Do you think this weapon belonged to the founder of the Circle?"

"I believe there's a possibility, but I also believe that we probably won't ever find out for certain."

I smiled, ignoring the temptation to sip from the ether through the pal'ether. I handed it back, wondering how Merwin obtained such a weapon.

"Why do you think he chose the name 'the Circle'?" I asked, marveling at the blade from afar.

"It's a good thing you asked while my husband isn't around," she chuckled. "Once he starts talking about it, he doesn't stop. The truth, as with the previous case, is that no one knows. All writings about the Maker were lost in the fire that consumed the Circle's first headquarters; what remains are just fleeting sources, recorded on paper by people who never even knew him, and, moreover, lived hundreds of years after his death. The theory my husband considers the most..."

She stopped abruptly, jumping to her feet and reaching for the katanas at her waist. It was just Wolf, descending the slope almost in a hurry. He stopped in front of us and whispered, "I found them."

"Let's leave everything here, and once we're done, we'll come back," Sparrow said.

I swallowed hard and rose, trudging reluctantly in the footsteps of the assassins that were already ascending. The exhaustion that had nearly brought me to my knees not long ago was gone, replaced only by fear. Another battle was ahead. Blood was about to flow again, and the memory of the Battle Near Blackstone was a constant reminder that it could very well be our blood. I hadn't prayed in many years, but as I climbed that wooded mountainside, I found myself uttering whispered prayers, tinged with fear, to Azerad and Fyrgon, the gods worshipped by those from the Coral Islands.

We walked for almost half an hour before voices could be heard in the distance. Laughter. Wolf signaled us to be silent. Sparrow felt for both her swords. A pale mist began to rise around us, engulfing the trees, then slowly slithered up the steep incline in front of us, ascending in the direction of our enemies. Or targets?

Sparrow grabbed my sleeve and pulled me onto a detour, through weeds and trees grown very close together. The mist followed. It didn't take long for me to lose sight of Wolf. We continued like that for a long time, our footsteps muffled by the cold drafts descending from the mountain.

The voices grew clearer. "It's not like I knew he wanted to stab me, but neither did he know I was wearing chainmail under my shirt," someone with a deep voice spoke, eliciting laughter.

"I imagine he wasn't glad to find out," the prince's voice resonated, and upon hearing it, I felt a pit opening in my stomach.

I had to try to save him. It was my duty to return the favor.

Don't die in vain.

"Let's just say he didn't imagine much after that," the man laughed.

"And now comes the good part," the voice of that wizard, Merwin, was heard. "The part where I myself appear in the story!"

"How suddenly the mist fell." This voice was a feminine one, cold and detached. Did it belong to the Black Queen.

"It happens often in these parts," another woman replied.

Sparrow and I continued to climb through the fog that enveloped us like a blanket until we reached a higher surface than where they were. I peeked out from behind the trees, and there, not far from us, sat eight people arranged in a circle. The mist slowly surrounded them.

One of them was very tall, wearing steel armor and carrying a massive battle hammer beside him. They also had a little girl, who stood between two redheads. The Shadow Walker was there too, standing close to one of the women, an archer. I saw both the Prince and Merwin, but the one who stood out the most was the Black Queen and her horns protruding from under her black crown of hair.

Weak strands of ether danced around us. When I noticed them, I almost jumped, but I soon realized they were coming from Sparrow. They were so subtle, so hard to notice. She was trying to mask our sound.

Someone from their group was speaking, but was interrupted by Aella, who rose cautiously, scanning the surroundings. Sparrow and I retreated behind the trees.

"This mist was born from ether," the same cold and calm voice was heard. It was Aella's voice.

"Yermoleth?" another voice asked.

I cast another glance at the silhouettes, which now seemed washed out and faded because of the murky ashy mist. They were all standing.

Without warning, Sparrow leaped away from me, bounding over the bushes in front of us and landing gracefully on the hard ground, then began to charge at them. I saw Wolf descending the mountainside, fleeing with the sword held above his head through the layer of mist that was too thin. If I could see him from there, surely they would see him too, being much closer. I couldn't understand what the assassin was thinking, attacking from the heights, when the thickest fog was on the steep descent leading downwards.

I stepped into the ether.

The Black Queen turned, her cold eyes falling upon Wolf's silhouette. There were too many for him, and Sparrow still had a distance to cover, so I acted as quickly as possible. I sent waves of magic around everyone, binding them, then with a wave of my hand, I threw them like puppets into the cloud swallowing the valley. I acted purely on instinct and perhaps threw them a bit too hard, especially the little one. Only Darion and Aella remained.

The Black Queen whipped the air with her hand, the waves shaping around her palm, forming incredibly complex patterns, giving rise to an ether beam. I gasped in fear, almost covering my eyes, but the projectile passed through Wolf as if he was made of air, evaporating him instantly into a cloud of smoke. It was just an illusion. The real Wolf appeared from the thick fog beneath, where I had thrown the others, and struck without hesitation. Aella turned and tried to evade, but far too slowly.

The assassin's blade cleaved through the Night's Daughter's throat. She collapsed backward, hands clutching the wound from which waves of blood flowed. He did it. He had taken the life of the Black Queen!

Darion drew his sword, unleashing a wild scream and sending a flurry of strikes at the assassin. He was furious, shouting and cursing, striking relentlessly, pushing the assassin further away from his beloved's body, which still struggled in the clutches of death. He was a skilled warrior, but nowhere near as good as the man from the Storm Islands, who swiftly thrust his sword towards his exposed leg. It sank deep into flesh, causing the prince to limp back like a beaten dog.

I could read the desperation and fury in his eyes. He wanted to run to her, to be by her side in her final moments, but he couldn't look away from the enemy.

From the mist burst the giant man with the battle hammer, wielding his weapon with wide swings to keep Wolf at bay. The assassin managed to prowl at him several times, like a wolf, but the katana was deflected by the steel armor, unable to pierce it. I caught him again in the ether and slammed him forcefully into the nearest tree.

Darion glanced at me, but only for a second, then he attacked Wolf again. Even so, it was enough to feel his regret and disgust towards me. Regret for letting me live. I clenched my teeth and whispered, "I'm sorry!"

The wolf's katana seemed to deflect another blow from the lion, after which it struck him again on the same leg. Darion cursed. It wasn't long before the assassin's sword whipped across his left shoulder, and then again across his leg as he tried to retreat. He trembled. It seemed like he could barely stand on his feet.

The giant attacked again, just as the assassin prepared to deliver the final blow to the prince. He had left his hammer in the grass and now confronted his opponent with bare hands. The katana struck uselessly against his breastplate, but the steel-gloved fist sent the assassin crashing to the ground with a resounding thud. That's when Sparrow arrived. She triggered a dazzling and deafening explosion of light, causing the warrior to shield his eyes, then executed a pirouette, striking with both swords simultaneously behind the opponent's knees. That part was not protected by steel, but even so, the woman's blows weren't enough to penetrate the padded material he wore underneath.

She danced around him, whipping him with a rain of blows much more fluid and expansive than those of her husband. While Wolf's fighting style relied more on immobilizing his opponent before delivering the final blow, Sparrow's style would inflict a thousand swallow cuts and leave him bleeding to death. That is, if he weren't wearing armor. The man drew two short swords from the sheaths on his belt, one on each side, leaping once again in the direction of the assassin woman, forcing her to step back.

Her husband was engaged in another fight, right beside her, against that man with black eyes. He couldn't help her.

I focused my attention on the battle hammer, lifting it into the air and noticed that from the tip of the weight emerged a sharp and flat point, like the blade of a knife. I threw the weapon through the air, striking the giant man in the back with that sharp point, and that was enough to bring him down to the ground. I put enough force into that blow to pierce through his breastplate. The assassin seized the opportunity, thrusting her blades towards the man's exposed face, but he defended himself with his hand clad in armor.

A spear of fire flew from the mists. Sparrow dodged it leaping back, barely managing to avoid the blow. Merwin appeared, stepping slowly, with serpents of fire dancing around his arms. It seemed as if the ground itself was catching fire wherever he stepped, and the power emanating from his body was terribly immense.

"Burn, filthy wretch!" he shouted, unleashing a torrent of flames in her direction.

The assassin dodged, sending a ball of lightning towards the wizard, who shattered it using one of fire. When the two spheres collided, the whole forest quivered. I tried to catch him again in my magical vines, but he sensed me, and my waves were shattered by his in an instant. I gasped in surprise and ducked to avoid a fire arrow he hurled at me with a flick of his hand, without even bothering to look. It nearly took my head off, exploding into a tree from behind. The blast made me stagger, but I managed to grab onto a trunk to my right before falling.

That wizard is much more powerful than I imagined. He is much stronger than me even without his pal'ether, so I didn't even dare to think what he could do with it.

Through the smoky river of the battlefield, I caught a glimpse of the prince's vague form, inching closer to Aella. Amidst the chaos, it was difficult to discern if the Black Queen had already drawn her last breath, for she lay eerily still, no longer moving.

Wolf kicked the Walker, sending him downhill, and rushed towards Merwin, but as he moved to strike, he suddenly turned, swinging his sword through the air, barely cutting off an arrow that shot from the thick layer of fog. The arrow, which was supposed to hit him in the face, deflected, piercing his shoulder instead. Merwin saw him and fired a fiery orb in his way, but at the last moment, he was able to draw an ether shield. The flaming sphere struck the invisible barrier, exploding violently with such force that Wolf was sent flying through the air, crashing into the thick stem of a tree.

Sparrow attempted to attack again but rolled to the side, avoiding another arrow flying from the mist, nearly piercing her neck. I tried to bind the wizard again, but as soon as I managed to gather the waves around him, I felt his magic unraveling mine.

He turned his head with a swift and abrupt movement, now facing me, his eyes blazing with anger. I leaped away just in time, the trees bursting behind me with a deafening bang, spreading tongues of fire and the smell of burnt wood everywhere. I fell to my knees due to the uneven ground I landed on, but I managed to rise in time and flee just before another fiery projectile flew over my head, so close that I could feel the warmth caressing my ear. Then another and another. Bolts of fire were whizzing at me, all striking the trees around and exploding, smoldering the branches for a few moments before extinguishing, leaving only black streaks.

I kept running like a scared rabbit dodging the stones thrown by mean children, looking back one final time before vanishing into the thick, misty clouds engulfing the valley. Darion lay over Aella's body, whispering something to her amidst tears. The little girl was running at them. The massive man stood with his back against the trunk of a tree, the hammer next to him, and a red-haired woman cradled his face in her hands. The other redhead stood beside the Shadow Walker, firing a final arrow through the mists, trying to hit something I couldn't see. Probably Wolf or Sparrow, as neither of them were there anymore.

The river of fog obscured my view, rendering my own feet nearly invisible. It wasn't long before I stumbled, tumbling down the steep slope, each jolt accompanied by the prick of thorny thickets. When Sparrow finally found me, I was trembling uncontrollably, cursing as I wrestled with the painful entanglement of thorns. With swift precision, she wielded one of her knives to hack through the thicket. After ensuring I could stand, she grasped my hand firmly and guided me down the slope.

The thrill of battle faded, and the heat of the ether dissipated, replaced by a sharp pain in my hip, likely resulting from the fall. As we descended at a brisk pace, I noticed Sparrow had a deep cut on her right cheek. She followed my gaze and whispered breathlessly, "An arrow. It could have been worse. Does your nose hurt?"

"My nose?" I wondered, touching my nose. I winced. There was a strong burning sensation halfway from the tip to the base.

"Deep cut," she said in a soothing tone, as if the words deep cut could be soothing. "Probably a kiss from the thorns."

"Bad kisser," I joked in a hushed voice. Surprisingly she laughed. "Where is Wolf? Mr. Wolf, I mean"

"He went ahead. He'll wait for us near the backpacks, then we'll look for a place to rest and dress our wounds."

"Is he hurt too?"

"Injured, but not seriously. However, we'll need plenty of rest and fresh supplies."

How heavenly those words sounded in my ear. *Plenty of rest.*

We descended for about ten more minutes until we reached the spot where Wolf was waiting for us. He was shirtless, with a strip of linen already tightly wound around his shoulder wound. He had another shallow cut on his cheek, likely from the blow of that massive man in steel armor, and his upper lip was split. His hair was loose from the usual knot, flowing down to his chest. He looked tired, even exhausted, but nonetheless, he smiled warmly at us.

"You did well, Saya, throwing them all out of my way before I attacked," he complimented me.

"I dare say the mission could have failed if it weren't for your quick thinking," Sparrow added, patting me on the back.

I didn't know how to react. I wasn't used to being complimented, especially by them. "Thank you!" I replied sincerely.

"And you did very well taking out that mountain of a man," said Wolf, getting up. "Fighting against such foes required a prolonged battle, and time was the thing we lacked the most."

"It seems I made the right call not sending you back to Romir," Sparrow laughed.

"We'll descend a bit until we find a more secluded spot, then we'll settle there to regain our strength. Maybe we'll stay for a few days, then we'll set out again on their trail to finish the task. There's one more left."

"Is Aella really dead?" I dared ask.

"She is," Sparrow told me. "And Darion is pretty badly injured, but not enough for us to guarantee he'll die if we leave him be."

I could hardly believe it. So many days lost on the roads that I started to believe this hunt would never end. But it was almost over. Parzival had been avenged.

The Black Queen is dead.

Revenge

Excerpt from Elena's journal, dated the twelfth day of the seventh month, Iureia, in the year six hundred twenty-three after the Conversion:

Messengers from my father's army arrived at the gates of Romir this morning, announcing the king's approach. Of course, I already knew all the details from the spies of my betrothed, who had not taken their eyes off the Frevian army since it crossed the Derahia border. That's what Larion said, however, I knew they were trailing the army since before that, because my spies, hidden among his spies, made sure not to omit any detail. He remained calm when Radagrim delivered the news, but I had a sudden fear that the serenity he displayed was merely the deceptive calm hiding the storm.

On that day, he chose to dress casually, wearing a thin blue silk shirt and a black pair of cotton pants. I chose a silk dress in a color as similar to his as possible, tight around the chest, shoulders, and waist, but with a billowing skirt that descended from the level of the thighs.

"Do you happen to know how long he plans to stay here?" Larion asked, combing his hair in front of the wall-mounted mirror.

"Probably a day, at most two. Trust me, I want him here just as much as you do, and Mom even less," I replied.

"Is she really that bad?"

"You have no idea. She could make Aella blush."

"So, you take after your mother," he commented.

I rolled my eyes, huffing loudly, as he started laughing.

"Queen Lenore, my mother, never treated me like I was her child, but I suppose that's fair because I didn't treat hcr like she was my mother either. Even my father ignored me a lot in childhood, spending all his time with Rorik. I practically grew up without them. Maybe you had a different relationship with your family, but mine was like this," I explained.

He took on a serious gaze. "I'm sorry."

"Don't be. I had Rorik by my side, and that was enough for me. We need to keep an eye on Jane these days. Even after dad leaves, because I'm sure my cunt of a mother will stay here for a while."

His face was etched with a scowl. "Killing someone under my roof would be quite reckless of them. That would force my hand."

"She won't kill anyone. It will be an accident. The poor thing will choke during dinner, or slip down the stairs, or maybe decide to jump out the window to check if she can fly. And we won't have any way to prove otherwise," I told him.

Larion waited in silence for a moment, adjusting his shirt collar. "I'm starting to love your family more and more. Anyway, now I must go talk to the lords. They've all gathered at Romir, and it's time to discuss what we'll do with Darion and the men he's gathering in the north. Then, we need to prepare for your father's arrival. Many have already started taking censuses of their subjects to see how many men are fit for war."

"Try to keep your swords in their sheaths. Is that the only way you men know how to solve problems: kill first, ask questions later? Let him fight with the wildlings until he gets bored and leaves peacefully, not harming anyone."

He hesitated for a moment, undecided whether to respond or not, then nodded. I waited a while longer after he left, trying again to figure out the growing void I had been feeling in my stomach for the last few days.

When I left my room, the halls were crowded with noble ladies, wearing their finest silks, hoping to catch the eye of some Frevian nobleman. Some might have succeeded; undoubtedly, they caught mine. This, however, should be a piece of cake, as the Derahian girls were beautiful and daring, and our men foolish enough to fall for the charms of a girl from a modest family. Or even a simple woman of humble status, why not, since Darion had done it, and Rorik as well.

"Princess Elena, a word if I may!" The one who spoke was Oswin, leaning against one of the walls near the door leading to the hallway where Beatrice and Jane resided. He seemed troubled.

"Of course," I replied, slightly puzzled by the seriousness and remorse in his brown eyes.

"Could we speak in a more secluded place?"

"Has something happened with Jane?" I asked in a hushed but hurried tone.

"No. I just came from their room. Lately, she seems to have gained some color in her cheeks and is more talkative, although today she seemed a bit down."

"I wonder what could be the reason?" I asked with sarcasm, for it was clear that the arrival of my father was frightening her. It unsettled me as well.

He gestured towards two doors beside us leading to one of the balconies attached to the walls facing the west. It was a secluded spot, shielded from prying eyes or ears, but not secluded enough to spark unfounded rumors. After we stepped out, he remained frowning for a few moments, uncertain, scanning the hills and plains towards the east. He sighed.

"Your father may be disappointed in me, but Jane is a good girl, and I can't do this to her, or to Rorik."

"Do what?" I asked in a hostile voice, catching onto the meaning of his words before he could respond.

It wasn't hard to understand. I had my suspicions from the beginning. Oswin had always been our friend, but his choice to stay in Derahia instead of following his king to Frevia had been inexplicable, uncharacteristic of him. But he stayed with a purpose. He stayed on my father's orders, to help us find Jane and get rid of her.

He took a vial from the pocket of his leather pants and placed it on the stone balcony.

"Black viper venom with ground poppy root," he said remorsefully. "It was for Jane."

I thudded the balcony railing with my fingers, one by one, trying to drown out the hatred and repulsion that consumed me. "I understand. If there weren't people in the hallway behind us, I'd gouge your eyes out," I said, trying to keep my temper at bay. "I thought you were my friend, Oswin, but you were actually accompanying us to... pathetic bastard."

My heart pounded with mocking anger in my chest, as I was trying to cool down my impulse. I grabbed the vial with my hand trembling and slipped it into a hidden pocket of my dress.

"Forgive me."

"You're sorry?" I muttered. "That is so sweet of you."

I abruptly rotated to face Oswin and slapped him as hard as I could, making several glances from the hallway turn curiously toward us.

"My brother would have... pathetic scoundrel... leave and don't you dare to come before me ever again," I whispered through clenched teeth.

"As you command, my princess" he said sadly.

He bowed, then left.

I was usually very skilled at hiding my feelings, but not today. People who saw me almost stepped aside, probably seeing my angry face and the hurried steps with which I marched down the hallway.

Jane was combing Beatrice's hair when I violently burst in. They both startled like scared mice, turning their heads at the same time.

"Where's the fire?" Beatrice asked.

I blew out all the air from my chest before responding. "Nowhere for the moment. Soon, in Oswin's room. Preferably with him inside and the door locked."

"You're up to big things," Beatrice teased me, biting her lip. "Should I ask what he did?"

"He didn't do anything." I would have liked to tell her he was actually my father's lapdog, but I didn't want Jane to hear such things. "Why do you think I need a reason to burn someone alive?"

"My mistake," she chuckled, and Jane forced a smile. Was she taking us seriously? I hoped not.

"Lovely dress, Jane," I said.

"Thank you," she replied sheepishly.

Jane had come to enjoy wearing the dresses given to her by Beatrice, but she was too stubborn or shy to admit it. Even so, she blushed at the slightest compliment. I sat down beside them.

"The King and Queen..." Jane began.

"They'll be here soon, but don't worry, they won't do anything to you. Neither of them would dare to harm anyone in Grayfang House. Maybe they could get away with it in Montrias, but not here."

I don't know if my reassurances convinced her, but the corners of her mouth lifted into a barely contoured smile. I waited with them for a while, occasionally feeling the vial of poison in my pocket and gazing at the unsuspecting face of the girl it was meant for. Maybe I had been unfair to Oswin. After the initial shock had passed, I realized that he had done the right thing and although he had initially intended harm, he had only been compelled by my father. Perhaps I would forgive him. But still, if the voice of reason hadn't urged him to do the right thing, he would have killed Jane and her unborn child.

The hollow feeling in my stomach made my throat feel dry. I had a sense that this void was caused by the things Jane had told me just a few days ago, things I hadn't yet mustered the courage to ask her about. Until today.

"In the night you heard Rorik talking to something in his room..." I began suddenly, but then I clamped my lips shut.

"Elena!" scolded Bea. "I don't think this is the right time."

"You're right, I'm sorry Jane," I sighed.

"Do you want to know what they were talking about?" she asked, almost calmly.

I nodded in silence. She took a deep breath, and Beatrice turned to her, taking her hand in hers.

"He was searching for a city. Rorik was searching for a city for that thing, whatever it was. The city where someone named Bhalphomet was bound."

"*Bhalphomet! What have you made me do!?*" the dread filled voice of Larion came back to me.

"Why?" I shuddered. It couldn't be a coincidence, it just couldn't. It was the same name Larion called out during that nightmare.

"I don't know, but finding that place was very important for that creature."

"Bhalphomet," repeated Beatrice. "What a strange name."

"Don't say it anymore," I urged her. "It sounds wrong. As if..."

"We shouldn't even know it," Jane added. "As if it shouldn't even exist."

"Frightened little girls," Bea burst out, not making any serious effort to counsel her own fear. "Burning Hells, Elena, why did you have to bring it up? Let's all agree that it does us no good to talk about such frightening things, especially when you're pregnant. Do you want to scare the little humans residing in your bellies? Besides, we won't solve anything anyway; we'll never know what happened that night."

"Agreed," said Jane. "Princess?"

"And I agree too."

"And perhaps tomorrow we can go to the Temple to pray, it would do me good," Beatrice said firmly.

"The erthals will fall on you from their paintings as soon as you step in the Temple," I said, and she started to laugh.

But I lied. I intended to find out who this Bhalphomet was and who the creature was that spoke to Rorik that night. I didn't want to force Jane into remembering more, although the details could have been useful, so I planned to insist with Larion. Or perhaps the Grand Master Radagrim knew something about it; after all, it was his job to know all sorts of things from all sorts of fields. I had a lot of digging to do.

I grimaced and loudly cleared my throat as Jane placed the comb on the table, then nodded approvingly as Beatrice hurried to align it parallel to the edge.

The sudden commotion in the hallway signaled that my parents had entered the town. Jane paled. I stood up, smoothing the folds of my dress, then told the girls, "I'm going to greet my family. So long."

"Good luck," Bea wished me.

I chuckled to myself, realizing how much I needed it.

Like a few months ago, the palace courtyard was filled with nobles, awaiting the King's arrival. The difference this time was that many were wearing steel armor and displaying hostile and somber looks, while the gates remained closed. It was a clear message to my father that he was not welcome. It was ridiculous, but men, in general, were often ridiculous. Some glanced at me out of the corner of their eyes, observing my reactions, but I showed nothing.

Larion stood with his hand on the hilt of his sword, wearing the same clothes he had earlier, studying the closed gate with an arrogant and smug smile. I approached him and slipped my fingers through his.

"Are you going to make him jump the wall?" I asked, nodding towards the gate.

"I hadn't thought of that, but it doesn't sound bad," he replied.

I clicked my tongue, intensifying the grip on his hand. "You're ridiculous, you know that? The relations between you and us are already fragile, do you want to..."

"You and us," he repeated, frowning at me. "My dear, are you with us, or are you with them? Maybe you're not on the right side of the wall."

He spoke loudly enough for others nearby to hear. I smiled at him, swallowing the response I had almost spat out in his face. He had gone too far with that.

A crossbowman from the defense wall turned towards us and made a wide gesture with his hand. Larion let go of my hand and marched towards the wooden stairs embedded in the wall, closely followed by Lord Alfric and Lord Lanre. I was surprised to see Lanre in Romir, as I hadn't seen him at all since the death of his daughter, and now, like the last time I saw him, he was wearing the same worn-out armor. Alfric, on the other hand, like my betrothed, wore thin clothes suitable for summer days.

The soldiers began to rotate the heavy mechanism of the gate, the metallic clanking of the chains filling the courtyard, drowning out the furious whispers of those present. My father rode proudly inside, clad in black armor himself, with the sword and crown encrusted with gold on his chest. He glanced over everyone in the courtyard, looking at them coldly, then paused upon me for a moment, giving a brief smile.

"King Alfred, welcome, my house is your house!" exclaimed Larion, opening his arms wide. He stood on the wall above the gate, looking down at my father.

"Thank you for the warm welcome, and I am honored to be a guest in your house," declared my father. His royal guard followed closely, mounted on their tall steeds, equipped as if for a tournament. "I would embrace you, as is customary, but I fear I am not tall enough."

Larion smiled. "We will have time for embraces. Please forgive me for waiting for you with the gates closed, but some precautions are necessary. It's not every day you wake up with an army at your gates, and I don't know what the custom is in such situations."

"If my army concerns you, King Larion, it will not remain in front of your city for long. Tomorrow, I intend to continue my journey north, to avenge my son and to avenge your father. And your daughter, Lord Lanre, and all those who have fallen. You are free to join me if you have bothered to put on your *shiny* and *polished* armors."

"It is gracious of you to invite us on your little stroll through the mountains, but don't call that revenge. When it's time to fight, we'll fight."

"Of course," my father replied conciliatory.

The army had set up camp at the city gates, but several nobles had followed my father inside, people I knew. And among them, rode my mother.

Her sly eyes found me the moment she passed under the archway of the gate. She immediately flashed a warm smile, accentuated even more by the dimples in her cheeks. How I wished I had inherited those dimples, but nothing of her had stuck to me, except for the chestnut hair, and even there, my color seemed much blander than hers. She wore a beautiful black velvet dress with a square neckline, and riding to her right was a woman I didn't know. She looked to be in her early thirties, wearing a fiery red dress, her hair the color of polished gold flowing in waves over her shoulders. She was strangely beautiful.

The atmosphere was tense. Larion descended from the wall and approached my father, exchanging a few whispered words amidst forced and strained smiles, lacking any semblance of tact. My mother's smile was sincere yet sickeningly sweet, revealing nothing and displaying only what she wanted to show. A smile I rcturned.

She dismounted her tall, black steed and came to me with quick steps, enveloping me in a tight embrace.

"My dear Elena, how much I miss you," she intoned with a sigh.

"I've missed you too, Mother," I replied, kissing her on the cheek.

That blonde woman came near us with feline-like steps, stopping behind my mother. She stood with her back straight and hands clasped under her abdomen, looking at me through jade-like eyes, displaying the faint trace of a smile.

"This is my friend, Merideth," my mother said, disengaging from the embrace and turning towards the woman.

Merideth made a short, graceful bow, never taking her eyes off me. Larion came shortly after, walking shoulder to shoulder with father, then bowed to mother and kissed her hand.

"Queen Lenore, it is an honor to have you here," Larion said.

"And it is an honor for me to meet you, King Larion. It's a shame that such circumstances have brought us together and not better ones."

"Better times will come. Elena has told me a lot about you."

"Only good things, I presume," she replied with a wide smile, glancing at me from the corner of her eye.

"Only good things. But let's not linger here; the table is set and the food is warm."

"I beg your pardon, but both Merideth and I are exhausted from the journey and have no appetite for food. It would be best if we retired to our chambers to rest for a bit."

"Of course," grumbled Alfred. "I have some matters to discuss with the king here, and I will join you later."

"Actually, we'll be in Elena's chamber for a while," Mother said in a tone that suggested she had already discussed this with me before making such a statement. Nonetheless, I nodded. "We have much to discuss, and there couldn't be a better time than now, isn't that so, my darling? Please instruct the servants to send our luggage to the chamber; we'll retrieve it later. Come, dear, lead the way!"

"Before that, I would like to have a look through the lady's belongings," Radagrim interjected, seemingly appearing out of nowhere.

He stood behind us, wearing a brown robe that covered him from head to toe like a sack, his face displaying that foolish grin he always bore. But despite the smile, his tired eyes fell heavily and sharply on Merideth.

"And why is that?" the woman wanted to know, raising her eyebrows.

"Precaution," the old man replied. "I know it's not proper to go through a woman's belongings, but I wouldn't want to take any risks. Not long ago, another wizard brought stolen pal'ethers to Romir without anyone's knowledge, and I wouldn't want such incidents to repeat, especially in times like these."

So, she is a witch! The new Melchior, I thought, pursing my lips as I watched her.

"I understand," mother said. "All our luggage is in that blue-painted carriage waiting in the town square. My belongings are there too, but I don't mind, feel free to look around. In fact, to avoid any suspicions, you have my permission to check through the luggage of all the newcomers."

"Wonderful!" exclaimed the wizard.

"It won't be necessary," Larion hurried. "Radagrim, it's not polite to suspect our guests."

"Politeness is a luxury we can't afford these days, Your Highness," Radagrim replied.

"You can only check in the belongings of lady... excuse me, but I didn't catch your name."

"Merideth," she smiled, looking at my betrothed rather unsubtly. I frowned.

"As you command," the wizard yielded.

I left there with my mother and the witch Merideth, heading straight to the room I shared with Larion. I didn't like the way the new witch smiled at him.

On the way, my mother began to tell me about how things were going in Montrias, speaking loud enough and smiling wide enough for everyone to see how good our relationship was.

"I noticed that your maids returned to Montrias," she said.

I inclined my head in an approving manner, then said, "Beatrice stayed."

"Lovely. Is she enough for you?" she whispered.

I dug my nails into my palms, and in response, I shrugged. We turned into a narrower corridor, which shortened the way, and she looked somewhat disappointed at the stone floor covered with old carpets and worn tapestries.

"Rustic," she commented.

"This is a hallway from the old palace over which the new one was built. It doesn't look like this everywhere, in fact, the palace is quite beautiful and..."

"Surprising!" she exclaimed aloud, then lean towards my ear and whispered, "did you come to that conclusion before or after your betrothed gave you a gift?"

I burst out, turning suddenly, and giving her a venomous look that made her smile. Merideth watched us in silence, without showing any expression.

"How long do you plan to stay here?" I asked sharply.

"Not as long as I would like, but not as short as you would like. I'm curious how you've organized yourself, but we'll talk more about that in the room."

To see how I had organized myself meant to pry into the influence I already had in Romir. It meant finding out more about the people who worked for me, who were my eyes and ears on the streets of the city and in the palace.

We climbed the spiral stairs that led directly to the hallway where my room was located. We walked slowly to the door and I invited them inside, reluctantly.

"Nice abode," mother commented, examining the room. "You've always had a great aesthetic sense, my dear. Don't you think so, Merideth? Everything is in its place."

Her hand slid over the pile of books on the table, then she tapped one of them with the tip of her forefingers, making its corner stand out more prominently than the others it was stacked upon. An evil, mischievous smile appeared on her face as I gasped with irritation.

"Eyes on me!" she urged when she saw me frowning at the pile of books. "Tell me about Larion."

"I'm sure your spies in Romir have already told you enough, why don't you tell me?" I growled, shedding all pretenses and appearances.

"You don't know how to keep him on a leash, Elena. That's what I've heard, and I hoped you'd tell me otherwise, but it is obvious that the Black Queen did a much better job than you, apparently."

"The Black Queen had a simple task. Darion is a fool, Larion isn't. Besides, Dad came here with the army, and I'm sure you don't agree with that, so don't tell me that I don't know how to keep my man under control."

"Oh, just shut up! Alfred is an idiot, but that's no secret to you." She flopped onto the bed. It seemed that Merideth was very close to her if she allowed herself to speak so openly. Merideth remained standing, a formal smile adorning her beautiful red lips.

I clicked my tongue. "Larion isn't, and probably that's no secret to you. Although sometimes I wish he were just like Darion."

"I've heard conflicting things about Darion. And I've heard he's already won a battle against you, so he might not be as stupid as you think."

"Mhm," I nodded.

"Oh, Heavens, Elena, stop looking at that book! Get a grip on yourself! But what am I saying, it's clear you can't control your urges. If you could, you wouldn't have gotten pregnant since you stepped here. What were you thinking, girl?"

I didn't respond. I couldn't think. All I could see was that cursed book. It was torturing my senses.

"Nothing," she replied with satisfaction, seeing the uncertainty in my eyes. "Let's go on."

She picked up one of the glasses arranged near the wine bottle on the table and turned it upside down. The thought that she was doing it just to cloud my judgment, to prevent me from thinking clearly so that I couldn't come up with convincing lies, infuriated me.

"Tell me about your spies. I've heard that Darion has hidden supporters throughout the city. In fact, throughout the country," she probed.

"I'll handle it," I replied curtly.

"How?" she pressed.

I stumped the ground, doing my best to refrain myself from charging at her. "That's none of your concern. These matters don't involve you."

"If I asked you to set fire to the Grand Temple tonight, would you have enough faithful people to do it for you without asking questions?" she continued, her tone challenging.

"Yes," I lied, my eyes defocusing from her face.

I didn't have such loyal people, not yet. And those I had used in the past weren't very reliable, and I wouldn't dare to ask them to do something so significant. Mother was right; I needed more capable individuals in my service.

"I don't know why I doubt it," she shrugged.

"Because you always doubt me," I replied coldly, then reached for the stack of cards.

My hand froze in the air, suspended just a finger's length away from the card that needed arranging. My whole body felt stiff, as if the air had solidified around me. I turned my head — the only part of my body that I could move — towards Merideth, who was watching me with the same formal and impersonal style.

"How dare you, you filthy whore?!" I shouted.

"Elena, Elena, where are your manners? We only want to help you," my mother said, rising from her seat.

My arms tensed as I tried to reach my nails into her throat but couldn't. "I don't need your help. Why did you come here?"

"You're as stubborn as ever, but we'll talk about this later," she said, heading towards the door. "When you've calmed down."

I almost collapsed when Merideth lifted the spell that had frozen me. I clasped my palms onto the table, leaning over it, and my heart stopped beating for a few moments at the thought that I had almost hit the corner of the table with my stomach. In that moment, I lost all sense of reason, and grabbing the first book that came into my hand, I spun on my heel and struck Merideth, who was already facing away from me.

The satisfying sound of the book's spine hitting the witch's head, striking it strongly, echoed in the room. The blow was violent enough to make her lose her balance, knocking her to the ground. Mother turned towards us, watching the scene with confusion, and then with something that seemed to be fear.

"What do you think you're doing?!" she growled, kneeling beside her servant. Her hands were trembling, and eyes shined with the familiar gleam of fear. Fear of what? Of Merideth?

"Ah, it felt so good," I said with a wide smile.

Merideth got up to her knees, looking somewhat amused, as she touched her temple. She brought her long slender fingers in front of her green eyes to see if there was any blood, but unfortunately there was no red stain on them.

"Well struck, young Princess. And some say knowledge isn't power," Merideth laughed.

"You're behaving like an animal, Elena," my mother said angrily.

"Remember, mother, that you're under my roof now," I said calmly. I took a step towards them, still holding the book in my hand, ready to teach the witch another lesson if needed. "And you, Merideth, are lucky I don't put your head on a spike for using ether against me! You won't have such luck twice in your life, I promise. Get out of here before I call the guards!"

Mother tried to say something, but the witch grabbed her hand, silencing her. A triumphant smile carved into my lips as the two of them retreated, leaving the room. I remained motionless for a long time after the door slammed shut behind them, staring at the thick covers of the book with a grin I couldn't contain. I still couldn't believe the expression on my mother's face.

I placed the book back on top of the others, ensuring they were perfectly aligned, then turned the glass back and gasped full of satisfaction, as things were now in place. As they should be.

"If only you could have seen the look on her face," I said to my little Rorik, rubbing my stomach. "You would have loved it, but I will remember the expression, and I'll show you when you decide to come out. If you're anything like me, you'll certainly enjoy hearing about it."

I could say that the meeting with my mother went better than expected, although I knew I won just a battle, not the war. The war was about to be a prolonged one, and the enemies too many to even try to count them.

The next item on my agenda was to exchange a few words with Master Radagrim. I traversed the Great Hall, emerging directly into the palace courtyard. From there, I proceeded towards the solitary, ancient tower that loomed adjacent to the wall, serving as the abode of wizards. In Montrias, the royal wizard resided in the same building as everyone else, but not here, in this desolate city that one day I would rule.

The wooden door of the tower swept aside under my push, revealing a dark hallway, which, after a few steps, widened into a large and poorly lit room. It had windows, but they were covered with a thick layer of dust, blocking the light from penetrating inside. Worst of all, the room was in complete disarray. Scrolls and books of all shapes and sizes were strewn everywhere, on every table and piece of furniture, and in some places, even on the floor. The room had three desks, all cluttered with all sorts of strange instruments and vials labeled with words in a foreign tongue, inscribed with odd glyphs rather than letters. I could have organized them, and perhaps even enjoyed the process. All those papers… it wasn't normal to keep them like that. My ears buzzed, feeling the urge to clean becoming stronger and stronger.

"Master Radagrim!" I called out, trying to look around as little as possible.

"*Elena!*"

It was a distant and faint voice, barely audible, calling me from the other side of the door. I shuddered, for whoever called had a voice similar to my brother's, Rorik.

"Did you hear that too?" I asked in a whisper, touching my belly.

I took a few steps towards that door, feeling like I shouldn't be there, and slowly pulled it aside, scrutinizing the interior. There was no one inside. *Then who called?* Dim light filtered through another small, narrow, and dirty window, casting feeble illumination on the sparse surroundings. It seemed as though something from within was devouring the light before it had a chance to spread. A bed was pressed against the wall to the right, and directly under the window was another desk with a small object covered with a brown blanket. To the right of the desk stood a wooden chest, its lid raised, and to the left, a tall black metal candlestick, about a meter and a half tall, adorned with half-consumed candles.

"Master Radagrim?" I asked, my voice weak and brittle. I was afraid, but I couldn't understand why. Was it fear itself I feared?

Something inside me screamed to turn around and leave as quickly as possible, but another part, almost alien, whispered to me to approach the desk. *Come closer.*

"One of the artifacts found in the chamber of the Black Queen," the old man's voice echoed behind me.

I flinched, letting out a small whimper as I turned to him. I gave him a grimace, but he seemed not to notice, quickly passing by me and heading towards the worktable. I followed him, and without realizing why, I reached out towards the object that awaited covered, and somehow invited me to touch it. Radagrim slapped my hand away.

"You'll be the second wizard I punch today," I warned, but he smiled gently.

"Do not touch it, princess, it is very dangerous."

"But what is it?" I asked, rubbing my hand.

"Something wicked, that's all you need to know. It will soon be sent back to the Circle, but until then, it must remain here."

"I thought I heard... my brother," I said, trembling.

His face was now dead serious. "It can mimic voices. That's how it lures people."

"I insist you tell me what it is," I said, trying to sound convincing, more for myself than for him.

"This," the old man said, pointing to the object on the table, "is evil. True evil, in its purest form."

"Spare me the riddles," I burst out. "I don't have time for this. Anyway, what would happen if I were to touch it?"

"If you try, I would probably slap your hand again. But if your skin touches it, you'd likely lose your mind, or die, or even worse, you'd end up serving it."

I took a step back from the table. "Serving it?" My neck felt dry.

"The one who speaks through the idol. The god imprisoned on the altar of his own temple, eagerly awaiting the day he will be free in the world again."

"There are no gods," I replied with a voice drained of conviction.

"*Elena,*" Rorik's voice sounded again, calling me from under that cloth. I shivered with mouth slightly agape.

"Are you feeling alright, princess? You look very pale."

"I'm fine. I'm fine."

He nodded his head, visibly concerned. The tense gaze of the wizard gave me the impression that he too was disturbed. This god he spoke of must truly be a dreadful thing if even a great master of the Circle feared it. I remembered how Kolan was frightened on the night he learned that Melchior had brought such an idol to Romir. The idol of a god. Even now, as I write these lines, I hear again and again that thing whispering my name with the voice of my deceased brother. I shudder at the memory.

Despite the fear I felt and despite the voice of reason in my mind telling me that I did not want such answers, I asked, "This god, is it named Bhalphomet by any chance?"

"No," the old man replied promptly. "None of them. But please, do not try to guess their names. If you speak their names, you will invite them, and they will answer."

"None..." I repeated. "But how many are there?"

"Five. We've found three of them, and two are still hidden somewhere in the world. But none of them are named Bhalphomet."

"*Elena!*"

The old man followed my terrified eyes, then placed another handkerchief over the idol, lifted it, checking several times that it was well covered, and placed it in a chest which he locked.

I pressed my hands against each other, to stop the faint trembling of my fingers. "What do you mean you found them?"

"We found the cities where their bodies are chained, princess. Now please, do not concern yourself with such matters that concern only wizards."

I blinked a few times as his words wandered freely through my head, then asked, "What if there's a sixth one?"

He kept silent, pondering, then asked back, "Why do you think that?"

I wished I could trust him enough to tell him about Rorik and about Larion's dream. I wished with all my heart. He seemed filled with the concern a parent has for his child.

"I don't know," I replied. "But what happens if you speak one of their names?"

"It's like an invitation to which they respond. Princess, if I may suggest, such knowledge would be better kept from everyone's ears. It can be dangerous."

"I won't speak of it," I promised. "But I don't understand, how do they know when we utter their names? How can they respond to the invitation if they're chained?"

"Let's step outside for a moment, get some fresh air."

"Answer my damn questions!" I urged with anger, then I gasped, bringing both my hands over my mouth, surprised by my own reaction. My stomach twisted. "I'm sorry," I muttered then. "I didn't mean to shout; I don't know what came over me."

"It's the creature. The demon. It senses the evil within our souls, amplifies it, and makes us submit to it. It burrows through our thoughts, seeks out our weaknesses, and uses them to destroy us. It feeds on the vulnerable."

"I'm not vulnerable," I told him.

"You are very vulnerable," he contradicted me. "It seems like you have a lot on your mind, and it also seems like you feel terribly alone, that you don't have enough trust in anyone else to share your burden. And that makes you very vulnerable, an easy prey for the demon. Let's go outside."

"*Margery*," the voice whispered again.

"Margery," I frowned at the wizard.

The wizard gestured towards the door, and I nodded, grateful to leave that room. The old man pulled out a rusty key from the pocket of his robe, which he struggled to insert into the door lock, turned it, then slipped it back in.

"Please excuse the mess," he said. "I was searching for something, but at this age, my memory doesn't serve me as it once did."

"I don't excuse the mess. I can't stand the mess. Please make sure I don't find it like this when I come back. It gives me a headache. And know that I'll come again to talk about these gods. We're not finished," I warned him.

"I eagerly await your return, Princess. Although, I would argue that such dark matters should be left to those who have already seen the darkness."

"Wizard's palaver," I retorted.

I felt my courage and inner peace returning after that fragile wooden door, blocked by the frail and rusty mechanism, separated me from that idol.

Why did it call me Margery? My name is Elena.

"If you truly want to know, I will teach you," he said.

"Of course you will," I replied. "Your mirror caught fire!"

He followed my gaze, unsurprised, as if what I said not only sounded perfectly normal but was also an event that happened regularly. On one of the three desks sat a square mirror, as large as a human head, leaning against the wall and seemingly reflecting the blaze of an invisible torch. The old man pulled a chair, sitting in front of that artifact, then reached out his hand towards it, making the redness disappear. For a while, I wondered if I should be there, and although a part of me told me that I had no business witnessing the affairs of wizards, another part kept repeating that the old man hadn't asked me to leave. So, I stayed.

In the mirror suddenly appeared the stern and harsh face of a man. It didn't take long for me to remember who he was. He was called Wolf, and he was that peculiar wizard who had left for the north on the trail of Darion, accompanied by his wife and their two apprentices, Parzival and Saya.

"Master Radagrim," Wolf began, "I see you have company. Princess Elena!" he greeted me, bowing his head.

"Elena is there?" sounded a voice from beyond... the mirror, and Saya's face appeared over his shoulder.

I approached the table, looking at Saya and Wolf with an astonishment I was completely unable to control. It seemed as if they were in a cave, and on the wall above them, thin strips of light extended.

"Is this a door?" I asked amazed.

"More like a window," Saya replied, smiling at me. "A communication pal'ether."

Wolf turned his head slightly at her, raising an eyebrow. She smiled, then sat behind him, continuing to watch me over his shoulder.

"You're injured," Radagrim observed with palpable concern.

The assassin pulled the edge of his shirt to reveal a patch of white fabric that kept him wrapped, covering his shoulder.

"I was hit by an arrow and the wound is deeper than I hoped, but other than that, we're fine. The wound is healing, slowly but surely."

"Where is Sparrow?" Radagrim then asked.

"I'm here, master," her voice sounded. "I'm preparing something to help clean and close the wound. Don't worry, we bring good news."

"Wonderful!"

"We crossed paths today and fought Darion and his servants. There were eight of them in total, and they even had a Shadow Walker among them." The old man's brow furrowed pensively. "We managed to seriously injure the prince, but we had to retreat and couldn't take his life. Instead, the Black Queen is dead."

My eyes widened in shock, betraying the turmoil I felt in my soul. "Are you sure!?" I burst out.

"Mr. Wolf slit her throat," Saya told me. "She didn't move anymore when we fled."

"She's dead, Princess," Wolf assured me. "She couldn't have survived such a cut."

Aella has been killed. The wretched woman who caused my brother's death and brought my betrothed's country to the brink of war has been sent back to the Burning Hells, where she came from.

"That is truly good news," I nodded in relief. I couldn't wait to tell Jane and Larion.

"Can you find the body?" asked Radagrim.

"They'll probably take it with them to bury somewhere or to burn it," Wolf said. "I'm sorry, master. But I'll tell you more when we return to Romir, after we manage to end the prince as well. The steel was perfect in the way only steel can be, but the hand that wielded it wasn't, so I can't guarantee that the wounds will shorten his stay in this world."

"It's a shame we can't even obtain her body to study it," the master remarked in a low voice.

"She bleeds just like humans, that's for sure," Wolf replied.

"Rest up," Radagrim told them. "Have you informed the Circle?"

"We'll rest, you don't have to tell us twice," Saya chimed in, a smile on her lips. Wolf chuckled.

"Saya, speak when you're spoken to!" scolded Sparrow.

"I apologize, Lady Sparrow."

"I've informed the Circle," Wolf returned.

"Then I should inform Larion as well," I said.

For a moment, I felt like asking if they could have captured Darion alive, for the sake of my betrothed, but it didn't take long for my mind to come back to my head. Darion had to pay the same price as the Black Queen, whether he was under her spell or not.

"Farewell, Princess Elena," Wolf said.

"And to you," I replied, smiling at Saya one last time before turning and leaving.

The bright sunlight momentarily blinded me as I exited the dark wizard's tower. The people in the palace courtyard were chatting in shady spots, seeking refuge from the merciless heat of a summer afternoon, which I couldn't feel. I felt cold. The news of Aella's death should have brought me joy, but I felt unable to be happy; I felt weak and chilled, frightened.

I crossed the courtyard with my arms wrapped around my body, trying to figure out if I was trembling from fear or cold. It was both. Was that creature, which spoke through the idol now locked in the wizard's chest, the same as the one Rorik spoke to? Did Rorik have such an idol? That had to be the most logical, or rather the least insane, explanation.

I stopped in front of the gates, took a deep breath, and cleared my mind. Then, with confidence, I stepped into the Great Hall. My father stood beside Larion, who frowned as he listened to his plans of clearing all the villages of the wildlings they encountered. He shut his mouth when he saw me halting in front of their table. I was consumed by dark thoughts, and the cold I felt outside only amplified them.

"My dear, are you feeling alright?" Larion asked me. "You're very pale."

More faces from the tables turned to look at me. "I... yes." I steadied my voice, then added firmly, "Yes, I'm fine. Master Radagrim spoke with the assassins, and he will probably come to inform you personally: Aella has been killed."

The entire table was plunged into a silence deeper than any ocean. A chill skittered down my spine as I drew in a deep breath, feeling the coldness no one could feel stabbing through my lungs. Larion gaze expressed a subtle, uncertain happiness, masked by a sudden anticipatory fear. He was thinking of his brother.

"Prince Darion escaped," I added. "Radagrim will tell you more, of that I'm certain. Now, if you'll excuse me, I must return to my room."

Larion nodded, but when he saw my unsteady gait, he suddenly snapped out of his trance, rising from the table. "I'll escort you," he offered.

It was pointless to oppose, so I reached out my hand to him. He exchanged a few words with my father before rising, but I was too lost in thought to hear anything they were saying. I felt like I wasn't really there.

"*Margery.*"

"Should I call the doctor?" he asked as we left the Great Hall.

"No, I'm fine. I just want to lie down on the bed, cover myself, and sleep until morning."

"You're cold, I'll call the doctor," he insisted.

"I said I don't need it, Larion."

"And I choose to attribute your response to delirium caused by... well, whatever you have now."

I smiled, rolling my eyes. "I'm fine, trust me. If I felt something was wrong, I would have gone to the doctor myself, I'm not stupid." Then, feeling the need to change the subject of conversation and at the same time to shift my thoughts away from that creature, I asked, "What do you think about Aella's death?"

"I'm glad," he replied after a long pause.

"It doesn't seem like it."

"You don't seem well either, but you say you are. Sometimes things aren't as they seem, my dear, but are better left that way."

"Don't call me 'my dear'," I whispered, then smiled broadly as we passed by some nobles chatting in the hallway.

"We'll go to the room, and you'll tell me everything that's on your mind, and maybe, just maybe, I'll consider forgiving you."

"Forgive me? But what have I done?"

I burst out angrily, pulling my hand away from his. "Are you playing dumb or are you dumb?"

I decided it would be better, both for him and for me, if he didn't respond. But Larion didn't have a very good survival instinct, so he replied. "Elena, I'd give up the crown if I could understand why women get upset every time they do. But nobody in this world has such powers, so please, tell me what I've done this time so I can apologize."

"I'd rather not," I replied sardonically.

He raised his shoulders in acceptance. "Very well, then I apologize in advance."

"Not accepted," I replied as we ascended the stairs. I realized that during the final months of the pregnancy, likely in the winter, I wouldn't be able to climb as many stairs as I could now.

"I'm glad Aella is dead, why wouldn't I be," he said after a while. "I just feel sorry for... you know."

"I know."

We stood in front of the door when Larion stopped, grabbing my hand before I could reach for the handle. I was ready to ask if he finally remembered what he had done, but then I saw him tensing up. His gaze was serious, dangerous even, as his hand moved to the hilt of his sword.

He pushed the door handle forcefully and barged in. Mother and Merideth were there. I was shocked, but more so because he had realized someone was in the room and I hadn't. It wasn't cleaning day, so whoever it was, certainly wasn't a maid. There was only one reason someone would sneak into the king's room, and the idiot chose to barge right in!

"You want more?" I asked Merideth, looking at the book on the table. "What are you doing in our room?"

"We just came to talk," mother replied.

"Poor timing, as usual. I'm feeling unwell and need rest."

"Oh, what's wrong?" mother asked, coming toward me and placing her hand on my forehead. "You're pale, should we call the doctor?"

"I don't need a doctor," I insisted. "I need rest. Alone."

"Queen Lenore, did she inherit this stubbornness from you?" Larion laughed.

"I'd like to know who she takes after too," mother shrugged. "If you want to be alone, then we'll leave, but I'll send someone with a bowl of steaming soup and some tea, because you're as white as snow."

I nodded and stepped aside, making room for them to leave. Merideth cast me a fleeting glance out of the corner of her eye before exiting.

"She seems like a lovely woman," he said, once we were alone.

"Lovely as a snake," I replied innocently.

I stretched out on the bed and closed my eyes, trying to figure out why they had sneaked into the room. They wcrc plotting something, that was clear. Larion sat beside me, playing with my hair. He opened his mouth to say something, but I was quicker. "You're on the wrong side of the bed."

He laughed. "I see. Not I know what I did! It's about what I told you in the palace courtyard, isn't it?"

I didn't respond, continuing to ponder why Mother and Merideth would have sneaked inside. Larion was speaking, stringing together excuses half-heartedly, words muttered in the background, of which I wasn't interested.

"Larion," I whispered, and he stopped, looking at me with a frown because I had interrupted his long string of excuses. "My journal, please bring me my journal."

He rose in silence and made his way to the library, where I hid my journal on the shelf. I kept it in a similar place in Montrias, and I wouldn't be surprised if Mother knew.

There were some of my secrets and many of my plans. I took the journal and flipped through the pages, trying to find any sign, anything, to help me realize that she had read it, but I didn't know what I hoped to see. If she was looking for Jane, that's where she would find her most easily.

"You look paler," he said.

"I want two guards stationed outside Jane and Beatrice's door, day and night," I told him.

"I'll send word."

"Can you do it now?"

"Do you think your mother...?" he paused, his eyes fixating on the door.

"As much as possible."

He shook his head from side to side, then laughed.

"You, women of the Tarrygold family, are completely mad. I'll send two guards. You just sit on the bed and stay still at least for today. Now excuse me, I need to return to the Great Hall. Aella may be dead, but even without her, there are plenty of problems I need to deal with. Heavens, too many. Should I take the journal back?"

I shook my head. "No, I want to write in it."

"Understood. So, do you forgive me?" he inquired.

"I'll think about it."

He chuckled, then came over and kissed the top of my head. After he left, I found myself staring out the window, over the city I would one day govern. I liked it. The light pouring over it from above was so warm and bright, yet it felt so cold.

The door to the room slid aside not long after Larion has left, and Merideth entered, carrying a tray with a bowl and a steaming cup. She came over, keeping her gaze on the ground, and placed them on the table.

"Are they poisoned?" I asked without turning my face from the window.

"No, Princess," she replied after a moment. "Would you like me to taste them for you?"

"Only if they were poisoned," I said. "But mother wouldn't have the courage, would she?"

I turned to her, raising an eyebrow, and she took a step back. She was either scared or a natural-born pretender.

"I'm sorry for what I had to do today," she said.

"Good for you. Now, out with you. Shu!" I waved my hand to the door.

"I'm sorry. But your mother... I'm sorry."

A smile appeared on my lips. "My mother, what?"

"Your mother would have been upset with me if I hadn't intervened. And I serve her, so I had to. She's not a very pleasant person when she's upset."

She looked at me imploringly. "When is she a pleasant person?" I asked. She smiled shyly. "How did you end up working for her?"

"My brother was very ill, and the treatment was very expensive. We come from a less than humble family, barely making ends meet. Your mother chose to lend me money for the treatment, and now I have to work for her, another seven months, to pay off my debt. I made a deal with the devil, and now I have to pay." She widened her eyes, then added, "I'm a fool, please, don't mind me."

She turned and started for the exit. "Wait!" I urged. "Your brother..."

She remained completely still and spoke in a low voice. "He died from the illness, the doctor said, but I believe someone poisoned him shortly after we paid for the treatment. I have a suspicion, but..."

I silenced her with a gasp. I knew my mother was cold and unscrupulous, but that is a ruthless way of acquiring a servant witch, even for herself. "And now you're working for her for free?"

"For the money she gave me," she replied.

"You've chosen the worst benefactor, Merideth. What if you were paid for your work?"

"I'm obligated to pay off my debt..."

"Yes, yes, and you will. You'll spend your time with her, find out everything she's up to, who she talks to, and where she goes, then you'll tell me."

"I can't do that, Your Highness, I'm sorry."

Her back was still turned to me, but her voice was faltering. I almost convinced her, just a few more pushes. "Lenore has taken advantage of you," I insisted. "She exploited your suffering and made you a slave, and you gain nothing from it. I can help you get revenge. What do you say?"

She thought for a long time before refusing with a shake of her head. I ran my hands over the fabric of my dress, feeling one of the many hidden pockets, and I pulled out a gold coin. I have such concealed pockets in all my dresses.

"Come on, Merideth, help me make her days miserable," I pressed.

"If she finds out..."

"If she finds out, I'll pay off all your debt, and you'll be free. What do you say?"

"Fine," she replied in a whisper, turning to face me.

Her face remained impassive, betraying a strange calm that seemed at odds with the tension I had heard in her voice just moments before.

"Now tell me, does the name Jane sound familiar to you?"

"Yes," she replied after a much too long pause. "She was your brother's lover and is pregnant with his child."

"Is Mom trying to find her?"

Another long pause.

"Yes, Princess."

"Call me Elena, please," I asked.

"Fine, *Elena*. Your mother is looking for her because she fears that now that Frevia's heir is no more, her child, be it illegitimate, may claim the crown when it grows up."

I frowned for a few seconds at the calm and composure she now possessed.

"Did she read my diary?"

"I can't do that, Elena. I'm sorry. I'd love to help you, but I need a longer time for consideration before getting on her bad side."

She turned and left the room in a hurry, leaving me smiling. It was only a matter of time before Mother's poisoned temper would push her back to me, and having a spy in the Queen's entourage was an opportunity I was going to take advantage of. She wouldn't make a move without me knowing.

With Aella dead, I no longer saw Darion as a threat. That left only my mother, and with Merideth's help, I would always be one step ahead of her. It couldn't be better.

"*Margery.*"

Yermoleth's Sanctuary

Merwin looked at me with visible concern, seeing my face change back into an angry grimace. I managed to restrain myself for a while, but the memory flashed back to me, as if it were all unfolding before my eyes again. The naked face of the assassin, the surprised face of Aela. The blow, the blood. And I was just standing there, too slow to save her. Too weak.

"I'll kill him, I swear!" I muttered under my breath, just to myself.

Aella squeezed my hand. "He'll die, but we don't have time to look for them now," she replied with her usual icy calm.

I still held her hand. Ever since Lyra healed her, I hadn't let go except when she got up to heal Regihold. When Lyra arrived at her side, I thought it was already too late, but Aella was a fighter and clung to life with all her might. But still, if Lyra were late even for a second...

In those moments I considered that wizard, Wolf, my greatest enemy. I wanted him dead with all my heart, and in my soul, an unquenchable fury burned, sealing away any other feelings, leaving in their place a void that would only be filled with his blood. I was going to kill him, I knew that. It wasn't clear to me how, or when, or even where, but I could already feel his blood dripping on the edge of the Heart of Dawn. He wouldn't receive forgiveness for this, even if he begged for it.

Aella seemed not to share my anger. She was as calm as ever, maybe even calmer. I insisted several times that we should track them down, find them, and kill them, but she opposed, saying we didn't have time to wander aimlessly through the forest. We had to reach Yermoleth.

It was the first time we had stopped to catch our breath since the attack. The sun was setting, plunging the forest into an eerie, deep, solitary silence. The wind blew cold that evening. We didn't speak much, but I could see Merwin tightening his cloak around him. Kayra scanned the forest with clenched jaws, wearing a stern expression, and at every little sound, her hand flew quickly to her bow. Lyra slept soundly in Regihold's arms, exhausted from the large amount of ether she had to consume to heal Aella. Yenna sat beside her, occasionally glancing up at me as if she wanted to say something, but probably refrained due to the anger I couldn't hide.

"Have you rested enough?" Aella asked.

"No," Merwin replied. "But it's better than nothing. And you... are you feeling alright? I ask because you seem to look terribly alright after what happened."

She nodded, then leaned back, scanning her eyes over us. For a moment, I could see a hint of weariness in her clear eyes. Everyone was demoralized.

"Regihold, how's your back?" I asked.

"I don't feel anything anymore. Your ice-eyed lady works wonders," he replied. "However, my soul aches because of the breastplate. It's pierced."

"We'll repair it when we find a blacksmith," I promised.

"Next time you get the chance to kill an enemy, don't waste it," Aella said, shooting me a sideways glance.

"Why would we do that?" Regihold wondered.

"Some have a heart too big," responded Aella. "A big heart is an easy target."

She spoke of the mercy I had shown to Saya Starfrost, a mercy that nearly cost all of us our lives. I regretted my decision and was determined not to repeat my mistake next time—if sparing lives can indeed be called a mistake. Of course, plans made at home don't always align with the agreement in the market, and decisions made in tense moments are often the most fragile.

We rose and continued to climb up the slope of the Demon's Fang, weaving through the tangle of firs, bushes, and moss-covered rocks, making the most of the last rays of light. We only managed to advance because of Yenna and Kayra, who always found another hidden path whenever it seemed we had reached an impassable thicket. We advanced slowly, but we advanced nonetheless.

The sun went down soon after and fatigue began to creep in, weighing down our eyelids and dulling our senses. Something was strange. At first, I thought it was all in my mind, but with every step I took and with every glance I occasionally cast at the others, it became increasingly clear that sleep was falling heavier on that mountain. I even saw Kayra stumble a few times, and the perpetually agile and sharp gaze of the Shadow Walker, now swept tiredly across the dark earth of the forest. The night was far too bright; the brightest I could remember. It was also cool, but not chilly; almost perfect.

The Black Queen's silvery skin radiated with a spectral and cold aura. She looked magnificent, and despite all that had happened that afternoon, she seemed happy, even confident.

"I love you," I whispered to her.

She turned and kissed me on the cheek, with a wide smile, almost uncharacteristic of her.

"The night here is... strange. Don't you think?" I asked.

"It's beautiful and soothing as only the night can be," she replied.

"Perhaps it would be wise to rest," Merwin suggested. "It's clear that Regihold can't keep up anymore and will soon fall asleep on his feet."

"This time I don't disagree with you," the giant chuckled with his voice sleepy. "I'm exhausted."

"Me too," Yenna agreed, blinking rapidly.

"Darion is right, the night is strange here" Mathias admitted. "I'm starting to believe that we are under the influence of a spell that is becoming increasingly powerful. It dulls our senses."

Kayra nodded, then shook her head a few times to wake herself up.

"Perhaps we're all just tired," Merwin suggested. "It's been a long day of fighting and almost constant walking. Plus, if it were a spell, I would undoubtedly feel it."

Despite the assurance in his voice, the slight frown with which he looked at Aella expressed an unspoken question, to which she merely shrugged, amused. Merwin raised his eyebrows in surprise. There was something different about her that night; everyone could see it, for she was never so cheerful and expressive in front of others. Most of the times not even in front of me. She withdrew her fingers from mine, then took a few steps forward, before turning on her heels towards us and smiling again, almost giggling. She looked exactly like a small child, preparing a jest for her friends.

"Merwin, please come here," she requested.

"*Please,*" I repeated in my mind, confused.

The wizard took a few cautious steps, then suddenly shuddered, jumping back with such force that he fell backward. "Burning Hells Aella! A Sanctuary!"

She burst into loud laughter, a laughter so strange, so beautiful, and so pure that despite the fatigue I felt, I too began to laugh.

"Yermoleth lives in a Sanctuary," Aella declared after she held back her laughter and wiped the tears of joy from her eyes.

Everyone looked at her with evident surprise.

"I'm not going in there!" exclaimed Merwin with a shudder. "Nothing, and I mean nothing, is more foul than a Sanctuary, a wound in the soul of the world, a place that the Great River avoids."

"You will enter," Aella reassured him.

As Merwin said, a Sanctuary was a place where the Great River was obstructed from flowing, a place where wizards couldn't reach the ether and couldn't use magic. But the children of the night did not rely on the Great River, and such a place had no effect on those like Aella or Yermoleth.

I stepped forward as well, suddenly feeling a part of my mind being torn away. I don't know how to compare the sensation, but it was as if my whole life I had been walking on water, and that night I set foot on dry land for the first time.

"High Heavens! This is strange," I said.

"I don't understand," said Kayra, coming quickly beside me. "How can you feel?"

"Only a wizard senses the ether," Merwin emphasized, still frowning. "You shouldn't feel anything."

"But I'm not a wizard," I laughed, looking questioningly at Aella.

"You're a Dreamer. You can see beyond the veil of time when you sleep, and this gift still relies too on the Great River. Like Lyra, you also use the ether, but in a completely different way from how a wizard does."

Regihold took a few steps, passing the invisible barrier that separated the Sanctuary from the rest of the world. Lyra stirred, lifting her head alarmed.

"What's happening?" she whimpered, her voice tinged with concern. As her gaze settled on Aella, a warm smile spread across her small, sleepy face. "You look so beautiful."

"Not as beautiful as you," Aella replied tenderly, then approached her and planted a gentle kiss on her forehead. "We're in a Sanctuary, my dear. Here, you cannot heal."

She jolted. "What if those people come back?"

Regihold carefully lowered her to the ground, his massive hand stroking her hair reassuringly.

"They won't pursue us into a Sanctuary," Aella reassured. "No wizard willingly enters such a place."

"Neither will I," Merwin insisted stubbornly. "Go on ahead, and I'll wait for you here."

I patted Regihold on his steel covered shoulder. "What do you say, should we carry him?" I asked.

"Don't even think about it!" burst out Merwin.

"We've already thought about it. Come on, I don't want to carry you all the way. I don't see what's so bad about it?"

"What's so bad? What's so bad? The fact that in that place, I'm cut off from the ether, that's what's so bad. Without the ether... I'm nothing, just nothing."

"Welcome among us," Kayra chuckled. "Come on, stop whining and let's go."

Merwin rose reluctantly and stepped into the Sanctuary, grimacing with every step. He shot Aella a reproachful look.

"Let's just get this over with," he muttered sharply, then said something under his breath, meant for himself alone.

So, we continued our journey, and I found myself continually astonished by the consistently cheerful demeanor of my beloved, her perpetual smiles, and the affectionate kisses she bestowed upon the little healer. Even Merwin had chosen to set aside the drama of being separated from his beloved ether, focusing his attention fully on her. He turned at me with a questioning expression, a look I had already received from Kayra not long before, and in reply, I simply shrugged.

We followed Aella for a few more minutes. I was listening to her speak in an almost whispered voice to Lyra, who seemed to marvel at every word she spoke. It wasn't long before we stepped out onto a stretch where the ground was very slightly uneven, almost flat, and the trees grew away from each other, making the moonlight seem even brighter. I noticed that there were many paths there, which indicated that the place was often traversed, unlike the rest of the mountain. And Aella's skin was almost shimmering. It always looked beautiful under the moonlight, but now more than ever.

Not far from us stood the largest stump I had ever seen, at least fifteen meters in diameter and another three in height. It was so huge that at first, because of the dimness of night, I assumed it was just a very large rock. I only realized it was more than that when I heard Kayra exclaim in surprise.

"This is the *house*," Aella declared.

"Does he live in the stump?" I asked.

"Under."

Kayra whistled, visibly impressed. "In Verdavir there are all sorts of strange, big trees, but I don't remember ever seeing one like it," she uttered. "This one would make even the mighty Giant Tree look like a sapling; it was probably three hundred meters tall before it was cut down, if not more. What kind of tree was it?"

"I wondered the same thing when I first saw it," Aella replied thoughtfully. "Let's go inside and find out."

"It's the last living remnant of the proud Yerdrasils."

The one speaking was Yermoleth himself. He appeared from behind the tree stump, wearing a shirt and a pair of trousers, both in various shades of green, as if sewn from tree leaves. His hair was as blue as the clear sky, long to the base of his neck, and his eyes glowed yellow as amber. His skin, like Aela's skin, was grey, and the face looked youthful, so that if I had not known better, I would not have given him more than thirty years. He had two pairs of horns on his head. Some of them were twisted, like the horns of a ram, and some went straight up, like Aela's horns.

"I'm trying to preserve her as best I can," Yermoleth said, placing his hand gently over the massive stump, "and I hope from the bottom of my heart that there will come a time when she can grow again. In a better world, perhaps—a world yet to come."

"As you predicted, I've come seeking answers," Aella said. "I need your help."

"To free your sisters, I already know, and I will help you in any way I can. Welcome!" He gestured towards some stairs carved into the earth, descending beneath the tree, and disappearing into the shadows of its roots… or her roots.

"Why do you live in a Sanctuary?" Merwin asked provocatively.

"I myself made this Sanctuary in this place, to protect the last Yerdrasil from the corruption of Yohr'Sherrat."

We all stirred, checking the surroundings and holding our breath for a moment, because we all knew the dangers associated with that cursed name and the creature that bore it. However, Yermoleth, without paying attention to our reactions, continued, "If his roots were to reach hers, he would corrupt and destroy her. As they did with the others."

"More care when you utter such names," Merwin cautioned him.

"We are in a Sanctuary; the First Gods cannot hear nor see us, for here the ether does not flow. Do not worry about them."

"What does the Great River have to do with the First Gods?" Merwin wanted to know.

The surprise in the nartingal's expression indicated that he expected us to already know such things. "They created it," he said in one breath.

Silence. No one uttered a word. A breeze made Aella's dress tremble. Lyra shivered, and Merwin moved his lips without speaking a word, trying to keep his composure.

"No," the wizard denied eventually. "I don't believe you."

Aella frowned. She didn't know this either.

"That doesn't make any difference," replied Yermoleth. "They created the Soul of the World, the source from which the Great River springs, and their power is tied to it; their corruption spreads through it. But let's go inside and talk more."

He looked at us with sadness and remorse, as if the weight of the news he had given us weighed most heavily on him. He gestured again towards the steps descending among the roots of the last Yerdrasil. Aella glanced at me with a questioning look, probably wanting to know if we would enter the house beneath the tree or not, and in response, I nodded.

"It can't be true," Merwin murmured. Kayra placed a hand on his shoulder, but he shook it away.

"Let's go inside and get some clarification," I suggested with care.

Merwin nodded absentmindedly and sprang off first in the footsteps of the nartingal, his face downturned and empty. Those stairs led to a dead end, a place where roots blocked the way forward, growing so close together that they practically formed a wall. As Yermoleth approached, right before our eyes, the roots began to move, retracting from the ground like a guillotine gate. Warm light spilled from within. Lyra exclaimed loudly in amazement, then squeezed through us and took Aella's hand.

The room, if it could be called that, was immense, illuminated by bright flowers growing from the roots that covered the earthen walls. It was incredible. In the center of the room stood a long wooden table with a single thick leg in the middle, which seemed to grow directly from the grass-covered ground. The chairs resembled woven reed baskets and were attached to the ceiling by a kind of vine, making it difficult to sit without swaying.

On one such chair in the corner of the room lounged a young woman wearing a green leather vest over a white shirt, a pair of brown trousers, and black boots. Her hair was in various shades of red and orange, resembling flames, and her eyes were yellow, with a pupil like a long, black reptilian line. When I saw her, I almost jumped, because I had dreamt of her before, and not just once. She tilted her head to one side, studying us silently, then quickly licked her upper lip.

She rose from her seat, leaving the chair swaying behind her, and approached with slow strides, stopping in front of me, never once averting her gaze, blinking often. Then, she closed her eyes and leaned her head towards me, remaining still, almost holding her breath. I frowned and turned to Aella, hoping she would enlighten me, but she seemed just as puzzled as I was.

"She is Arya of the drakars. She wants to greet you," Yermoleth clarified.

"I greet her too," I said confused.

"Well, greet her then," he laughed. "You have to touch her head. With your forehead," he hurried to add, seeing that I was about to pet her.

Considering that I had no choice and wanting to move on to discussions more quickly, I closed my eyes and pressed my forehead against hers. This made her giggle, opening her eyes and looking at me with a childish smile.

"*Sher venyak*, you don't know how to greet, do you?" she asked with amusement.

"I confess I've never greeted anyone like this before," I said, still keeping my head against hers, unsure of how long I was supposed to remain in that greeting. It was a pretty awkward situation for me.

"Do you want me to show you how it's done?"

I hesitated for a moment before reluctantly giving my approval. "Sure."

I immediately regretted my response as Arya headbutted me, hitting my head with such force that I almost lost my balance.

"Heavens!" I exclaimed, rubbing my forehead and staggering back a few steps.

Regihold burst into laughter, and Merwin followed suit.

"Who greets like that?" I snorted.

"I do," she replied, after a few moments of hesitation, making the laughter of the two even louder.

"She does," Merwin repeated amidst laughs. "Regihold, go get greeted!"

Aella lowered her head to hide her subtle smile.

"*Shalikhr!* We usually only greet one member of the *flyjhar*, not everyone, sher venyak," Arya explained.

"*Shalikhr,*" Merwin struggled to reproduce. "I don't know what it means, but I'm sure I've been called worse."

"Especially by women," Regihold jumped in.

"*Shalikhr* is a way of telling someone they're wrong or don't know what they're talking about," Yermoleth explained, "and *sher venyak* means short life. Arya has slightly different customs than you, as you've noticed already."

"Slightly different would have been if she greeted with her left instead of right," I said, still rubbing my head. "You have a very strong head, lady."

My remark seemed to deepen her confusion; she stared at me with those snake-like eyes, mouth slightly open, head tilted to her right shoulder.

"Compliment," clarified the nartingal.

"You also have a head strong like the scales of Tiamat. It was a pleasure to hit it," Arya said solemnly. Merwin and Regihold stormed into laughter again, as if they had forgotten the words Yermoleth had spoken just moments ago. Even I almost let out a smile, seeing the seriousness and puzzlement with which she spoke. "Although," she continued, turning to Aella, "it might have been more appropriate to greet you, *eshz venyak*."

"You greeted the right person," Aella assured her. "It seemed to me he needed a good greeting."

Arya blinked, then licked her lips again.

"I've wanted to meet more *eshz venyak* ever since my mother told me about the Age of Eternity and the world before the One Who Must Be Forgotten rose."

"The One Who Must Be Forgotten?" I asked, and immediately the whole aura of the room darkened.

"Yes," she replied, then fell silent.

"Let's all take a seat," suggested Yermoleth, gesturing towards the table with chairs descending from the ceiling. "Take a seat, come on, leave your cloaks off your shoulders, and I'll bring you something to drink. I only have fruit syrup and water, but they will do. Maybe we should also have a more proper introduction, since we didn't get that chance upstairs. I'm Yermoleth, and this is, as I said before, the young Arya of the drakars."

We all introduced ourselves and sat in the chairs that slowly swung under our weight. Lyra was all smiles, giggling continuously while Aella used her ether to sway her chair. Arya, although she appeared human, was not a human being. This was evident to everyone, I was sure, although no one voiced their doubts. "*But what could she be?*" I remember wandering. "*What does drakar means?*"

Yermoleth approached a wall, and the roots retreated from his path, revealing a small room into which he entered only to emerge a few seconds later with a wooden tray containing several wooden glasses. He handed each of us a glass, smiling cheerfully.

"I'm sure I've guessed everyone's tastes," he said.

"You certainly did for me," acknowledged Mathias.

"Wild strawberries," commented Aella. "I can say the same for me."

Mine smelled like peaches, and the thought took me almost instantly to the perfume Arlieth wore most often. I raised my eyes, looking at him reproachfully for a few moments, undecided whether to confront him or not. In the end, I silently nodded and said nothing more.

Merwin took a deep breath, then shrugged with feigned indifference and said, "You said the Great River was created by the First Gods. Please explain to me how it's possible for those demonic creatures to have created something so pure, because I find it hard to believe."

Part of him didn't want to hear Yermoleth's answer; I knew that because a part of me didn't want to hear it either, and I didn't love the ether as much as he did.

"Wouldn't you want on such a beautiful night to talk about beautiful things and leave the pain of tomorrow."

"We'll still be here tomorrow," replied Aella.

Merwin snorted. "Thank you so much for deciding on behalf of those who could be directly affected by such a revelation, sparing us the burden of making such a decision."

Aella frowned, then nodded. "The decision is yours, then," she agreed.

The wizard scowled at Yermoleth's calm face, then turned his gaze to one of those glowing white flowers, which cast warm light throughout the room. He was undecided.

"We'll talk about this tomorrow," he finally said and we all nodded at once. "Today, I just want to know if you're absolutely certain that what you're saying is the pure truth and nothing else. Just that."

"I am sure. I was there, seven thousand years ago. The day the Soul of the World was created was supposed to be a day of great celebration, both for humans and for us, but the truth is that there has never been a day of greater mourning, and there probably never will be, as long as this world will endure. Our proud race, which was ordained here at the same time as the world, meant to watch over it and help it thrive, like a gardener... our entire race, slaughtered in one day." His face darkened, and his voice deepened, the friendly tone being drowned in the anguish brought back by the memories. "The Calamity, the Destroyer, the One Who Must Be

Forgotten... deceived us all." He stood silent for a while, his eyes gazing at his clenched fists. He opened them, then spoke in a milder tone, "But yes, to answer your question, I am sure they created the magic you use."

"How will this affect me?" Merwin wanted to know.

"As long as they are imprisoned, it will not affect you in any way. When they are free, stay away from their filth, do not sip ether without a protective amulet around your neck."

"Where do I get one of those?"

"You will receive one at the right time, not a moment sooner."

"Right," he said, then chuckled. "How ironic that the first wizards used the very magic the First Gods created against them."

"Humans didn't defeat them alone," Arya asked half-amused, her little forehead wrinkling. "Surely you don't attribute all the credit of that victory to yourselves, do you?"

"I don't know much about the War of Shadows," Merwin admitted. "Yermoleth is right, I can wait until tomorrow, because today has been full to the brim. Let's talk about happier things."

"I won't say a word until you taste the green apple syrup I prepared for you," Yermoleth told Yenna.

"Mine is not bad at all," Regihold encouraged her.

Yenna nodded, then sipped from the wooden cup, but without taking her eyes off the nartingal. "It tastes like memories," she said. "From when I lived in the valley, before I was taken by the mountain people."

I don't know if she noticed my surprise, because after that she didn't say another word. I would later learn that the reason Yenna spoke the common tongue so clearly was that she had lived in Derahia as a child, being abducted at the age of only seven and raised in the mountains. Regihold seemed to already know.

"You have a very beautiful home," Mathias told him after the silence became heavy.

"For a *rothzhak*," Arya laughed, her voice sharp and high-pitched. "The old man lives underground like a mole."

"Please excuse Arya," Yermoleth told us, "she's at that unbearable age where the rebellious side takes control." Arya was about to comment, but the nartingal raised a finger to silence her. "Don't even think of telling me you're not rebellious, especially now that you've just run away from home."

Arya licked her lips again with a quick movement, but said nothing.

"You mentioned you were seven thousand years old," Kayra said. "Tell us, what was the world like back then?"

"Oh, it was wonderful. Yerdrasils grew everywhere and rose so high that almost reached the stars. Our seven kingdoms were absolutely magnificent, a beauty this world was doomed to never see again. It was almost perfect, but no one even realized it."

"What happened to the Yerdrasils?"

"The First Gods destroyed them because they were beautiful and pure, and they hated anything too pure to be corrupted, they hated anything clean. They would have destroyed her too if I hadn't made the Sanctuary around her. The Faceless Ones cut her down, but not from the root, preferring to give her a slow and painful death. Instead, I offered them exactly that. One day she will rise again, but now she fears, for if she were to grow and her branches were to extend outside the Sanctuary, she would fall into the clutches of the enemies, and then the last Yerdrasil would be lost. A bleak prospect."

"I'm sorry to hear that," Kayra said. He silently caressed the tabletop as if trying to soothe a wounded friend. The flowers on the walls began to glow brighter.

"She's alive; she feels us, hears us, and sees us."

"Are you the last of your kind?" Mathias asked.

"Yes. The last one I knew of passed away over a thousand years ago, giving her life to save a mortal. I roamed the world far and wide, hoping to find others, but I'm probably the only one left." He sighed, then looked at Aella with tired smile. "And now, of course, there's them."

"Do we have you to thank for all the suffering Aella endured seven hundred years ago?" I asked sharply.

"And for the fact that she's now by your side instead of dead, yes. I needed other daughters of the night, for my mother had seen in a dream that the First Gods would be destroyed by one of them. The problem was that after the War of Shadows and the Great Oblivion, there was only one left, and she hated me and chose to live in solitude, somewhere on the land now called Frevia. I didn't know how much I could rely on her, so I began to work and experiment, seeking to bring back my people. And I succeeded, though the cost was great. I knew about all the atrocities your ancestor, Arika, would commit, yet I steeled my heart and chose to pass all my studies to her. She had the courage to do things that were beyond me."

I clenched my jaw, prepared to raise from the chair, but Aella caught my forearm. "To massacre tens of thousands, to test your theories?" I called him on it.

"Yes," Yermoleth nodded with pain. "A great price, but the blood shed then will redeem the world one day, you'll see."

"How do you know that Arika was my ancestor?" I asked. "I don't remember telling you that. And how did you know about the peaches? Are you reading my mind?"

"I know that Arika is your ancestor because I can feel her blood flowing through your veins. Your blood is Arika's blood, and her blood..." he shuddered. "Well, I remember it. I am not your enemy, believe me. Perhaps my hands are stained, but until the pains are over, we will all wear the same marks."

"The past is in the past," Aella said with an icy voice. "You gave Arika the sword, and she wielded it."

I lowered my hand over hers, sensing her mood. She was sad and angry, but I couldn't tell if the anger was directed at Yermoleth or at the past.

"Rather, I gave her a reason to use the sword she already had. But, as we've repeated since we met, let's leave discussions of death and pain for tomorrow."

We remained in that room for a while longer, and Yermoleth told us about creating a Sanctuary. I can't say I understood much of what he said, but the whole process was similar to building a dam. It took a lot of power to create it, and even he could only repeat the process only once in a few years. He told us that for the past six thousand years, he had worked tirelessly, creating a vast Sanctuary in Frevia, which already stretched for dozens of kilometers and which he expanded continuously.

"Why?" I wanted to know.

"A refuge where we can retreat when the One Who Must Be Forgotten returns, and the Shadow covers the earth again. There will come a time when we will need such a thing. A last scrap of land where the sun will still shine, a last kingdom for humanity."

I already knew he was talking about the Last Sunset, the day when the Enemies of Humanity would be free again, and the sun would darken forever, leaving the world in an eternal night. If the First Gods were to be free again, a Sanctuary was the perfect place to hide, as according to Yermoleth, they had no power there. Many questions raced through my mind that night, but although the wisdom he carried suggested he knew all the answers, I chose not to voice them yet. Was the Enclave of Knowledge real? Who was that Khyalis, whose name kept popping into my mind and evoking fear? Who was the One Who Must Be Forgotten, whom he called the Calamity and the Destroyer? Why were the

First Gods imprisoned and not killed? Did he know who Deoa was, the voice that spoke to Lyra?

Yenna and Regihold were the first to admit they were tired, so Yermoleth opened a door, if it could be called that, as there were only moving roots, revealing a hidden chamber. Inside, the branches from the walls intertwined to form a bed. Regihold began to laugh heartily, and even Yenna's face was adorned with a vague smile.

"Is it the tree doing this, or you?" Aella wanted to know. "I see no trace of magic, no waves, delicate or dull."

"She," replied Yermoleth, caressing a branch of his root chair.

Lyra also went to bed, followed by Merwin, who seemed too tired to sleep and rather pensive. In their room, two beds also sprouted down, one large for the wizard and one small, covered with all sorts of colorful shinny flowers. Lyra squealed, clapping her hands and running around Yermoleth, who stood in the doorway, before throwing herself onto the soft bed of intertwined roots.

"We're not going to get her out of here easily," Aella told me, with a hint of a smile.

"Certainly not," I agreed.

Kayra laughed, then rose from the table, and Mathias followed almost instantly, as if he were her shadow.

"Lyra is very fond of you, and I can see that you are fond of her too," Kayra said. "You already talk as if you were her parents."

She turned her back on us and walked towards the room that appeared in another wall. Mathias bowed briefly before disappearing after her. Although the Black Queen remained silent, the smile she didn't try to conceal told me that the archer's remark brought her happiness. She cast one last glance at the place where the roots had covered the little girl's room before her gaze settled on my face.

"As if we were her parents," I repeated.

Yermoleth took a seat at the other end of the table, silently studying us. Arya was still there, crouched on one of the swing chairs with her chin resting on her knees, her fiery hair being so long that it almost covered her completely. She hadn't spoken a word for a long time.

"I think you must be very tired," Yermoleth said.

"We are," I replied. "Thank you for your hospitality!"

"It's my pleasure. I haven't been visited by humans in over a hundred years."

"I suspected you weren't human," I addressed Arya.

"Of course I'm not human," the girl laughed, then licked her lips again.

"But... what are you?"

"I'm a drakar, isn't it obvious? You can tell by the eyes, just as you can tell that Aella and Yermoleth are eternal lives.

She settled her head back onto one of her shoulders, looking at me calmly. The light from the flowers on the walls grew dimmer, as though the very tree itself was preparing to sleep.

"I've never seen a drakar before," I admitted.

"Of course you have not. If you had encountered one, you wouldn't be here now, talking to me. There has been enmity between my kind and yours for over six thousand years, ever since the Shadow War ended. Mother despises you as much as she despises the trolls, and that's saying something, because we loathe the *rothzhakayr* with all our might. Vile, wretched, treacherous creatures!" she spat, almost trembling.

"Then it would be wise to stay away from your mother," I chuckled.

"But unfortunately, we're headed straight towards Shartat," Aella said, then turned her head to me. "Drakar, in the old tongue, means dragon."

I darted my eyes to Arya's face, finding her looking sleepy. "Heavens! Are you a dragon?" I whispered.

"That's what I said," Arya laughed. "You have quite a strong head, I would have thought it hid a sharper mind."

Yermoleth saw my bewilderment, so he said, "Like us, the drakars can take human forms whenever they wish."

I was left gaping in amazement, wondering if Larion would ever believe that I was sitting at a table between two children of the night and a dragon who deemed me slow-witted. I could hardly believe it myself, yet there I was.

"Why do you hate humans?" Aella wanted to know.

"Dragons are hypocrites," Yermoleth quickly interjected. "Don't take it to heart, her mother doesn't like me either, and I'm a child of the night. They hate humans and trolls because of the sins they themselves have committed."

Arya, filled with frustration, opened her mouth to defend herself, but Yermoleth raised a finger and shushed her. The girl closed her mouth with a snap.

"You know I'm right," said Yermoleth, "besides, you wouldn't have any reason to hate either of them. Your mother was only a little older than you when the War of Shadows ended, and you were born just three hundred years ago—you were not around when the trolls accepted the Gift and you were not around when the humans awakened the One Who Must Be Forgotten, therefore, your hatred is, if anything, unreasonable."

"I don't despise humans, and when I've eaten some, it's only because I wanted to see what they taste like! As for you, Mother has reasons to dislike you, *taher va zshyrack*. You could have killed the Temptress, yet you chose to spare her life."

"*You've eaten humans?*" I was about to ask, but Yermoleth spoke again, "And I would make the same choice every time, ever again. I can't harm her, but you wouldn't understand."

Yermoleth's face was now grim and ominously foreboding, and no matter how carefully I observed him, I couldn't discern whether he was struggling with anger or doubt. Or perhaps both. Whoever this Temptress was, she was a highly sensitive subject for him, so I refrained from prying. Aella, however, was not as tactful.

"I haven't heard of the Temptress before," she said.

"You couldn't have," Yermoleth replied. "I sealed her away when the War of Shadows ended."

"Who was she?" she persisted.

"A friend, that's all you need to know for now." He rose with slow, weary movements. "We'll discuss more in the morning, including the reason for your visit. May the light of the stars bathe you."

After this farewell, he walked away from us, heading for the stairs leading outside, but not before gesturing towards the room where we were to sleep.

"Does Yermoleth sleep outside?" I asked Arya.

"Sometimes," she replied. "But especially on the nights I bring up the Temptress. He doesn't even like me to call her that, but that's what everyone calls her. "

"Then maybe you shouldn't call her that. You're not empathetic."

She didn't bother to hide her grimace as she said, "No, I've told you before, I'm a drakar."

"Who was the Temptress?" I pressed after a long time of watching her with my lips pressed together. Arya always looked somewhat comical to me, beautiful and slender, with her cheeks perpetually flushed and her face often contorted in confusion.

"She was one of the Immortals, the champion of the One Who Must Be Forgotten, and also his most powerful servant."

"I don't know who the Immortals are," said Aella.

"The ancient monarchs. The champions of the First Gods and those who led their armies during the War of Shadows. How is it that you're older than me, yet you still know so little?"

"I lived among humans; there was no one to teach me. I thought I knew enough, but it turns out I knew very little. I've never heard of the Immortals, the Temptress, or the disputes between dragons and trolls. I could listen to you if you have more to tell me."

"We, drakars, don't fancy idle chatter," Arya replied in a tone that suggested she couldn't care less. "Yermoleth will tell you everything you need to know tomorrow, and he'll be glad to do it because, like you, he enjoys using his mouth. I prefer to use mine mainly for chewing."

Aella nodded. Although her face was like a blank page, I was certain that Arya's impolite refusal didn't sit well with her. To some extent, it amused me, but I refrained from showing it. Arya stood up, taking a few steps away from the table, then curled down on the grass covered ground, just like a cat.

"Don't you have a bed?" I asked. She chuckled as if I had said something amusing but said nothing in response.

We bid her goodnight, to which she only frowned, then went to our room and sat on the gently swaying bed. It was more comfortable than I had expected, despite appearances.

Aella hugged me and with a flicker of her powers she made the bed wobble gently. The ceiling was adorned with small, bright white flowers, so tiny that they resembled the stars dotting the sky outside from our bed.

"Today, Aella... it was too close," I began.

"It was, but we've gotten through that. Those wizards probably consider me dead, and that will give us an advantage over them when we decide to strike."

"If you were... I would have lost everything, you know that?" I asked, holding her tightly in my arms.

I didn't want to imagine the direction my life would have taken if she had died that day.

"Don't dwell on what might have happened. We'll get rid of all our foes, of all that wish to harm us, even if that means the entire world. And then, we will have peace."

I closed my eyes, holding my breath for a time.

"When will all of this end?" I asked with tiredness in my voice. "Every day I wake up with the hope that we'll make it through, and I go to bed realizing that we're sinking even deeper into this madness. I'm exhausted."

"I wish I had answers like that. Everything would be simpler if I knew what tomorrow holds, but I can't even know what the next moment will bring. You wonder when it will end, I wonder when it will begin, for I fear that the worst may not have even started."

I held her tighter. She did the same. I remember feeling so small, so weak, and insignificant that night, and I sensed that she felt the same. So we simply remained there, enveloped in silence, hugging each other tighter and tighter. Soon, her hands began to roam across my body, seeking to deepen her hold, to draw me closer, and I responded in kind. It wasn't long before she whispered in my ear, "*I want you!*"

I discovered soon that the vines and roots holding our bed were surprisingly strong. I had expected them to snap at any moment, but they did not yield.

It didn't take long for us to fall asleep afterward, as we watched the fragile light of the false stars, struggling desperately to keep the darkness that surrounded them at bay.

Just like us.

World Soul

That night I had had no nightmares and no prophetic dreams, for I was free, disconnected from the Great River that brought me such visions. Aella was still asleep when I woke up. I couldn't tell if it was morning or still night because of the heavy darkness in that windowless room, but I felt rested. I kissed her on the forehead before taking my clothes that were scattered around, grabbing my sword, and pulling my cloak over my shoulders. Then I headed towards where I remembered the door to be, for my usual training.

I ran my hand over the roots covering the walls for a while, but I couldn't find any opening. After a few moments, I started to worry that Yemoleth had deceived us and taken us prisoner, but then I glanced at Aella and calmed down, thinking that she could destroy the entire tree if necessary. I don't know if the tree heard my thought or not, but right after, I reached into a thorn. I jumped back, almost cursing, biting my tongue just before the words escaped my mouth.

I laughed softly, then decided to try another approach. "*Lady tree, if you can hear me, please let me out,*" I thought, not really expecting anything to happen. To my surprise, *she* heard me. The roots began to retract with a sound like the faint murmur of a stream, or perhaps like two fine fabrics being rubbed together.

I hurried to get out, fearing that the roots would descend back from the doorway, catching me in the wall and putting me in the awkward situation of asking for help, being halfway in the room and halfway in the main hall. The flowers covering the walls shone faintly, spreading a dim, cold light, like the glow of a pale moon covered by faded clouds. Moving quickly through the dim light, I stumbled over Arya, who was sleeping on the floor, nearly losing my balance. I could swear she wasn't in the same place where she had fallen asleep, and I could be right, since I was soon about to find out that she moves a lot in her sleep. I quickly tucked my head between my shoulders, expecting her to jump out of sleep and scold me in a typical feminine manner, but she made no gesture to suggest she had felt the boot ramming her ribs.

I knelt beside her, putting two fingers against her neck to feel her pulse. Her skin was feverishly hot, and the pulse very slow. "*Did I hit her too hard?*" I panicked.

"Arya, wake up," I whispered, starting to shake her violently.

For a few moments she didn't move, then shivered violently and opened her eyes. Because of the darkness, her pupils were more than just black lines on a yellow background—they were oval.

"*Sher venyak*, what's happening?" she breathed, grabbing my hand.

"You're burning up," I told her.

She smiled wearily. "Thank you. I'm sure you're burning like the flames of Methuselah too."

With that, she closed her eyes once more, curled up, and drifted back to sleep in mere seconds, leaving me crouched beside her, puzzled by her rhythmic, slow breathing. I realized she likely mistook my concern for a compliment and returned it in kind. I considered this a fortunate outcome and withdrew slowly, carefully watching my steps to avoid stepping on Yermoleth or any other oddities that might be sleeping nearby.

"*Can you please show me the way out?*" I asked the tree in my mind, almost chuckling at the sheer thought of it.

A new doorway appeared beyond the living curtain that drew aside, revealing the shadow-covered steps that climbed out of the nartingal's house. The chill of the night flowed in like water rushing through a broken dam.

It was still dark, and despite the brightness of the shining sea of stars above, I could barely make out much. Dawn was approaching—the night is always darkest before the first light.

I began to train under the scarce light, practicing broader attacks and, perhaps in many cases, less practical ones. I tried to quickly transition from defense to attack, then defense again, to change guard as often as possible, blocking blows aimed sometimes at the head and sometimes at the legs. For that's how he fought. The Assassin. The man I swore to kill. The man I had to kill.

It was futile.

I couldn't defeat him, not in such a short time. He moved like the cold, sharp wind blowing over the frozen winter river. You couldn't fight something like that; it was perfect. I would need years of training to stand up to him, but I doubted I could negotiate with destiny about that. The gods will bring him back against me when they decide.

His shadow, which I projected dancing among the others, won every time. Wolf, they called him, although that certainly wasn't his real name. I had briefly studied the fighting styles of the people from the Storm Islands and was fairly certain that the man used the Wolf style. This style is known for its swift, lightning-fast movements, targeting the throat or feet to incapacitate its prey. I also deduced that the woman likely employed the Sparrow style, characterized by fighting with two weapons—considered the most challenging of the eight styles due to the exceptional coordination required between arms and legs. That's why they called her Sparrow, that must be it. I thought about all of this while the shadow of the Wolf kept cutting off my legs again and again.

Burning Hells!

"You fight very well," I heard Yermoleth say. He was perched on the giant stump.

"Not well enough," I replied between gasps.

"You are not perfect, but I ask you: who is?"

"My opponent." I didn't like to admit it, but I saw myself forced to, for this was the plain truth. I was inferior to him, not to mention the fact that he was a wizard. I was fighting a battle I couldn't win.

"Stay with me," he requested. "Let's hear the night's song together."

His horned silhouette, with eyes burning yellow in the night like two lit coals, reminded me of Yohr'Sherrat. Of the night I stood before the demon. The heat I felt in my body from training dissipated in an instant, and the sweat droplets covering me turned as cold as ice. From the stump emerged several large mushrooms, growing diagonally, one higher than the other, somewhat like steps.

I climbed carefully and slumped beside him.

"You're much more modest than I was at your age, I can admit that much," he said. "And much, much more mature. When I was your age, I used to consider myself perfect. It wasn't until I met *her* that I realized how far from perfection I was."

I raised my eyes to the starry, unclouded sky, resembling an endless, cold lake speckled with shimmering stones. "The one Arya calls the Temptress?" I asked.

He grimaced at the mention of the name—I caught that from the corner of my eye—then smiled, heavy with sadness.

"Yes. I met her seven thousand years ago in the place now called Verdavir. Much has changed in the world since then, even the face of the world itself. Did you know that the Verdavir of that time had a climate like that of today's Derahia, and Derahia was just a dead and frozen land? Only the ice shadows lived there; soulless demons, born from the darkness where the light of the stars does not reach. Descended into our world and rested in those frozen hells, probably reminiscent of them to the coldness of the void. Beyond Redat, to the north, temperatures were slightly higher, but still freezing cold, and there proudly stood one of our kingdoms. Its inhabitants loved the chill. '*There is no night more beautiful than the night on the Realm of Eternal Winter,*' they used to say. It seems that the winter they spoke of wasn't quite so eternal, but it will come again, it will surely do, for such are these cycles, like day and night and like ebb and flow and like the seasons. But what am I saying? I'm rambling off on tangents; that's what I do if you don't stop me in time."

"Are these ice shadows the First Gods?" I asked with a feigned smile.

"No, but perhaps they are not, nor have they been. No one remains in this world who has encountered them. But no, if we are to believe the tales, they have been here since before the First Gods, even before Creation itself. From another Creation! But let's return to concrete matters." He sighed deeply. "I was telling you about her. As I was saying, I found her in Verdavir, wounded, trying to escape from the legionnaires of the Rewanian Empire. Just her and her dog, Furry, limping through the forest. She had such a good soul, Darion. She would have given her life for... anyone. She had no trace of selfishness in her, believe me. She was everything I could never become."

The hair on my neck stood as I felt like the wind stopped blowing and the forest went still. "What was her name?" I asked in one clipped whisper.

"Khyalis."

I almost jumped. Tightening my cloak around myself, I nodded in silence. "What happened to her?"

"She found the First Gods. You see, she was a human being, and she drew her power from the Great River.

Believe me when I tell you: she was powerful. She almost knocked the mountain onto my head when she saw me the first time," he laughed, watching the dance of the leaves under the night wind that started blowing again. "Such power was not meant for the beings of this world. One day, at the command of a witch, she delved too deep into the ether river and there she stumbled upon the One Who Must Be Forgotten, the most powerful of the First Gods and the one who orchestrated the downfall of my kind: Bhalphomet the Destroyer."

The name sounded strange, as something never meant to be heard, or rather never meant to exist. Like a piece left in front of an apparently complete puzzle.

"I'm sorry," I said trying to hold a shiver.

"In time, she began to change. Every time I saw her, she was less herself, but more cruel and evil, more of Bhalphomet's corruption was crawling into her soul. There is no greater pain in the world than to see someone so dear, dissipating more and more until nothing remains. The true Khyalis probably faded away long ago."

"Still, Arya says you refused to kill her when you had the chance. Why?"

"Do you really have to ask that? I hoped that maybe, deep down, there was still a shred of the woman who blushed when you reminded her how beautiful she was. Besides that, tell me, Darion, what would Aella have to do for you to harm her?"

"You're right, I couldn't," I admitted. "Do you think the First Gods can be destroyed permanently?"

"That's the only thing that gets me up in the evening."

For what he had done to Aella, I considered Wolf my greatest enemy. I could only imagine the depth of Yermoleth's hatred for the creature that had taken Khyalis away from him. That hatred kept him alive; it was a wound that even millennia had failed to heal.

"Then we'll vanquish them," I said with a confidence I didn't know I had. Confidence and fury. All the evil that had happened to me was caused by them—by Yohr'Sherrat especially.

"Words forged in steel," he smiled. "Let's go inside; the sun should rise soon." He yawned and stretched. "At this hour, I usually go to sleep, but since you have a different sleep schedule, a rather strange one, I must say, I'll stay awake to tell you everything you need to know."

The children of the night from ancient times used to sleep before sunrise and wake up before sunset. They did not like the day. Once, I heard Yermoleth saying that the sunlight was too noisy for him, too restless compared to the silently melodious moonlight. Aella later confirmed that the nartingals could hear the breath of light.

"The moon seems strange here," I remarked, fixing my gaze on its glowing form.

"Wait until there's a full moon," he chuckled. "Did Aella react strangely?"

I hesitated, recalling her behavior from the previous night. Even in bed, she had seemed different—more feral, noisier. "Yes."

He laughed. "If you're not accustomed to it, too powerful moonlight can have the same effect on us as too much wine has on you."

"Was she drunk?" I asked, my smile widening.

"Yes. You should have seen the first time Arika brought them here. They were just children back then, barely able to keep their heads straight. The moon shines brighter over Yerdrasils."

"I should bring her here more often," I said, and we both started to laugh.

"The wizard and the girl have already woken up," he told me. "Go to them, I'll follow after I get a chance to meditate for a few moments and banish the shadows from my heart, lest I bring them into the house. That usually unsettles *her*," he added, touching the wood he was sitting on.

I nodded and went back down the mushroom ladder, then down the steps dug into the earth. Inside, as Yermoleth said, Lyra and Merwin were waiting for me. Arya was still sleeping under the seemingly cheerful light of the magical plants that now shone with more vigor.

"What's with the gloomy faces?" I asked.

"*Deoa* spoke to me," said Lyra. Her eyes seemed unsure, and her tiny mouth twisted with sadness. "She told me that today we will part from you, from you and Aella. I don't want that."

"Are you sure?" I asked, then crossed the room in a few large steps, sitting down beside them. "Maybe it was just a nightmare."

She nodded, then got up from her chair and climbed onto the table, coming in front of me and opening her arms, waiting for a hug. I picked her up with soft movements, placed her onto my lap, then gently kissed her over her golden hair.

That's how Aella found us when she left our room. She didn't say a word and made no effort to ask why the little one was upset, most likely knowing everything we had talked about. Kayra and Mathias came next, and just a few moments after them, Regihold and Yenna appeared. I was surprised to see Regihold without his usual steel armor, or at least chainmail, wearing only simple, thin clothes.

Regihold opened his mouth ready to speak, but lost his momentum after bumping into Arya, who was still sleeping a few steps away from the table. He fell to his knees swearing and quickly turned back to the frail body of the girl with fiery hair. Just like the first time, she didn't even stir.

"She's not dead," I assured him. "She's just a deep sleeper."

"Are you sure, Master Darion?" Yenna asked. "It doesn't seem like she hears us."

"Yes," I replied. "Perhaps we should move her out of the way, so we don't stumble over her again."

Regihold nodded, then leaned down and lifted her up.

"She's so small, weak, and pale," Regihold said. "Aella, could you take a look at her? She seems to be feverish."

"She's fine, Regi, trust me" I reassured him.

He hesitated for a few moments, looking unconvinced at the young woman sleeping in his arms, then nodded. He carefully placed her on one of the wider chairs, large enough for her to lie down, placed a finger under her nose to ensure she was still breathing, and then turned back to us with slumped shoulders.

"She's fine," I repeated after Regi sat down. "I also stumbled over her when I left the room and woke her up, but she fell asleep again in seconds. We just need to watch where we step when she's around."

"Like having a cat," laughed Merwin. "Have you had cats before, haven't you?"

"*I've had a dragon before,*" I almost said, referring to the reptile I bought when I was a child.

"Deoa spoke to me," Lyra resumed after each of us took a seat. "She told me that today our path will separate from Darion and Aella's."

"Why would he do that?" Kayra asked immediately.

Lyra puffed, her small hands clenching around my forearm. "I don't know. But he has always been right about everything he said, so we should listen to him again," she said, the last words uttered with great difficulty.

"Well, what about everything he said earlier, about the Last Sunset? Is that no longer valid?" Merwin asked.

"I think we've done our part," Mathias said harshly. "Yesterday in the forest and two weeks ago near Blackstone. Maybe that was his plan for us."

"His plan," Aella repeated sharply. Her bright eyes sparkled with anger, but when they fell upon Lyra, they expressed only sadness.

"Maybe," Merwin began, but was interrupted by a muffled thud.

It was Arya, who rolled off the chair, falling to the floor. She was still asleep, lying on her back, mouth slightly open in a very delicate and soft snoring. If Yermoleth hadn't mentioned she's three hundred years old, I would have guessed she was around twenty.

"I say we wake her up before she injures herself," Merwin suggested.

Then came Yermoleth, appearing from behind the living door separating the room from the stairs leading outside. He walked slowly, hands behind his back, face still burdened. Stopping, his yellow-burning eyes scanned the room. He displayed a smile as his eyes halted on Arya, then said, "Arashkigal, wake up, it's morning."

To everyone's great surprise, the girl woke up, rising confusedly from her slumber, then stretched like a cat and yawned loudly. She stood up, murmuring something with her low, sharp voice, then sat down next to us, leaning on the table with her elbows, face resting in her palms.

"Did you sleep well?" Merwin wanted to know.

The girl nodded but kept silent. She seemed to be struggling to stay awake, as dragons cherish their sleep immensely.

"Young lady, I must admit, I envy your deep sleep and tough skin," Merwin laughed.

"Compliment," clarified Yermoleth when the drakar looked at him questioningly.

Arya smiled friendly, then said, "And I envy your long slender hands too, you can probably snatch the little creatures with ease."

The wizard let out a faint smirk, but managed to maintain his composure, seeing the solemnity on the girl's facc. He said, "My lady, snatching little creatures is my most favorite activity. Sometimes I even dreamed about it."

"Me too!" she exclaimed with a wide smile.

We all managed to hold back our laughter, and that was a miracle in itself.

"Do you happen to have coffee around here?" asked Regihold after clearing his throat. Yenna shot him daggers, as she still feared Yermoleth.

"No, but if it is energy you need, I might have something better," replied the nartingal.

He disappeared for a few moments into his pantry, then returned carrying a tray of food, with several other trays laden with glasses and bottles floating behind him. Everything was made of wood. He poured a greenish liquid with a dense consistency into each glass, then smiled at us expectantly. It didn't look very appealing, but the smell reminded me of green apples, so I was the first to try it out.

"It's good."

"It is," Regihold approved after mustering up his courage to sip, "but a coffee would have been nice."

"Stop bargaining!" scolded Yenna.

Yenna feared that if one asked for something from the demon, the demon would ask for something in return. The food brought by Yermoleth consisted of all kinds of vegetables—some fried, others plain—and fruits.

"No meat," Regihold remarked with disappointment.

"Those like me do not consume the corpses of other beings," Yermoleth replied smugly.

"And be careful not to be deceived by his words," Arya warned Regihold, "for he will be angered even if you eat them while they are still alive."

"That's even worse, Arashkigal!" Yermoleth grumbled.

She pursed her lips but said nothing more, as again, the nartingal raised his forefinger in the air.

The food wasn't bad at all, but it wasn't the kind of food suitable for a long journey, which was exactly what awaited us. The children of the night, of course, didn't have such problems as humans, because they could go for a long time without feeling the need to consume food, and when they did, even a few apples would fill their stomachs. Arya, whose full name was Arashkigal, had been living with Yermoleth for a while, and once every few weeks, she had to leave his den to procure more substantial food.

After the meal, Yermoleth made all the trays float back into the chamber from which he had taken them. He opened his mouth to speak, but Lyra beat him to it, "Can we go outside, in the sun?"

"Whatever you want," Aella said, pinching her cheek.

Yermoleth didn't seem thrilled, but he didn't object either. We all stepped out into the slightly cool morning air, and Yermoleth gestured towards the mushroom stairs leading to the top of the Yerdrasil stump. Lyra seemed unsure, so I carried her up. In the daylight I could see that the top of that stump was perfectly smooth, almost like it had been polished with a saw. It was the middle of summer, and the sky above was blue and clear, with a few white clouds like wisps of smoke scattered to the south. Towards Romir.

After we all settled down, we could see Yermoleth heading towards a dark boulder, almost flat on the surface, about two meters long, nearby. It was the only one without moss growing on it, and I would soon find out why. Yermoleth reached out his hand towards the rock, and a river of flames poured from his palm, lashing it.

"Do your people have a grudge against boulders?" Merwin asked Aella with sarcasm, arching his brow.

Arya stepped out of the house, wearing only a pair of white pants that ended above the knees and a strip of material of the same color wrapped around her chest. The nartingal stopped that stream of flames and turned to face us, approaching briskly, while Arya, without a second thought, sat on a stone. I saw horror on Kayra's face and heard a gasp of amazement coming from Yenna's lips, as that rock was probably burning terribly.

But Arya just let out a satisfied sigh, stretching out on her stomach, with her arms under her head.

"That girl..." Mathias began.

"She's a dragon in human form," Aella explained.

Suddenly, all the eyes fell upon her, but no one dared to utter another word. Yermoleth sat down beside us, sighing.

"I owe you explanations," he said.

I still remember how my heart suddenly raced, even though I didn't understand why. I watched as a strand of blue hair moved on the nartingal's forehead, orchestrated by the cool breath of the mountain, and I thought that I was about to acquire knowledge so valuable that there was a real chance we would be the only human beings to possess it. That thought was both heartening and despairing at the same time.

"Seven thousand years ago, the world was very different. Yerdrasils were common, and people knew of our existence and sought our advice in everything. At least some—the wise ones or those seeking wisdom. There was order and beauty in everything, for it was our duty to maintain it, ordained by the Creator himself, and that's what we did."

"What Creator?" Aella wondered.

"One of the great mysteries, I dare say—the voice that ignited the stars and gave shape to souls. Many heard it during the First Dawn, and among them, seven were chosen to govern this world. Seven nartingals rose, crafting magnificent kingdoms for their people, wonders never seen before or since; they captured the celestial light in glass and the pure ether in stones. Our kingdoms spiraled up around the great Yerdrasils. It was a time of peace, where even dragons and trolls were friends. I do not claim that all was perfect, but I see that the world will never witness such an Age again. The Age of Eternity."

He lowered his head, looking at Arya, who seemed to be asleep, then turned back to me and continued, "The humans had their kingdoms too, of course. There would be much to say about the societies of that time, about their customs, and about how things worked, but if I were to tell you, we would be here for years and years and I still wouldn't finish. Humans were just humans; they multiplied quickly and killed each other just as quickly. Not much has changed for them since then, I dare say, at the risk of upsetting someone."

"It hasn't changed," I agreed.

He frowned, raising his gaze to the sky. The morning sun hid behind a cloud, and nature fell silent for a few moments. The stillness was so deep that I thought I could hear the blades of grass bowing under the cool breeze. When Yermoleth began to speak again, his voice sounded like the sharp wind announcing the storm.

"The beginning of the fall came when our sages noticed that some humans had everything they needed to use magic, but their bodies were incapable of generating it. A flaw in the Creator's perfect plan, some said, and others said it could actually be a test for us. The most powerful of these seven ancient rulers had come up with a plan: to create a wellspring of magic so powerful that any ether-sensitive human in the entire world could use it. They began digging from within each kingdom until they reached a common spot, deep in the flesh of the earth, where they agreed to place the source of that river of ether, the World Soul."

"I don't understand," Merwin told him. "You said the First Gods created the World Soul, and now you say these kings of yours did."

I understood, and judging by the blank look on Aela's face, I could tell she did too. I understood, for I stood before Yohr'Sherrat when he revealed himself in his true form, and I could see that in appearance his face looked like that of a crippled, misshapen nartingal.

"The names of these seven rulers were: Azariel, Sharaleth, Gorgoth, Kir'Zaled, Xeneloth, Yohr'Sherrat and Bhalphomet."

"Burning Hells!" Merwin exclaimed, jumping to his feet. "The first Gods were children of the night!"

Everyone was astonished, their mouths agape and eyes widened in wonder; Everyone except me and Aella. We both remained cold and expressionless, not even stirring.

"I had barely seventy years back then," Yermoleth continued, "and at that age, we were still considered immature and young. I hailed from Arsharis, the kingdom that floated around the seven Yerdrasils of the sea, governed by the mighty Queen Gorgoth. On the day the Soul of the World was to be created, my family and I were supposed to be in Nayr'Lohdra, the kingdom of the One Who Must Be... the kingdom of Bhalphomet. But we encountered problems on the way, which delayed us greatly, ultimately saving our lives." He let out a harsh laugh. "We were heading to Nayr'Lohdra to celebrate thirty-three thousand years since Creation with my mother's family who lived there. My grandmother was one of the originals, like the seven, created by the Creator Himself, not born from others like me. I was very upset that I wouldn't witness the creation of the World Soul. Kings of men from all over the world gathered in our palaces to see with their own eyes this wonder that was about to change the course of history forever. And it did. The seven began to work at noon, each from their own palace, from a different corner of the world, sending their power to that common point deep beneath the earth. When I first felt the ether flowing, we were close, with Nayr'Lodrha looming in the distance."

He threw his head back and sighed in anguish.

"But something was wrong. I could instantly feel that the new ether was not pure, and so did my parents. Probably every adult among our race managed to feel this, but not the children, who jumped into the Great River as soon as they felt it."

Aella let out a surprised gasp, realizing what that meant.

"One second", said Yermoleth, then shuddered, as if a sudden chill had struck him. "That's all it took, no more; just one second and the ancient Nayr'Lodrha, the first city of this world, disappeared in a burst of light. It didn't take long for us to learn that this was the fate of all. All our cities were gone, tens of thousands of souls evaporated in a heartbeat. The Great River was not meant for nartingals, only for humans. Bhalphomet, the crown of Creation, the strongest and purest creature ever made, deceived us all!"

A deep silence fell over us, and all I could hear were the beats of my own heart. Aella once told me that if a nartingal were to sip from the Great River, they would die in an explosion violent enough to destroy Romir. Lyra was pale and her eyes were filled with tears. How could it not have occurred to me that such matters were not proper for her? The girl was not even ten years old. I took her hand, and she looked at me with sorrowful eyes.

"You want to go from here?" I asked her. "We can go gather some cones?"

She shook her head and hugged me tightly.

"Where our kingdoms had stood, the ground was dead and cracked, full of craters. The whole world was in chaos, broken, for almost all the kingdoms of men were left without rulers. At the time we didn't know that Bhalphomet had deceived us, we assumed it had all been a mistake. Almost three hundred years passed before we discovered that the seven were still alive, forming new bodies in the World Soul. It wasn't even us who found out, but a human woman, a witch, how you call them nowadays. She sank too deep into the river and unwillingly woke Bhalphomet. From there to the Age of Shadow was only a matter of a few centuries."

Another long pause followed.

"They rebuilt their cities, but not the glorious edifices of yore, but macabre and maddening structures in which their new servants lived, creatures born of the hatred and insanity that had engulfed the Creation. We managed to find more nartingals, we tried to fight back, but it was all in vain. There was no way of winning a conventional battle against them, for no matter how many shadow creatures we killed, they would always make more. We stormed Arsharis, my home, and killed Gorgoth. But their power was too great, and death only gave her power over the Realm of Eternal Night. A new world to consume."

"Arlieth is there!" I snapped, making Lyra flinch.

"Gorgoth is bound now, both on this world and beyond it," Yermoleth told me. "She has no power, or at least not enough to do harm. After that failed attempt to destroy them, we retreated to a lonely mountain where we created a Sanctuary. We began to organize, write everything down, and devise a plan to rid the world of them for good. Human sorcerers could no longer use magic, for as long as the First Gods were free, they would take over anyone who sipped from the Great River. The first step was to create pal'ethers to filter out the corruption, for we badly needed as many sorcerers as possible. After that, we went around the world looking for survivors and brought them there, gathering an army."

"This sanctuary," Aella interrupted him, "was it the Enclave of Knowledge?"

When Yermoleth nodded, I could see a flame flare in her beautiful glowing eyes. She had always dreamed of finding that legendary place.

"We figured there was only one chance the world could get free of them, and that was to seal them off and block their access to magic. Thus began the War of Shadows, spreading across the centuries. The final battle was an organized effort down to the last detail. Nartingals, humans, dragons, and the last remnant of trolls, fighting side by side in a last desperate struggle. We split up and attacked all of them at once, defeated them and managed to restrain their access to the great river. But Bhalphomet was too powerful."

"If he's as strong as you say, how come I've never heard of him?" Aella wanted to know. "Neither him nor Azariel."

"Neither have I," Merwin admitted.

"You haven't heard of him because of the Great Oblivion, because we succeeded. I'll explain. We were in his city, the new Nayr'Lodrha, and it was very clear that we could not hold out much longer, for we could not bind him as we did with the others, and his champion, Khyalis, was organizing armies to come to his aid. If they had destroyed our blockade, it would only be a matter of time before the First Gods were free again. I lead the final battle against Khyalis, while the human sorcerers began to prepare a perpetual spell, a song meant to lull him to sleep. And they succeeded! Bhalphomet the Destroyer fell, and the last charge of his subjects failed. We have won. But to stay asleep, the humans had to not break the spell for even a second, otherwise he would rise again. And that spell still continues today in a ritual unbroken for millennia."

"This spell," Merwin said with a hoarse voice, "seems somewhat more fragile than a woman's temper."

"It is, but we had no other choice, no other way. After the war ended, we tried to erase the memory of Bhalphomet from people's hearts through another spell, one greater and more complex than anything done before. The Great Oblivion. The last nartingals used the ten most powerful pal'ethers to create the waves, and the spell was so demanding that no one survived. But it worked, for the memory of the One Who Must Be Forgotten was no more; not even the First Gods remembered where his city was.

He laughed bitterly for a few moments.

"Those pal'ethers were powerful enough to alter their minds—to some extent, admittedly—and they were all originally in the possession of the Destroyer. What valuable weapons they would have been if they hadn't been destroyed during the spell. All but one, which became unusable afterwards. If you speak Bhalphomet's name outside a Sanctuary, you will not attract his presence, for unlike the rest, he is forced to sleep. You see, victory against the Shadow was the most ardent desire in the soul of every living being, but when we obtained it, it did not bring us the happiness and peace for which we longed, because from his deep slumber, Bhalphomet whispers, awaiting one who will hear his call. A grim prophecy, but one that will come true. The First Gods will be unleashed again, and the world will plunge into darkness, then they will be destroyed forever. The world must bleed before it heals. My mother foresaw their destruction, vanquished by a daughter of the night who will shatter the very Soul of the World. But there was a problem. There was only one female left from our species, and she wasn't very cooperative. So, I ended up spending six thousand years searching endlessly for a way to create more. And that brings us to you and your sisters."

Aella kept fer face blank, not betraying any shred of emotion. She placed a hand on Lyra's shoulder, pulling her closer and kissing her forehead thoughtfully.

"Why haven't you destroyed the Soul of the World by now?" she asked after a few moments, fer eyes fixed on the canopy of leaves and branches above.

"Because we couldn't find it. But you will."

"Me, or one of my sisters, I suppose."

"A daughter of the night, that's what my mother saw in her dreams, but I saw something more precise: you and Darion standing in front of it."

"*Deoa* was right!" burst out Lyra, receiving a harsh glare from Kayra. The archer's eyes then fell on me, her face tensed.

Yermoleth hadn't bothered to ask who *Deoa* was, and in that moment we all took it as a relief, instead of wondering why.

"How could we find it?" I asked grimly.

"If I knew, we wouldn't be having this conversation, and the First Gods would be no more," Yermoleth laughed. "You will find a way; of that I am certain. But now, enough about all that has happened. Let's talk about what is to come, about where the road will take you."

"Before that, you must tell me where I can find the Library of Aratheea," Aella insisted.

Yermoleth pondered a few seconds, his slender fingers tapping in the trunk beneath us. "I cannot do that, because you need to stay alive, and if I were to tell you, you would go and die," he said with some harshness. "There lies dangerous knowledge, spells powerful enough to rip gates even into the Realm of Eternal Night. After the war, we created a protection system to defend all that knowledge, and... well, we made it too efficient. Not even I could step in there without being torn into pieces. Perhaps, one day, I will tell you, and perhaps one day I will help you sneak in there, but not now."

Unwillingly, I chuckled briefly, wondering what kind of ward they could have created that was strong enough to keep the nartingal out. At first glance, Yermoleth didn't seem like a threat at all—if not for the horns, Lyra might have appeared more intimidating than him. He wasn't particularly tall, had little muscle on his lean body, and even his clothes screamed 'harmless.' Yet, he had fought against the champion of Bhalphomet and won. There's a fair chance that, in those days, he was one of the most powerful beings roaming free in our world.

"You mentioned heading to Shartat," he said.

Arya suddenly raised her head, like a cat sensing when you approach with food. She straightened up, staring at us silently.

"Yes," Aella replied. "We want to free my sisters. Do you think the dragons will allow us?"

"Arashkigal?" Yermoleth asked.

"It depends on Mother's mood," Arya replied. "If she's in a good mood, she'll kill you quickly." She frowned, then continued, "Anyway, she wouldn't allow so many humans to approach the mountain, that's for sure, especially the one who waters from the First Gods' filth. Not alive, anyway."

She was certainly talking about Merwin. He gave her an ugly look, but didn't say anything, and the drakar didn't react in any way. The truth is, even if he said, it wasn't easy to offend Arya, because most of the time she didn't understand insults. This also worked the other way around, as she was excellent at unintentionally offending others.

"What do you suggest we do?" I asked.

"Try to reach the mountain unnoticed," Arya said. She lowered her head on her left shoulder, thoughtful, then continued, "It won't be easy for you, daughter of the night; my kin will sense you. Even I can sense you from here."

"I might have a solution for that," said Yermoleth.

"Even if we managed to get there, we need the key," Aella pointed out. "Do you know anything about it, Arya?"

"It was found not many seasons ago by Mother," the drakar replied, adjusting her position on the stone. "At best, she still has it."

"At best," I repeated. "What's the worst?"

"Beithir," she simply said. I noticed how she curled her fingers into fists after uttering that name.

"The main thing," Yermoleth intervened when he saw me ready to ask who Beithir was, "is to find out whether Rei Khulsedra has the key or not. That would be the easiest. If the key isn't there, we should plan the next steps and start considering the worst."

"Probably," Aella acknowledged. "And Khulsedra is..."

"Mother, and also the *Rei* of the northern dragons, the Queen" the drakar replied.

I scanned the surroundings, shuddering at the mere thought of approaching the dragons with ill intent, especially since, according to legend, they were hoarders. To steal from them might be considered one of the gravest crimes one could commit against these creatures. Merwin seemed detached from our discussions, likely still pondering over Yermoleth's revelations. Should we destroy the World Soul, the First Gods would be vanquished forever, and with them, magic itself. A world devoid of magic—High Heavens!

"If she had the key, where would she keep it?" I asked abruptly.

She swiftly brushed her tongue against her upper lip before replying, "In Saherdrakar—our house in the heart of Shartat."

"There must be something else we can do," I suggested. "Something more rational than sneaking into a dragon's den."

"It's not the den of a dragon," Arya said. "It's the den of all dragons."

"Will you help us?" Aella asked her.

Arya pondered the question for a moment, then shrugged. "How?"

"You're a dragon, can't you sneak in and take the key?" she said.

The drakar opened her mouth in shock. "No," she replied coldly. "I wouldn't like it if someone stole the things I've been lying on, so I can't do it either. If my mother slept on the key, it's hers, and I have no right to take it unless she gives it to me. That's been the law since Methuselah and Tiamat, the first of our kind."

"But maybe you can help them in other ways," Yermoleth suggested.

"I don't want to talk to Mother. She's a coward. They all are, old and with no mind. Worse, with troll-like minds!" Her body trembled with disgust when mentioning the trolls.

"But you don't have to steal anything," Aella said. "Draw the dragons out of the lair, and we'll snatch it. After we free the Daughters of the Night, we'll bring it back to her."

Arya pondered for a few more moments, then nodded. "I'll do it. We leave tonight, then. I'll take you near Shartat, and from there we'll figure out what to do next."

"You'll take us?" I asked. "Meaning we'll fly?"

"I'll fly, and you'll hold onto me."

My mind could barely process the thought that the feeble, flushed-cheeked girl in front of me would soon transform into a giant dragon.

"To fly on the back of a dragon," Merwin said dreamily.

"I'm afraid you can't all go," Yermoleth cautioned. "I have a pal'ether, a blanket that could cover two people and shield them from the eyes and sensitive nose of the dragons. But only one. It would be too risky for more than two of you to go."

"Just as *Deoa* said," Mathias added. Again, Yermoleth pretended not to hear, and none of us paid attention. "It seems that in the end, we'll have to part ways."

"Master Darion?" Yenna asked.

"There's no other way," I told her. "We have to part ways today, but we'll find the village on our own when we return."

"Yenna is coming with us," Regihold told me. "Isn't that so?"

"I'm not sure, I might, if Darion allows me, of course. After all, I don't have a home anymore since we moved in with the Blood Wolves."

"Of course I allow, Heavens! Which way will you go?" I asked them.

"South," Kayra replied. "But how far south, I can't say; we need to discuss and vote."

"It seems our paths finally diverge," Merwin said sadly. "I started to like your company, and no doubt you will miss mine."

I felt Lyra jumping from beside me onto the staircase made of mushrooms below. She descended almost running, then disappeared among the trees. Aella stood up, stepping down from the stump in a few long strides, then headed in the same direction Lyra had fled.

"Drop Lyra at the village," I requested.

"No way!" Kayra shouted.

"And what if she wants to stay?" I asked.

"She's a child, she doesn't know what she wants!"

"If she wants to leave with you, she's free to do so, but if she wants to stay, she'll stay," I said.

"At the risk of having to extract an arrow from my backside, Darion is right," intervened Merwin. "The girl feels better with him and Aella than with us, and besides, months of traveling back and forth aren't suitable for someone her age."

"We can't leave her in a village full of savages, Merwin. We don't even know if he and Aella will ever return."

"Savages!?" Yenna snapped at her.

"We will return, don't you worry" I assured Kayra coldly.

"Why don't you stay with Darion, and that way you can all raise the human cub together?" Arya asked.

"Well..." Merwin began, then fell into thought for a few heartbeats. "That's a brilliant idea, mean lady!" Arya smiled and frowned at the same time. "We can spend the winter in Darion's village."

"I'll leave you to decide, but you'll take her away only if she wants." I stepped down from the stump of the last Yerdrasil, passing by Arya, and followed in the direction Aella went. I found them immediately, sitting embraced on a mound of earth not far from the nartingal's house. I gripped the hilt of my sword as I made my way through the bushes, swearing that I would sooner give my life than allow anything to harm either of them.

Another oath I wouldn't keep.

"Lyra will stay with us," Aella told me in a commanding tone, without even turning to me. "Both of us want that. We'll settle somewhere, build a house, and she'll live with us. I want nothing more."

"Neither do I," I confessed, sitting down beside them. "Would you like that, Lyra?"

Looking back, I realize my decision wasn't based on rational thought; rather, it was shaped by the emotions that had grown within me. I had come to love Lyra dearly, beginning to see her as my own daughter—an odd notion considering I was only twelve years older. Unbeknownst to me, we had become a family, and in such times, that could only be seen as a weakness.

"Yes," she replied, fighting to keep her tears at bay.

"Maybe the others will agree to stay with us," I said, hugging them both.

In our absence, the group unanimously agreed to winter in my village, the village of the Black Lions, and will decide in the spring where to go next. This decision pleased me, and not only because I needed strong allies around me in that grey period, but also because I considered each of them to be my friend. Merwin was to confess to me later that he was going to propose the same thing, being very curious about how my story with the Daughters of the Night would turn out.

It was already midsummer, and I was sure that Alfred's army had already reached Romir, if not even at the foot of the Redat Mountains. I was right; the Frevians were already in Romir, and that day they were set to march north. However, as I would later find out, they had to extend their stay in the capital for another four days due to the sudden disappearance of Princess Elena. A disappearance for which I was accused.

As evening approached, Aella seemed less and less convinced about our departure, and I prayed for her doubts to be voiced, because I wanted nothing less than to reach that mountain. The part that worried me the most was that we were going to rely heavily on Arashkigal, whom I not only didn't know, but also seemed quite adept at giving the impression that you wouldn't want your life to depend on her. I caught her more than once during that day doing strange things, rolling in the grass or starting to dig into the ground with her bare hands, without any warning. Aella watched her, frowning, probably thinking of ways to make our lives as little reliant on the young drake as possible.

Yermoleth brought us the pal'ether, which looked like a simple brown blanket. Pal'ethers were just objects imbued with magic, having various shapes, sizes, and utilities. We covered ourselves with it, and Arya began to laugh, saying that not only could she no longer smell

Aella's scent, but she could barely see us anymore, because the cloak could change its color to blend in with the environment. I decided in my mind, more as a bravado, that the cloak would be more useful to us than any distraction Arya would cause.

"She'll forget about us and run off to chase some mole," Aella told me a few hours before sunset, watching Arya suddenly prowling in the forest.

We spent the rest of the day in Yermoleth's house, but after sundown we all went out, preparing for our departure. I was already tired of farewells and was determined that this would be the last time circumstances would force me away from the people I cared about. No longer was I to be a prisoner of circumstance.

"We'll wait for you in the village," Merwin said, hugging me tightly. "Safe flight to you!"

"Bring me some dragon meat to taste," Regihold asked, embracing both of us.

"Farewell," Mathias said.

Kayra simply nodded silently at first, but then she also came to hug us. "I have something to tell you," she whispered in my ear, while holding me, her words scarcely above a breath.

I hesitated, my entire body tensing before I could muster the courage to ask. "Something that could be a distraction?" I murmured in a whisper. I felt the gentle pressure of her chin on my shoulder as she nodded. "We can talk more when we get back," I declared, pulling away from the embrace that had lingered too long. I couldn't afford to be distracted on Shartat.

"We'll be waiting for you, Master Darion," Yenna told me, but my eyes were still resting on Kayra and Mathias.

Then I saw Arya, her naked body seeming pale, bathed in the bluish moonlight, walking towards us with a feral grace. She was beautiful in an untamed, almost ethereal way. Her clothes, neatly folded, were cradled in her arms. She bent down, gently placing them upon a patch of grass, before turning away from us and taking a few deliberate steps.

Yenna nudged Regihold in the shoulder, seeing that his gaze lingered too much on certain parts of the girl's body. Fortunately, Aella was more forgiving, understanding that I wasn't made of stone.

"The girl is full of surprises," Merwin said. "You're in for quite a ride!"

Arya burst into flames. Her hair ignited first, then her whole body began to glow like the light of a thousand torches under a cloudy sky. The flame grew in intensity, and her silhouette, now just a black shape, became increasingly faint through the wall of light. The entire transformation lasted less than ten seconds, and when the flames subsided, Arashkigal was waiting for us in her real form.

The dragons were arguably the most majestic creatures to have ever lived, as fearsome and beautiful as the ancient Frevian steel. Her horned head was large enough to swallow me whole, and her claws were long and sharp enough to pierce through Regihold's armor without difficulty. I had dreamt of her on the first day after escaping from Romir. With a hint of amusement, I realized that everyone was holding their breath, including Aella.

"I am ready," the drakar spoke with a deep yet beautiful voice.

She stopped in front of us, extending her massive head towards us, and I reached out, stroking her hard, scale-covered skin. The air that came from her nostrils was hot and often accompanied by coils of smoke. She opened her mouth to reveal her fangs, long and sharp like spears, then, with a quick flick of her tongue, she licked her snout. Lyra began to laugh and approached, placing a trembling hand on Arya's head. The red scales shone, showered in the abundant moonlight.

"Please come back quickly," Lyra pleaded suddenly, turning to face me and Aella.

The little one struggled with tears, and looking at Aella's face, she wasn't the only one. The Black Queen knelt, hugging her tightly one last time before climbing onto Arya's back. I kissed her on the top of her head and promised her we would meet again soon.

"Thank you for being with us until now. We wouldn't have made it this far without you," I said to my friends, right before grasping some of the spikes that protruded from the dragon's back, using them as handholds to climb atop her back.

Arya, who had until then been resting on her belly, rose on all fours, flapping her wings a few times. "Haven't you forgotten anything?" she asked.

I instinctively felt for my sword before realizing that the question was actually directed at Yermoleth.

"No," he replied gruffly.

"Old weakling," she scolded him, emitting a guttural grow right after. "You're just delaying the inevitable."

"Don't poke your snout into another's burrow," Yermoleth retorted.

I had no time to dwell on their exchange, for Arya spun around, darting between the trees before taking to the sky with a few mighty beats of her wings. I felt a lump in my throat as my hands gripped the spikes on her back so tightly that I wondered if I might be hurting her. After she managed to climb high enough, she spread her wings like a bat, gliding smoothly. It didn't take long for me to get used to it.

The night was clear, and we were just a reddish shadow slipping through the air, beneath thousands of stars. I started to laugh as Aella, who was sitting behind, embraced me. The next day we would once again test our luck, willingly throwing ourselves into the claws of danger to see if we could escape with our lives once again. But tomorrow was still far away, and I refused to think about it because in those moments, I was happy.

Kidnapped

Excerpt from Elena's journal, dated the thirteenth and sixteenth days of the seventh month, Iureia, in the year six hundred twenty-three after the Conversion:

The morning came with the scent of peach jam and cherry syrup. But not the morning of today, but the morning of the thirteenth, which, I still find it very hard to believe, was three days ago. I woke up with Mother, closely followed by her little dog—and hopefully mine too—Merideth, and two other maids carrying a tray laden with foods and drinks. Maids from her personal suite, as they did not wear the usual clothes of the servants from Romir. Larion had already left. Suppressing the urge to send them away was no simple feat, yet I acquiesced to share breakfast with them.

"Oh, how I would love for those wizards to kill Darion too," Mother said to me. "Your father should return with the entire army, without even having reached the mountains. Ah, Heavens, it would be divine!"

"We both agree on that," I chuckled.

"I'd tease him for the rest of his life," she added dreamily.

"The death of the Black Queen is indeed a joyous tiding," Merideth added, sipping tea.

The woman had been giving me fleeting glances ever since she entered the room. She was probably ready to accept my offer.

"It is, but there are other enemies we must rid ourselves of," mother replied. "Others who, though seem innocent as mice, given enough time, will turn into full-fledged rats and raid the pantry."

She spoke of Jane and the child she carried in her womb, trying to pry information from me, to make me reveal things she already knew from my journal. But I knew she had read it. The fact that she didn't realize I was the one in control brought me a foolish sense of satisfaction.

"Don't worry, mother, one way or another, I intend to rid this place of all the rodents," I replied with a smile cunning enough to imply I was speaking about her, yet sweet enough to seem like I was trying to conceal it.

"Very well, my dear," she chuckled. "Do so!"

She smiled detachedly, looking at me with a certain air of superiority that reminded me that, though I had the upper hand, Mother was the more skilled and experienced player, so any mistake on my part could cost poor Jane her life. But I won't make mistakes. The first step will be to find a hiding place for my journal, one where Mother won't find it.

The breakfast passed without much of a fuss. Mother told me about the ladies of the Derahian court and how easy it was to extract all sorts of gossip from them. She recounted a few unimportant rumors that had been circulating lately, watching my every reaction with the attentiveness of a cat. She sought to gauge how much I already knew from what she told me, and she also hoped to coax a smile from me when presenting certain falsehoods as if they were true. Her aim was to test my finesse in the social machinations of the great houses. I endeavored to seem as gullible as possible, taking care not to make it obvious that my credulity was feigned. I was privy to every murmur at court, knowing already which rumors held weight and which did not. I remained one step ahead of her.

After the meal, her servants who had likely been waiting outside the door were summoned to take the plates, and then Mother and Merideth left. Merideth forgot her short-brimmed blue hat on the bed, so I changed out of my nightshirt and, responding to her indirect invitation, went to bring it to her.

Her chamber was next to Mother's in the guest wing of the palace. I entered without knocking, an act that caused Merideth to leap from her seat at the table and spin to face me, dropping into a hasty curtsey. Chimes. Affixed to the door's interior, clanged with an overwhelming volume.

Extending the hat towards her, I said, "I believe you've left this behind."

"So it seems," she smiled.

I surveyed the room. "These chimes are damn noisy, and I notice you've put them on the windows too, why, if my ask?"

"No, you may not," she retorted with a smirk, her expression then shifting to one of grave solemnity. "They're a precaution—to ensure no one enters the room undetected. Please, take a seat, Princess Elena."

"In my own residence, Merideth, surrounded by palace guards? I understand the need for door chimes, but windows? This room is perched so high above the ground. Who, pray tell, could possibly infiltrate through the window?"

"Not who, but what," she answered, her laughter breaking through as she noticed my puzzled expression. "They're ornamental—simple decorations. You find them loud and strange, yet to me, they're charming. I'm glad you're here, for I am ready to accept your proposal, if it's still on the table."

I settled onto the bed while she drew her chair near, positioning herself before me. The dress she wore was red and fitted snugly to her body. She always wore red. Even the jewelry she wore was adorned with fiery rubies.

I smiled warmly. "Shrewd decision. You'll have no cause for regret, I assure you. Unlike Mother, I understand the value of loyalty and offer more than hollow promises."

She crossed one leg over the other with nonchalance, the slit of her dress revealing almost the entire foot. "That remains to be seen," she mused. "We must devise a more secure method of communication; the queen's suspicions will soon be aroused by our clandestine gatherings."

"I've already thought about that, and I have a solution," I replied. "Be my lover."

She blinked. "Princess Elena..."

"Not for real, silly," I laughed. "I doubt Mother hasn't already told you about my... more unusual tastes, and you're a very attractive person. It wouldn't be hard to convince her that I've taken a fancy to you, and she'd probably make you play along. She'd have you stay close to me and find out things I plan to do, and you'll tell her everything I tell you to say. How does it sound?"

Lost in thought, her hand drifted absentmindedly along her bare leg. Her laughter echoed faintly at the sight of my half agape gaze, prompting me to avert my eyes hastily, a warmth possibly rising to my cheeks. Damn, she is beautiful; it won't be hard to pretend to like her.

"It could work, but it's a higher risk than I'd be comfortable taking," she replied, still smiling.

"I'm taking a risk too. A big one."

She raised her thin, golden brows. "How so?"

I chose my words with care before speaking. "The risk that Mother might have already sent you to me and that all the stories you've told me are just fabrications to make me trust you, when in fact you're only telling me what she wants me to know."

She smiled at me and leaned closer. "How will you know if I'm on your side or playing both ends?"

I leaned to her, mirroring her smile. "Oh, dear Merideth, I may be only eighteen, but I know how to play this game very well. Has Mother told you about

Lord Sigmurd Fraindolle from my father's personal guard?"

"No, Princess," she responded with a little more caution now.

"He thought himself clever too, playing both sides, pretending to inform me about the king's plans when in fact he was only telling me what Mother wanted me to hear. Do you know where he is now?"

"No, Princess." Now her tone was serious.

I smiled, leaning more, and pinning her down with my eyes. "He's enjoying eternal life under the light of Azerad."

"I understand," she replied, then chuckled briefly, somewhat tensed.

"I'm your friend as long as you're my friend, no more. We have a common enemy, and that's the best motivation to be friends, isn't it?"

"Best motivation." She leaned back.

"You'll tell Mother that I suggested you stop by tonight for a glass of wine. She'll encourage you to do so. You'll come to my room, and we'll discuss the next steps together. Does that sit well with you?"

"Yes. We may proceed with your plan, but tonight you'll need to pay me to ensure you're true to your word and that I'm not risking my life for the same amount I'm being paid now."

"With pleasure. I have to ask you one more thing before I leave. Mother is trying to find a way to get rid of Jane and wants to see how capable I would be to defend her, isn't she?"

She halted for a moment, looking at me with trembling eyes beneath her golden crown of hair. She was afraid to tell me such things, but I could almost feel how much she longed to do so. "Yes."

"I'll be waiting for you tonight," I smiled at her.

She nodded, then escorted me to the exit, closing the door behind, the chimes ringing aloud.

Immediately after leaving the witch's room, I went to Beatrice and Jane. I was glad to see that my future husband had taken seriously what I had told him the night before, and two sturdy men, dressed in the Grayfang family uniforms, were stationed in front of the door. They bowed their heads to me and took a few steps aside, making way for me to enter.

Beatrice and Jane were waiting for me on the bed.

"Your Royal Highness," Beatrice began with a vibrant sneer on her face. "Have you finally come to take us out so we can relieve ourselves and sniff some fresh air?"

"Why are there soldiers at our door?" Jane asked.

"For your protection," I told them plainly.

The girl covered her belly protectively, shifting her gaze from my face to the door, then to the bright light pouring in through the open window.

"Shall we go for a walk?" I asked.

Bea nodded almost instantly, jumping off the bed. "I would love to leave this room, but please, check first if our noses are still as wet as they should be. And don't forget the leash."

She hated being restrained with Jane, but I didn't have the nerve to go over why it was important for her to do so again, so I ignored her and turned my attention to Jane.

"I'm not feeling well," Jane said. "I'd like to stay in the room today, if you don't mind."

Normally, I would have dragged her out without discussion, but Father's army was still in front of the city, and I preferred not to take any unnecessary risks.

"If you think that's best for you, you can stay," I said. "Today, Father will leave Romir to hunt ghosts, and things will return to normal. You heard that the Black Queen was killed, didn't you?"

The shocked expressions on both their faces were answer enough.

"And Darion was injured, but the worm managed to crawl to safety," I continued. "Probably the Circle's assassins will crush him before Dad gets there.."

Jane's eyes filled with tears at once. Tears of happiness. "Thank Azerad!" she said gratefully. "Rorik is avenged."

The thought of my brother instantly sent me back to the wizard's tower, where that creature he called 'a god' called out to me with its voice. I brushed off the thought.

Margery.

"Rorik is avenged," I echoed, feeling the hair on my neck rising. "Are you sure you don't want to come outside with us?"

"Not today, thank you very much."

There was no reason to worry about Jane as long as she stayed indoors, with the soldiers stationed at her door. Although I didn't realize it at the time, her refusal to follow us and my reluctance to force her probably saved her life.

Beatrice and I left, stepping into the palace courtyard and settling on a secluded bench. Larion was speaking with that Toader Veleront, and no matter what the boy was saying, my betrothed did not seem pleased at all.

Oswin broke away from a group of soldiers wearing Frevian uniforms and approached us jogging. He wore his chainmail shirt, cinched around his waist with a belt, and a pair of thick wool trousers, entirely unsuitable for such a sweltering day. He bowed deeply, the chainmail clinking softly.

"Are you getting ready to head north?" Beatrice asked before he could speak.

"Yes. We'll leave before sunset." His voice was rough as unchiseled stone.

"I hope you break your leg," Beatrice thundered abruptly.

Her words were, despite appearances, gentle. She didn't yet know what Oswin had done, or what he was planning to do.

"Thank you very much. I hope to receive what you wished for me, and you ten times as much."

Beatrice snorted, and he began to laugh.

"Was it my father's idea to march at night?" I asked.

"Probably," Oswin replied. "But it's a good idea. The road is wide and straight, and the day is too hot."

"Am I to understand that you've come to apologize again?" I asked.

"Apologize? But what did he do?" Bea asked, her brows nearly touching in the middle of her forehead.

"I'll be heading North for who knows how long, and I would have liked for us to part on better terms," he said. "After all, I'd like to think we were friends."

"But what did you do?" my friend insisted.

"He stayed in Romir to help us find Jane, because my father ordered him to find and kill her," I replied in his stead. "That's why he was discussing poisons with the old woman, and that's why he was more than willing to waste his time with us. Isn't that right, Oswin?"

Beatrice made no sound. She hardly even changed her facial expression, as if she hadn't heard.

"But I didn't do it," he emphasized. "I came and told you, didn't I? I couldn't harm the girl, believe me. You believe me, don't you, Beatrice?"

"Stop speaking my name," Beatrice said, her voice barely a whisper.

"So how do you want me to address you?" he asked, trying to lighten the mood. "I have some ideas, but..."

"How could you?" she cut him off, barely concealing her burning anger. "Jane is oddly annoying because her face is so similar to Elena's, yet she barely utters a word. But if you had harmed her, I swear by Azerad, I would have plucked your eyes out with my own nails!"

"I couldn't," he reiterated. "But fine, hate me."

He turned to leave.

"Wait," I urged. "Let's go to an inn and eat. It's not even noon yet, and we have plenty of time before you leave. You can explain everything there, and you'd better rehearse your speech because if I don't like it, you won't return to the palace alive."

"That's fine by me," he smiled in relief, still glancing at Beatrice, who was glaring elsewhere. I quickly went to Larion to inform him of our plans and invite him to join us, but he declined, citing that his day was already too busy with court affairs.

The streets were busier than I would have liked, and the smell of sweat was ingrained in the air just as dust was embedded between the cobblestones. It didn't take long for me to regret not taking a carriage from the palace. I despised the crowds and the disorder. The cursed disorder of the streets of a cursed city; nothing compares to it.

"I forgive you," I said. "But you still have to convince Beatrice."

Beatrice frowned, ready to say something, but then my thread of consciousness was cut. That was the last memory of that day.

The next thing I remembered was fear. A fear unlike anything I had ever experienced, one that nearly shattered my mind and stopped my heart in my chest. A terror so intense, it could kill. I remembered whispers. Names. Bhalphomet!

Fragment of memories.

Beatrice crying in Oswin's arms, Oswin telling her he loves her. People. Clad in white robes, seated in a semicircle in a dark room. They screamed as flames erupted from their eye sockets. Chants. Shadows. A voice—low, guttural, cruel, rumbling through it all. *Darion. He wants to take the key. He must be stopped. Beithir will go. Beithir will stop him.*

I flinched, feeling a sharp pain in my head, and woke up to a dirty dog bent over me, gently licking my face, its tail wagging quickly. I was in a ditch. I didn't scream immediately; it took me a few moments to convince myself I wasn't dreaming, pinching my hip just to be sure. The sun was still shining, and the first thought that came to mind was that I must have slipped and somehow fallen into the ditch.

I screamed.

The dog reared onto its hind legs before turning and vanishing into the bustling streets. I hurried to my feet, my gaze darting around in alarm. My clothes bore the stains of dried blood, drawing looks of revulsion from the passersby. Where were Oswin and Beatrice? What in the world had transpired? As I rose, confusion, anger, and fear washed over me while people gave me a wide berth. Only fragments of memories returned to me—mere fragments.

"What the hell is wrong with you people, can't you see I need help!?" I screamed.

Everyone ignored me, and for a moment I started to wonder if maybe I had died and now I was just a spirit. A man quickly convinced me I was still alive by hurling a few curses in my direction. "Go back to the brothel you escaped from, you piece of shit!" he snarled, spitting at me.

"I am Princess Elena Tarrygold and I'll have your head on a spike for that!" I yelled.

"And how many pieces do I need to spread your legs, Princess?" the man laughed.

I stepped back, climbing out of the ditch and avoiding that disgusting creature of a man who was leering at me. My dress was torn in several places. With horror, I realized I wasn't on the same street where I had been with Oswin and Beatrice just moments ago. Was I even still in Romir? The Grayfang banners, hanging limply on the wall of an old building, confirmed that I was probably in one of the poorer areas of the capital.

"Which way to the royal palace?" I asked a passerby, and she recoiled, avoiding me. "I am Princess Elena," I repeated with a broken voice.

Someone shoved me out of the way with a brutal push, causing me to stumble to a wall.

"Darion is going for the key," I whispered, trying to figure out if those words were a memory, or just a thought.

I groped myself to check that my dress wasn't torn in any of my private areas, then started walking aimlessly, hoping to run into a soldier to lead me back.

"Beithir will stop him," I repeated to myself in confusion. What key? Who was Beithir?

Those men with burning eyes... was that just a figment of my imagination.

"You seem lost," a man blocking my path said.

I tried to sidestep him, but he grabbed my arm and pulled me closer, growling.

"Let go," I snarled, ready to poke my fingers into his eyes.

He released his grip on my arm and took a step back before turning away and walking off briskly.

I turned around to find a tall man dressed in full reddish-golden steel armor standing behind me. He held his simple helmet under his arm, and his appearance suggested he was around forty years old, with red hair and beard, complemented by black eyes. There was a sense of concern evident in his gaze.

"I can take you to a doctor if you need one," he suggested in a gentle voice.

"I am Princess Elena Tarrygold, and I command you to take me to the palace," I said, attempting to keep my voice steady.

"I am Ser Aldric and I serve no Queen, King, or Princess, but only Azerad. But you are in luck, for Azerad commands me to aid the needy."

He shrugged off his heavy cloak, blue as the sea, and draped it over me. I was about to tell him that if he didn't have a lord, he couldn't be a knight, but I quickly decided that an argument wouldn't be the wisest course of action, given my situation.

"Do you mind?" he asked.

I nodded, half-absently due to my thoughts and fear, and he bent down, lifting me in his arms.

"Where are we, Ser Aldric?"

"In Romir, Princess. Your father's and your betrothed's soldiers have been searching for you for three days."

"Three days?! What day of the month is now, Ser?"

"The sixteenth. You disappeared three days ago with Lord Oswin and your handmaiden."

"Oswin and Beatrice..."

"They have not been found yet, as far as I know, but I could be wrong."

"Heavens..."

"Azerad has watched over you. He will watch over them too, if that is his will," the wandering knight said.

I remained silent, trying hard to process what had happened, but no matter how hard I struggled, I couldn't remember anything but those fragments and fear. But fear of what? Bhalphomet? Those whispers. What language was that?

"My child!" I screamed, placing my hand over my abdomen.

A wave of guilt washed over me as I realized I had nearly forgotten about him. He should have been my main priority.

"We will reach the palace as quickly as possible," he assured me, quickening his pace.

I frantically felt my stomach, but I couldn't feel any injury or scar. I needed to see a doctor urgently!

As we approached the palace, the road was increasingly crowded with soldiers. Most of them had the two lions of House Grayfang embroidered on their cloaks, but I saw enough who bore the crown of our house. A commander from Romir, riding a white stallion, cut across our path, giving us a bored glance before grumbling, "Get out of the way, move to the sides. Don't you see we're trying to do our job?"

Idiot. He left before taking another look at us, while Aldric quickened his stride through the huddled soldiers who were 'looking for me.' Only when we reached the gates did the soldiers recognize me, rushing towards us while others ran to alert the doctor.

Aldric passed me to the guards who had carried me to the palace cabinet.

"May the erthals watch over you!" he said to me, smiling warmly before we parted ways. I was still wrapped in his cloak.

The doctor examined me from head to toe, concluding that apart from a few bruises on my arms and legs and some broken fingernails, I had no serious injuries on my body. Nothing of concern and nothing to indicate that the child's condition was in any danger. I ordered him out of the office because I could feel the horror creeping over me and felt I would soon burst into tears. I didn't want anyone present when I cried.

As Larion burst through the door, he discovered me curled up on the examination table, my knees tucked tightly to my chest, whimpering. His appearance mirrored my distress—beard unkempt, hair tousled, and weary eyes shadowed by deep, furrowed lines. He rushed over, the door slamming shut in his wake, and enveloped me in an embrace.

"What…?" he stammered.

"I don't know," I told him amidst sobs. "I don't know anything. I want to go to my room, Larion!"

"We'll go..." He stopped speaking when my hand struck his cheek. I was shaking. "Why?" he asked.

"That knife! That damn knife!" I screamed through my teeth.

"What knife?" he asked in a panic, then followed my gaze to the doctor's instruments on the desk, waiting neatly in order. All except the scalpel and something that looked very much like a fancy spoon. He breathed a sigh of relief, then broke out of the embrace and walked quickly to place them next to the others, as was normal.

"Is that better?" he asked.

"And the books, please, look how he left them... I don't want to see them anymore. Arrange them or burn them!"

"Whatever you wish," he said, hurrying over to the books that were haphazardly placed on a table in the corner of the office.

When he finished, he looked at me with concern, waiting for my verdict. I approved. He returned to me.

"The doctor says you're fine and that you don't remember anything. He also mentioned that your hands look like you've been trying to dig or scratch something."

I lifted my hand, observing the state of my fingers. Despite the doctor's efforts to clean and bandage them, the memory of broken nails and ingrained dirt lingered vividly in my mind.

"I can't remember. I don't know anything. Beatrice was with me! And Oswin too! Hells, make me stop crying!"

"I don't know how," he replied. "Let's go to the room and talk there. Whenever you're ready."

I cried uncontrollably for almost half an hour, maybe more or maybe less, during which Larion just held me in his arms, comforting and kissing me almost incessantly.

He was scared. I hadn't seen him so scared since the Night of the Blood Moon.

After we got to the room, Father visited us immediately, accompanied by Ser Duncan, Oswin's brother. Later, Mother and Merideth came as well. They spoke to me, but I was absent-minded. They kept insisting that I remember what happened, as if I, with my narrow woman's mind, wouldn't have thought to do so. I don't remember much of what they said, I don't remember how they talked to me, and I didn't realize how visibly worried they were. I was too tired to care.

After a while, Larion lost his temper and sent everyone out.

"My wife needs rest, and so do I," he told them. "I haven't slept in three days. Come back tomorrow."

They exchanged a few more words before leaving, but I was too disoriented to understand what they were saying. I felt dizzy, drowsy, and the bruises on my hands had started to sting.

"Thank you," I said after everyone left the room.

"From tomorrow on, you'll only leave the palace if you're with me," he said, without looking at me. He spoke gently, but still authoritatively.

"We need to find Oswin and Beatrice," I told him. "They could be injured... or worse."

"The soldiers are still looking for them. If they're in Romir, we'll find them, but we'll find them ourselves, not you. You're the smartest person I've ever met, Elena, and I think it's as clear to you as it is to me that someone wants to harm us. Someone kidnapped you, for one reason or another, then wiped your memories and let you go."

A shudder skittered down my spine. "The hand of sorcerers no doubt," I replied. "But whose sorcerers? And why?"

"Only one thought comes to mind, and I don't want to voice it," he said, his face stern, filled with pain.

"Darion," I replied in his stead.

"Revenge for Aella's death. Perhaps he believes I'm responsible for it, and Heavens, I wish I were. I wish I had been the one to slit the Black Queen's throat."

"But I was left alive. Why would he do that if the Black Queen is truly dead?"

He pondered, his fingers curling into a fist. "Maybe she isn't, I don't know. Maybe the assassin was mistaken, or maybe it was someone else entirely, not him or his servants. Anyway, one thing's for sure: you won't leave the palace without me and a retinue of guards."

"Fine," I conceded.

"If I had lost you too..." he began but didn't have the strength to finish the sentence. He went to the window, gazing thoughtfully over the streets shining silvery under the moonlight, hoping I wouldn't see the tears in his eyes. "You have assassins in my city, you scoundrel?" he whispered, full of hatred.

"*Darion wasn't to blame this time,*" whispered a part of me inside my mind, but another, much more logical, told me that nothing else would make more sense. Could it be true? But what about the rest of the fragments I remembered?

I recalled my first interactions with the prince, and no matter how much I tried to find a clue about his true intentions, I couldn't see him as anything more than a conceited and infatuated fool. I wish it had been him responsible. Heavens... how I wish.

But the fear... the terror I felt made me believe that greater, darker forces than Darion Grayfang were at play.

The Mountain of Dragons

I was flying beneath the silver sky, burdened by millions of stars painted in a rich palette of colors, ranging from pale white to fiery red, with the cool night breeze blowing in my hair and Aella, holding me in her arms. It was like a dream come true, because for as long as I could remember, I had dreamed of riding a dragon. A foolish dream, anyone would say, for dragons lived in the deepest wilderness and despised humans, but that never stopped me from continuing to wish.

But I couldn't relax. I felt as though I was standing in the middle of a frozen lake, and a multitude of sharp, strident sounds indicated that the ice was cracking beneath me. I had felt this before, and it always preceded bad things, but never with such intensity. Often, I found myself gazing over the rows of trees that from above looked like mere dark spots of color speckled on the mountainous surface, trying to memorize the path. I couldn't understand why, but an inaudible voice screamed in my mind to do so.

After several hours, we began to descend, flying very close to the peaks of the trees. Sometimes we descended so low that I feared the drakar's feet would hit the top of some too-tall fir, but she always avoided them.

"We're getting close," she growled. "Hold tight, I wouldn't want us to be seen."

In front of us stretched the immense silhouette of a mountain, covering half of the night sky, blocking the already faint light of the stars. Flying at low altitudes was much less smooth, as Arashkigal made many abrupt turns, trying to avoid some trees that rose like spears from the midst of the forest. Sometimes she descended very low, gliding gently over a river that probably originated from the heights of that mountain, named Shartat; other times she suddenly soared over certain portions, after which she dived back just as quickly.

It was on this mountain where my ancestor, Vlad Grayfang, sealed the Daughters of the Night, sparking a civil war against his twin brother Jared.

"I wish things were simpler," Aella whispered tensely.

"Would we have still flown on the back of a dragon if things were simpler?" I asked, making her burst out in laughter.

"I guess not."

Arya landed softly on the bank of the river. She bent down to allow us to slide off her back, then waded into the water and began to glow, transforming into a ball of fire that dwindled in intensity with each passing moment, until all that remained was her human body, naked and frail. Thin trails of smoke emanated from her fiery hair. The water sizzled around her body. With delicate steps, she made her way to the shore, her smile broadening and laughter ringing out each time the waist-high currents nudged her off balance. Halting before us, I shrugged off my backpack and presented her with the clothes. She accepted them, setting them carefully upon the earth, then offered me the band of fabric meant to be secured tightly around her torso.

"Tie it," she asked.

I turned to Aella, who nodded without betraying any emotion. Taking the fabric from Arya's outstretched hands, I carefully wrapped it around her torso. Once secured, she donned her attire in silence.

"Thank you for bringing us," I said after we all sat down on the riverbank.

"It was better than waiting for you here," she replied. "It would have taken you at least a week to get here with your short legs."

I exchanged a quick glare with Aella behind Arya's back, both our faces frowned.

"The prison of my sisters is at most five hours away," said Aella, looking at the shape of the mountain ahead, "but that's not where we're going now. Arya, tell us more about the other dragons."

"What exactly?" she asked.

"First of all, how many are there?"

"When I left, there were over two hundred. Many summers and winters have passed since then, but I don't think the number has changed much."

"How sociable are they?" Aella continued.

Arya blinked several times, moistening her lips as a bat fluttered overhead. She shook her head a few times, as if she forced herself to focus. "You'll have to describe to me what 'sociable' means."

"It doesn't matter, your answer is explanatory enough. Tell me more about your lair. How big is it?"

"Very big," Arya responded with a smile, as she slapped her left-hand palm with the forefinger of her right.

Aella tightened her lips. I could see her blue eyes flickering nervously.

"You said that the key is in the place where your mother sleeps," I reminded her before Aella could speak. "Can you give us some details to help us find it?"

"Yes."

We waited for a few moments, but Arya didn't utter a sound, her stare appearing lost over the turbulent and dark waters of the river. Dragons weren't very talkative, and most of the time they took questions too literally, but back then I didn't know such things.

"Well... are you going to tell us?" I added, seeing that she had no intention of responding.

She flinched, like she'd forgotten we were still there. "Yes. Our den is what you would call a city, similar to what you would call a village, but larger. Or so I've heard, as I've avoided getting too close to your settlements, especially the big ones. And when I did venture near, it was only for food, bargaining, or taking treasures—as long as a human hadn't slept on them, of course. Our city was dug inside the mountain by the ancient trolls, those who had not yet accepted the Gift and still possessed more wit than a stone."

She kicked a stone, watching it roll into the river, then giggled.

"Strange 'Gift,'" I commented, but she ignored me.

"Mother lives in the farthest building from the city's entrance," she continued. "It stretches from floor to ceiling and has a red Flame-Stone above the entrance, the only one of that color. Even a blind *rothzhak* would see it."

"A Flame-Stone you said..."

"Yes."

"What is it?" I asked her.

"What?"

I sighed and closed my eyes tightly. "The Flame-Stone, Arya. Can you describe it, please?"

"I feel like what you're asking isn't what you really want to know, *sher venyak*. Do you want to know if I can describe it, or do you want me to describe it?"

"To describe it," I clarified, opening my eyes and staring at her still confused face.

"Your speech is strange," she said, shrugging. "Flame-Stones are crystals that glow. Trolls knew how to make them before they accepted the Gift."

"I must ask," interjected Aella, "what is this 'Gift'?"

"A lie that they were foolish enough to believe, a lie that we would have never believed. The One Who Must Be Forgotten promised them eternal life, and they accepted, but it came with a price. Now the trolls are nothing but simple animals."

I have seen trolls before, and just as Arya said, they were mere animals. I never thought of those creatures that turned to stone in the sunlight as being more than that.

Aella remained silent. Many ominous and unsettling tidings we received in those two days. That Bhalphomet, orchestrator of the Last Sunset, the most powerful among the First Gods, was somewhere in the world, sleeping in his city under the burden of a spell that must not be interrupted. One mistake was enough for the Forgotten One to wake. One mistake and a new Age of Shadows would come. One mistake.

But still, if it had worked for six thousand years, why wouldn't it continue to work?

Someone will hear his whispers, Yermoleth said, someone will be called, will answer, and awaken him. Someone would bring doom. All these will happen, all must happen, that's what the nartingal seemed to believe, and that's what the *Deoa* believed. And we were in the center of it all.

I dragged myself behind Aella, slipping my arms around her as we both fell into silence, our eyes fixed on the blurred reflection of stars in the tranquil water along the riverbank. I immediately noticed the tracks left by Arya's paws when she was still in her dragon form, on the sandy ground by the shore. They were so large. What could I do against such a beast? How could I keep Aella safe? I had to keep her safe.

She raised her hand and placed it over mine, which was still wrapped around her.

"You're very beautiful when you're concerned," I told her.

"I'm not concerned," she almost startled.

"You're very beautiful when you're trying to lie to me." She laughed, then turned and pressed her lips against mine.

Arya was still beside us, silently watching the playful ripple of the river. She made no sound. We could have made love right there beside her, and she wouldn't have noticed, thinking it was another meaningless ritual practiced by us, the small and strange beings without wings or scales, which she neither understood nor desired to.

"I have a bad feeling," Aella whispered to me as she pulled away from the kiss.

"So do I. Worse than in times past."

"*Maybe we should go back,*" I wanted to say, but I swallowed my words. A reddish aura came from beyond the eastern peaks, reddening the few bluish, wispy clouds that shrouded the mountains.

"It will dawn soon," I observed.

Arya stood up. "Follow me, we've lingered enough," she requested, departing ahead.

The dragon's mountain was challenging to traverse on foot. The paths that were very rare in the forested landscape of Shaitahar Canair were almost entirely absent on Shartat, for no creature that did not seek death deliberately would approach the territory of the dragons. Even the birds' chirping was weak and listless, as if they were doing everything possible not to disturb the masters of that mountain. I have never seen any forest so still.

It didn't take long to see the first dragon. Aella sensed it before it appeared. I saw her long ears twitch briefly, like a cat's, then she dropped to the ground and pulled Yermoleth's cloak over her. The dragons could feel her easily, but not me or Arya. Immediately we saw a green shadow pass like lightning overhead, making the branches of the trees rustle fearfully in the wind and send their leaves like spring rain over us. Then, a guttural grow pierced the forest in the distance.

"Heavens..." I shuddered, instinctively reaching for my sword.

Aclla poked her head out from under the cover, her ears pricked up, trying to catch any sign that the beast was returning or that another was nearby. She stood up, her cloak draped over her shoulders, and changed her appearance, resuming her human form. I hadn't seen it since Bragovik.

"It'll be easier for me to hide without horns," she said.

"Can't you shrink?" I was curious.

"Shrink?"

"So I can carry you in my pocket? It would be easier for both of us to hide..."

She started laughing, then pinched my cheek and walked ahead.

"So, no," I told myself.

That dragon that darted overhead seemed much bigger than Arya, probably an adult. I murmured a brief prayer before resuming my journey on their trail. The ballads I grew up with often spoke of a simple method for a human to vanquish a dragon: thrust a long spear into its chest just as it prepares to breathe fire. At that moment, the dragon's armor is said to soften, heated by the intense flames wrapping around its neck and chest. For a moment, I observed Arya, her waist-length red hair undulating with each stride, and contemplated if it may be wise to ask her. I decided not to.

"We'll just go through the forest, as far as the road allows," Arya informed us after a while. "They'll never see us if we walk under the trees, that is, unless they sense Aella. Stupid drakars!"

"It doesn't seem like you're very fond of those of your own kind," I observed.

"I'm not, and I would have preferred not to come back here, but Yermoleth believes that you two will vanquish the Destroyer, so I had to come to make sure you don't die."

"What do you think?" I asked.

She stopped abruptly, causing both of us to bump into her. She made no effort to conceal her doubt as she turned back to us.

"I trust Yermoleth," she finally replied, then resumed walking. "More than the others, anyway, but not completely."

"What did you mean when you asked if he hadn't forgotten something?" Aella asked.

I shared that curiosity. From her expression, it seemed Arya was already perturbed by the '*excess of chattering*'.

"He was supposed to give you a blade of ameterium, like the one your friend dressed in steel carries. It was foretold that... actually, it's not my place to tell you such things; he should tell you when he desires."

She was probably talking about the Bringer of Dawn, the spear embedded in stone that Regihold had stolen from a temple in Verdavir.

"What's the use of an ameterium blade?" Aella asked, and Arya laughed.

"Only with it can you kill an Immortal." The tone in which the drakar spoke indicated that even a child should know such things.

"It was mentioned that the Immortals led the armies of the First Gods during the War of Shadows. What happened to them?"

She raised her shoulders in a subtle shrug. "They probably died."

I burst into laughter and even Aella chuckled. "Immortals," I repeated.

"When the First Gods awaken, they will return too. Yermoleth told me that the last one he can confirm is dead, Drakyr, was killed over a thousand years ago. Besides him, there is only one left. Aveloth, who may already be dead, as she is constantly hunted by a tamed Screamer."

Aella's brows narrowed as she noticed my flinch.

"Aveloth; I've heard that name before," I explained. "When I was attacked by Sihad, I heard one of them mentioning her name. They seemed to fear her. If she really is the Immortal, I suppose she won't be very friendly."

"Of course not!" Arya burst out. "Weren't you paying attention to what I told you?"

I winced, narrowing my eyes. "I was being sarcastic."

"Oh, I'm sorry to hear that," she said uncertainly. "I hope you feel better."

I nodded, but remained silent, contemplating what the implications of the new information might be. The wizards of Sihad had said that if they failed, their Master would send Aveloth. They had failed. Did that mean Aveloth was already in Romir?

"*High Heavens, take care of yourself, brother,*" I prayed.

The scree of that mountain was particularly steep in places, but Arya knew plenty of shortcuts. She had lived there for over three hundred years and proudly claimed to know every bit of it as well as she knew her own scales. The journey had not been an easy one and unfortunately for me, like Aella, the drakar never tired no matter how far we walked.

Before noon we made our first and last stop of that day. Arya told us that we were approaching the edge of the forest and were about to cross an open field. The forest ended in less than a hundred meters, leaving a wide expanse of deeply uneven ground, dotted with bushes, which we had to walk through before reaching the next group of trees. Arya assured us that if we made it through safely, we'd only have a wooded path all the way to the den. I shifted my gaze several times along the line of trees on our side, hoping to find a spot that was close enough to the other, but nothing was in sight. The situation didn't look very good.

Defeated and despondent, I pulled out the last pieces of meat I had just as the roar of a dragon pierced the silence, causing the appetite I thought I had to vanish. I scanned the skies, as much as I could see through the canopy of treetops, but there was no creature in sight. Another roar echoed from the north, and in response other such growls came from the west and south. Aella pulled her cloak over her head, leaving only a small hole to see through.

"Do you sense me?" she asked Arya.

"Barely, and I'm right next to you. Yermoleth did a very great work."

"How do you suggest we pass?" I asked, looking over the barren terrain toward the forest beyond.

"We run," Aella replied. "As fast as we can. Every time we see or hear a dragon, we throw ourselves to the ground, cover ourselves, and hope it doesn't land on us."

I didn't like the plan. It was far too risky, and I could see in her eyes that she felt the same. "Arya, what do you think is the best course of action?" I asked.

"Cross at night," she replied thoughtfully. "In such open terrain and with such light, even an old drakar would spot you." She pondered for a moment, then spat, "Even a troll!"

"Couldn't we find a spot where the forests meet?" I asked. "To avoid crossing openly."

"There is such a place at the base of the mountain," Arya acknowledged. "We can descend, but it's too steep for you to climb on the other side. If you can't grow wings, the only way is through here."

"We'll cross after sunset," Aella decided at last.

"It's still a bold scheme. Everything is dicey, it's like we're bluffing and hoping for the best hand every time. I don't like it, Aella," I voiced my doubts after a while."

A mocking snort escaped Aela's lips.

"If the Daughters of the Night were with me, we could have a rest stop right in the middle of that field without worrying about a thing. We wouldn't have to wait for the right hand, we could simply burn the cards."

The drakar didn't seem interested in our chatter, still eyeing the tree line on the opposite side as if trying to calculate our odds, which, judging by her sour expression, weren't very good. In the event of a fight, would Arya fight on our side? Unlikely, after all, the dragons are her family. If a dragon were to attack us, it would be best to kill Arya with a swift swing before she could transform. I shifted my focus back to her, watching her rosy-cheeked, unblinking frown, and immediately hated myself for the thought.

"I'll try to fall asleep," I told the girls and sat down on the grass, folding my cloak under my head. "I already began to stop thinking straight."

The sleepless night was beginning to take its toll. Aella lay down too, clinging to me, then pulled Yermoleth's cloak over us.

"I should get some sleep too," Arya said, then let out a loud yawn, stretching her slender hands. "I'm going to look for a rock heated by the sun. I'll come back to you at sunset, don't get out of the woods."

"Why would we..." Aella began.

"We won't, thank you," I quickly stepped in.

"I should have gone with her to see where she'll be sleeping," Aella said after Arya disappeared. "I'll go later to look for her."

"Are you worried she'll sleep too much?"

"Aren't you?"

"Well, yes. She sleeps so deep, one may take her for dead," I laughed.

"Let's go after her," Aella requested after a few moments of consideration.

We found her asleep on the edge of a ravine, on a moss-covered, almost flat boulder, and sat down a few feet from her on the least steep piece of ground we saw. I was exhausted and it didn't take long for my body to go numb and my eyelids to go heavy. As I almost dozed off, the memory of Arya rolling off Yermoleth's chair popped back into my mind. I stood up, cursing under my breath.

"Can't sleep?" Aella asked.

"I'm moving Arya from there. I wouldn't want her to shift in her sleep and fall into the chasm. Heavens... how could she have survived three hundred years?"

I lifted her off the cliff and placed her between Aella and me, figuring that this way, whichever way she rolled, we couldn't lose her. Sleeping against a drakar was not an easy thing to do, especially in the middle of summer, as her skin was hot. After a while, I managed to doze off for a few moments but was quickly awakened by Arya, who spun over and hugged me. I pushed her back, but the girl was very insistent and kept moving, either shoving me or Aella.

So it happened that I was able to fall asleep only in the evening, though only for a brief period.

I found myself in Romir, in an old and dark room, with orange curtains covering the windows. In front of me stood a man with a long, gaunt face, who, except for his chestnut and curly hair, bore a striking resemblance to that wizard I had slain, Melchior. He had a black patch over his right eye.

He was seated at a long, rectangular table that stretched across most of the room, with high-backed chairs on either side, and next to him sat a tall, suave, brown-haired woman wearing a simple, pale green dress. She seemed dressed so as not to stand out, but even so, I recognized who she was, despite not having seen her for many years. Queen Lenore.

At the far end of the table, with her head bowed in her lap, sat a young, dark-haired woman wearing a blue dress stained with blood. She appeared to be asleep, or perhaps dead—but then why would she be seated in the chair? Her cheeks were scarlet, looking like she had cried tears of blood. I didn't remember her right away, but eventually I realized she was that maid I'd seen so often following Princess Elena—the one called Beatrice.

I approached, waving my hand in the queen's face, but she couldn't see me; I wasn't there. I circled the room, peering through the corner of the dusty window covered with curtains, but except for my family's banner that was boarded up on some of the buildings, I could see little on the street to indicate where I was.

I flinched as the door opened, creaking recklessly, and a tall blonde woman in an elegant red dress stepped inside. Both the queen and the man with the patch over his eye rose, bowing deeply to the stranger. She ignored them, making her way over to the dead-looking girl, who didn't even seem to be breathing, then kneeled.

Beatrice suddenly tossed her head, twitching, then grinned, baring her bloody teeth. She had no eyes! It looked as if someone had driven a hot iron through her eye sockets. I drew my sword.

"What tidings do you bring, child?" said Beatrice. For every word she mouthed, I could hear a second, much deeper voice repeating it.

"No doubt anymore; it's him we're looking for," answered the woman in red.

"At long last," the girl spoke, and the demonic voice pouring from her flesh echoed the words.

"But still, I fear the princess may be a problem," the woman continued.

The eyeless girl leaned her head back, breathing heavily and muttering unintelligible words. I approached; my sword ready to slice the red woman's head off. Could I harm her?

"I can dispose of that little parasite any time you command," Lenore declares.

"Not yet," mumbled Beatrice, prolonging each word, then suddenly dipped her head with a spasmodic bow.

And the second voice repeated. "Her death will do more harm than good, for now."

Lenore nodded submissively but failed to hide the displeasure on her face. What princess were they talking about? Elena? Why would Lenore want her own daughter dead. I've heard enough. I spun on my toes, swinging my sword down towards the bowed head of the woman in red, but the blade went through her as if made of steam.

That creature in Beatrice's body raised its head, and its hollow, burnt eye sockets stopped looking directly into my eyes, making the air freeze in my lungs.

"Your time will come, Dream Watcher."

All heads turned in my direction, though I don't think any of them could see me. I cut the air again, this time passing through the eyeless girl to no avail.

I fell; the floor became a well of shadows that swallowed me in moments, blanketing me in utter, relentless darkness. I couldn't even see the fingers I was holding in front of my eyes, and I could barely remember them. It was like when I touched the obsidian idol.

"No!" I screamed, kicking my fists and feet in vain through the blackness.

The mist lit up. Two colossal flaming eyes watched me from the realm of shadows, scorching my soul and destroying my sanity with each dying moment. It was trying to break into my mind. Without much thought, I placed my left hand on the cold tip of the sword and pushed as hard as I could.

I jumped out of my sleep, almost screaming in horror.

"Another nightmare?" Aella was awake; she probably hadn't slept at all, and from what I could see, the shadows of the trees hadn't shifted position a bit, meaning I hadn't napped for more than a few moments. I just nodded, then prayed she wouldn't ask me what I'd been dreaming about. Such dreams, if it really was a dream and nothing beyond that, would unsettle her, and that was the worst time to concentrate on anything other than crossing that meadow.

I nodded and turned on my side, restraining my wince when I saw a deep wound in the palm of my left hand. "*Now even dreams can kill me,*" I said to myself with dread. Aella had to know, I was going to tell her, but not then, not that night.

Was that blonde woman Aveloth? As for the other one, the one who looked like Melchior, my intuition told me it was none other than Aethelred, the supposed leader of Sihad. That girl though, the one with the burning eyes—what was she?

Arya woke up just before sunset and didn't react in any way when she saw that she was no longer in the same spot where she had gone to sleep, or that she was now sitting between us, as if that was something that happened to her regularly.

"It'll be dark soon," she remarked, stifling a yawn.

I followed her to the edge of the forest, scanning that land bathed in the last rays of the day. My ancestor, Darriwill, had come to this mountain more than four centuries ago, after fighting a battle against his brother Vlad, in Romir. He had managed to steal the key that could open the dungeon of the Daughters of the Night, but was discovered by the dragons and killed before he reached them. I feared I would end up sharing his fate.

I turned to Aella, whose eyes were darting about, searching for the best route over the crevasse and bush-covered terrain. Though night passage was safer, as the sight of the dragons suffered, it had the same effect on me. I relied almost entirely on her.

"It's quiet," murmured Arya.

She was right. I realized I hadn't heard anything else to indicate the presence of a drakar nearby.

We gathered at the edge of the forest as the light in the sky faded and the darkness began to deepen. All three of us were holding our breath. The silence was complete; it was as if the wind had stopped breathing.

"Now!" Aella ordered.

Arya ran ahead, while Aella and I were close behind her, running hand in hand. We were running like we had never ran before, and I was struggling with the urge to take my eyes off the road to watch the sky for dragons. The terrain was much more rugged than it appeared from the forest, and the gullies that cut across the road at every turn were much deeper. The drakar eased her pace after a while, then stopped completely when she reached the edge of a ravine.

I began to wander my eyes across the dark heavens, but the moon's sickle sank behind the ragged clouds, blinding me even more. Aella pulled my hand to the right, but the drakar grabbed my other hand and pulled me in the opposite direction. The Black Queen's icy eyes fixed on Arya's.

"It's too steep that way," Arashkigal said. "Follow me."

"I'm not leaving myself in your hands, you sleepyhead," Aella whispered through her teeth.

"The road stops there," Arya insists. "You cannot cross."

"Go your way and we'll see you on the other side," Aella retorted.

Arya let go of my hand and stood still for a few moments, watching us descend the slope with small steps, then muttered a few words in her own language and followed us. I could see the black outline of the earth descending to a point, then rising again on the other side of the ravine. The path narrowed, and the darkness became denser because of the edges of the ravine into which we descended.

We almost fell. Arya lunged from behind, placing a hand on each of our shoulders and pulling us back just before we stepped into the pit that was initially hidden by the inclination of the path. It was a dead end.

Aella turned to Arya and whispered, "Lead us."

We turned back and followed the path indicated by Arya. It was longer and more winding, but in less than thirty minutes, we reached the other side of the crevasse.

"I shouldn't have called you sleepyhead," Aella told her. "I'm sorry."

"Why?" wondered Arya. "I like to sleep."

It wasn't the only chasm on that terrain, but the next few times we followed Arya and made it across safely. The road was strenuous and my legs were about to give out, but there was no time for breaks, not there.

After we passed the last pit, we found ourselves not far from the shadow line of the forest on the other side. I almost laughed, thinking I would finally be able to rest my legs.

"Dragon," Aella hissed, pulling me to the ground and placing the cloak over us.

Arya ran a few steps and threw herself into a tall bush, disappearing into the shadows of the thicket. I tucked the edges of the cloak under my toes to prevent it from being blown away by the wind, just as the powerful flaps of wings became audible. Each stronger than the last. It was heading straight for us. Had it seen us? Aella placed her left hand on my cheek, her right anchoring one of the corners in place. The outline of her body was vague in that darkness, but her eyes gleamed intensely.

The dragon was close.

The cloak rustled as the dragon flapped its wings near us, coming to a stop and landing over us, the ground trembling under its massive paws. I thought it would crush us beneath its weight, and it almost did, missing by only a few steps, then took a few long strides before halting. Its muffled roar reverberated in my chest.

"*Don't move,*" Aella spoke in my mind.

I slightly lifted the edge of the cloak, looking up at the drakar that stood not twenty meters from us, sitting on its hind legs, tail wrapped around its body and wings tucked back. It was larger than Arashkigal, with jade-blue scales.

A short while later, another flutter of wings could be heard, and it didn't take long for another dragon to land beside the first. The latter was smaller, but still larger than Arya. Her scales were as red as flames, and on all four horns that adorned her head, she had large golden rings attached.

"*Rei* Khulsedra," the sapphire-scaled beast spoke, then bowed its head. From the voice, I could tell it was male.

The very queen of the dragons of the Redat Mountains stood before us, Arya's mother. She bowed her head too and struck the blue drakar's head forcefully, causing a loud thud that sounded like two boulders colliding.

"Mahrays mat, shaflakir perentra tru sahr stahro luren," replied Khulsedra, then her tail flashed and slapped the other one across the muzzle.

Both dragons burst into such powerful laughter that it made my lungs vibrate, then the blue one rushed to bite her neck, but the queen was quicker, pulling back and slapping him again with her tail. I clenched my teeth when I saw the gigantic blue tail, thicker than a tree trunk, flashing above. The cloak danced because of the wind, almost flying off us. Fortunately, the beasts didn't notice.

Khulsedra lifted her snout towards the sky, and her neck began to burn as if it were metal heated in the forge of blacksmiths. She breathed out a stream of fire that slithered like a shining column towards the stars above, and the blue one followed suit. The two fiery streams illuminated the entire forest before gradually fading. The dragons continued to speak for a while longer, unaware that the three of us were just a few steps away from them, listening. I wouldn't know how to reproduce the words they exchanged, not even now, after fighting so many years side by side with them, but Arya assured me that none of their conversation was of interest to me. Those moments when we stood in their shadow passed like hours, but Aella insisted that it all lasted less than ten minutes.

Khulsedra leaped a few steps in the opposite direction, then soared upward, while I muffled a silent prayer. The other one rose on its hind legs and took flight with a few strong wipes of its wings, the air currents blowing us in the opposite direction, like a ragdoll. In a frantic effort, I groped for any hold through the cloak's fabric, clinging tightly to Aella as we tumbled.

"Heavens..." I breathed out in a hushed tone when we came to rest, perilously close to the maw of a crevasse.

Aella, now beneath me, looked in the direction where the two dragons had disappeared, seeming slightly uneasy, then let out a shuddering gasp. The sleep potion! I quickly got up on my knees, dropping the almost empty backpack from behind and starting to search through the clothes piled there. It was still there, still in one piece. I breathed a sigh of relief. Arya crawled out from under the bush where she had hidden, smiling at us.

"We're good," Aella said, taking my face in her hands and kissing me tenderly.

We retreated under the shelter of the trees, casting a final glance at the now empty sky before plunging deeper into the forest. Another brush with death, and given our destination, it was reasonable to anticipate it wouldn't be the last.

The path was becoming too abrupt and too difficult to navigate at night, so we decided to find a place to rest until dawn.

"Rest?" Arya exclaimed in surprise. "But we slept all day."

"You slept all day," Aella corrected, her calm demeanor masking her emotions.

"We stood guard," I lied. "Was that red-scaled dragon your mother?"

"Yes. *Rei* Khulsedra. Tomorrow, I'll have to face her again, to lure her out of Saherdrakar," Arya said thoughtfully. "You'll have to hurry, I don't know how long I can keep them following me, or if they'll all come. Some may still stay inside, so be careful."

Aella was about to respond, but then she noticed the cut on my left palm. "Is the wound on your hand from earlier?"

"I cut myself on the sword," I lied.

She did not believe, I was sure, for at that age, I could clearly see it in women's eyes—the subtle way of saying: "*you lie.*"

For a heartbeat, I felt as if those burning eyes from my dream flickered among the trees, but I blinked them away. I was losing my mind. Aella noticed my flinch and took my hand, holding it for a moment before letting go with a scowl, without saying anything; another gesture I momentarily disregarded.

We found a patch of flat ground devoid of shrubbery where we settled down quietly. I didn't like our chances of success at all, but there was no point in voicing my thoughts, as I could read the same things on Aella's blank face.

"I can try to break the prison door, although I doubt it would be possible," suggested Aella.

"You'll draw my kindred to you if you do," Arya said.

"It's too dangerous, and we have no guarantee that the door can be destroyed," I told her. "It's also too risky for you to enter the mountain, as you'll have to move with that blanket on you, and it will weigh you down significantly." I paused briefly until I saw Aella squint, then I added with the most authoritative voice I owned, "I'll go alone."

"Have you hit your head?" Aella retorted.

"He's right," Arya reinforced. "Beings like me can sense you very easily, but not him; he's like any other animal. You, however, would be like a Flame-Stone in the deepest darkness."

"I don't need the cloak," I told her before she could say speak. "If the dragons were to return and I were still there, I could find a way to sneak out, but not you; you'd have to stay still with the blanket on your head."

"No. We're going together."

She wasn't about to give up, this stood written all over her beautiful human face, but still, I pressed on. "Don't let emotions control you. You know that's the best solution."

"No." Her calm seemed to be hanging by a thread.

"Aella, we should..."

"No!" she shouted, clenching her fists. "We're going together, or I'll go alone!" Her voice thundered with such force that we instinctively searched the heavens, peering through the openings between the tree branches overhead.

I was right and she knew it just as well as I did. I had been considering this possibility ever since I learned about the dragons' sharp senses regarding ether, but I hoped that Yermoleth would have a better solution than a damn blanket. I had to go in alone; Aella would have been a danger to both of us. I laid my hand over the backpack, feeling the shape of the sleep potion through the thick material, then I smiled at Aella, nodding.

"We'll go in together," I lied.

Saherdrakar

Aella woke me long after the first glimmers of sunlight had reflected off the gray peaks. Arya was hunched over what looked like a campfire, with nothing on but those sleep shorts and that tight strip of cloth around her breasts, gorging herself lustfully on a bird. Raw. Blood dripped between her fingers, onto her rosy chin, and the sound of chewed bones made me swallow hard with disgust. When she noticed that I was awake, she offered me the bird, raising an eyebrow in question. Some feathers were stuck to her fingers, due to the sticky blood running down her forearm to her elbow.

"I'm not hungry, thank you," I said.

"I have one roasted for you," Aella told me.

"In that case, I might try a bit."

That morning, I ate bird meat with the vegetables given to us by Yermoleth, without much appetite. Several times I heard roars and powerful wing beats, reminiscent of thunder, and each time a gap opened up in my stomach, completely cutting my hunger. We were close to the den.

"Let me go alone," I insisted again after finishing eating.

"Darion, hold it! I've already decided. You're clumsy and careless, be thankful you can come with me."

"Fine."

Arya got up and went to a stream that ran a few hundred meters below us, to clean herself of the dried blood.

I raised my eyes to the morning unclouded blue sky, then back at Aella. "Arya said her mother lives in the farthest building from the den's entrance," I said, "with a shiny red stone right above the doorway. Once in her room, we'll split up and look for the key. Describe it to me, please."

"It's as big as my forearm, made of a golden alloy with markings on it; you can't miss it. As Arya would say, even a troll would spot it."

"Alright," I chuckled.

Aella nestled through the tall grass, covering herself with pal'ether, and at once the brown blanket turned green like the grass she was sitting on. I knelt beside her and kissed her forehead.

"What do you think of Arya?" I asked her.

"Hard to say. She seems trustworthy, but she seems very empty. Like she has no interests or doesn't know what her interests are. I wouldn't put my life in her hands, much less yours, but right now we have no choice but to rely on her."

I walked over to her and took her in my arms.

"This morning I thought of Lyra," she told me in a voice weaker than a gust of wind. "What life would be like if... when we come back. If she would like to live with us, if we would be fit to look after her. I feel like I shouldn't even dream of such things, like they'll never happen."

"I've also become afraid of dreaming," I admitted. "But after today, after we leave this cursed mountain, things will settle down. We're nearing the end of the journey."

Arya returned shortly and retrieved her neatly packed clothes from the trunk of a fallen tree. She always liked to pack her clothes with extreme, extreme care.

"Are you ready?" she asked us.

I hardened my heart, and tried to steady my heartbeats as I casually made my way to the backpack. I couldn't afford to appear anxious, or else Aella would sense it and grow suspicious.

"Just need to have a little more water," I told them.

I said that because Aella would hear the liquid flowing, and I feared she might turn her head. She sat with her back to me, covered in Yermoleth's cloak. I pulled out a linen shirt, then retrieved the sleep potion and poured as quickly as I could over the fabric.

My blood froze as I heard Aella sniffing the air. I was running out of time. I let the potion fall and lunged at her before she could turn, pinning her from behind and pushing the potion-soaked shirt in her face. She began to struggle and whimper, digging her nails deep into my forearm, but my grip was far too strong.

"I can't put you in such danger," I whispered as I felt her last bit of strength leaving her. "I'm so sorry."

I laid her body carefully on the grass, kissed her forehead once more, then covered her with the cloak. She was going to be safe, I kept telling myself, for the place was too thick with trees for a dragon to land there. Even so, I hated myself for what I had to do.

"Let's go," I told Arya, who remained completely passive and watched.

"You made the right decision," she encouraged me, each word framed with unwavering certainty.

I nodded but didn't respond. I wasn't in the mood for conversation. Despite her stature, the girl was swift, and even during the day, it was hard for me to keep up with her. The mountainside was very steep, and in certain sections, we had to crawl on all fours, clinging to moss-covered boulders and bending branches.

The forest ended on a plateau in front of a massive rock wall that rose almost vertically, blocking half the sky. In that wall was the mouth of a cave so massive, that at first, I thought it was a gorge. From its depths, two dragons took flight, their silhouettes gliding above the treetops before vanishing into the valley beyond. A weariness overcame me, a deep exhaustion that I couldn't attribute solely to Aella's absence or my proximity to the potion. Perhaps it was a mixture of both.

I looked around at the ridges and forests stretching in all directions, as far as the eye could see, and I was struck by an even stronger sense of despair. "*High Heavens... I am so far from home.*" I considered that I might die that day, far away from where I grew up and the people I had lived with for the past twenty years, and probably no one would ever know my fate.

"There's the entrance," Arya told me. "I'll go inside and try to get the dragons to follow me. When you see them coming out, run as fast as you can."

"I will."

"I hope you're fast, Darion, very fast, like a deer every time the wind blows from me to it. If the dragons come back, there's plenty of places you can hide, think like a mole, *sher venyak*; those damn beings always find a way to get away from me. And keep your eyes peeled, there may be more left in the den."

"How hard will it be for me to reach the building where your mother lives? How far will I have to run?"

"Quite a distance, but you'll see it as soon as you enter. There are steps you'll have to climb and steps you'll have to descend. I hope you have strength in your arms." Her hands felt my arms under the shirt material. "You should be able to handle it," she concluded.

I frowned. "Strength in my arms to climb and descend stairs?"

"They're big," Arya said. "There are also steps for small creatures like yourself, but not towards my mother's room. Stop thinking about Aella, focus on what you have to do, like when you're foraging for prey, otherwise you'll shorten your already short life even more."

"I know. How will you lure the dragons out?"

"Simple. I'll tell them I saw trolls heading up the mountain."

I parted my lips, pausing as I gathered my thoughts. Was that truly the extent of her scheme? Merely a simple lie? "Do you think it'll work?" I finally asked.

"Of course it will work! Only that I mentioned it, and I feel like going to check if it's true."

"Alright then," I laughed nervously. "Go get changed." She began to undress. "Or you can do it here," I added, shrugging.

"I will return," I promised Aella in a whisper.

Arya emerged naked from the cover of the trees, and right before my eyes, her reddish hair began to blaze, then her body began to glow, and after a burst of light, an immense red dragon remained in the place where she had been. She rose with a few flaps of her wings and disappeared into the heart of the rock, immediately swallowed by darkness as if plunging into an ocean.

"As soon as I see the dragons coming out of the cave, I will run with my own cloak pulled over my head," I said aloud, imagining Aella was beside me. "It's not magical like yours, but it's gray enough to hope that from above I'll be mistaken for a stone. If you were to come with me, we would have to move very slowly, and you would have to always stay close to the ground. We'd lose too much time."

Arashkigal's plan worked, because before long I saw the dragons swarming out of the den like a flock of bats. The one flying ahead was Arya, followed closely by the *Rei*, then dozens and dozens of them, dragons of all colors and sizes.

I patted my sword again and said a quiet prayer, unsure which of the two I was relying on more, then started sprinting. The path was almost flat to the cave entrance, strewn in places with huge boulders. I ran as fast as I could, feeling my neck too tense to look around, keeping only the entrance in front of my eyes.

I was nearly three hundred meters away when I heard a roar coming from inside, followed shortly by the shape of a beast with green scales, soaring from within with wings spread wide. I threw myself on my stomach next to a boulder three times my height, praying. It seemed that I relied more on prayers, for in such circumstances I felt them more useful than the sword. "*Azerad listened,*" I thought as the dragon had not seen me, gliding like a ship on the waves of wind. I didn't wait, just jumped off the ground and kept running. I was thankful for the little respite, for my chest was already burning.

I reached the base of that cliff wall and turned to scan the sky. I could see dragons flying in circles in places over the woods, like birds of prey. A wide, road-like path climbed seemingly carved into the rock to the entrance. It was very sheer, and after running for a few minutes I began to feel like every step I took might be my last. Beams of light flickered on and off in front of my eyes, and my legs trembled, but I didn't stop until I was a few steps from the opening.

Just then, when I was ten steps from the entrance, two more dragons soared out. I threw myself to the ground, struggling to calm my breathing, but my body was fighting hard not to faint, forcing me to take as big a gulp of air as I could, as often as I could. The beasts could not see me, for I was almost pressed against the rocky wall, and they flew swiftly away without looking around. I forced myself up, but my right leg gave way, causing me to fall to one side due to severe exhaustion. I clung to the side of the mountain and waited a few moments before I managed to hold my breath. I had to keep going. I had to get back to Aella.

I forced myself to rise and continued at a running pace. The mouth of the cave yawned into a tunnel that stretched about fifty steps ahead, wide and tall enough to accommodate a castle. Inside, I could see faint points of light—probably the Flame-Stones—and faintly outlined shapes carved into the rocky walls. I ran until the tunnel opened into a colossal cavern.

It was so high that I wondered if clouds might form beneath the vastness of that gallery. Columns of rock rose in several places, spanning from floor to ceiling. The buildings seemed to have been cut directly into the mountain, polished and smoothed in such a way that they no longer seemed to be made of stone. There were houses, fit for dragons, yet they were indeed houses, adorned with all sorts of ores and minerals in vibrant colors. Some had reddish streaks, others yellow, others had walls in different shades of blue, or green, or silver, and the Flame-Stones shone everywhere, including on the ceiling and columns. Such a stone was slightly bigger than a full-grown human.

But of all the pieces that littered the chamber, one stood out, being larger and more radiant than all the others. It was red like freshly forged iron, while the others were white, yellow, or orange. Arya was right, it wasn't hard to see. There, the queen's chamber awaited me. And the key.

I almost lost all hope seeing how far the place I needed to reach was from where I stood, and for a moment I even began to consider whether it would be better to turn back and try something else. But then I remember the fight, the assassin, the cut. The soldiers who led us out of Romir to kill her. Alfred and his army that was about to massacre thousands of people living in Redat. I needed the Daughters of the Night.

I leaped from the vast corridor that served as the gateway to the city, scanning my new environment for any lingering dragons, yet none were in sight. Flanking me on both sides stood rows of buildings. They had no doors, only openings like archways that led directly inside. Ahead were steps descending towards the center of Saherdrakar, each at least two meters high. Fortunately, to the left and right of those massive steps, there were some normal ones, just right for humans.

I continued to run, leaping over two or three steps at a time, holding my breath each time I passed by the entrance of a building, afraid that I might see the hungry head of a dragon peering at me from inside. In the wall alongside which I was running, I could see grooves large enough to hide in if necessary. It was a pattern that repeated consistently on all the buildings along that avenue, down to the circular center of the city, and from there it repeated on the buildings along the street that ascended to Khulsedra's den. That was good because I could sneak even if the dragons returned, running from one such crevice to another.

The statue of a dragon decorated the center, where the streets that cut through the rows of buildings converged. I could have crossed that portion by running in a straight line, it would have been the fastest option, but I didn't feel safe to remain exposed in that place, so I walked while sticking to the walls of the buildings scattered along that circular square. Sometimes the wall disappeared, opening into wide streets of almost twenty meters, if not more. The city was marvelous, and I found myself wishing I could stroll through it freely, without fearing for my life.

I tried to be as silent as possible, stepping with my heel and arching my foot in such a way as to make as little noise as possible. Everything was quiet in Saherdrakar, so no matter how quietly I tried to move, it wasn't of much use. In a quiet room, even a mouse's step was noisy.

I began to climb on the broad, inclined avenue leading towards the queen's chamber, which was much more difficult than descending. Every time I felt like I was losing my breath, I took refuge in a crevice in the walls, where I counted to a hundred, then emerged and continued to run. I didn't know if those shapes had a role beyond aesthetics, but I was grateful to the ancient trolls who decided to put them there. Several times I turned towards the city entrance, looking at the beams of light streaming inside, stretching to the center, fearing that soon I would see the dragons returning.

"*Darion, you idiot!*" Larion would say if he knew what I was doing, while Arlieth would shake her head and murmur, "*My foolish prince.*" The thought of them and the days that would never return brought a smile to my lips and tears to my eyes. I stopped, retreating into another narrow slit in the wall to wipe my moist eyes. I had probably been there for an hour, and I was about to waste another hour trying to get out. Things didn't look good at all, and Aella could wake up at any moment.

I took a deep breath, trying to clear my mind, and continued to climb until I reached the top of those stairs flanking the bigger stairs that surrounded the avenue. The Flame-Stone marking the entrance to the queen's lair gleamed in front of me. I almost tasted the sweet flavor of victory. Too quickly, though.

A stiff sound of something heavy being dragged across the floor came from my right, making me turn with a quick spin and reach for the sword. A dragon! It lay curled up like a cat, covered with its long wings, while its tail lazily waved, sweeping the floor. It was gray and at first glance seemed to be very old. I froze. There were at least thirty more meters to run for the great stairs leading to the queen's chamber. I couldn't turn back, not when I was that close.

I walked, as running would have been too noisy, keeping my eyes pinned to the dragon. I didn't know if it was asleep and fluttering its tail from its slumber, or if it was trying to fall asleep, but either way, I had no intention of disturbing it. With each step, I repeated in my mind all the prayers I had heard at the Temple, hoping that the eyes of Azerad could see me even in the heart of that far-away mountain.

I reached the base of the stairs, which, as Arya said, were not made for humans. I had to gather momentum and jump, hitting my foot against the wall of each step, and trying to throw myself as high as I could. My fingers barely reached beyond the edge, and it took all the strength I had left to pull myself up. There were fifteen such steps. After each one, I turned back to the creature that still hadn't heard me, then to the mouth of the cave, and when I made sure no dragon was in sight, I gathered momentum and climbed another one. When I reached the top, I could barely lift my arms. It was going to be much easier to go down.

The wall in which the queen's building was carved was so smooth that it gleamed, covered with glimmers of gold and bronze. Dragons with rubies for eyes were sculpted on the left and right sides of the entrance, like two sentinels. Two rows of columns adorned the last stretch of flat ground leading to the entrance of *Rei* Khulsedra's chamber.

The sleeping dragon suddenly lifted its head, sniffing the air noisily. I ran on tiptoes, not looking back, and plunged into the queen's chamber, sticking to the inner wall, eyes closed and ears pricked listening. The dragon growled. I could feel it rising on all four. I had to hide. The queen's room was huge and looked very much like the warehouse of a merchant who didn't discriminate in the goods he sold. There were piles of objects, clothes, paintings, furniture, statues, books, boulders, weapons, gold, pieces of armour, a cart... she had everything there. It goes without saying that dragons liked to hoard things.

I hid behind a tower made entirely of books, some so old that the writing on the cover or spine was long since legible, and listened with my heart in my throat as the dragon's footsteps grew closer.

The drakar stopped in front of the chamber, continuing to sniff like a hound. It hissed, uttering a string of mumbled words, then sniffed again. I needed to find the key and flee from there; if it sensed me, it meant the others could too when they return.

"Khyalis!" the beast roared, halting just short of crossing the threshold. The name momentarily paralyzed me, and before my eyes, a vision of a woman appeared. She wore tattered black attire and a white mask streaked with red lines, resembling cuts freshly made in flesh. The vision was so brief that when it passed, I wondered if I had really seen anything.

Returning to my senses, I turned my focus back on the beast, realizing it was a male drakar.

A wisp of smoke carried by the dragon's breath snuck into the room. I slipped through the piles of things, some so large that they would have buried me alive if they had toppled over. There was an order in all that disorder; the armors, swords, and metallic objects were all piled up in one corner. There had to be the key there, I assumed.

"I can smell you, serpent!" growled the dragon in the common tongue, stepping with one foot into the room.

Some weapons and armors were old, rusty, but others seemed to be fairly recent additions to the queen's collection. I stepped carefully among the jewels, weapons, and breastplates on the ground, searching for the key. The dragon couldn't see me because of the piles of things between us, but I could see his shadow cast on the floor, through the colossal doorway. Why did he think I was Khyalis?

It stepped again, inching even closer. I gave up searching for the key, hoping instead to find a spear long and sturdy enough to thrust into his throat. Perhaps I could strike him hard enough to gain an advantage. But Heavens! I was in the dream of any warrior, mountains upon mountains of weapons, and I couldn't find any sturdy spear. The dragon approached, his guttural growls resonating within me, compelling me to draw my sword with trembling hands.

"My name is Darion Grayfang!" I shouted. I had to talk to him. I doubted I had any chance to escape from there, and I was sure that if I waited any longer, he would discover me.

"Grayfang, indeed," his words seemed as carved from stone. "I've heard that's what you call yourselves now, you *abominations*! For many years, we have tried to wipe those like you off the face of this world, and here you are coming alone into our lair like a dumb sheep."

"I came for the key that rightfully belongs to my family," I said, stepping out from behind a pile.

The dragon laughed mockingly, bringing his head closer to mine. Now that I could see him up close, it was clear that he was old. I could see it in the worn features of his face, in the tired yet threatening gaze, and in the faded scales. Once he had been as red as Arashkigal or the queen, but his steel-hard skin had lost its shine. I wondered what old meant for these creatures. Nine thousand years? Ten? Perhaps more?

"The key," he said with bitterness. "You, a Cursed One, have come to steal from us! The beats of your tainted heart disgust me, die!

I leaped back just as his massive jaws snapped through the air in front of me, then I struck him with the Dawn's Heart over his muzzle, to no effect; his skin was thicker than any armor I've seen. He was big and slow, and fortunately for me, he wasn't going to breathe fire, risking destroying the queen's belongings. I ran for the exit, through the piles of 'treasures,' as the dragon's head snaked above, searching for me through that labyrinth of everything.

Clutching a hefty shield of some lightweight metal, I sprinted toward the exit with all my might. As I neared the threshold, the dragon cast aside a heap of timber and unleashed a torrent of fire—nothing lay ahead that could ignite. I huddled behind the shield, the force of the inferno staggering me. Fire roared in every direction, the shield's iron grip searing my flesh, eliciting a cry of pain, yet it withstood the assault. As the flames abated, I dropped the shield with a resounding clang and bolted outside, weaving between the pillars to reach the grand staircase I needed to descend. The dragon gave chase, spewing another fiery gale, but I evaded it, taking refuge behind a stout column.

"How long do you intend to play this game?" he asked as the flames dwindled.

"Until you tire and fall asleep," I admitted in a whisper, flexing my fingers that had grown numb. A crimson mark etched across both my palms, a lasting imprint from the shield's handle seared into my flesh by the relentless heat. "I don't know what you think of me, but you're wrong!" I shouted afterward.

"Me?! To be wrong?!"

"You don't know me."

He slipped his head between the columns, forcing me to step back onto the path, grinning as he realized I had nowhere to run. The queen's chamber lay behind him, and the key was probably hidden somewhere among the heaps of objects. I had failed.

"I know the blood flowing through your veins better than I know the blood of my own progeny. Blood doesn't change! I have made killing those like you the purpose of my life. Thank you for willingly coming here to offer one last pleasure to an old drakar. Now burn!"

He opened his large mouth with a low roar, ready to incinerate me, when I felt the air vibrate and a blinding explosion of light erupted between us, so powerful that everything I had seen before was engulfed in whiteness.

"*Turn around and run!*" Aella screamed in my mind. The dragon howled furiously, and I felt the ground tremble as he collapsed backward, just as blinded and surprised by Aella's intervention as I was.

I tried to run in the direction where I remembered the stairs to be, hearing the sounds of the dragon thrashing behind. Though I couldn't see her, Aella was there, in the middle of the city, next to the dragon statue. More explosions erupted behind, loud and bright, deepening the shadows that my eyes struggled to discern.

In the center of the city, before the towering dragon statue, stood Aella. The old drakar screamed in fury, crashing into the columns with thunderous booms, likely startled by the cascade of explosions, groaning words in his tongue. I later learned from Aella that she hadn't intended to kill him but merely to disorient him.

I was still partially blind, but as I approached the first step, I noticed the drop and managed to stop just in time. Aella lifted me into the air using the ether and pulled me toward her with great haste. The loud flapping of wings signaled that the dragon was rising from the ground, gliding after me with a singular desire to finish what he started and end my life, like an eagle pursuing a swallow.

Whenever my nephews hear that story, they look at me in awe, wishing they could experience such thrills themselves. I tell them each time that I would trade that life without hesitation for the life they live now. They refuse to believe that these stories are better read than lived, dismissing my desire for a peaceful life as a result of my old age.

I turned mid-air to face him and screamed as the air ignited with light, the sound so deafening that everything went white, leaving only a high-pitched screech in my ears. The dragon fell from that last explosion, slamming into the wall of a tall building before crashing onto the stairs below. It took a few moments for the whiteness to fade enough for me to make out faint shapes in my vision, and a few more before I could feel the ground beneath my feet again.

I was trembling. Aella hugged me tightly, but I could barely see her. Although I could tell she was trying to say something, I couldn't hear her over the ringing in my ears.

"I'm sorry," I tried to whisper, but as Aella was to tell me later, I shouted it out loud.

I could see the dark shape of the dragon sprawled on the city steps, and for a moment I thought he was dead. He whipped the air with his tail a few times before rising on all four and shaking his head, then turned towards us, fuming with fury.

"We need to get out of here," I urged Aella.

She didn't react, calmly watching the beast slowly descending to us, like a cat preparing to pounce on its prey. I grabbed her hand and tried to pull her in the opposite direction, but I immediately understood why she didn't budge. The dragons were coming back! We were trapped.

"You shouldn't have come," I said.

"You're a big idiot," she replied in a calm voice.

So many dragons. Their forms were barely distinguishable to my still blurred eyes, yet that was of no consequence, for their presence was unmistakable. Dozens upon dozens of them, their roars reverberating through the city.

"Do you have a plan?" I asked her.

The ringing noise had almost disappeared, but my vision had not fully returned, although I was seeing better with each passing moment.

"We negotiate," she stated nonchalantly. "Should that fail, I'm left with no alternative but to kill them."

"There are over a hundred."

"I know," she replied with an icy voice. "I won't be pleased to take so many lives."

Blood Sin

Although Aella seemed confident, I for one was almost certain that we wouldn't stand a chance of escaping alive. The dragons had begun to circle us, soaring overhead like hawks.

"Back!" growled the old one, who was now very close, poised to charge. "I'll be the one to kill them!"

It lasted only a split second. The dragon leapt. Aella raised her hand, ready to strike, ready to kill. Arya flew like the wind past us, and slammed the dragon full force, then they rolled together to the edge of that city square, hitting the bottom of the stairs, in a tangle of scales and fangs. The young ruby dragon loomed over the beast, growling like a feral dog poised to tear out its throat.

"What is happening here?" thundered Queen Khulsedra, annoyed, landing between us and the two dragons fighting.

She turned her head toward us, the rings on her horns catching the light of the Flame Stones and sparkling brightly.

"A daughter of the night and a..." she paused, sniffing the air, and her furious expression became overt. "Cursed One! Grayfang!" She pronounced the name like a curse.

"We came for the key," Aella said calmly.

"All you will receive is death!" Khulsedra screamed, furiously stomping the ground.

With a flap of her wings, Arashkigal launched herself into the air, landing above us like a mother protecting her cubs. She arched her back and folded her wings, ready to pounce on the queen herself. More and more dragons encircled us, prepared for battle, ready to tear us apart.

"Yermoleth has spoken! They are the ones who will bring back the sun!" declared Arya.

"No wonder Yermoleth would say such things about him, given the blood that runs through his veins. His kind are better off dead, and so is the nartingal that hides beneath the Yerdrasil."

Their hatred for me was already filling my glass, yet there was nothing I could do against a dragon. "Arika was a murderer, but I am not guilty of her crimes," I said calmly, exhaling a deep sigh.

"Arika?" Khulsedra wondered. "Is that another name of the Temptress?"

"What are you trying to say?" I asked almost voicelessly.

Even Aella seemed shocked, and for a moment Arya lost her composure, lowering her head slightly and looking at me with uncertainty evident on her face. The Dragon Queen seemed to believe that I was the descendent of Khyalis, the woman who awakened the One Who Must Be Forgotten and commanded his armies into the War of Shadows.

"You didn't know, did you, daughter of mine, about the evil you bring among us?"

"I..." started Arya, then yelled, "Darion is our ally! He is not the Temptress, and I won't allow you to harm him for the things he didn't do."

"He is not the Temptress," Khulsedra repeated. "Yet, I sense her presence emanating from within him, the same stench she had, the same Malice. It's as if I see her now, daughter of mine, walking arrogantly on our lands, killing mercilessly everything in her path. She killed my offspring, the first brother of yours, while looking into my eyes, grinning. She knew I couldn't do anything to stop her."

She took a step forward as Arya's deep growl reverberated through my body, making me shudder. She seemed poised to charge at her Rei, her own mother, just to keep us safe. I could catch glimpses of the expressions on the reptilian faces surrounding us; they were filled with doubt and indecision. Yermoleth's words, delivered through Arya's lips, weighed heavily on them.

"Do you dare to oppose me, daughter of mine?" the queen asked. The dragons around inched closer.

"If that's what it takes for those who will bring the sun to live, then yes," responded Arashkigal.

Rei Khulsedra lowered her back, preparing to pounce on her own daughter who refused to back off. I regretted how wrong I had judged Arya, thinking she would betray us at the first opportunity.

"We come as guests to your house, great *Rei*, and you attack us?" Aella thundered suddenly. "Come a little closer, I beg you, and I will sip from the Great River. You won't have to worry about my husband's blood anymore, for it will disappear, along with this 'city of yours' and these 'subjects of yours.'"

"You wouldn't dare," Queen Khulsedra said with her voice just above a thought.

The atmosphere tensed to a standstill as Aella murmured, "There is one way to find out." At her words, several dragons recoiled, their lethal fangs bared. "Attack me!" she challenged.

"Perhaps we should listen to her, *Rei* of mine," another dragon spoke with a calm voice, articulating each word perfectly, just like humans spoke the common tongue. It was the dragon with blue scales that we had seen yesterday.

"I didn't expect to hear troll words from your mouth, Volthrax," Khulsedra snarled, keeping her cold gaze fixed on Aella's eyes.

"Perhaps you're the one speaking troll words, Mother," Arashkigal intervened.

"How many of those here have witnessed the War of Shadows?" the queen shouted. Less than thirty dragons growled in response, including the one named Volthrax.

"If you had seen that world and the horrors the Enemies were capable of, the grace and majesty of Tiamat, the mother of all dragons, and the abomination she became. If you had seen the Temptress summoning the storm and bringing down the dragons from the sky like mere birds, you would understand. But few of those from back then still breathe. You, daughter of mine, are young and unripe."

"And you are far too ripe," Arya retorted, trails of smoke escaping her lips as she talked.

"I was there, my Queen, and I saw all that you speak of," Volthrax said in a neutral tone. "It was you and I who attacked Tiamat and Darkyr through the hordes of traitors, you and I who struck her down before she reached our forces. That's why I would think twice before killing those who could be our only escape from such a future. Even if the one who said this is Yermoleth."

The queen shot him a deadly glare before abruptly turning her attention back to Arya, who had nearly seized the opportunity to attack her. With a resigned sigh, Volthrax used his tail to slap Arya across the face.

"Arashkigal, stay put!" he grunted.

Khulsedra straightened her back, stepping out of the fighting stance. Her daughter followed suit.

"Very well, Volthrax," the queen said. "I will heed your advice, even though I did not ask for it and I bear no need of it." She turned back to me and Aella, her large, yellow-red eyes piercing us. "Speak, and perhaps I will let you leave with your lives."

Arya nestled protectively around us, arching her thick tail behind and gently pushing it beneath our knees, prompting both of us to sit on it like a makeshift chair.

"As I was saying," Aella spoke, "we came for the key. My sisters have been imprisoned for too long."

"Was the sun in the sky when you sneaked your way here like two thieves?" Khulsedra wanted to know.

Aella pondered for a moment, before demanding, "Speak your mind, lizard!"

"The girls will remain imprisoned until the Last Sunset comes," Khulsedra declared. "You will receive your key then and only then, daughter of the night. Not sooner, not later, but precisely when the time has come. I knew one of you had broken free, and that makes me wonder: how did you manage it?"

Aella's eyes flashed with fury.

"She was freed by a clan leader," I quickly interjected before Aella could worsen the situation. "He's the one who left the key in front of the prison, and I assume it reached you from there, mighty *Rei*."

The queen nodded, her approval accompanied by a low, vibrating growl.

I still remember how terrified I was, surrounded by those creatures that could stomp, burn, or eat me at any moment. Aella appeared calm, or at least she tried her best to hide her unease, so I followed her lead.

"The prison is hidden," Aella emphasized. "How did you know where to find it?"

"Vlad Grayfang and I had an agreement. I was the one who allowed him to build it on my land, so of course I knew where it was. I wouldn't have permitted him to construct it if I hadn't known where he intended to do so. It wasn't a deal I took lightly, eternal life, but despite the tainted blood running through his veins, I could see that he was right. He agreed to leave the nartingals on my land, to give them up to me, and I had to guard them, to forget he existed and promise not to attack his city. As if such things can simply be forgotten!"

"And protected us you did," laughed Aella.

"I still don't understand how that human could have sneaked into the prison without my knowledge and left with you. It shouldn't have been possible; I should have been alerted immediately."

"Yet, it was."

The Dragon Queen's gaze was fixed on the Black Queen, yet she looked far beyond her. "Yet it was," she echoed.

"And you found the key conveniently left at the entrance, yet you didn't even bother to check if we were still there. For all you knew, you could have been guarding an empty tomb."

"I couldn't step in myself; it was part of the agreement with Vlad. However, I peered in from the threshold and noticed that one of the rings was missing." Rei narrowed her eyes, her massive head approaching us. "You escaped from the yoke, I see."

"The key belongs to Vlad," said Aella dryly, then gestured towards me, "and rightfully belongs to his descendant, Darion. Besides, I'm sure Vlad has already slept on it."

"Are you scoffing our customs?" the queen thundered, her tail lashing through the air like a whip.

Aella shrugged with a mocking smile on her face.

"Perhaps we should consider their request, my queen," Volthrax quickly interjected, before the queen made matters worse. "Let's hold a council with all the elders and decide together if we should fly with the wind or against it. We have all seen the signs, and we all know what is coming. All I ask is for caution."

Some of the dragons snarled their approval, while others shook their heads, watching us with hostile eyes and bared teeth. *Rei* appeared defeated. It was clear she was not in a delicate situation at all, as Aella held the power to destroy her entire city in just a few heartbeats. She had to give in. She was going to give in.

"So it shall be. We will deliberate and then make a decision. Until then, daughter of the night, you and your mate are welcome in Saherdrakar. No one will harm you until I say so, provided, of course, that you keep your snout to yourself."

She cast us one final glance before turning her back and flying off to her chamber. Volthrax had the same relieved expression on his face that I had on mine. He turned and followed her as well, joined by other dragons, including the old one that chased me. The ones that remained quickly lost interest in us, going off to wherever.

Aella took my burned hands and healed them, causing some of the remaining drakars to growl at us, but no one dared to intervene. Since childhood, I had yearned to behold dragons—the majestic creatures of myth and legend. But now, standing before them, I felt a pang of disillusionment. These ancient beings, revered for their power and wisdom, exuded an air of arrogance and heedlessness.

Arya leaned down, gesturing for us to sit on her back, then rose, gliding above the buildings until she reached one not far from the queen's, colored in shades of pink, yellow, and blue. She plunged through the doorway and landed abruptly on the floor, almost knocking us over. After we dismounted, she said she was going to fetch our backpacks, then darted out the door before we could say anything else.

"You wouldn't have destroyed the mountain, would you?" I asked Aella once we were alone.

She was gazing absentmindedly through the massive archway of the door, toward the city illuminated by the Flame Stones outside, deep in thought. "Yes," she replied after a while.

Then she turned to me and slapped me so suddenly and forcefully that I almost lost my balance.

"You have some explaining to do," she thundered, her tone burdened with anger.

"I deserved it," I told her, rubbing my cheek.

"Of course you deserved it, you idiot! What was going on in that head of yours? Should I break it and look for myself?"

"Be my guest."

She snorted furiously. "I understand your judgment, but it was a huge mistake. You let yourself be blinded by emotions and made an irrational decision that put you in danger and forced me to run without any plan into the den, putting me in danger as well. You can't think rationally, but now is neither the place nor the time to talk about it. But we will talk, rest assured." Her voice grew hoarse from the lengthy tirade, barely managing to push out the final words before drawing in a deep breath.

I tilted my head, scanning the room. Like the queen, Arya also had a bunch of stuff gathered there. Including a bed. I walked slowly and sat on it, smiling. It seemed to be in good condition.

"We won," she told me in a cold voice, sitting to my side. "She will give us the key, she has no choice and she knows it."

"Yes. Just so you know, I feel very..."

"Don't bother. Save your apologies until we're no longer in hostile territory and I can properly hold a grudge against you." She looked around the large room. "I've heard that dragons like to collect things, but this... look at all those mirrors, and they're all broken… and that's a mill wheel. Why would someone steal a mill wheel?"

"Because she didn't have one?" I shrugged. "Many years ago, I remember a farmer whose abode lay close to Redat, coming to the palace complaining that someone had destroyed his mill and stolen the grinding wheel. Dad refused to help him, and the treasurer called him crazy, without mincing words. I think we finally found the culprit."

We both started laughing. Arya returned shortly after, resuming her human form, and retreated to a corner where she had several neatly packed piles of clothes. She pulled out a simple white dress that ended just above the knees. Aella glanced again at the mill wheel, chuckled, and then went to Arya, wrapping her in a warm hug.

"Thank you for defending us," she said.

"You're a good friend," I told her. "We owe you."

She smiled warmly, visibly pleased and delighted with the compliments, then sat on the floor in front of the bed. Aella returned to bed.

"I think Mother will give you the key," she said.

"We think the same," I admitted. "You… have skulls in your room."

"Yes," she replied proudly. "I have skulls from all the animals I could find: goats, sheep, cows, horses, beavers, humans. I haven't managed to catch any moles yet, but I won't let them slip away much longer; I'm already learning to dig better."

I smiled, remembering how suddenly she had thrown herself into the grass, starting to dig, in front of Yermoleth's tree. She had sensed a mole.

"You also have pal'ethers here," Aella observed. "Where did you get them?"

"For some things, I bartered with the clansmen or the horse lords from the north, for others, I stole them, and quite a few I found in the forest. Especially the stones. I found them in the forest and liked them."

"May I look through the… treasures?" Aella asked.

"Mhm," Arya responded after a moment of thought.

Aella's fingers traced the contours of a wooden staff, plucked from a collection of timbered artifacts. She regarded it in hushed contemplation. Intricate symbols etched into its surface sprang to life with a soft glow, illuminating the dim space as she raised it aloft.

"How did you do that?" Arya asked, astonished.

"It's a battle pal'ether," Aella explained. "It helps you make waves of destruction easier, although I wouldn't dare to use something like that. I like to have complete control. It's Yerdrasil wood, from what I see."

Arya told us she found it in a farmer's yard and stole it because she liked the symbols engraved on it. She also had a few globes and mirrors, all pal'ethers, but Aella couldn't figure out what they were for as they were destroyed. Despite everything she had said about how much she hated her family, she seemed more than delighted to be home. Dragons were very territorial creatures and liked to fill their nest with all sorts of things they found interesting. I couldn't help but wonder if she had bargained with someone for that bed in the room or simply stolen it. If she had stolen it, she probably had no idea humans sleep on these things, which for her made no sense.

As the night approached, the Flame Stones' light began to diminish, much like the glowing flowers in Yermoleth's house. Outside, in the city, the drakars still prowled, their eyes sharp and watchful, casting fleeting glances as they flew near the doorway.

A green dragon stopped at the entrance to Arya's room and waited a few moments until she finished telling us about how sometimes it was better to feed in human form, as you needed less food to feel full. When she noticed him, she frowned for a moment, then gestured for him to come in. The beast stepped inside and took on his human form.

He appeared to be a young man around twenty years old, tall and thin, with hair as green as a grasshopper's back. He hugged Arya, and she pushed him aside gently.

"I am Falkor, the older brother of Arashkigal," he told us excitedly, stretching his neck.

I stood up and bumped heads with him in greeting, then he embraced me tightly, laughing. He was naked.

"Second oldest, but we don't talk about the first," he added.

He let go, his face breaking into a broad grin, and then took a seat beside Arya.

"Why aren't you talking about the first one?" I wondered, seating back next to Aella.

"He was the reason I left Saherdrakar," Arya told us. "He's a traitor; a pathetic traitor who made us a laughingstock, and mother refused to pursue and kill him for his betrayal."

"Pursue him to Rhal'Ellieh?!" Falkor exclaimed. "We would have pointless losses, why would you care if Beithir lives or dies."

Beithir. Arya mentioned that name once before, at the Yerdrasil. She was afraid he might steal the key. I remembered that Rhal'Ellieh was the name of the city where Yohr'Sherrat was sealed.

Arya's small fist hit the ground she sat on. "Because he betrayed us, and because he was family! The Beithir of now killed the Beithir of then, our brother. He deserves to die for that, and I will kill him. I will break his neck and feast on his heart!"

"I missed the flame in your soul, sister of mine," Falkor said.

Falkor stayed with us long after sunset, telling us about the new names he found for some constellations—very uninspiring names, I may add, but I said nothing. He also said about some people from the clans who got too close to the mountain, and about how a drakar female named Saphira that suggested *lepwiht to him*, which, to my understanding, meant mating.

Later, Arya and Falkor showed us the mountain. I rode on the green dragon, Aella on Arya, and other dragons, small and large, flew around us. That night was like a distant dream. We didn't visit the prison of the Daughters of the Night, as Aella refused to reveal its location to others, but we were taken to the crest of that mountain, where, under the celestial tapestry, we exchanged tales and musings until weariness claimed our spirits.

When we returned, Saherdrakar was asleep. The Flame-Stones were pale, almost extinguished, and there was not a dragon in sight on the streets or above them. Dragons cherished their sleep.

"Can I suggest *lepwiht* tonight?" Aella whispered to me when we were on the mountain peak, but when we arrived in Arya's room, we both succumbed to exhaustion in moments. Arya nestled on one of the larger boulders she had there, laughing at us and calling us *soft beings* for choosing to sleep on a bed.

So, we all fell asleep, for after all, we were safe in Saherdrakar, the city of dragons. Then, Beithir attacked.

The Siege of Saherdrakar

The dream I had the night before, where Queen Lenore, that woman whom I believed to be Aveloth, and that man—who was in fact Aethelred—appeared, made me ponder. My dreams could penetrate the thick fabric of time, allowing me to see the future, but would it work in the opposite direction? Could they also unravel the past? So, I thought of Romir, of my home, and the times when I could truly call it that. *My home.* I longed to see them all—Larion, Arlieth, my mother, father, grandfather, my friends, the men from the barracks. Those days will never come again, I accepted that, but in my dreams, they could still be true. I just had to figure out how; how to choose which direction to look, how to wield my gift instead of being led by it.

But I dreamt of nothing.

"Darion!"

The voice that called me belonged to a man, calm yet with an undertone of urgency. It was diluted by the waves of sleep, yet still clear as if whispered directly into my ear.

Another spectral whisper clung to my consciousness, this time clearer. "You're in danger, Darion. You need to wake up! Wake up!"

I stirred, opening my eyes, and seeing the high ceiling of the dimly lit room. A divine and pure song, so beautiful and soothing that I almost fell asleep again as soon as I woke up, echoed in the cool air of the underground city. It was more beautiful than any choir I had heard before, almost as melodious as Arlieth's song. Almost magical.

I caught a movement from the corner of my eye, smooth as a breeze over a field of daisies, inhumanly delicate. A woman. She was naked, pale, with long chestnut hair down to her small breasts and red, glassy eyes. She slipped inside with feline, elegant steps, almost tiptoeing among the waves of that liturgical chant. She was heading towards our bed. Everything about her seemed to scream 'danger.'

I tried to get up, but my body refused to listen; I tried to scream, but my lips were sealed, and my tongue numb, as if I were paralyzed. The woman stopped at the end of the bed and swept her blood-red eyes over us.

"You're awake," she remarked with a certain sadness. Her voice was honeyed and laden with emotion, like that of a maiden on her wedding night. "Don't you like our song?"

I muttered something incoherent, as I couldn't seem to move my lips at all.

"Poor creature… I would have wished to offer you a long and peaceful end."

She let herself fall, sliding off her feet so smoothly as if she had no weight, laying on top of me. Her pale fingertips brushed my cheek, then kissed me tenderly on the lips before revealing her long, sharp fangs—fangs that could easily tear into my throat.

In those moments when time seemed to stretch and life felt as if it were about to end, I remembered the nights when Arlieth, Larion, and I would sneak into the deserted observation tower with candles and blankets to share scary stories. I used those nights as an excuse to hold Arlieth under the blanket, pretending to be frightened. She would be so engrossed in the stories that she often didn't notice my hand straying where it shouldn't, but eventually, she would realize, and her face would turn pink. She never pulled my hand away. Many of the stories we told featured creatures from ancient legends, like ghouls, whisperers, and spirits. But also dhampirs—bloodthirsty beings from the Dacryen mountains. The tales varied, but when I saw that creature, my mind immediately jumped to those beings from our tales. A shiver coursed through my paralyzed body as my eyes remained locked on the approaching fangs.

"Aella!" I managed to scream at last.

The woman startled, her eyes widened in astonishment, indicating that I shouldn't have been able to utter any word, let alone to yell. When she turned to Aella, she gasped, finding herself gazing into the crystal eyes of the Black Queen. In an instant, she was lifted off me and suspended in the air, her face exploding, struck by a beam of ether. A warm rain of blood drops fell upon us, as the disembodied body collapsed a few meters from the bed.

"Screamers!" Aella uttered with disgust, jumping out of bed.

I struggled to get up, feeling that melody enveloping the Saherdrakar numbing me, alluring me back to sleep. That was the effect the dhampir's song had on living creatures, it impaired their judgment and senses, that is if they were awake, and if they were asleep, it locked them into a full, dreamless slumber.

"Shadow creatures," she explained, "by the hundreds. We are under siege!"

"They've come for the key," I muttered sourly, massaging my temples.

The dhampirs are strange creatures, fierce and deadly, built to murder. They can kill you in moments, but their preferred way of working is to prolong death as long as possible. They cripple their victims, either by severing their tendons or stunning them with their song, then slowly suck their blood, talking to them all the while. They like to take on human forms and chatter with the dying.

Without warning, Aella sent a lightning bolt into Arya's sleeping body, causing her to suddenly jump in her seat in confusion. We couldn't have woken her up any other way, especially with the dhampirs singing in the city.

"Screamers," she muttered as soon as she heard the chorus, then jumped to her feet and glanced briefly at the disembodied body of the woman.

"We need to wake up the dragons," Aella said, her voice full of urgency.

"No chance," Arya responded, shaking her head to wake herself up better. "Not while the Screamers are screaming, unless we go to each one and snap them with lightning."

"We don't have time for this."

A black shadow darted through the door, circling the room like a stray bat before swooping towards me. Aella hurled a wind sphere at it, the burst of energy causing me to stagger and making the beast crash onto the ground, a few steps away from me. It somewhat resembled human beings, with skin as black as tar, sharp ears, and fangs almost too large to keep its mouth shut. Its long arms seemed particularly powerful, covered in thick muscles, and its claws were enough to pierce through simple armor.

It quickly recovered from the impact, as if it were just a minor fall, and got up, charging at me with its arms outstretched. I retreated backward, slashing with my sword, cutting off a few fingers with the first strike, then splitting its face in half with the second, dark-red blood cascading from the wound.

"Beautiful," Arya commented, seeing the lifeless body of the monster collapse to the ground.

I shifted my gaze from the girl's headless body to the creature.

"This is their true form," Aella told me.

"Heavens..."

The Heart of Dawn was an exceptional sword. With an ordinary weapon, it wouldn't have been easy for me to cut through a dhampir's muscles and bones.

Aella and I went out first, giving Arya time and space to take her dragon form. The city was full of them, I could see their silhouettes in the dimness of the gallery under the fading light of the Flame-Stones. Some hovered above, slicing through the air, others perched on the tall buildings, their forms bent in reverence, voices raised in an otherworldly chorus. My gaze swept the vastness of the cavern, lingering on shadowed corners beyond the reach of my mortal sight, and I exhaled a frosty sigh. "There are several hundred of them at least."

Aela's eyes glittered like two polished stones, and a slight tremor moved the air around her.

"Many of them can't fight; they can't afford to interrupt the song. We can hold our own against them, if need be, but our target is him."

I traced her gaze to the figure of a man stepping out from Khulsedra's chamber, draped in a long, grey robe with the hood drawn over his eyes. The beams from the red stone atop the archway danced upon a metallic object at his belt, the size of a long knife—it was the key, I could see even from that distance. His gait was unhurried, almost indifferent, and in his wake trailed a dozen dhampirs, her black winged forms making them seem like shadows.

We ran down the flight of stairs leading from Arya's room to the street, steps fit for human feet, then ran up the avenue leading from the Queen's room to the city center.

Arya's angry roar shook the buildings. She flew over us at speed, making my cloak and Aela's dress billow in the wind, then caught a dhampir in her mouth and tore it to pieces with a flick of her head. She sent a burst of fire toward other monsters singing on a building, then vanished beyond the tops of the colorful rooftops. She passed among them like a hawk among beetles, spreading death in all directions.

When we got to the main road, I saw that man waiting at the bottom of the massive staircase leading to the Queen's room. The screamers were perched on the steps and on the surrounding buildings, their glassy red eyes watching our every move.

"Someone has already slept on that key," I told the stranger. It was clear that he was a dragon. I could see it in the eyes that looked at me devoid of any emotion from under the hood's edge. He seemed dead, absent, soulless.

He twitched, his mouth crooking into a wicked smile. "I think... I would like... to kill you," he uttered in a low voice, barely audible due to the distance between us.

"I will snap your neck little bird," Aella thundered, sending a beam of ether at him.

A dhampir leaped swiftly from the front step, taking the full blow, then collapsed to the side with a smoking hole in its chest. It still lived, struggling for every breath due to its destroyed lungs. The man took a step towards the dying monster.

"You have fulfilled your purpose," he said without any inflection in his voice. My heart seized in horror as he brutally extinguished the dhampir's life, his heel grinding into its skull with a sickening crunch, dark blood staining the earth. He turned to us, his yellow draconic eyes reflecting the shining of the stones. "As for me..." He covered his face with the palm of his right hand. I could see the furious, mad grin through his clenched fingers that seemed to dig into his skin. "My purpose is to suffer!" he screamed, shaking with all his might.

His barely visible face lit up, flames now bursting from the hood as if he had a torch for head. He was transforming. Aella struck again and again, but because of the distance, the dhampirs had time to throw themselves in front of the projectiles, receiving the gift the Black Queen intended for the dragon. The man exploded, and in the place where he had been standing a huge black dragon rose.

The shadows behind him rattled, making sharp sounds, somewhere between the moan of a pig being slaughtered and the snicker of metal rubbing against metal. I turned toward a small, narrow street that opened between two buildings a few steps behind us, thinking we might have enough time to sneak through. It was too narrow for the dragon to pursue, and Aella could create an ether field arcing around us to keep the monsters from reaching us until we could find a way to wake the other dragons.

But she had no intention of running, I could read the determination in her cold eyes.

"We can win," she said simply, as if reading my thoughts.

I nodded in silence, trying to empty my mind completely, as Master Anduin had taught me. Though it wasn't easy. I didn't understand why the shadow creatures had attacked right then; I didn't understand why that dragon hadn't just stolen the key and fled, why it had waited there in human form. Whose voice was it that woke me, why did it wake me? Another question formed at the edge of my subconscious, one that made me grip the sword handle tightly in my palm and grit my teeth in anger. Yermoleth knew I was Khyalis's descendant, I was sure of it, yet he did not warn me. Why?

The air vibrated just like on the Night of the Blood Moon, and dark clouds emerged above us, between the buildings and the stone ceiling. I pushed aside the long string of questions, focusing on the enemies ahead.

"Beithir!" Arya shouted, laden with anger.

"*Of course,*" I thought. The dragon before us was Beithir, the elder brother of Arya and Falkor, the one whose soul had become entangled in Yohr'Sherrat's tentacles.

Arashkigal was coming to us from the center of the city, furiously beating the air with her long wings, closely followed by a swarm of screamers, and the old stones were trembling beneath her fury.

Beithir was over two thousand years old, a seasoned warrior, a born killer; powerful, cruel, merciless, and since he had switched sides, completely mad. But this was the first time he'd stood before a nartingal... and he made the mistake of underestimating her. He pushed the pavement with his hind legs, his claws leaving marks in the cobblestone, lunging at us, but five red lightning bolts erupted from the clouds above, whipping his back and striking him to the ground with a deafening thud. Wisps of smoke rose from the beast's wounded back, blood stains visible over its dark scales.

For a few moments, time seemed to freeze. The creatures remained silent, Beithir unmoving, and the only things that could be heard were Arya's wing beats, drawing nearer, and the lightning bolts tearing through the clouds of that subterranean city. The black dragon lifted his head, his reptilian face twisting into a strange mask interweaved of pain, madness and amusement. He laughed, or at least I think he did, because the sound that came from his throat sounded like two boulders colliding, causing my heart to stop in my chest.

"My dear sister," he grumbled with a voice framed in pain. "End me!"

Arya passed above us, slamming into her brother with great might and rolling together onto the base of the high steps. She stood atop his back, sinking her teeth into his neck, and tearing at his obsidian scales with her dagger-like claws. He laughed and roared simultaneously, struggling to shake her off. A chain of lightning struck the stairs behind them, unleashing loud explosions and incinerating all the dhampirs who appeared poised to pounce on Arya.

Then Aella unleashed the storm. The sky lit up with explosions of reddish lightning, streaking in every direction and consuming the shadows chanting on the rooftops in blinding bursts of fire and light.

A dhampir descended upon us, its movements a blur of predatory grace, and in a heartbeat, it bore down on Aela. I blocked its path, driving Dawn's Heart into its gaping maw, amidst its sharp fangs. Due to its swift descent, the blade emerged halfway through the other side of its head, piercing its sturdy skull. With a forceful tug, I freed the blade, just as another screamer hurtled from the shadows of the nearby edifice, its sights set on the spell-weaving Aella. I pivoted on my heel, weapon tracing a deadly arc through the air, and delivered a blow to the creature's neck with such ferocity that it nearly disarmed me. Its lifeless body rolled at the feet of the Black Queen, while its severed head was flung aside. It struck the building's wall with a sickening thud before rolling down the cobblestone street, leaving a trail of dark ichor in its wake.

"Protect me," Aella demanded, her eyes closed.

I positioned myself in front of her, spinning the weapon a few times to flick off some of the black blood from its blade. More creatures descended before me, crouching on all fours, their fangs bared in a silent snarl and backs arched in a predatory bow, ready to pounce.

"Come and meet your end!" I urged, severing the throat of the first beast that stepped closer.

I pushed the blade into the other's chest, but the creature shoved itself into the weapon without even flinching. Its black claw sliced through the air, aiming to carve my face, but I jerked my head back just in time. I attempted to withdraw, but the beast grabbed the hilt with its left hand, then drove the claws of its right hand into my arm.

"You want it, fiend?!" I howled in pain, starting to twist the weapon in the wound, slamming the creature to its knees and forcing it to release the handle.

I tore Dawn's Heart from its chest and with the next strike, severed its head from its shoulders. Before I could regain my stance, another creature slammed into me with its shoulder, sending me flying several meters into the air, cutting off my breath. As it lunged, I directed the sword's tip into its heart, impaling the creature mid-assault. I kicked the shadow, pushing it out of the blade, then felt for my left arm, sensing the places where the claws had pierced my skin. My eyes flickered and my muscles tensed as another one plunged at me. I performed a pirouette, narrowly avoiding its attack. It missed me by a mere whisper, crashing hard against one of the stone house walls.

Arya leapt from her brother and began to shake like a wet dog, covered in dhampirs biting and tearing at her relentlessly. Beithir turned, striking with his tail in our direction. I leapt towards Aella, hugging her tightly and collapsing together with just a breath before the long tail whipped through the air above us, slamming into the wall of a building. With reflexes honed by fear, I managed to slide my hand beneath her head just as we crashed, cushioning the impact against the hard stone floor.

Arashkigal dived down, blasting her brother with a burst of fire before seizing him, rolling together in our direction. I was still pinned over Aella, so I pushed with my feet, and we spun several times before getting out of the way of the two dragons, who passed by us in a flurry of tails, scales, and claws. She gasped as I stole a quick kiss before leaping to my feet, extending my hand to help her up.

More dhampirs landed around us, poised to charge, and in that moment, I started believing that our luck had finally run out. We were completely surrounded. My eyes darted to Aella for a second, wondering if she had enough power left for a new barrage of lightning, but she seemed exhausted too.

Then, shattering the stillness, a roar seething with fury rented the night asunder—another dragon. That's when I realized the song had stopped and the dragons were awakening. Aella's relentless onslaught silenced them. Despite the searing pain in my left arm, I almost let out a squeal of joy.

Beithir kicked his sister, knocking her off him, then rose and flew towards the exit. Arya immediately rolled to her feet, and surged after her brother, beating the air like an oarsman battling against the current.

"Wait!" Aella shouted at her, but the young drakar was already too far away.

The remaining dhampirs, more numerous than I had expected, considering the number of charred and severed corpses littering the streets, set off after them like a swarm of insects.

The crooked smile on Aella's face didn't reflect in her eyes, which glinted with fury. She punched the stone wall beside us, letting out a loud curse. Falkor landed a few steps away, his gaze sweeping disdainfully over the carnage strewn about. He tried to ask something, but Aella cut him off. "Take us on your back! Beithir stole the key, we have to stop him."

Though visibly confused, the dragon scooped us both up in one scaly hand and placed us on his back, between his two wings, without asking anything. Before we could even settle properly, he took off for the exit.

"Quickly!" Aella shouted. "He's heading towards Rhal'Ellieh!"

I sheathed my sword back into its scabbard so I could hold onto Falkor with both arms. More dragons were emerging from buildings, taking flight behind us. Dhampir corpses were everywhere, strewn on the ground, burnt and torn apart, mostly around spots where a black ash stain decorated the earth. At least a few hundred had perished. Aella had slaughtered them. She stood at the back, her arms wrapped around me, tense and uneasy.

"Faster!" she thundered.

"Did you kill them all?" he marveled.

"She and your sister!" I yelled back, trying to cover the wind's whistle.

Falkor flew at very high speed, his powerful wings pushing relentlessly. I could barely breathe because of the air rushing at me, forcing me to tilt my head for each breath.

As we exited the city, I could see Beithir disappearing into the dark clouds to the north, closely followed by Arya and the dhampirs, who from that distance looked like a flock of bats.

"Faster!" Aella thundered.

"We are going fast enough!" I shouted back, pressing my right hand against the wound on my shoulder once again. I had blood on my fingers.

"We cannot afford to lose the key!" Aella yelled back. She looked drained and exhausted, having consumed a lot of ether during the battle.

"Arya!" I screamed. "She is our main concern, not the cursed key!"

Falkor was doing everything he could, for when we plunged into the tangle of dark clouds, the other dragons were far behind. The starlight faded away, along with the silver glow of the crescent moon, as though we had descended into the maw of a colossal beast. It felt like stepping into another realm, where even the wind's whistle seemed to hush. Around us were only the shadowy forms of the clouds, dark gray or outright black, like smoke.

"I don't see anything," I whispered. Aella remained silent.

A column of fire sprang to life in the distance, like a lightning bolt piercing the storm, and extinguished in just a few moments, followed by the roar of a dragon. It was Arya. She seemed in pain. She screamed once more, this time with even greater intensity. Then, a chilling crack sliced through the air, and as abruptly as it had begun, her roar was cut off—silenced as swiftly as a taut thread severed by scissors.

"Arya!" Falkor shouted.

"We need to descend from the clouds!" I yelled, "we can't confront Beithir here."

"Keep flying!" Aella shouted at him.

"Descend!" I urged again, this time full of fury.

"We can't afford to lose the key!"

"To hell with the key, we'll lose our lives!"

We had barely finished speaking when a squeal, like the sound of brittle wood giving way, echoed from our right, and before we could react, Beithir emerged from the darkness overhead, seizing Falkor by under the jaw with his fangs. I leaned over, gripping tightly onto two smaller spikes on the back of the green dragon, as we began to fall, spinning through the layer of clouds with the black dragon dangling from us.

"I could kill you, brother!" Beithir shouted as we plummeted, his voice muffled by Falkor's neck clamped between his fangs. "But it's not your time to die here. Not yet! Your fate will come. Death claims everyone eventually."

Beithir released him, pushing off Falkor's chest with his feet and disappearing, swallowed by the shroud of darkness. Falkor regained control, straightening his body and gliding through the dense clouds, with no visibility.

"Brother!" he shouted. "Let's fight into the light, where I can see you!"

"We are good," Aella whispered to me with a shaken voice.

I had barely begun to nod in response when a screamer materialized from the void, its claws sinking into my flesh, wrenching me from Falkor's back. Aella tried to hold onto me, but everything happened too quickly, even for her to generate waves of ether to pull me back. In an instant, I was lost, falling from the dhampir's talons through the darkness, my back burning with pain. I couldn't even scream due to the shock.

The wind was hissing next to my ear, rendering me deaf, and the canopy of darkness blinded me. Another dhampir flashed past me, just a shadow among shadows, mowing down my leg with its claws before fading again. I drew my sword from its sheath, cursing.

As I fell from the clutches of the cloud sea, the forest below unfurled like a dark tapestry, rushing up to meet me. There were parts where the clouds were pierced by the moonlight, emerging on the other side like pillars of silver holding the black sky in place. The monster dashed at me again, swooping in with wings wrapped around its body and talons outstretched like deadly spears. I twirled in the air, cutting deep into the shadow's flesh. My sword was pulled from my hand, embedded in the back of the screamer who was now falling without an arm and a wing.

Falkor and Aella had no way of finding me in time. In those few, possibly last moments, I thought of Lyra and Aella. Of the life I might have had if the whole world hadn't been against me. The Circle's assassins, Romir and Frevia, the First Gods—my list of foes was endless. My desire was not for bloodshed but for seclusion, for a quiet existence away from conflict. Perhaps therein lay my failing. Aella understood from the start the truth I had refused to acknowledge. We were at war. Not just with the kingdoms of men, but with the gods themselves.

There was nothing more I could do, so I simply closed my eyes, allowing myself to fall face down, feeling the tears of anger overwhelm me. In my mind, came that vision from Yohr'Sherrat: Aella, Arlieth, and I lying in the same bed. Despite everything, I couldn't help but smile.

Something slammed hard against my back. Two dark arms grabbed me from behind, and a pair of wings swelled above me. A dhampir!

I felt my heart rise into my throat as the speed of my descent abruptly changed. I was carried through the woods, crashing into several branches that snapped upon impact, before being released through the tall grass and stopping with my back against the trunk of a tree. The dhampir, unmistakably female from her facial features and the contours of her breasts, settled in front of me, studying me with scrutiny. She was not black like the others, but had a very dark shade of gray, and on her chest, between her breasts, she had a peculiar symbol tattooed, resembling a thin triangle piercing several circles.

I was intact but defenseless, the sword remaining lodged in the corpse of the dhampir who had attacked me in the fall, lost somewhere in the forest. However, this one didn't attack. She scanned the forest, seemingly listening, then tucked a strand of black hair behind her sharp ear. Tied to her right leg, above the knee, was a dagger sheathed in a brown leather scabbard. She leapt and soared with a flutter of her wings, disappearing between the trees.

"Thank you," I whispered, confused but grateful.

I immediately noticed with astonishment that a part of me regretted surviving. "I was denied a quick death," I said in a whisper. I was exhausted, and the wounds from the battle throbbed with pain.

I burst into laughter.

"Creator," I murmured. "That's what Yermoleth called you. You're not finished with me yet, are you?!" I shouted, my eyes darting around desperately. "Azerad, I'm speaking to you! Can you hear me? Do you enjoy the spectacle I'm putting on? Are you entertained by the souls I've sent your way? Just wait—I'll send you the whole world!"

The Purpose of Evil

Excerpt from Elena's journal, dated the thirteenth and seventeenth days of the seventh month, Iureia, in the year six hundred twenty-three after the Conversion:

I stood on the northern wall of the city alongside Jane and Larion, watching my father's army marching from the fields outside the capital. There were so many of them, like finely coordinated ants heading for the crumbs that had fallen from the table. I smiled at the thought that they were too slow, and that a little sparrow would steal the last bits before they reached them. From above, it seemed like I could wipe them all away with a simple wave of my hand. Perhaps Aella could have, but she was dead. She had to be!

We were flanked by thirty men in chainmail armor, their backs adorned with long green cloaks bearing the Grayfang house crest. Mother stood in front of the wall, kissing her husband one last time before he rode along the column of marching soldiers. It was clear to me that Father was curious about the secrets and treasures those mountains hid, and my brother's death had been a well-justified opportunity for him to dig.

In the city, hundreds of soldiers went from door to door in search of Lord Oswin and Beatrice. We did everything in our power to find them, but deep down I doubt we would. I felt nauseous all morning, but I couldn't tell if it was because of the tiny creature forming in my belly or the guilt of not remembering what had happened when I was kidnapped. I felt useless.

Still, I needed to figure out what to do with Jane, because since Beatrice was missing, she had to sleep alone, and she didn't like it at all. Neither did I. During the days I was absent, Larion often stopped by to make sure she was fine. Though she tried not to show it, she was terrified because she had come to see Bea and me as her only friends, and in one day, she had lost both of us. But I came back, and despite everyone's doubts, I was alive, so I don't see why they couldn't be too. I wasn't ready to lose Bea. I could never be, not her.

Larion inclined his head, his gaze lingering on my features for an unnecessarily long moment. 'Are you feeling well?' he inquired, his hand gently covering mine, resting on the stone battlement.

"I think so," I sighed.

"Do you want to sit down? Do you want us to go back?"

"I'm fine, Larion, you don't have to fuss over me. But thank you for caring. Jane, what about you?"

"I'm fine, Princess Elena. Thank you." Jane made a curtsey.

"Tonight, we'll have dinner in the Great Hall," Larion said. "Except for Lanre, all the big nobles of Derahia will be there, and I'd like them to see you; to see that we're not defeated and that we're not afraid. But only if..."

"I will come," I assured him.

And I had to go, I had no choice. He was right; if Darion was responsible and had spies in our court, he needed to know that we were not afraid of him, that we were not afraid to show our faces. But I doubted it was him, and with every passing moment, doubt turned into certainty. But if not him, then who? And why am I so cold?

Darion. He wants to take the key. He must be stopped. Beithir will go. Beithir will stop him.

"Can we return to the palace?" I asked, a shiver coursing through me. Suddenly, the brilliant golden sun seemed to cast a mockingly cold light upon us. A cold only I could feel.

Larion nodded absentmindedly. He stared thoughtfully at the faint shape of the mountains looming in the North. His brother was there, alone and wounded, with the Circle's assassins on his trail and my father's army on the way. His days were numbered, and my betrothed understood that as well as I did.

We descended from the wall and entered the carriage waiting for us at the bottom of the stairs, but before it departed, I saw Merideth approaching, waving at us. She wore a marvelous red silk dress, tightly hugging her body, leaving her right shoulder bare, and her blonde hair was loose, a few strands flowing in waves over her bosoms. She was blessed with extraordinary beauty.

"Princess Elena, Your Majesty," she said, bowing solemnly. "Do you have room for one more?"

"Of course, please come in," I invited her.

I sat beside Larion, and she sat next to Jane in front of us. Silly Jane edged away from her as if she were on fire, or as if she found her alluring lavender perfume repulsive.

"Why isn't Mother coming?" I asked her.

She lowered her head and bit her lip thoughtfully, then replied, "Your mother wants to stay and see all the soldiers disappearing into the distance, but she told me I could wait for her back at the palace. You've probably heard that a lot since yesterday, Princess, but thank Azerad that you've returned unharmed. Your mother has been crying incessantly."

"Poor thing," I muttered, rolling my eyes. "I'll pray she gets over this trauma soon."

Her lips, red as rose petals, curved into a sympathetic smile that didn't quite reach her amused eyes. For a moment, her attention shifted from me to Larion, then back to me.

"Shall we pray together?" she asked.

Larion nearly let out a chuckle. He probably thought I was planning to sleep with her, because I hadn't told him yet that she had agreed to report to me every move of my mother. I was eager to seize any opportunity to glean insights from Merideth about my mother's actions during my absence.

"I don't see why not," I replied, shrugging. "Let's meet this afternoon, what do you say?"

"I'll come to your room," she said, pausing for a long moment, then added with a smirk, "for prayer."

"Radagrim will want to see you later," Larion reminded me. "He wants to consult with you privately before the Circle wizards arrive."

"The Circle wizards?" Merideth's face contorted into a delicate, small frown.

"Yes," my betrothed replied. "Ten in total. After the Battle Near Blackstone, the Tower of Fire decided it would be advisable to have a more serious force in the city until things settle down. Quite pointless, if you ask me, especially now with the Black Queen dead."

"I see," the woman said listlessly. She brushed a golden strand of hair from her face. "Please excuse my gloomy face, but simple wizards, are not well-regarded by the dogs from the Circle. They only like those who know how to sit when told."

Larion laughed. "I assure you they won't give you any trouble. If they do, you can come talk to me, and we'll sort it out."

"Thank you," she said, visibly relieved. "The only thing I miss about Erop is the weak influence the Circle holds there."

She adjusted her position on the bench, causing Jane to startle and pull herself closer to the carriage wall.

"I suspected you were from Erop; that or Merik, " Larion chuckled. "Because of your accent."

"Accent?" she exclaimed, surprised.

"Yes. You don't have any. With me, you can tell I am Derahian by the way I pronounce certain words, or with the girls, you can hear they're from Frevia by the way they speak, but not with you."

"Interesting," she replied, pronouncing the word with a hint of Derahian accent.

Larion laughed. "You're quite good at it," he complimented her. "I, for one, can't change my accent at all without sounding ridiculous."

"I traveled a lot in my youth."

"Youth?" Larion raised an eyebrow.

"Are you curious?" she asked him in a tone that was too personal.

"I know better than to ask a woman her age."

I didn't like how she looked or smiled at him. For the first time in many years, I felt a faint pang of what could be called 'jealousy'. I took my betrothed's hand and placed it on my stomach, and he turned somewhat surprised, as if he had forgotten I was there.

"Jane, how long did it take for yours to start moving?" I asked, then turned to Merideth. "I'm beginning to think mine is just lazy. Probably takes after his father a lot."

"Four months, Princess," Jane replied, still keeping her face down, pressed against the carriage's wall.

"In other words, it'll take a while," Larion said, placing a kiss on my cold cheek. Why was I so cold?

"You're probably looking forward to meeting the baby," Merideth said, her gaze fixed on my belly.

"You have no idea," I replied.

She smiled at me, and I almost gasped of anger. She was too beautiful. She'd better be more reserved in Larion's presence.

Larion jumped suddenly, almost hitting his head on the low ceiling of the carriage. His hand went to his weapon. He was holding his breath, I realized. He sat back, pale-faced, then spoke with a hazy smile, "Excuse me, for a moment I thought I heard something.

"Like a whisper?" the woman in red swiftly enquired. She was the only one of us who didn't startle along with Larion.

"Mhm," Larion nodded. "Probably something from outside."

Merideth's warm smile quickly spread across her face, and for a moment, I thought I saw tears glisten in her eyes. As soon as we arrived in the palace courtyard, she hurried to her room, bidding us farewell with a playful Derahian accent that elicited another laugh from my betrothed.

Larion turned to me, still sporting a foolish grin, then said, "I need to meet with Lord..."

"Do as you please," I cut him off.

"Did I say something wrong?" he asked, confused.

"Nothing," I replied, trying to mimic Merideth's voice. "Now, please excuse us, Jane and I will go inside."

"Sometimes I can't understand you," he said, defeated. "Jane, do you have any idea what I did?"

The girl looked from me to him for a few moments before shaking her head no.

"You sold me," I told Jane in an annoyed tone as soon as we were apart from Larion.

"I'm sorry, but I don't want to get on the king's bad side," she replied.

"And you want to get on mine? Jane, I'm the most horrible thing that ever set foot in this palace."

She put on a small, feminine smile, already accustomed to my jokes. Not long ago, such words would have made her cheeks match the color of her hair—white—while begging for thousands of apologies.

"I believe the red witch is very close to stealing your title, Princess. There's something rotten about her, I can feel it deep in my bones, and when I feel such things, I never miss."

"It's just in your mind," I reassured her. "But don't worry, I don't trust her either, but I need her help.

Uncomfortable situation, but these are the only ingredients I have to make soup with."

"Why not throw away what's spoiled? Better to have less soup than to get sick to your stomach."

Passing through the Grand Hall, I saw Ser Aldric, the knight who had helped me reach the palace yesterday, sitting next to Arlieth's younger sister, Aethelwit, at a table in the center of the hall. I assumed he had come for the reward offered by Larion for bringing me safely, so I pulled Jane in their direction.

"Ser Aldric, I believe your cloak remained with me," I said.

The man turned to face me and smiled with a warmth almost palpable. Rising to his feet, he bowed gracefully, the chainmail beneath his reddish-golden steel plate armor softly clinking as he took my hand. Despite the padding on the palm of his steel gauntlet, his touch felt nearly as cold as I was. He pressed a gentle kiss to my hand, then repeated the gesture with Jane, causing her cheeks to flush a deep shade of rose.

"Princess Elena, I am delighted to see that you are well," he said, his tone sounding too sincere. "As for the cloak, you will do me a great honor if you'll accept it as my gift."

I looked at him doubtfully, then said in an indifferent tone, "Have you already collected your reward, Ser?"

"Reward?" he exclaimed, raising his eyebrows. "I was not aware of any reward, but I couldn't say I need it. I have done Azerad's will, and that was reward enough."

"So you don't want the money?" I prodded. "One thousand gold coins."

"I don't need so much money. As you can see, my pockets aren't deep enough," he chuckled. "But there's an orphanage in the northeast part of the city, on Star Street, that isn't in very good condition. Besides that, there are a few streets in the same area where the houses are almost falling apart. Those people are very poor. It would bring me great joy if you were to use the reward money to fund the necessary repairs. I'm sure there is more than enough."

I regarded him with wide eyes, struggling to conceal my astonishment. After all, what normal person would relinquish such a substantial sum of gold pieces so readily?

"I will do that," I replied.

He smiled, made another courtesy, then sat back next to Aethelwit.

"Ser Aldric," I insisted, somewhat stunned, "a thousand gold coins mean a great deal. It would allow you to live a more than comfortable life without ever needing to work again. Are you sure you don't want the reward?"

The man lowered his head, concealing his smile, then rose again and gave me a somehow disappointed smile. Apparently, courtesy didn't allow him to speak to me while seated.

"There are things more valuable than money, riches that those who consider themselves 'wealthy' never get to own. I can say that I have a rich life, but not in material things, in something more precious. However, if the reward money burdens your treasury too much, give it to the people in the city who truly need it."

"Very noble of you," I said, trying not to show, or voice, my doubt.

A more fitting word would have been 'mad,' not noble. I was still surprised by how easily he had refused such a prize for which others would sell their souls. It was as if he lived completely disconnected from the real world. He turned to Aethelwit, then back to me, and his red eyebrows arched as if he had just had an idea. His eyes sparkled mischievously. "Princess Elena, since you're here, could you help me and my new friend, Lady Aethelwit, solve a problem?"

I shifted my gaze to the serene face of the girl, who smiled excitedly at the idea. "What is it about?" I asked.

He patted the empty chair next to him. "Come, take a seat, and I'll tell you."

It didn't take long for me to notice, with a hint of amusement, that none of the people around the table were eating. They were all sitting with their faces in the plates and their ears pricked up, enchanted by the charisma of this preacher in shining armor. He probably knew. He was damn tenacious, I noticed that pretty well.

"So," the man began, "this morning, I unintentionally overheard a conversation between a young lady and a priest of the Temple. The lady was asking the priest some very important, very valid questions; questions that I'm sure any person asks at some point in their life. But the priest was treating the issue superficially."

"He told me," Aethelwit started, then frowned for a moment before continuing, "he told the girl that a true believer should not voice doubt; that his duty is to believe and keep his mouth shut."

"That's what he said," the man nodded sadly. "That's the problem I've seen not just here, but in most Temples I've visited: priests shy away from tackling the tough questions, the very questions that yearn most for an answer. Aethelwit, do you remember the question that young lady asked the priest?"

"She wanted to know what the purpose of evil is, why it exists," Aethelwit answered.

"It's simple," I replied, perhaps without giving it more than a droplet of thought.

"Is it?" the knight asked, his eyes widening in astonishment. He was very expressive.

"There's no purpose," I replied with certainty.

"Lady Jane, what is your opinion?"

"I haven't thought about it before," she admitted, embarrassed.

"And that's perfectly normal," the man encouraged her. "I didn't think about such matters at your age either. Are there any other opinions?"

"Is Azerad testing us?" asked a servant who pretended to sweep nearby.

The man slapped the chair's armrest and said in a friendly tone, "Come on, take a seat here, don't stand over there. 'Azerad is testing us,' you said. You'll hear this most of the time when you ask a priest, but that's not an answer, it's just a way to avoid responding."

I clicked my tongue, adjusting my position before speaking. "I see you're trying to suggest that you have the true answer."

"Rather that the true answer is complicated," he began, his face becoming serious, "Evil exists because it is necessary." I couldn't help but let out an almost mocking smile, to which he responded with another friendly smile. "What would a world without evil be like?"

"Perfect," replied Aethelwit thoughtfully.

"Impossible," the man corrected.

"I wouldn't want to offend you..." I began.

"You couldn't," he interjected in the same warm tone.

"Your answer is foolish," I replied, annoyed. "If Azerad existed, he could make evil disappear. If he couldn't, he wouldn't be all-powerful, as the priests claim he is. You're saying that evil is necessary, meaning that Azerad can cure the plague, but won't, right?"

"Exactly," he replied, his eyes wandering over the surprised faces at the table. He smiled. "But before I explain what I meant, Princess Elena, I have a question for you." I rolled my eyes, as I never liked religious debates. "Is it good for people to have free will?"

"Of course," I replied.

"Good, a firm answer; very well. Could I still be free if I didn't have the freedom to do certain things that others might consider evil?"

"No."

"Do you understand now? Evil and freedom go hand in hand. You can't have one without the other. Azerad chose to give us total freedom. Some use it for good purposes, others for evil purposes."

"I understand," said Aethelwit, smiling.

"Now, I'm sure that everyone here, having both the freedom and the desire to do good, will not wait and will not hesitate to do so, because neither will those who have the desire to do evil."

"Very beautifully explained," Jane complimented him.

"I haven't heard that explanation before," I admitted.

"I hope it's satisfying enough. Lady Aethelwit, it was a pleasure to meet you, and I hope to see you again during my short stay here. Now, I must take my leave."

His explanation had indeed been a good one, and his oratory talent had also helped. Until then, I had seen very few people speaking with greater passion than him. If that man was just a charlatan or a hypocrite, he was a damn good one. But what charlatan would give up a thousand gold coins?

Master Radagrim was already in front of the room when me and Jane arrived there, hunched over, wearing the usual black robe of the wizards, and carrying a small black sack of cloth behind him. Sensing our presence like an old hound, he turned to us, wrinkling his face into a smile.

"Princess Elena! My Lady!" he said, bowing in turn before me, then before Jane.

"Master Radagrim," I greeted him. "The King told me that you wished to see me."

"That is indeed so, but forgive me, I would prefer it to be in private, or if that's not possible, just us and King Larion."

"I can leave," said Jane, bowing before me.

"Or I can come back later, it's no problem," said the wizard, with caution.

"I would like to see you now, Master. Let's get this over with. Jane can wait a few moments." I looked at Jane and she nodded.

"I'm afraid it might take more than a few moments. Many moments, I dare say."

"Perfect," I sarcastically uttered. "Jane, would you mind if we continue the discussions another day?"

"No," she said, then hugged me. "I hope to hear well from you."

I invited the master into the room and gestured for him to sit on the bed. He breathed a sigh of relief, setting down the sack tied with a cord.

"There are too many stairs in this palace for someone my age," he chuckled.

"There are too many even for someone my age, Master. Can I offer you a glass of wine?"

"Thank you, but I must decline. I haven't drunk wine in so long that even its smell would make me tipsy."

"Larion told me you wish to analyze me. Excuse me, but could you tell me what this examination entails?"

I never relished being examined by a doctor, and I anticipated that being examined by a wizard would be ten times worse. While wizards might not wield pointy tools like doctors, their methods seemed infinitely more daunting.

"I will use a pal'ether to try to unlock your lost memories. It's a process that can be very simple and easy to perform, but it can also be very complex. I've never been good at such spells, I hope I don't do something to make it explode."

"Make it explode? Are you talking about my head?"

He began to laugh. "Please forgive me, I couldn't resist making such jests. To lighten the mood a bit, as it seems quite dreary in here."

I burst into laughter for a moment. "You got me with that one."

He pulled a smooth-edged, yellow metal bar, thickened in the middle, from the bag and placed it in his lap.

"So, it's not dangerous?" I asked. "The thing you're holding in your lap looks remarkably close to some toy a woman might use for... it has a funny shape, that's what I mean."

The wizard's gaze fell upon the pal'ether as if he had just noticed it for the first time, then he raised his shoulders.

"The examination itself is not dangerous," he replied, ignoring the last remark. "What could follow after, however, might be. But let's not dwell on those things until we get there; what's the use of worrying in advance?"

"Before we begin, may I ask you something?"

"Of course."

"What do you think is the purpose of evil?"

The old man furrowed his bushy eyebrows, bringing them together just above his nose, and a faint smile appeared on his face.

"I must admit, I wasn't expecting such a question. Not at all, actually. It's commendable that you're concerned with such important matters. Scholars have been seeking an answer for centuries, perhaps millennia, and I'd be lying if I said I have it, but perhaps I can share my opinion."

"Your opinion would be sufficient."

"The line that defines human evil from good is a very fine one, very blurred."

"In other words, it's subjective?"

"Exactly! Think about the death of the Black Queen, which happened quite recently. We would say, rightfully so, that it was a happy event, but Darion surely sees us as the villains who assassinated his beloved. Each person has their own evil."

"The thought that Darion would believe that we are the evildoers, especially after everything he has done, is as amusing as it is likely. But what you say seems fair."

Radagrim was right, and his opinion did not contradict that of Ser Aldric, but rather complemented it. We commit evil because we have the freedom of choice, and each of us perceives it in our own unique way.

"I hope I've helped."

"You have. Now we can get to work."

The wizard drew in a deep breath and fell into a pensive silence for a few moments. Rolling up his long sleeves, he cleared his throat and motioned for me to step closer. With his right hand, he grasped the rod at its thickened middle part, causing the ends to glow pink, while his left hand positioned it on the crown of my head. Under different circumstances, such a spectacle might have struck me as comical, but in that moment, it was disconcerting. After lifting his hand from my head, he returned the object to its sack and retrieved a worn book with leather covers.

"It's indeed a spell," he said, disappointed and tired. "A powerful one. I felt like I hit a wall. Whoever did it, is not just any wizard, and they wanted to make you forget no matter what you might have seen. I don't like it at all."

For a few moments, I felt a wave of nausea rising from my stomach to my throat, and the roof of my mouth dried up as if I hadn't drunk water for days. I can't say whether it was due to fear or as a side effect of the spell the wizard cast, but I leaned towards fear.

"Can anything be done?" I asked.

"There's always something that can be done, please lie down."

I stretched out on the bed, and he moved up, positioning himself level with my head, then opened the book in the middle. He flipped through page after page until he found whatever he was looking for.

"The pages are blank," I murmured.

He smirked. "Not for me. It's a useful pal'ether in a lot of situations, but especially in breaking curses like this one."

"Do you have any suspects?"

"No. Honestly, I don't even think I know a wizard powerful enough to do something like this on their own. But the way the waves were woven seems to suggest just that—all was done by a single individual."

"Heavens..."

"Don't worry, Princess, soon the wizards sent by the Circle will arrive here, and they're all specialized in battle magic. I'll deal with this spell even if it's the last thing I do," he promised.

He is so old that it may very well be. "Thank you!" I replied.

"I'll need you to clear your mind of any other thoughts, and I'll try to extract the memories hidden by the spell."

"It's hard for me to do that," I admitted. "Not to think about anything, I mean. But I'll try."

I closed my eyes, staring at the blackness and focusing only on my breathing, nothing else. The old man placed his hand on my forehead, then let out a long sigh. A warm breath traversed my body, starting from where the wizard touched me and slowly spreading to the tips of my fingers.

"I feel warm. Is that normal?" I asked.

"Yes. But I still need you to clear your mind. I'm stuck, not by magic, but by your own thoughts."

"I am trying. But I don't like the idea of you digging through my thoughts, you know?"

"That's not my intention, Princess. That's why I told you it would be best if your mind was... free."

He withdrew his hand from my head as if I had tried to bite him, and turned his eyes to the window, leaving me feeling thoroughly embarrassed. Struggling intensely to avoid dwelling on compromising thoughts, I fixated precisely on those memories I wished to conceal. Particularly, my first night with Beatrice and Lady Anne Grielburry.

"I'm sorry," I muttered, feeling my cheeks flush.

"We can try another day," he suggested.

"No need, I can do it. Let's try again."

"Probably, I'll need the help of my colleagues from the Circle to get through this," he replied with a grave tone, restarting the spell. "I'm not sure if I'll be able to tear through this alone," he responded.

"I hear whispers," I said, trying to delve into a distant memory.

"Very well! What do you hear?"

I focused intently. "Names, I think" The muffled sounds gradually grew clearer. "Someone is uttering names: Gorgoth, Xeneloth, Yohr'Sherr..."

"No, no, no! Don't say any of those!" he yelled, horrified.

With a force unexpected for his age, he rose from the bed and hastily reached for the sack, pulling out a bunch of thin sticks, each palm-length, which he then threw onto the table.

"What is happening?" I asked just as a heavy aura fell upon the room. I felt watched. I began to scan the room, shifting my eyes from one corner to another, but the feeling only intensified. It was as if someone else was there. A whispered voice emerged in the background of my mind, distant, terrifying, as if all the evil in the world was concentrated in each syllable. The words were almost inaudible, spoken in a language I never heard, nor dreamed. An amalgam of sharp consonants and guttural sounds, with far too few vowels.

Radagrim lit the sticks and began to recite quick, whispered incantations. His eyes darted frantically around the room, and the shadows began to deepen and elongate around us, stretching out like claws, reaching for our own shadows. The old man spoke louder and louder, almost shouting each word, and I withdrew even further into myself, trembling with the deep chill in the room. The same old fear I remembered gripped me, and the whispers took shape, becoming clearer and clearer.

"*Margery, the farmer princess*," a deep, guttural voice echoed in my mind.

"*You may step through shadows,*" another voice uttered, much sharper and grimmer.

Then everything abruptly faded away, along with the shouting incantations of the old wizard, who looked at me with a face marked by exhaustion. He breathed heavily.

"Do not utter those names again," he urged. "They are the First Gods! The creatures I told you about not long ago."

"What do they want from me?" I almost screamed. "Why do I remember their names? To remember them, I must have heard them..."

I was terrified, and I wasn't even trying to hide it, nor could I. Radagrim had told me that their names were like an invitation, and I used them, drawing the creatures there, in my room. But if I remembered their names, it means that... someone spoke them in my presence, in the three days I was absent. My captors.

"They probably don't want anything from you, but we'll find out. I promise we'll shed some light on this."

"I'll talk to Larion to get you a room nearby, that tower is too far," I said. "If I need you again..."

"Very well," he interjected. "Although, now they won't return unless you call them again."

"Rest assured I won't. High Heavens and Azerad above! And what do you mean probably they don't want anything?"

"I just think you were in the wrong place at the wrong time," he suggested. "That's why they wiped your memory, because you stumbled upon things your captors wouldn't want you to know. But they couldn't kill you, because you're the princess, and that would..."

I gasped. "You mean Beatrice and Oswin..."

"No, no, no, don't dwell on that. Everything I said was just a spur-of-the-moment guess, nothing more. But anyway, dark things happen in this city. Too dark. We'll have to talk to the King."

The door to the room slid open slowly, making me startle, and the old wizard's face frowned as he caught sight of the beautiful and young face of Merideth. She entered the room uninvited, a smile on her lips, but her smiling expression turned to concern as she saw my face.

"Is something wrong?" she asked. "It smells like smoke in here, did something catch fire?"

The old man packed his pal'ethers back into the bag just like a child who was gathering up his toys before letting others lay eyes on them. Merideth, completely uninterested in them, didn't even look at Radagrim, coming straight to me.

"You are very pale and cold" she whispered, touching my forehead with her palm.

"I'm fine," I replied with a voice that seemed to indicate that I wasn't convinced myself.

"Princess Elena learned some worrying tidings; tidings that do not concern you," Radagrim told her. "Princess, I think we're done here. I will go immediately to speak with the King, with your permission, of course."

"Very well," I said, trying to hide a tremor.

"We'll have a more extensive discussion when the rest of the members of the Circle arrive," the old man said, his eyes fixed on Merideth. "All specialized in combat magic."

He bowed before me, then turned his back and walked away with swaying steps.

"A very unpleasant person!" said Merideth, seeming stung by his last remark, watching him go.

"He's just trying to figure out what happened to me while I was away," I replied.

"That's no excuse. He made a point of mentioning that those wizards know how to fight just to scare me, as if who knows... I'll say no more." Her lips were just a straight line across her face.

I wasn't in the mood for wizardly debates. "*You will step through shadows*." What was that supposed to mean? And why do they keep calling me Margery? The voice of this one was different from the first one that spoke to me through the idol.

"Do you need to be alone?" asked Merideth, seeing that I was absent.

"No! You can stay. Did Mother try anything while I was away?"

"As far as I know, no. She was too worried about your disappearance to bother with Jane."

"I understand."

I shuddered again, remembering the shadows stretching through the room as if the sun had set right then and there.

"You are not well," she simply told me.

"No. Whoever kidnapped me, they are very bad people. And they still have Beatrice. Poor girl, she has such a fearful character."

"Whoever kidnapped you," she wondered. "Do you doubt it was Darion?"

"I'm almost certain it wasn't him. There's another player in this game, one much more dangerous than Darion, but I can't figure out who." I shuddered, and thought, "*Or what?*"

I even had a strange feeling that bastard, Darion, was fighting the same enemy, but I wouldn't dare to voice such thoughts even if I were alone, let alone with her, for it was pure insanity. *'Darion is going after the key.'* Well, I hope he finds it and shoves it down your throat, and you die together!

"Can I help you in any way?" she offered.

"I don't know. Why do you think evil exists?"

Merideth fell into thought. "I don't think it exists. I believe there are needs and ways to fulfill them, and also believe that the weak tend to call the strong 'evil.'"

"Interesting response."

"Can I help you with anything else?"

"No. I just wanted to find out if my mother baked anything while I was gone. I think I'll try to get some sleep."

Merideth stood up, bowing, then headed towards the exit. However, she stopped before pressing the latch and turned her head to me. Probably I was still pale, because she said, "Do you want me to stay with you until you fall asleep?"

"As you wish," I said, trying to sound indifferent.

She smiled as if I were a little frightened child, then came over and sat on the edge of the bed.

"You can lie down," I said, pulling myself aside.

"I don't know what that wizard told you, nor do I insist on finding out, but it's clear that he really scared you," she said, settling in.

"I'm not scared, Merideth, I'm unsettled. There's a big difference."

"As big as a grain of sand?"

"Perhaps."

All of a sudden, she turned to me, a soft smile playing on her lips. "I have a story on my mind, Princess. Would you like to hear it?"

"Of course."

The Cursed One

Once upon a time, in a faraway land, there lived a beautiful queen—fair as a rose, wise as a serpent, and wealthy as a dragon. But this story is not about that bitch; plenty of tales, poems, and ballads have already been written about her. No, this story is about the youngest of her progeny, a girl named Avelanora—the Blessed One, a name bestowed upon her even before she was born.

However, her name was her only blessing, for she had been born with a very rare disease, one that was slowly eating away at her flesh, day by day. She lived in great pain; every second was pain, every breath was pain, every wish was one of death. At the age of seven, she had to be covered in bandages to prevent herself from bleeding to death, as new cuts were opening in her skin every day, some of them very deep. Bloody, stinky bandages that had to be continuously changed by the servants who prayed for the same thing she did: her death.

Her siblings developed a particularly cruel hatred towards her. They called her Aveloth, the Cursed One, and once people caught wind of that name, everyone started to use it. The name Avelanora was the only blessed thing in her pitiful life, and they took it away and sealed it beyond their mockery, beyond their disgust and hatred. They liked to pinch her and shove her, because even the softest kiss came with a lot of pain for a body as frail as hers(dash em)not that she ever received any kisses, but she could dream, couldn't she? Aveloth despised them, unable to comprehend how anyone could take pleasure in inflicting pain on others.

She believed they were malevolent, doing evil for the sake of evil, but later she realized she was wrong. As I said, they had needs and found a way of fulfilling them. What is with this confused, sweet frown on your face? I'm talking about the need for power, the need to feel strong and dominant; and what better way of feeling big than by stepping over the small ones?

So, Aveloth had always been alone, always in suffering, tortured, betrayed not only by the world, but by her very own body and probably by the gods. She should have died long ago, but something kept her alive; maybe it was the pain, maybe the hatred, maybe the longing for revenge, but she craved and craved for that something day and night, moment after moment, while awake and while dreaming.

One day, when she was seventeen, her parents took her for a ride in the carriage. They draped her in black clothes and left the palace under the cover of night, urging her to move faster through the royal hallways, as they did not want to be seen in the company of the Cursed One. Their whispers were sharp, filled with disdain, and the few servants they passed turned away, pretending not to notice them. Aveloth shuffled along, her bandaged feet dragging, her heart aching not just from the familiar physical pain but from the humiliation of being hidden like a shameful secret.

Every step was agony; her skin was covered in so many cuts and bruises that her body was slowly withering and dying. Despite all the hatred that surrounded her, a flicker of happiness bloomed in her heart. This was the first time they had ever taken her outside the palace. She was about to see the world!

They rode in the carriage for hours upon hours, in near silence, until the sun climbed high in the sky and then dipped below the horizon, only to rise again. Every jolt and bump was a source of pain, yet one eye shed tears of sorrow while the other glistened with joy. She saw foxes darting through the underbrush, a graceful deer prancing through the trees, and a myriad of colorful insects she hadn't known existed. Until now, her only encounters with bugs had been the flies buzzing around her whenever she tried to sleep, drawn by the strong odor of her bandages.

Then, the carriage stopped, and the perhaps too silly girl stepped outside full of hope. It was a misty, moody swamp, but even so, she loved it. She did not get to take more than a few steps when the hounds of the soldiers accompanying them attacked. Her parents just stayed and watched with so much indifference as she was being mauled, dragged like a puppet into the swamps.

"I didn't quite have that in mind, but I guess it works," her father said with a shrug... with disgust. She didn't even cry or yell. She didn't even ask for help. No help would come, so why bother? Then she saw it. Her mother shed a tear. Was that compassion? Was she caring for her? She was dragged over the edge of the road, casting one last glance at her family, smiling for the last time. Mother had really shown her a tiny bit of compassion, more than she had ever received, and she had seen that; now no one could take the memory away from her, perhaps not even in death.

But that would not be her death. A big, giant gray wolf jumped out of the shadowy forest like a specter, killing the hounds like they were nothing, before cuddling next to her and starting to lick her wounds. A woman came soon after, dressed all in black, wearing a white mask resembling a scarred face.

"Poor child, you have lived in such darkness that even the tiniest firefly shines like a sun to you," she said.

"Can you give me death?" she asked the strange woman, with the last shred of life she had left.

"But you died so many times already. I can give you life instead. What is your name?"

She was tempted to say: 'Avelanora,' but the Blessed One had died so long ago, drowned in the hatred and the rage the Cursed One was swimming in.

"Aveloth."

That woman touched her, and for the first time in forever, she felt no pain. She felt warm.

"The most unfitting name for such a beautiful woman."

Beautiful? She? Since when was the putrid, bandaged body, without a strand of hair, beautiful? She was a monster, cursed with life.

That woman helped her take off her bandages. She felt no more pain, and when the patches fell off her hands, she almost screamed. The cuts and scars were gone! No more pain, no more stench of death. She was normal. She even had hair. She cuddled down like a puppy, hugging herself, too scared that anyone would take that away from her, just like they did with everything else. So, she cried, and she cried for hours, while the masked woman stood there, gently caressing her hair.

"I had my share of scars too," the woman said. "That is why I'm keeping this mask, to remember of my own days of suffering, to not forget what I once was."

"Why would one not want to forget suffering, for it is such an evil and sorrowful thing to remember?" Aveloth whimpered.

"There is no such thing as evil, my beautiful child. As for why, there is power in pain and sorrow as there is in love and joy. Even greater."

She took out her mask, revealing a beautiful face, maybe the most beautiful Aveloth had ever seen—one that seemed vaguely familiar, though she couldn't recall from where, her mind clouded as it was in those days. Her eyes were green like the forest, her hair black as the starless night, her nose small, her chin delicate, and her smile so tempting that even the most pious and reserved individuals, whether men or women, would fall for her.

"My name is Khyalis," she told Aveloth.

"Like the Empress," Aveloth remembered.

That was the name of the Empress whose empire had almost took over the entire world.

"This is because, my sweet friend, I am the Empress."

She quickly made a bow, a very stiff one, for she was too afraid of sudden movements, of new cuts that may open in her skin. They always came with great pain. But not then, because then she was cured. She stared at her hands in disbelief, terrified that she might be dreaming, afraid she would be awakened by the woman who came to change her bandages, whose face she could no longer even remember.

She left with the Empress, and not far from the swamps awaited another carriage, with hundreds of soldiers flanking it, holding the imperial banners that danced in the wind—the violet serpent over the black background. No one looked at her with disgust anymore. She could barely hold her tears in place, until alone with Khyalis in the coach, where she cried again for hours.

"*What if this isn't real?*" she kept asking herself.

The face that looked back at her from the mirror belonged to a stranger. She was supposed to be a walking corpse with inflamed, reddish skin full of cuts, not a beautiful young woman; this was what she had always been. Her oldest sister used to bring a mirror into the room and force her to look, asking why she just wouldn't just die. She despised mirrors, but not after she was healed. She felt like she could stare at her reflection for years and never get bored of that face.

Surprisingly, the imperial caravan was heading toward her former home—or rather, her prison. Khyalis was set to meet with her father, the king, regarding a peace treaty between his kingdom and her empire. By a twist of fate, she crossed paths with Aveloth. Her family did not recognize her when they reunited; her sisters even praised her divine beauty. Yet, for some reason, she felt nothing. Just days earlier, she would have wept tears of joy for the slightest compliment, but now she was overwhelmed by a deep emptiness. That emptiness would later give way to a growing hatred.

"You are as beautiful as the painted graves," she told her sisters.

It was her time to watch her siblings, her parents, and her servants with disgust, for they were all weak. They did not know pain nor the power it brings. And, you see, there was one more reason Khyalis came to her in that swamp. She could touch the ether, not only dipping her fingers in the Great River but reaching all the way to the bottom. She was powerful, almost as powerful as the Empress herself, who was the most powerful witch to ever live.

While at the palace, Khyalis taught her to wield magic, and she was learning so utterly fast. When she left for the Imperial Palace, her new home, she left a small present for her beloved family. A curse—after all, she was the Cursed One. Soon, everyone from that palace developed the same disease she once had.

She met them again in five years, just some bloody pieces of meat, covered in bindings, still wearing their fine clothes and expensive jewelry. Painted graves. She revealed her identity before partially healing them, doing so only to ensure their suffering would continue. Aveloth then seized the kingdom, eliminating anyone who dared to oppose her.

As queen, she enjoyed a long and prosperous reign, surrounded by power and riches. Frequently, she would descend to the prison, taking pleasure in the torment of her former captors. By healing them only to let them wither again like old flowers under the scorching sun, she derived satisfaction from their ongoing agony. Despite their repeated pleas for death, Aveloth took delight in their suffering. Although Avelanora might have shown them mercy, they had killed her. Unbeknownst to them, their own actions had created the Cursed One, and they were tortured by their own deeds.

For a while I remained silent, chewing at her story in the back of my mind. I said, "I know a particular knight who would have said that Avelanora became the very thing she despised, enslaved by the same circle of hatred that broke her. But damn ser Aldric! She gave them what they asked for."

She was about to respond when mother pushed the door aside and stepped in, wearing a serious and alarmed expression. Uncharacteristic. She rubbed her hands spasmodically, something I hadn't seen from her since childhood, from the moments when she argued with dad.

"Merideth, I would like to discuss something privately. Now, if possible," her voice sounded off. As if she was trying to sound authoritative but couldn't seem to appear anything other than submissive and scared.

Merideth stood up and made a bow.

"Of course, my Queen," she said, looking at her from under her golden eyebrows.

"Has something happened, Mother?" I asked.

"No, Elena!" she snapped. "Anyway, nothing concerning you."

A smile escaped me as they left. Regardless of what had struck her, she seemed terrified, and that was delicious. "*Nothing concerning you,*" she told me without knowing that soon I would find out everything from Merideth.

Soon, I fell asleep, and Larion woke me at sunset.

"Good morning," he said, raising his eyebrows and leaning over me.

I pushed him aside, rolling away from him. "Is it morning already?" I asked, confused.

I could hear the corners of his lips contorting into a smile. He brushed a strand of hair from my face, then leaned down and kissed me. "No, my dear, the sun has just set. You told me you would have dinner in the Great

Hall, but if you want, I can let you continue your hibernation."

"No, no. I'll come. You go ahead and I'll join you in no time."

"You'll fall asleep on duty the moment you step out the door. I'll be waiting," he insisted.

I got up and changed my dress, trying to keep away from his teasing pinches, the story of Merideth coming back in my head. Her tone seemed so personal as if she was talking about herself.

Simply taking off my dress was enough to make him lose control, and that always amused me. The atmosphere quickly changed as I sat down to arrange my hair. He looked at me with some concern, the shadows caused by the flames of the chandeliers braiding through his black hair.

"I spoke with Radagrim," he said with a sigh.

"And what do you think?"

"That it's time for him to stop poking his dusty nose into old books and fairy tales. Has some powerful magic user wiped your memory? Coincidentally, such a witch slipped away from under the noses of four dozen soldiers, massacring almost all of them. There, mystery solved."

"Are you suggesting that Aella is still alive?"

"Be it her or some other creature like her. But she is not a goddess, as the old fool claimed, but a cursed woman. If you cut her, she bleeds and if she bleeds, she can also die. Those 'gods' Radagrim believes in are nothing more than aberrations that exist only in the weary minds of those with too much idle time on their hands."

"When I spoke their names, the shadows began to stretch across the room, Larion, as if they were alive. I've seen them with my own eyes."

"That, Elena, is something either caused by the ether or those artifacts of Radagrim, or maybe the sun simply hid behind a cloud. Don't give me that look, it's madness! High Heavens, it's complete madness. First, my brother loses his mind and flees north with a savage to gather an army, and now... this. I don't know what in the Burning Hells is happening to this world. Here's what we'll do: say their names. Show me, and I'll believe you."

I shuddered, their voices coming back to my head. Those whispers. "I wouldn't do it again even if I were to die!" I almost cried. "If you don't believe me, it's strictly your problem."

"How would you expect me to believe that? Malevolent ancient gods sealed away millennia ago, that somehow hear when you utter their names and that came into your room. Do you hear yourself?" I didn't respond with words, contenting to a simple nod. He buried his head in his hand, visibly exhausted. "Whatever it was," he continued, "it's over. You know? What was worse has passed."

I nodded again, though in reality, I felt that what was worse hadn't passed, but on the contrary, it was yet to come. The end of the day would prove me right.

Despite this, I made sure to maintain a smile on my face as I descended into the Great Hall, offering a warm greeting to everyone I met. The smile I wore was as genuine as I could manage. At times, I found myself envious of Darion's ability to treat the courtiers with such effortless detachment. Like him, I didn't care much about other people's opinions, but unlike him, I couldn't afford to do whatever I pleased without thinking dozens of times about the possible consequences and how they might affect me in the long run. He didn't care about any of that. He was a man that lived in the '*now.*'

We sat at the table at the head of the hall, surrounded by the most prominent nobles in the entire country. I sat to the right of my betrothed, with my mother to my right. When I asked her where Merideth was, she snapped at me like a dog when someone tries to steal its food. Something had frightened her.

I tried to remain present, but my thoughts drifted far away throughout the night. The melodies sung by the bards became distant echoes I could hardly grasp, and the faces of the nobles who approached me faded into a blur. In my efforts to remain courteous, I offered wide smiles and nodded incessantly, but it was likely evident to all that something was amiss with me.

It was past midnight when Larion and I rose from the table to leave the hall. As I was bowing left and right in salute, like a well-dressed animal, it occurred to me how pathetic everything was. I didn't like them, and they didn't like me, but we all had to pretend to be on good terms just for the sake of pretense. If that isn't madness, I don't know what is.

Chaos broke loose as a beggar, clothed in tatters and smeared with blood, burst through the grand entrance of the hall. I couldn't hold back a surprised gasp as I realized that those sanity-stripped eyes belonged to Oswin. He was swinging a crossbow left and right like an axe, causing the nobles to jump aside, while the soldiers sprinted behind him, yelling commands.

His lips quivered, struggling to shape words that refused to come forth. Tears carved paths down his cheeks as he hoisted the crossbow, now pointing its threatening promise directly at my betrothed's chest.

"No," I whispered, stretching my hand as if I could stop him shooting.

"*He must die,*" I discerned from his trembling lips.

Larion shoved me aside just as the bolt hurtled towards him, piercing his chest and causing him to stagger a few steps before collapsing onto his back. A scream tore from my throat as I fell to my knees beside him, surrounded by commotion and screams erupting all around.

"Please, please, I beg you, stay with me. Please, Larion, don't leave me alone, please. Someone do something!"

Mother was by my side, her expression a canvas of horror and fear, as if Larion embodied her entire reason for being. Trembling, she whispered under her breath something between a prayer and a curse. Doctor Jared arrived in haste, kneeling beside him, and inspecting the wound with a pale face.

Larion remained conscious, his gaze never shifting from my face, his lips forming a bloody smile. With a trembling hand, he reached out towards my face, while the other clutched around the golden zerath he took from Arlieth.

"Do something, don't just stand there!" I implored the doctor, but he merely shook his head. There was nothing to be done; the bolt had pierced his right lung. It was now just a matter of seconds, perhaps minutes.

The hall spun around me, the voices of the nobles reduced to distant whispers, their words shapeless specters struggling to reach me through my nausea. I collapsed onto my side. I was deaf, but I could still see someone brutally pushing everyone aside, running barefoot on the cold floor, and almost falling face down just a few paces from me.

Merideth.

She moved with the urgency of a mouse, hastily placing her hand on my betrothed's chest, causing him to jolt as if struck by lightning. Sound flooded back into my ears, and I rose back to my knees.

"Please help him, please!" I pleaded with her.

Though his eyes remained open, his body trembled under her touch. She seized the bolt in her fist and yanked it out forcefully.

"This is not..." Jared's voice faltered as he reached for her hand.

"Back off!" Her scream pierced the air, and in an instant, the doctor was hurled across the room by an unseen force, crashing into a cluster of nobles.

She pulled the bolt out, and then his body began to glow, his skin knitting back together as if he had never been wounded. The witch fell onto her bottom, her expression weary yet relieved, before nodding at me.

"The king is fine!" she declared for all to hear. "He just needs a few days of sleep. And privacy. Please, everyone out of the hall!"

I hugged Merideth, still crying like a child, then settled beside Larion on the cold floor, cradling him in my arms and listening to his breathing. His eyes were shut, trapped in a peaceful slumber, and his wound was gone. Merideth assured me multiple times that he was completely healed, that he would sleep for a few days, before simply awakening.

Except for his uncle, Alfric, everyone else left, escorted out by the soldiers. I discovered, just after the initial shock had passed, that Oswin slit his throat before the guards could apprehend him, leaving us forever unaware of his motives or the details of this attempted assassination. At that moment, I didn't even care why.

Shortly thereafter, Larion was carried to his room, still sleeping, while I awaited the arrival of the City Guard Captain.

"Your Highness, I arrived as swiftly as I could," the old man wheezed between gasps for air.

He wore armor painted in red and green, with the two lions of the Grayfang family embroidered on his green tunic. I preferred the previous captain, the young one, but he had lost his legs during the Night of the Blood Moon.

"Yet not swiftly enough," I half-mumbled with a cold voice. "Your king almost died, and your men did nothing to prevent it. How is it possible that an armed madman could burst in and shoot the king in front of everyone? Explain."

He cleared his throat. "I'll conduct an official investigation and find out what had happened, all the details…"

"Are you deaf," I whispered, silencing him, then slammed the door and stood up. Mother, who was seated not far from me, smiled. "I'll tell you what happened. Treason! Damn treason! How else could you explain the incompetence?!" I yelled at him.

"Princess…" Alfric began, but I cut him off.

"I want all the guards that served in the Great Hall arrested for treason and assisting the assassin, right now! Every single one, including those who guarded the entrance on the outside. For what in the Burning Hells are we paying you?!"

The captain nodded grimly, his back straight as a pole.

"Heads will roll for this," I warned him. "And yours might just be the first."

"Forgive me, Princess," he muttered with a deep bow. "I will…"

"You have done enough. I'll take it from here. You just do what you did when the King was in danger. Relax. Escort the former captain to his cell," I ordered my men. They quickly surrounded him, taking his weapon and leading him towards the exit. He didn't even try to protest.

"Larion would not be happy that you replaced the city guard with someone from your entourage, Princess," warned Alfric as soon as the guards led the prisoner out.

"We'll see about that pretty soon."

"As the King is unable to rule, the next one in command is me, Elena. I hope you won't forget that. Next time, think twice before making such hasty decisions on your own."

My mother huffed a laugh. "The King is not unable to rule. He is just sleeping."

He glanced around the room and quickly noticed that our men outnumbered his, and besides, I had Merideth. He rose from the table and bowed.

"You are right," he said. "We shall talk more in the morning."

"I care for you, Uncle Alfric; you are like family to me already. That's why I won't let you leave the palace until the King awakens. The streets are dangerous. If Oswin could sneak in here, who knows what else could be out there, waiting for victims."

Alfric Grayfang grinned at me. "Am I your prisoner?"

"My guest, Uncle."

I was no fool. Allowing him to leave was a risk I was not prepared to take, as he could muster a few thousand soldiers in no time. Who knew what he could have done under the pretext that the king is dying, and I am trying to plant my own men in his ranks.

His men lowered their hands on their sword handles, and mine followed suit. Merideth rose, the candle flames flickering.

"Thank you for your care, Elena," he said with a wide smile, then burst into laughter. "You are right, I will spend the night here."

"Then it's settled."

Everyone breathed again. Alfric was soon escorting to his room, but not before casting one last glance at me and then at Merideth, his eyes flickering with muffled rage. My instincts had never been at ease with him, and now, with the power he wielded, he could effortlessly claim the palace, seize the throne, or worse, end Larion's life in his vulnerable slumber. He was the only one that had such power, and I refused to risk it.

"Very well," my mother complimented me as we headed towards our rooms.

"Do you think he would have done something against Larion?" I asked.

The halls were filled with soldiers. All the Frevian soldiers that remained in the city were now in the palace.

"No. But why risk it? A toothless dog won't bite."

"Oswin…"

"He is dead," said Mother.

"Yes, but why? Have you seen his eyes? It looked like there was nothing there, no life. Only madness."

"Our men will try to find out more, but I doubt we'll ever know what got into him."

I thanked Merideth once again before entering my room. Larion was still sleeping, his shirt torn away because of the bolt, still bloody. Two maids awaited in the corner of the room.

"You can leave," I told them. "I'll call you back if something comes up."

After they left, I took off all my clothes and rested next to him, my head on his chest, just listening to his beating heart.

"I love you more than anything," I told him.

After that I broke down, wrapping my arms tightly around him and crying away all my tears. The moon's silver light spilled through the window, tracing the archway's form across our chamber, its slender beam creeping onto the bed to enshroud us in its ethereal glow. Maybe this city is indeed cursed. Or maybe I am the cursed one.

Apart

Beithir, Yohr'Sherrat, Wolf, Sparrow, Alfred, Aveloth, Aethelred... Larion.

I repeated the list every few steps, feeling a deep pain in my chest at the mention of my brother's name. But that was the truth and denying it wouldn't do me any good. From that day on, no more lies. Especially not the lies I kept telling myself, the lies I hoped that if repeated enough times, would come true. I was at war. I needed the Daughters of the Night, so the first name that needed to be crossed off that list was Beithir, because he had the key.

I unraveled my shirt, which I used only as a piece of cloth, wrapping it around the wound on my back, which seemed to be the deepest, and threw it into a bush. It was too torn and blood-stained to wear anymore. I couldn't find my cloak anywhere, probably caught on the branches I passed through on landing, and more importantly, I couldn't find my sword. I had lost a lot of blood, but under the morning rays, I realized that the tears finally seemed to have closed.

Beithir, Yohr'Sherrat, Wolf, Sparrow, Alfred, Aveloth, Aethelred... Larion.

Aella was in Saherdrakar, I hoped. She had to be there. The dragons circled the forest for hours after the battle, but none heard my cries. I didn't know if Beithir had escaped or not, but given the events leading up to my fall, that seemed the most plausible scenario. And indeed, as I was about to find out, that's what happened.

I was half lost. Every path I could find disappeared as soon as I began to climb from the base of the mountain; no road led anywhere. The Dragon's Mountain was a bastion of nature. I had the sensation that I was somewhere on the opposite side of where I ascended with Arya and Aella, which made sense because we climbed from the southeast, and Beithir retreated to the north. I spent the entire day wandering through the woods, trying to cross it, and at night I fell asleep at the foot of an old tree in a clearing.

I wasn't worried about being attacked by anyone, as not even the animals dared to approach that mountain. However, mosquitoes were a different story, and I was bare-chested, defenseless against them, wearing only a pair of trousers—torn above the right knee—and boots. I didn't dream anything that night, or at least nothing prophetic; nothing to remember.

In the following morning, I got closer to the spot where I thought I had climbed two days before. I limped in only one direction, or at least I hoped I did, but it felt like I was going in circles, and I feared I hadn't strayed too far from where I fell. From the place where that dhampir saved me. Heavens.

Beithir, Yohr'Sherrat, Wolf, Sparrow, Alfred, Aveloth, Aethelred... Larion.

Yermoleth? Was he supposed to be one of the names too? The bastard knew that the dragons could sense me, he knew, and he chose not to say anything. Saya? I spared her life, and she took advantage of it to try to kill me. Yorric? How long until he makes a move against me?

I collapsed at the end of another trail, exhaustion taking its toll on me—another dead end. I heard some dragons roaring in the distance, but it was too far to even attempt to cry. A long scar spread across both palms of my hands from the handle of the shield that got seared into them. Even if Aella healed me, the scar remained.

"Short life?" a voice came from my right.

I turned sharply to see two dragons, both shaded in greens and yellows, each of similar sizes to Arya, lying in a clearing. The one who spoke first appeared to be female.

"You're alive?" the other exclaimed, sounding like a male.

"I wasn't sure, but if you can see me too... I suppose."

They both burst into an unnecessary loud laughter, then pounced closer like two puppies, shaking the ground of the tranquil forest.

"Falkor told us you fought for us, *drakari apahr riak*, friend of dragons," the female said, lowering her head towards me. "He said you fell from his back. Tell us, how does life's flame still burn within you?"

"I flew," I joked, and the two began to laugh again. I bumped my forehead against her massive head, crooked at me, responding to her greeting. "Forgive my tired greeting, but I'm a bit weary; it's not easy to fly without wings. Could you take me to Saherdrakar?"

I was in good spirits, for once again, despite the odds, I had survived. I would return to Aella, lick my wounds, and prepare for the next battle. Or so I thought then.

Amarut and Daghra, the two dragons, argued for a while about who should carry me on their back, but in the end, Amarut conceded and left that honor for his sister. As expected, Beithir escaped with the key. Arya lost a horn in the battle, but otherwise was fine. No dragon died during the attack, because Beithir avoided killing at all costs, so as not to attract the retribution of dragons to Rhal'Ellieh. Despite this, Aella continued to insist on attacking the city and retrieving the key, but Khulsedra refused to endanger her kin.

"The Daughter of the Night was angry, and so was Arashkigal, the Bane of Screamers," Amarut said, flying very close to me and Daghra. "They left for Rhal'Ellieh a few hours ago to retrieve the key themselves."

I almost choked on air. "What?"

Amarut licked his snout before starting to repeat. "They left for Rhal'Ellieh a few…"

"Why? Why didn't you stop them? How could Aella leave without me?"

"We couldn't stop them, for they did nothing against *Rei*'s wishes, and we couldn't pursue them either, for it was forbidden. Why would the daughter of the night wait for your return, when you, after all, were dead? She cried a long time by your corpse before burying it, but there was no point in waiting for you, because no one ever returned from the Realm of the Blue Moon."

"Until today," corrected Daghra.

"I wasn't dead, Heavens! What do you mean 'my corpse?' What are you talking about?" I yelled, trying to cover the flurry of wind whistling next to my ear.

"Yesterday, when the sun was nearing halfway to setting, we found the burnt corpse of a man," explained Amarut, "and next to it was your sword, stuck in the flesh of a screamer. Humans seldom venture near this mountain, and the deceased was charred almost to the bone, unrecognizable. It was clear to everyone that it was you."

"But it wasn't! We have to go after Arya and Aella; they need help."

"We can't intervene, that's *Rei*'s will, and we are her *dharzgad*. We must obey if we want to remain so. We'll leave you at Saherdrakar, friend of the dragons, as you asked, but we can't do more than that."

"You can't...," I muttered bitterly, but I didn't say anything more. It was pointless.

I let myself fall forward, lying on my stomach, embracing Daghra's back as I gasped out my sorrow. I had accepted that the evil had not ended, truly accepted it; I had acknowledged the possibility that enemies seeking my death lurked everywhere, and I had even felt eager to confront them all. But not alone.

It was clear that I couldn't find Rhal'Ellieh without the help of the dragons. I had to convince them to assist me. The two dragons understood my pain, for they remained silent for the next few minutes, until we entered the city. I didn't dare to linger too much in thoughts and cry over my fate, because that would have been of no use.

The dhampir corpses were no more, I noticed as soon as we entered the cave. All the dragons flying in the vast expanse of the underground city, upon seeing me on Daghra's back, remained gaping-mouthed and confused, as if they had seen a ghost. For them, that's exactly what I was.

Daghra left me with Amarut in the center of the city, next to the giant dragon statue, while she went to inform the queen. I had more change of clothes in my satchel, which should still be in Arya's room, but I didn't have any other cloaks. Many dragons gathered there, either staring at me in silence or whispering muffled sounds to those nearby.

Khulsedra didn't seem surprised to see me alive at all; in fact, I dare say she didn't care.

"You're alive," she remarked.

"And in dire need of help, mighty *Rei* Khulsedra. I need to get to Rhal'Ellieh as quickly as possible. Aella and Arashkigal, your daughter, are there, and I fear they are in great danger."

The golden rings on Khulsedra's horns flickered as she stepped into the barrier of light flowing through the colossal cave maw, all the way to the center of the city. "You are free to go," she said.

I kept my face as clear and unbothered as I could, determined not to show any signs of faltering. "I was hoping you would accompany me…"

The queen growled, interrupting me. "And why, short-lived one, did you hope for that?" she inquired.

"Your daughter..."

"She chose to leave despite my insistence; her fate is not in my hands. She has chosen her own path, it's up to her whether she can traverse it or not."

"At least take me there..."

"We will not approach those accursed lands," the queen insisted.

"But they attacked your kingdom!" I yelled, losing my composure.

Rei took a few steps towards me, her breaths deep and heavy, visibly fatigued by the necessity of words. Dragons didn't particularly enjoy prolonged conversation, often finding it to be an irritating habit of the creatures who couldn't find solace within themselves.

"They came and they stole, but they didn't kill anyone; they even lost hundreds of their own. If they had taken the life of even one dragon, then we would have hunted them like animals, but they didn't. Our blood did not spill, but if we go where you want us to go, it will flow like river water. You fought for us, and I am grateful to you..."

"I'll do something on your gratitude!" I snapped.

Her eyer narrowed. "Is that an offense?" she wondered.

"A compliment, great *Rei*. I hope you'll accept it with open arms. Ever since I can remember, my greatest dream has been to meet the dragons. I relished the stories about you, the legends of your courage, wisdom, and power. It seems there is not a shred of truth in the old tales."

The queen scowled, her growl reverberating through the air, causing the dragons around us to begin whispering amongst themselves. I scanned over them, meeting their gaze without a hint of fear. Reason was already drowned in

"You're all cowards!" I raged as loudly as I could, the word 'cowards' echoing through the city, bouncing back to us multiple times. "You have no authority whatsoever, anyone can come into your domain and do as they please, and you won't lift a finger to stop them."

"Your words are filled with venom, human. Be careful where you spit them," she warned me.

"Of course, for I cannot harm you. You find courage in the face of the weaker ones, but when faced with a worthy opponent, you cower like a rat. So much for your courage!"

Rei turned her back on me, flicking her tail like a whip above my head, perhaps as a warning, then took flight for her chamber. I cast one last glance at the dragons standing in a circle around me before heading in the direction of Arya's chamber.

"What are you still standing around for?" I shouted as I walked away. "Go find a hole to bury your heads in, until others fight your battles for you."

My backpack was still in Arya's room, and thankfully, Aella's cloak was there too. She didn't need it much anymore since she already had the blanket from Yermoleth. I changed my pants, choosing to keep the empty sheath attached to my belt, then grabbed a new shirt and collapsed in the corner of the room, a move that made all my wounds protest at once. I stayed there for a while, clutching Aella's cloak to my chest.

"Heavens... what have you done, Aella? Why couldn't you wait, at least a few more hours?" I whispered.

The only one I could still ask for help was Yermoleth, and he was far to the west, at least a week away. I couldn't afford to waste any more time. I got up, enduring another wave of pain from my injuries, slung my satchel over my back, and began limping towards the exit. I had no other choice.

The Flame-Stones shimmered brightly in the morning light. I knew I had to hurry, so I ran to the stairs leading to the exit, passing several dragons who had stopped talking, silently watching me. Some of them were barely bigger than a horse and seemed fat and clumsy. Probably babies, I thought. The pain in my leg became sharper with each step.

Aella believes I was dead. Now she is heading towards Rhal'Ellieh, hoping to retrieve the key from

Yohr'Sherrat. I had to repeat all these events in my mind several times to reassure myself that they had indeed happened.

I left Saherdrakar with a bitter taste in my mouth, without looking back, determined to never have anything to do with the dragons again. I was planning to run all the way to Yermoleth. I knew which direction to take, and I had a few landmarks that I had taken note of when we came on Arya's back.

It felt pointless. Aella and Arya would reach Rhal'Ellieh and probably return before I even get close to Yermoleth.

Volthrax, the azure-scaled dragon, landed not far from me, blocking my path. I halted, sinking into the not-so-tall grass, my fingers tracing the contours of my injured leg. Pain radiated from the wound—the dhampir's talons had struck deep.

"What do you want now?" I mumbled at him.

"To return your sword," he said, extending one of his claws. The Heart of Dawn lay in his blue palm, like a needle in the hand of a human. Next to her was a white crystal shaped like a spike, as long as my palm and three fingers thick. "A piece of a Flame-Stone," he explained when he saw me looking at it. "It was struck by one of your mate's lightning bolts; I thought it might be useful to light your way."

I felt a hard-to-describe relief, holding the Heart of Dawn in my hand again, but also a pang of guilt for forgetting to ask what had happened to her. I grabbed the crystal, which didn't seem to glow at all, and stuffed it into my rucksack.

Volthrax was still there, watching me.

"Will you help me?" I insisted.

"I would like to, but..."

"Then help me! Arashkigal is your daughter, isn't she?"

"My offspring, yes."

"And that means nothing to you? A father should defend his daughter. If my daughter were in danger..."

I froze, mouth agape, staring as struck by lightning at the great dragon. I was talking about Lyra, and the words flowed out of me so naturally as if it were the plain truth.

"I promised I wouldn't, and a drakar keeps his word, guards it with his life," said the dragon. "I'm sorry, but I can't help you here, and you can't make it there on your own. My advice is to stay with us until they return."

"Thank you for the advice," I replied sarcastically. "That's what the voice of reason tells me too, but lately I've made a habit of not listening to it."

"I know what you're talking about, short-life, for that's how I was when I met my *Rei*. A fool stumbling after her tail. Your Aella doesn't have a tail, if I saw correctly, but you understand the purpose of my words. I'd tell you it'll pass, but seven thousand years later, I'm in the same situation," he chuckled.

"I don't like you, Volthrax, and even if I did, I don't have time for chatter right now," I said, rising again.

The dragon lowered his head, blocking my path just as I was about to run past him. "Too bad, human, for I like you. You seem like a brave one."

"That's exactly why I don't like you. What kind of parent leaves their daughter in danger for fear of their wife?"

"You don't know our customs, and there's no time to explain..."

"And above all, I don't care. Goodbye."

"I can take you part of the way," he hurriedly added before I started running again. "You're heading towards Yermoleth, right?"

I kept silent for a few moments, staring blankly at his face. He had two big pair of horns on his head, like Khulsedra, but also two smaller ones, along with numerous spikes spreading across his scaly neck in beautiful patterns. Some of his scales even had white tips. He claimed to have been alive during the War of Shadows, making him over several thousand years old. He was ancient.

"Does your *Rei* allow it?" I teased him.

"No," he replied honestly, unfazed by my mockery. "That's why I'll only take you part of the way, but even that will cut a good few days off your journey."

"Even so, I won't have enough time," I laughed bitterly. "They might have even arrived already."

"Don't worry, Darion, they may be women, but they're not fools. They'll stop at the base of the mountains and travel on foot from there, I know it. The Enemy has many spies keeping watch, especially in the light of recent events, and they won't stand a chance if they burst in there hoping to come out alive. They'll sneak in, slowly but surely. Well, 'surely' is a bit of a stretch, but the purpose of my words is: you have enough time to find them."

"Let's go, then."

He bent down, but he was too large for me to climb onto him, so he extended his paw and after I stepped on it, he lifted me and settled me on his back. I had to take a few steps, praying he wouldn't make any sudden movements until I got closer to the base of his neck, right between his wings, where I could grab onto some small spikes. If I were to fly on the back of a dragon, it would be preferable to have something to hold onto.

Thus, on that midsummer morning, I left the Mountain of Dragons on the back of Volthrax, filled with anger and sadness, without the key and more importantly, without Aella. We flew in silence, both of us lost in thought.

We landed a few hours later at the foot of a mountain, and in front of us, among other mountains, I could see the peak of the Demon's Fang. It was still far away. At least four days' journey, if I was lucky. I slid down from him, feeling for my sword and backpack once again.

"Bring the girls back," he asked, staring at me, his head lowered on one side.

"I'll do everything I can, but I need you to do everything you can too," I said. "Talk to *Rei* of yours, convince her to assault the Enemy."

"Oh, I could convince the wind to stop blowing or the fire to burn less fiercely, more easily than *Rei* Khulsedra when she's determined to say she's made a decision."

"Then we will die there. I dreamed it, Volthrax, and my nightmares come true. You might be our only chance. I will do everything I can, but it may not be enough."

"I will try to help you..."

"Don't help me, help your daughter."

"Take care of yourself, Darion Grayfang," he told me, then turned on his hind legs and took flight, the trees bending under the currents created by his wings.

"And you of yourself," I whispered, watching his blue shape disappear into the distance.

Allies and Promises

Then I ran. I didn't know if I was going the right way, I just knew the mountain was ahead and that's where I had to go. I tried to avoid hiking over the mountains that got in my way, but often it wasn't possible, as the trails I followed through the forest continued over the ridges that I wanted to avoid. I spent most of my days running, until I felt my leg giving up due to the injury caused by that dhampir, and the nights walking, when the road and the starlight allowed me.

During that time, it was a new moon, which only made my progress at night even more difficult. I came very close to stepping into a pit even with the light of that Flame-Stone crystal given to me by Volthrax. I could ignite it anytime with a simple thought, and I could make it shine brighter or dimmer, but I avoided using it too much for fear of attracting the attention of the clans living in those regions. For the same reason, I avoided sleep as much as possible. In that wilderness a quick nap could turn into the sleep of forever.

In the first night, I truly believed that was the case. I closed my eyes leaning against the thick back of a spruce, resting only for a few moments, when I felt a strong prick in my chest, on the right side, like an arrow. I spun back on my legs, almost collapsing on the slope and drew my sword, scanning the almost complete darkness of the forest. There was nothing, and I wasn't hit by anything. It was just in my mind.

From then on, I gathered some thorns from a thicket and passed them through the collar of my shirt, so that whenever sleep stole over me and my head drooped onto my chest, I would wake up whimpering, with the spikes either pricking my beard or my chest.

"I hope you're well, Aella," I whispered each time I looked at the thin, crescent moon, wondering if she did the same.

I didn't trust Yermoleth, but he was the closest thing to an 'ally' in my situation.

Three days had already passed. The little food I had ran out on the first day, but I had plenty of water. The lack of sleep was the worst. I became clumsy, and it was increasingly difficult to think clearly. Some paths I walked seemed freshly traveled, and often I felt like I heard footsteps or voices coming from the forest. I still wouldn't know now whether I actually heard them or if it was all in my slumbering mind.

Despite the thorns, on the third day I fell asleep as soon as I sat on the roadside, and I woke up just before sunrise, with red stains on the white fabric of my shirt and a few spikes I had to pull out from my neck. Despite the pain, I was grateful that I managed to fall asleep, and more importantly, to wake up. There was no mountain between me and the Demon's Fang anymore. I was sure that in less than two days, I would reach Yermoleth.

I regretted leaving my bow in the Yerdrasil, as it would have been more useful for hunting than the handful of stones I gathered from the forest, with which I couldn't hit anything. "*Soon, I'll have to tighten my belt,*" I remember thinking.

It was the middle of the fourth day when, during a break, I heard voices coming from down the trail where I was waiting. I stood up and hid behind a tree, and shortly after, I could see two men climbing up the slope, accompanied by three women and about a dozen horses tied together, each carrying several bags attached to the saddles. One of the men seemed to be around forty years old, short and bald, with a long blond beard reaching down to his chest and striking blue eyes that stood out even from that distance. The other was tall and solid, with hair black as coal, and long down to the base of his neck, greasy. The short man wore his sword at his waist, while the other wore it on his back, attached to a strap that went across his broad chest.

For a moment, I wondered if it would be a good idea to step out from behind the tree and ask them for food. The past few months had given me an unshakable confidence in my own abilities, a foolish sense that whispered to me that if it came to a fight, I could easily kill the two, even hungry and weakened as I were, for they didn't seem dangerous. At least not to me, who had fought wizards, dhampirs, and dragons. But I didn't step out; I decided it would be better to let them pass, to go their way, and I would go mine. I didn't resort to attacking and killing passersby for food.

The bald man stopped and turned his head toward the tree behind which I was hidden. That's when I realized that my backpack was still visible, leaning on the tree. I stepped onto the path, trying to appear steadier on my feet than a limping dog, holding my hand over the hilt of the Heart of Dawn.

"Keep walking," I said threateningly, giving them a cold stare.

The bald man clapped his hands, a lupine smile creeping onto his lips. "Well, well," he said. "What do we have here, a lost traveler?" His accent sounded very similar to that of the mountaineers. Usually, the accent sounded funny, but something in the man's voice lent it a menacing edge.

"Are you planning to rob me?" I asked calmly.

"Depends," he replied. "Do you have anything worth stealing?"

"No."

"Then no." He paused, rolling his eyes with a smirk, then glanced down at the Heart of Dawn. "But still, the sword you carry looks good."

"She's cursed, you don't want her," I said, shrugging. "Her or me, but I prefer to believe it's her."

"Ah, in that case you're right, I don't want it," he laughed. "I like you, kid, what's your name?"

"Call me whatever you like," I said.

"You wouldn't want me to pick a name. I'm inventive, ask my wives."

My attention shifted to the women, they expression indicating that their understanding of the common tongue was somewhat limited. "Darion," I replied, holding his piercing gaze.

He came a few steps in my direction, almost swaying, while the tall man adjusted the leather belt that crisscrossed his chest, causing the sword strapped to his back to shift slightly to the right—positioned for a swift draw.

"Where are you headed, Darion?" asked the man approaching. He stopped when I half drawn my blade.

"The Demon's Fang. Though I might have gotten a bit lost. Maybe you can guide me, what do you say?"

"Why would you head to such a place?" he inquired. "Maybe the name is not suggestive enough, but there lives a… demon."

"He's a friend of mine."

I hope.

He burst into loud laughter, then took a step back, and the women behind him shifted uncomfortably, as those people avoided that mountain with a more than religious devotion. Two of the women appeared to be close to his age, while the other seemed younger than me by a few years. The tall man with the long black hair didn't change his expression at all, not even his position. He watched the whole exchange with an empty, unfriendly stare.

"Listen, he's friends with the demon! You don't speak our language, do you? You only speak the common tongue, I can tell by your accent you're not from around here, you're from the valley, outside the mountains," said the bald man.

"You're mistaken there," I replied, pushing the sword back. "I know all the curses in your language, and my pronunciation is perfect."

"Then you know the essentials."

"What's your name?" I asked.

"Ragar, and the little one next to me is Byrgulf, my brother," he said, gesturing to the tall man. "He doesn't speak much, he can't, and he doesn't hear, but he has good eyes and a quick hand. It's enough for me to nod in your direction, and he'd take your head."

"Then I'll do everything in my power not to upset you, Ragar."

The man laughed again, tilting his head back.

"Are you hungry?" he asked when he stopped.

"I'd be lying if I said no."

"Good, we were just talking about sitting down to eat. Well, I was talking; my companions aren't much for conversation. Lucky, I ran into you, otherwise I would have choked to death on all the words I had no one to say. Stay with us, I'll let you feast on the scent of each piece of food before I shove it in my mouth.

"After three days on the road without any food, I'll gladly accept that too," I said.

"Where are you coming from?"

"Shartat."

Ragar squinted his eyes, studying my face for any sign that I might be joking, and when he found none, he giggled like a shy kid. "Ah, I like you, you know? You're crazy, and I'd watch my back if I slept next to you, but I like you, damn it! My dear, prepare the meal!"

He clapped his hands three times, prompting the women, who seemed almost trained, to spring into action in the blink of an eye. The man sat down in front of me, then unsheathed his sword from his belt and placed it halfway between us. The other, Byrgulf, did the same, and the unwritten code of warriors compelled me to follow suit. The women brought out various dishes from the saddlebags and a few pots, then made a fire at the edge of the trail, a few meters away from us, whispering in their language.

"Where are you coming from, Ragar, and where are you heading?" I prodded.

"I've been negotiating with other... savages, as you valley folk call us. And I'm heading back to my village."

"Selling or buying?" I asked.

"Trading. Although I did have something I tried to sell, but I couldn't find any buyer worthy of my goods," he began to laugh.

"And what would that be?" I inquired.

"Fight me," he said. "A duel until one of us bleeds. If you win, I'll tell you."

"And if I lose?"

"I won't tell you."

"Seems fair to me," I said, shrugging.

Ragar made a few hand signals to his brother, then grabbed his sword and headed out onto the path. I did the same. The younger girl placed a pot of soup on a black stand above the fire she had made and looked up at me. Her blue, curious eyes watched with a hint of fear from beneath her chestnut hair.

"*Tagur'elrumra,*" I told him.

"*Tagur'elrumra,*" he answered.

That was a promise that we wouldn't kill each other during the fight.

Ragar analyzed me for a few moments, then looked at the girl and winked. He spun back and attacked. His strikes were slow and clumsy, and I easily parried each of them. He didn't seem like a skilled swordsman at all, so after just a matter of seconds, I fully engaged, slipping my blade under his guard, attempting to stab him in the leg. I expected the fight to end there, but the man lifted his leg and stepped on the flat of my sword, causing me to lose my grip.

I let out a surprised grunt, taking a step back. His eyes were just as merry. He had toyed with me, pretending not to know how to fight, and disarmed me in moments. He nudged the sword at me with his foot.

This time the fight was completely different. His strikes were fast and precise, and every step he took seemed carefully calculated. He was a very strong warrior. Several times I came close to winning and so did he, but I couldn't manage to land a hit, and neither could he. Ten minutes later, we were both panting, and the fight was still not over. I regretted not tying my hair back before the fight, as the unruly strands kept getting in my eyes, and I had to sweep them away with quick swings of my head. Ragar didn't have that problem.

After we separated from another intense clash, he said, "You know what? Screw it, let's call it a draw, what do you say?"

"I agree. You fight well. I didn't expect to see such warriors in these lands," I admitted.

"I could have won at the beginning, you know that? But I gave you one more chance because I realized you're a warrior and I wanted to see what you're capable of when you fight with more heart."

"How did you realize I'm a warrior?" I asked, flopping back onto the grass, and taking a big gulp of air. My lungs were burning, and the wounds on my back, arm, and left side began to sting excruciatingly. Yet, I didn't even flinch.

"By the way you move. It tells everything about you. By the way you move your eyes and hide the tension in your body. You don't want me to know when you're about to strike next. Right now, you seem calm, but still not relaxed at all."

"I didn't trust you at first, but now I do."

I was speaking the truth. Our little duel made me trust him, and something told me he came to trust me as well.

"I wouldn't want you as an enemy, but I'd like to have you as an ally. You see, I haven't told you one thing about myself. I am Ragar Sharpstone, leader of the Dragon Scales clan," Ragar revealed.

"Nor would I want you as an enemy, Ragar, and I haven't told you one thing about myself either. I am Darion Grayfang, leader of the Black Lions clan."

A storm of loud, harsh laughter descended upon Ragar. I laughed too.

"What were the odds?" he asked among the roars. "I'll tell you, they weren't, yet here we are. I've heard talk about you and your clan. It's said that even after winning battles against other leaders, you continued to provoke other members to fight you."

"It's true."

"It's also said that you're crazy."

"It's possible."

I turned to the young woman and noticed once again that she was watching me. Ragar smirked dully.

"She likes you; do you see that?" he whispered to me. "Otherwise, she'd keep her eyes off you. What do you think?"

"She's beautiful," I admitted.

"Tell me, Darion, why are you here instead of with your clan? Have you truly been to Shartat?" he asked.

"As I said."

"There are dragons there."

"I know, I snuck into their den. I was looking for a key, Ragar, but someone stole it before I could. Now I want to reach the thief, but I need the demon's help for that," I told Ragar.

He leaned slightly towards me, tense, unsure whether to laugh or not. "Why?" he asked, his curiosity palpable. "A key for what?"

"For a prison," I explained, leaning towards him as well, fixing him with my gaze. "I'm trying to release nine demons into this world, nine like the one I'm heading at."

The women behind him were eavesdropping, as they were now pale, and even the young one lowered her gaze to the ground.

"Why?" he asked again, deeply shuddering.

"I'm gathering an army. I have many enemies and few allies."

"You're mad," Ragar whispered, then smiled widely, revealing his teeth.

"As rumored," I whispered back.

"I don't know whether to take you seriously or not. You seem more unhinged than me, and I think it's the first time in my life I've said such a thing. I'm almost tempted to do so, even tempted to follow you to see if you're telling the truth, but I can't."

The women immediately brought the food. The two older ones sat on either side of Ragar and Byrgulf, while the younger one came and sat next to me.

"I told you; she likes you," grinned Ragar. "She is my daughter, Odeth. She understands your language as much as a dog understands simple commands, but you don't need more from a woman, do you?"

I nodded, taking the bowl Odeth handed me, then began to eat quietly. The food was absolutely delicious, and I was so famished that I ate three portions.

"You haven't told me, Ragar, what were you selling?"

"I'm still considering whether to tell you or not; after all, you couldn't make me bleed. Should I tell you? Should I not tell you? You know what? I'll tell you, but not now." Ragar raised his finger towards the sky and widened his eyes. "I believe our meeting here, between the breasts of nowhere, was more than a mere coincidence. I think it was the hand of the gods! If that's the case, then we will meet again and then I will tell you."

"Sounds fair," I said.

"Actually, why don't we make things more interesting and at the same time push the hand of destiny a little?"

"I don't see why not."

"Let's make a deal, Darion. I'll offer you a horse today, whichever one you want, to help you get wherever you need, and if fate brings us together again by the middle of next summer, you'll be obliged to buy anything I have to sell. Of course, if it's still for sale, and if you can prove to me that you really are the master of the Black Lions."

"So, am I a worthy buyer of your goods?" I mumbled.

"We'll let the gods decide."

I pondered for a few moments. I needed a horse, but I wasn't about to sell my soul for it. "What's the price? I'd like to know in advance whether I can afford to pay a debt or not."

"No price," he said. "At least, nothing material."

"My soul, then?"

His eyes narrowed. "No. If the rumors about you are true, and you really are who you say you are, then I'm sure you've already sold it to the one called the Black Queen. Am I right?"

"Perhaps. So, am I supposed to receive something for free without paying anything? Something doesn't add up; is this good cursed?"

"As far as I know, no."

I looked again at the horses grazing on the edge of that trail, thinking about how much such an animal would help me save time on the road. I stood up, surveying the shape of the path that stretched downward on the slope, then wound along the edge of the forest to the distant, green foothills of Demon's Fang. It was barely noon, and I realized that if I accepted his offer, I could reach Yermoleth by nightfall. Probably sooner. The wound on my leg began pulsating once more, heightening the allure of his offer.

"Fine, I accept," I said.

Looking back, on one hand, it was foolish to willingly become indebted by accepting a gift from a man I had just met, but on the other hand, the arrangement didn't sound bad at all, and there was a serious chance I might never encounter that man again, or at least not until midsummer next year. But Ragar was right: fate had brought us both there.

He took out a knife and cut his palm, then handed it to me, and I followed suit. He shook my hand, then led me to the animals, letting me choose whichever one I wanted.

I stayed with them for a while longer, and Ragar told me about his clan. They numbered almost five thousand people and were likely the largest clan in those mountains. Rarely did mountain people manage to form groups larger than a thousand individuals, often either ending up killing each other or drawing Derahia's attention to them, but Ragar had succeeded. I wondered if Romir knew about such a force hidden in his mountains. Probably not.

I chose a black stallion, quite spirited, the man told me, but it was the strongest and most rested of them all. The women untied the bags, leaving only the saddle and reins for me. I hugged Ragar and shook hands with his brother, then bowed my head to the women and left. Odeth still watched me with a certain insistence characteristic of girls when they try to convey a message you don't understand. The warrior had been right to some extent, though I didn't know it at the time. Whether it was the hand of destiny or the gods, Ragar and I were destined to meet again.

The horse was swift. I descended along the verdant path to the foot of the mountain and rode towards the Demon's Fang. The road was good, and despite the trails becoming scarcer, the almost flat land covered in grass made my journey very easy.

Evening was rapidly approaching when I realized I had climbed too high and passed the Sanctuary. Yet, there was no cause for concern; to the north, I could see

Yermoleth's forest, separated from me only by a river. I found myself on a grassy slope, devoid of trees. The rhythmic beat of my horse's hooves echoed as I trotted towards the edge of the forest, where it parted on either side of the river.

In my foolishness, I allowed myself to revel prematurely in a victory that had yet to be won. Already, I envisioned my arrival at Yermoleth.

At that moment, I caught a glimpse out of the corner of my eye, a glint of crystal, akin to a shooting star soaring above the verdant field. But I was too intoxicated by the illusion of success to react in time. The animal's head exploded, drenching my shirt in blood, as I plummeted to the ground, managing to free my leg from the stirrup just before it could be trapped. I scrambled to my feet hastily, groping my body to ensure I was still intact. Fortunately, the horse's sturdy skull had absorbed the full force of the magical projectile that was not even meant for me, as the one who fired it preferred to kill with the sword.

From the forest, Wolf, closely followed by Saya, sprinted in my direction.

Sihirokhori Moro

Excerpt from Saya's journal, dated the twentieth day of the seventh month, Iureia, in the year six hundred twenty-three after the Conversion:

... the afternoon sun hid behind a white, puffy cloud when Mr. Wolf returned to the clearing, and Sparrow had just put the mushroom stew on the fire for the meal they called dinner, though it was barely more than a late lunch. It was good that we had moved closer to the Sanctuary and no longer needed to make the daily journey of several hours.

The woman lifted her head from above the pot and raised an eyebrow askingly.

"Still there," Wolf replied. "He hasn't left the Sanctuary. His friends had left, but he stayed inside. Either that, or he grew wings and took flight," he said with a hint of amusement in his voice, then slumped down beside me, his hands resting on his knees.

"Or he died from his wounds," Sparrow suggested.

"Unlikely, but not impossible. I've seen people die from less. Maybe it got infected."

The possibility of Darion's death became increasingly real with each passing day, as did the chances of us entering the Sanctuary to verify the kill. What a terrible thought! A wizard should never step in a Sanctuary. Four days ago, we mistakenly crossed the threshold, and the nausea that enveloped me—ripped from the comforting embrace of the ether—defied description. I felt alone, abandoned, and weak, as if my very strength was melting away, like a piece of wax dropped into a raging fire. A shudder skittered through me at the mere thought.

Besides, the chances of them accidentally heading for a sanctuary in the middle of the mountains were slim. It was clear that they knew about it, it was clear that it was their destination. I couldn't shake the feeling that if we delved too deeply into it, we wouldn't come out. Wolf and Sparrow were warriors and avoided relying on the ether more than necessary, but I could see the uncertainty even on their faces when the idea of stepping beyond the Great River's reach was proposed. Proposed by Sparrow, of course.

"Today," Wolf began, "we'll stroll along the Sanctuary's border, see how far it stretches, and tomorrow we'll pervade it to check if Darion is truly dead."

"Then we'll return to the Circle," Sparrow added, looking at me to gauge my reaction.

But I had none. It was somewhat funny because just a few days ago, I felt overwhelmed by a mix of melancholy and relief at the mere thought of leaving the wilderness behind. Yet now, I felt nothing. I was engulfed in sadness, but couldn't grasp why, as if I sensed that nothing would not end in our favor today.

"How's your shoulder, sir?" I asked Mr. Wolf.

"Completely healed," he replied, tapping it with his forefinger.

Sparrow clicked her tongue, gasping. "Such a liar you are!"

"What will you do once it's over?" I asked shortly after.

"We step down, let others fill the gap," Wolf said cautiously, watching his wife.

"We step down," repeated Sparrow, somewhat disappointed. "But you call a gap what is really a crevasse, and you think a few droplets could fill it. As you said, we'll buy land somewhere near a lake and live like ordinary people. Maybe we'll even get a dog or a cat, what do you say, my dear, what would bring you greater happiness?"

She spoke the words forcefully, with a faint hint of anger in her thin, sharp voice like a blade. It was clear as daylight that the assassin woman was not at all pleased with the idea.

"Just as we promised we would," Wolf said, raising his shoulders.

Usually, I avoid getting involved in other people's disputes, but today I couldn't resist.

"You don't seem very enthusiastic about the idea, Mrs. Sparrow," I remarked, quickly tucking my head between my shoulders to dodge the sharp glance she threw my way.

"That's because she's not," her husband said calmly. "My dear Ashin seems to believe that a day without feeling the breath of death on the back of your neck is a wasted one."

Sparrow almost flinched when her husband spoke her real name. It was the first time I had heard it.

"My dear Daesoh is already envisioning retirement," she said. "But fine, if that's what we decided, that's what we'll do. The wolf will turn into a mere dog."

Ashin and Daesoh, those were their real names. At the moment, I was glad they had told me; it made me feel closer to them. But now, at the end of this cursed day, I wished they hadn't. How badly everything had turned out…

He laughed. "You may call me that, if you desire."

"May I ask why you don't use your real names?" I asked.

"You already did, didn't you?" the witch-assassin stung.

"It's part of our culture," Daesoh explained. "We believe that sometimes names can be dangerous. We only use them around people we fully trust, and that's a very, very small circle."

"Am I in that circle too?" I asked, perhaps too enthusiastically.

"It seems so," Sparr… no, Ashin replied uncertainly.

"Yes," Daesoh said. "The past month has probably been a nightmare for you, and yet you're still here, still smiling. And your skill with telekinesis is unmatched even by the greatest of masters. I was speechless when I saw you lifting that boulder after the defeat near Blackstone. I may even dare to say that no one, ever in recorded history was as powerful as you."

I just sat there, bemused, unable to respond. No one in the recorded history. How could that be possible?

"You could be Ant," Wolf said with a lupine smile. "Because you're small and lift such heavy things."

"Ant," I echoed, almost laughing.

Wolf, Sparrow, and Ant—it sounded strangely funny.

"It would be a fitting name," Sparrow laughed. "Do you know what the word for ant is in our tongue?"

I shook my head.

"Saya," she responded, and both laughed at my shocked expression. I was an ant, it seemed. "But don't rest on your laurels," Sparrow cautioned me. "You still have a lot to learn."

"Like all of us," Wolf added.

"How to plant potatoes and take care of the animals?"

Her husband's smile vanished from his face in an instant. He stood up, looking at her reproachfully, then said, "I won't fight this battle today. Saya, come with me. Help me inspect the perimeter of the Sanctuary. We'll take a walk and be back in a few hours, before it gets dark."

I rose almost instantly and slung my satchel over my shoulder, the one where I kept my journal. I hoped to find another blackberry bush on the way, like in the past days.

Wolf crossed the clearing in a few strides and lifted his wife's chin, catching her in a long kiss. At first, she tried to pull away, then relented and kissed him back. When they broke apart, her cheeks were as red as fire.

"I can go alone," I offered, hoping to give them some time for themselves.

"Wolf will accompany you," she insisted. She pushed her husband aside and directed her attention to the sizzling and pleasantly smelling contents of the pot.

I waited for him, and then we left the well-covered clearing together, slipping through the dense green wall of trees. We walked in silence for a while, and not only once did I have the sensation that something heavy was pressing on my shoulders. I rubbed my ears.

"I felt too sorry for you to leave you alone with her, especially when she's in one of her moods. It's not a fate I wish upon anyone," chuckled the assassin. "Not even my enemies."

I didn't know how to respond. He was a cheerful man, but every time I made a joke, I was rewarded with a nasty look from his wife.

"Thank you," I replied, displaying a crooked smiling.

"Don't be fooled by her severity, that's how she shows she appreciates you. She always says that pampering dulls a student's senses."

"It means she's trying her best to keep mine sharp," I remarked.

Wolf began to laugh. "Both yours and mine."

I started laughing too, but my laughter quickly died down when I caught my foot on a bush and fell to my knees.

"I won't miss this mountain," I said, sitting back down to free my foot. It was usually a slow process.

Wolf knelt beside me and untangled my foot in a few nimble movements.

"Thank you," I said, grabbing his hand and getting up. "It seems like you two have known each other for a long time. May I ask how you met, if it's not too personal?"

"It's too personal," he replied, his expression turning serious. Then he smiled. "But Ashin isn't here, so I can tell you. I worked for her father since I was a child."

"Did she come from a wealthy family?"

"Her father was a shogun, something similar to a lord here. Our country, Tokero, was ruled by six shoguns. Each had the right to govern their province as they pleased, but there were also some common laws that had to be respected by all of them. The most important, you probably know, is that any form of magic is completely forbidden, and any practitioner must be killed on the spot."

"It must have been very difficult for you to live in such a realm," I said.

"It was, but I survived. I heard about the beautiful Ashin from the night she was born; I was five years old then. But I met her for the first time only fifteen years later, when I was twenty. I was a simple guard stationed at the gates of Bueyong, the biggest city in the province governed by her father. That day was one of the strangest days of my life. I saw her walking down the street, accompanied by her handmaidens and guards. Custom dictates that you bow your head when a member of the shogun's family passes by you, or else you lose it, but I was unable to take my eyes off her. She was radiant. That was the first time I saw another person sensitive to ether. And it was the same for her because she stopped in her tracks and stared at me wide-eyed, with amazement. The next thing I knew, I was on the ground with a katana at my throat. I would have been killed if she hadn't asked them to spare my life."

He stopped, his eyes scanning the perimeter of the forest with vacant eyes. He cleared his throat, resting his hand on the katana's hilt.

"After that day, I dreamed of her incessantly, both with my eyes open and closed. I was sure that she was glimmering, but I could not understand how that was possible and why I was the only one to notice. The social boundaries on the Storm Islands are much stricter than on the continent. Someone like me has no right to even look at someone like her, let alone speak to her. The sentence was death. The punishments there are more severe than here, and death could be served for almost anything, even for laughing too hard or not bowing deeply enough."

"Shells and crabs!"

"Sometimes, there is beauty in such order. Most of the time it's madness."

"What did you do after?"

He couldn't conceal the melancholy behind his grimace. His gaze felt heavy yet gentle on my face, reaching beyond me to those distant lands and back to those turbulent times.

"I knew how to fight; I wouldn't have made it to twenty if I didn't. My parents died when I was very young, and those places aren't very kind to orphaned children. More than once, I found someone sneaking into my house during the night. Poor souls, they lost their lives trying to rob a house that had nothing but four walls and a ragged blanket." He paused for a long moment, then continued, "My plan had been to become a soldier in the palace guard, so I could get close to her. I couldn't talk to her or even look at her when others were around, of course, but I could steal a glance when no one was looking. I wanted nothing more than to see again, to understand what that radiant aura was all about."

"Was it hard to find work at the palace?" I inquired.

"Very. I had to give up all my money, down to the last coin, just to be considered for the job. And the trials were merciless; many even lost their lives during them. Anyway, most were kicked out at the writing and reading parts, but I had learned that a few months before. The real challenge, though, was the physical tests. Not everyone was accepted into the palace guard, but I kept my head above the waves and kept swimming. The examination lasts for three months, and at the end of those three months, we are given the chance to either accept the position or opt to become a *shikori.*

"Did you accept the position?"

He raised his hand to stop me. I hadn't even realized that I was one step away from entering the Sanctuary. My eyes wandered beyond the visible, catching glimpses of the faint blue waves that covered everything like a blanket—everything except the Sanctuary, which repelled them like a barrier. With a gesture, he indicated to the right, then moved forward, and I followed closely, eagerly awaiting his response.

It took a long time before he answered. "No."

"No?" I squinched. "But you fought so hard for it."

"I saw her again as soon as the trials ended. We were brought to the palace to decide our future, and she was there, walking with her handmaids through the palace courtyard. She looked as if she were not from this world. Everyone averted their gaze, but like the first time, I watched her almost bewitched. My master noticed and quickly came over to elbow me. '*Head down, you idiot. They will kill you*' he whispered angrily. '*I'd die happy,*' I told him. I still remember the beating he gave me as soon as Ashin passed by us. That man cared a lot about me."

"You, people from the Storm Islands have a strange way of showing love."

For a moment, I feared that I said something inappropriate, that my loose tongue worked against me once again, but he just leaned his head back, laughing aloud. He was a prisoner of those social castes for so long, that he came to hate them. He didn't believe in them anymore, and he saw me as his equal, even though he outranked me by far. To be completely honest, I didn't even know his rank in the Circle; he was no Grand Master, yet he possessed knowledge only available to them.

"I don't disagree. After seeing her that day, I realized I couldn't bear to be stationed somewhere in the palace and not even be able to look in her direction. I had to become a *shikori*."

"A *shikori*?" I asked.

"A fighter in her father's personal retinue. Like a knight here. Always around the shogun and, of course, always around her. There was only one test to pass for this. One that usually was completed in a single day. In the last two years, no one had survived it, and as far back as I can remember, I can't recall more than five people who did."

"And you put yourself in such danger just to have the right to look at her?"

"She was worth it."

For a few moments, I felt saddened, because I knew I would never be seen that way by a man, but I tried to push the thought away. I turned my glance to the trees adorning the mountain above, beyond the invisible boundary of the Sanctuary, hoping the assassin wouldn't notice the tears forming in my eyes. I doubt he missed them.

"What was the test?" I asked, ignoring the lump in my throat.

Wolf paused. I turned to him just in time to see his lips quivering and his face wrought with a stern, pale expression. He looked scared. No, for a few moments, he seemed terrified.

"To stare a demon in the eyes and live," he said in such a low voice that even the soft whisper of the wind seemed to outspoke him.

I gasped, frowning in thought. "Metaphorically?"

"No," he said plainly.

"I don't understand."

"I believe I've told you enough. Not even the Circle would agree to divulge such information."

"The Circle? But what does it have to do with your story?"

"The story... it contains elements that the Circle has forbidden."

"Please don't stop here. You've really piqued my curiosity. I won't divulge anything you tell me to anyone; I swear."

The assassin raised his shoulders thoughtfully. I hadn't seen him like this before. Traveling with him over the past month had led me to believe he was prepared for absolutely any situation, but the demon from that memory still haunted him, even now after so many years. The breath he let out was uneven.

"We called it *Bakemoro*, the Black Demon," he replied, pronouncing the name with great difficulty. "Of course, that wasn't its real name; we didn't know its true name, and I'll be forever grateful for that. The creature was chained in the depths of a pyramid in... the heart of a city in the north of the Storm Islands."

My mind raced back to Prince Darion and the conversation he had with Ashin before the Battle Near Blackstone. "*I can describe him in great detail. The shadow stretching over the entire world...*" Fingers of cold crawled down my spine, making me shudder with all my might. The First Gods. This is how they called them.

"A city," I echoed in a soft whisper. "Are there more?"

"There are others," he acknowledged. "Possibly five, but the Circle only succeeded in locating only three."

My breath caught. "Why five?"

"Because we know of the existence of five such creatures, but we've only succeeded in finding three."

"What are they?"

"No one knows. All we know is that there was a time when they were worshipped by people all over the world, but someone managed to imprison them. We don't know how, or who, but they did it, and those spells can't be undone."

"And if they are?"

I was surprised by the tremor in my own voice. I couldn't understand why I was afraid, whether it was the restraint in his tone, or was it something else, something more than that?

"Many have tried," he told me. "It's impossible. Powerful spells were cast in the past, ones that we couldn't even dream of replicating in the present, not even through our most potent magic and artifacts."

"Why would anyone want to do such a horrific thing?" I asked with too much anger.

"I wonder the same," he said. "But I'm deviating from the story, aren't I?

"Mhm," I nodded when my foot slipped. Wolf rushed and caught my hand just before I fell to my knees again. "Thank you."

"A *shikori* was supposed to possess complete control over his mind. The test entailed standing on the edge of the pit within the black pyramid, where it lay imprisoned, and gazing upon it. A watcher stood by to ensure your eyes remained open, confirming you were focusing down. Twenty-two of us undertook the trial during that period. One by one, they walked to the precipice, only to succumb within mere seconds and to fall in the darkness with large smiles on their faces. Some even laughed."

"You were probably terrified."

"I was," he admitted. "But I went there, I looked, and... I'm here, so I survived."

"You won't detail further?" I asked in one breath.

"Curiosity is usually very good, Saya, but in certain cases, it can be dangerous. Any wizard from the Circle would tell you that." He remained silent for a few heartbeats, then continued, "But it is more dangerous to have questions that nobody answers, because you will search for answers on your own, and that search can lead you to dangerous places. *Bakemoro* was massive. I saw its dark silhouette contorting in the darkness of the dungeon, its eyes burning into mine from his horned face. Every second passed like an hour, maybe slower. My whole life flashed before my eyes, unfolding rapidly like a book being flipped open. It was as if I was remembering everything in a single breath, except I wasn't the one remembering; it was it, the demon. It was digging through my mind. Then everything changed. I wasn't there anymore. I was on a farm, by a lake, and in front of me... was Ashin. But don't think it was just that, just a page stuck in the book of my life. That creature rewrote everything, I could remember yesterday and the day before yesterday and last week, even the day we got married."

I stumbled again, and Wolf caught me once more. We were now at the edge of the forest, facing a field covered in vivid green blades of grass, speckled with flowers of all colors. The sun hung in the sky, promising us at least another hour of light. For the first time in my memory, I felt grateful for it; for the light. Isn't it strange how we, humans, take something as precious as light for granted? Moreover, we end up living under its glow and enjoying the warmth it provides without ever considering how impossible our lives would be without it.

"Would you like to sit down?" he asked me.

"That would be nice. I'm quite clumsy," I replied.

"Ashin invited me to step towards her, and I almost did. But the memory of the first day I saw her came to me just before I placed my foot on the ground. The monster had made a mistake. My Ashin is shining. I stepped back, and the world *Bakemoro* had built crumbled in an instant. I was back there, at the edge of darkness, and the creature was staring at me from the depths of his pit. I have never felt such fury in my life, and to this day, I don't know if it was my hatred or the creature's, poisoning me. When the overseer told me that time was up, I pushed him aside and remained there, looking the monster in the eye, to show it that I was not afraid. I stood there for almost a minute, and before I left, I spat into its dungeon. That is the greatest form of disrespect you could show someone."

"How well you've done!" I exclaimed, almost jumping up.

He smiled, but only for a moment, then his face turned serious again. "When I departed, the demon spoke to me in my mind, its voice akin to... boulders clashing against each other. It said: 'what you witnessed will never be yours.'"

"That's why you covet the farm so dearly... by the edge of a lake?"

"Yes," he said blankly. "In any case, I was accepted as a *shikori*. They named me *Sihirokhori Moro*, the One Who Defied the Demon. I was granted a chamber in the palace and a substantial monthly stipend, but undoubtedly the greatest prize was being able to see Ashin. I caught her stealing glances at me on several occasions, yet I never knew the reason. I was unaware of the magical signatures. I didn't realize that in her eyes, I shone too. We couldn't speak to each other, it wasn't allowed, so we settled for exchanging fleeting glances every time we felt safe to do so. Two strangers living under the same roof."

"When did you first speak to each other?"

"Two years later, we found ourselves at the shogun's vacation house. A group of bandits, or so we believed at the time, attacked the building. My duty was to defend the shogun, but as soon as I caught wind of the attack I ran straight to her room, positioned myself in front of the sliding door, and waited. The cries of the battle dragged nearer, and I feared I may not be good enough to defend her. By then, I was already proficient in the wolf's fighting style. I killed over twenty people by the end of that day and was bleeding from a thousand cuts, but she was unharmed. She emerged from the room, surveyed the hallway strewn with corpses, then looked at me and said, '*you shine.*' I replied: '*so do you.*' Then we both fainted. Me, from the blood loss. She from witnessing the bloodshed."

I opened my mouth and narrowed my brows, searching on his face for any sign that he may be joking. "Lady Sparrow fainted at the sight of blood?" I asked, unable to conceal the surprise in my voice.

"Don't let her know I told you that, or she'll slit my throat while I sleep."

"My lips are sealed," I emphasized, then we both started laughing.

"I woke up in the hospital with bandages all over my body," he said. "The shogun personally came to thank me for defending his daughter instead of running straight to him like the others did. Personally, I expected to lose my life for it, but I can't say I wasn't satisfied with how things turned out."

We shared another moment of silence, observing the wind as it danced through the leaves and the warm rays of the sun casting shimmering auras upon the peaks to the north. On the most distant ones, I could see snow glimmering like silver atop their summits.

"I can't wait to hear how you found out the glow came from ether," I said enthusiastically.

"For several more weeks, things returned to normal. But I remained sharp, as I knew that attack was just the first droplet, the real wave being yet to come. But until then: I first met her in particular during a summer night. It was well past midnight, and I was sitting in the misty gardens, meditating. Like many nights at that age, sleep eluded me. I saw a figure, very stumbling I must mention, moving through the walls raised by the hot vapors coming from the springs. For a moment, I thought it was a boy, because of the clothes she wore, until I saw that familiar glow. I ran to her, worried about what she might be doing out so late, alone and with no guards. 'Why do you shine?' she asked me before I could speak. 'I don't know, but you do too,' I responded."

Wolf scowled, rising abruptly, then looked at the treeless valley before us. I stood up as well, following his glare. I couldn't see anything.

"Do you hear something?" I asked.

He reached for his katana, the cold steel glittering in the bathing rays. The faint shape of a rider formed on the green canvas of nature, like a brown stain.

"Darion," Wolf whispered.

Defeated

My blood ran cold, and like a deer sensing the approach of a lion, I instinctively took a step back.

"Don't look," Wolf whispered in a soothing voice, so calm, untouched by even the slightest tremor. Taking lives had become routine for him, as had fighting. It was clear from his eyes that he saw Darion not as an opponent, but as a victim—just another name to cross off the list before moving on. "It might not be pleasant to watch."

"I'll stand by you," I assured him.

The distance between Darion and us was shrinking by the moment, the not-so-tall grass flying up from his horse's hooves like catapulted debris. I couldn't see his face clearly, but he seemed confused, as if he'd just realized he wasn't where he needed to be. He tugged at the bridle, bringing the horse to a halt, then scanned the forest—without noticing us—and turned toward the river. Beyond it lay the Sanctuary.

I was about to warn Daesho, but a white flame was already hovering above his palm like a dancing, formless liquid that shimmered strongly. The waves of ether were crafted with such incredible precision—truly the work of a master. A quick flicker of his hand and the bolt of crystallized moonlight flew over the field, so fast that Darion didn't even attempt to dodge, probably not even noticing it.

I could swear I saw his eyes widen just before the spell struck, sending him rolling across the uneven ground, his horse, lying headless not far behind, struck directly by the spell. I could swear I saw his eyes widen just before the spell struck, sending him rolling across the uneven ground. His horse lay headless not far behind, felled by the projectile. Despite the fall, Darion seemed unharmed, and Wolf looked almost relieved he hadn't killed him with magic—like his blade thirsted for blood. In just seconds, he was back on his feet, casting a quick glance at his horse before turning to face us with a murderous grimace. Wolf sprang from the forest's shadowy cover, sword in hand, and sprinted downhill toward him. Whispering a quick prayer, I followed.

As I drew closer, I could see only a tempest of fury and rage on the prince's face, emotions he seemed to struggle to contain. With a controlled motion, he drew his sword from its scabbard, the cold metal gleaming in the sunlight as if freshly pulled from the forge.

"You coward!" he thundered. "Damn your spells! Fight like a man! Do you carry that sword just to lean on it or to scratch your back?"

The Wolf's run transitioned into a brisk walk, eventually coming to a stop not far from Darion, holding the slightly curved sword with both hands. I could only see his back, straight as a pole, but it was not hard to envision his gaze. Cold. Blank. Deadly.

"Drop your weapon now and surrender!" demanded the assassin. "I can see you're already wounded. Give up, and we'll take you back to Romir, where your fate will be decided."

He was right; I noticed Darion limping as he adjusted his stance, preparing for battle.

"Surrender?" he echoed with a harsh laugh. "This time, you piece of filth, only death awaits."

He surged forward, his sword thrusting through the air, being deflected by Wolf's katana in a whirlwind of sparks glimmering in the evening light. Wolf attacked next, attempting a thrust of his own, but Darion jumped aside and tried slashing his face. Wolf pulled his head back, narrowly avoiding the swinging cut by a hair's breadth, then took a few steps back, his calm unwavering.

Darion's eyes turned to me, sparkling with a fury that sent icy spiders crawling down my spine. "Run, you hag! I will butcher your dog, then come for you." There was nothing but hatred in his voice. I couldn't blame him for that; he had spared my life, and I had come to harm him.

The prince stepped in again, thrusting only the tip of his sword at Wolf, which he deftly deflected before stepping back once more. Darion wanted to persist with the attack, but as soon as he approached, the Wolf lunged at him, reversing his feigned retreat. After pushing Darion's blade aside, Daesho's katana pierced his left shoulder, undoubtedly aiming for his neck but missing due to the rebel prince's quickness.

He groaned like a stabbed pig, his grimace etching lines of pain across his face. His eyes darted to his new cut for just a moment before locking back onto Wolf's. At first sight, it did not seem a very deep wound, and as he prowled his opponent, he rotated his shoulder a few times, to test its mobility.

"Your brother cares for you!" I yelled. "I talked with him. Drop your blade please, it is not too late."

He whispered something, but I could barely make out his words, as his voice was so low. What I thought I discerned was, "*It had always been too late.*"

Darion started pushing Wolf back, pressing with a flurry of savage strikes. He looked just like the wildlings who ambushed us near Blackstone, his face and clothes splattered with blood—more from his horse than from himself. The unraveled black hair swung with every slash while his eyes gleamed fiercely.

The clang resounded so loud, the sparks shone so bright, the very nature itself held its breath—as did I.

This time it was a slash that bit into Darion's flesh, not a piercing, like in the first encounter. It struck above his right knee, not very deep it seemed, as the prince successfully limped away from Wolf.

"I can bind him," I yelled to Wolf, uncertainty creeping into my voice. "Should I?"

In the aftermath of another violent clash, both warriors retreated, their swords poised with the tips nearly touching, a breath away from one another.

"Look at him," Daesho urged, nodding toward our opponent. "He's nothing but a rabid dog, driven only by the desire to kill. He is beyond redemption, worthy only of death."

Wolf charged this time, his katana striking the prince's straight sword with ferocious speed and power. The prince could barely parry, each clash bringing him dangerously close to being torn open. I had witnessed men meet their end by the sword before, not far from the edge of that forest of Blackstone, not long ago. It was a gruesome sight and an even more wicked fate; one I prayed the gods would spare anyone from enduring. Many didn't succumb to the blade with the first strike, and a sizable number persisted even after the second. As I watched Darion in battle, I found myself pondering how many blows he would endure before finding his eternal rest, liberated from the poison the late Black Queen had poured into his soul, finally at peace.

The resemblance I once glimpsed between him and the king had faded entirely. He was no longer Larion. Instead, he was consumed by hatred, rage, and malice. Wickedness emanated from him like black ink from an octopus, leaving him broken and destroyed—a monster.

This time, he jumped back, blinking rapidly a few times. After taking a deep breath, his tense posture relaxed for just a moment. He pushed his left foot slightly forward, holding his sword with both hands to his left side, slowly inclined, the tip pointing to the ground. His breathing steadied, and he waited, not tearing his eyes away from Wolf.

The assassin adjusted his grip as well, now holding the sword with his right hand above his head. As if understanding what Daesho was about to do simply from the way he held his blade, Darion raised his sword with both hands, the tip now aimed at Wolf's chest.

They stared at each other like two card players, each trying to guess the opponent's next move. Daesho gripped the sword with both hands, now holding it sideways, while Darion turned the tip back toward the ground again, just as he had initially, except this time it pointed slightly to the left. They both held their breath, and Wolf's cold gaze gleamed with an acknowledgment that Darion was not his usual adversary but a very skilled opponent worthy of his skills.

Then it happened. In a flash, quicker than a heartbeat, so swift that if I had blinked, I would have missed it Wolf's eyes flashed as he lowered his body, the sword descending toward Darion's left foot. The prince feigned a parry, but at the last moment, his own blade swung upward with great speed. He allowed his opponent to strike his foot, sacrificing it in exchange for a lethal blow. The cold steel katana sliced bone-deep into Darion's left thigh, but not before his own blade tore open Wolf's throat.

Daesho's body spun, collapsing onto the grass, his head almost detached.

"No," I muttered in shock.

Darion seized the black handle of the blade still embedded in his leg and wrenched it out with a rageful roar. His black eyes fixed on me, piercing my soul like two spears. Despite his injury, he limped a stride in my direction, but I wasted no time. Summoning a wave of ether, I bound his body, and in a surge of desperation, I tossed him a long distance across the field, like a puppet discarded by a petulant child. He slammed into the slope, rolling several meters before finally coming to a halt.

Wolf was dead. He really was. It was incomprehensible then, and it remains so now. He was Daesho, the greatest warrior of our time, perhaps of all time, and more than that, a formidable wizard. He was *Sihirokhori Moro*. Yet he had been slain by a mere mortal, one who, above all, was wounded. How could this be?

The prince rose, now far from me, his leg trembling under his own weight, the sword gleaming in the burning-red rays.

"You monster! You killer! You wretch!" I cried, my vision blurred by tears as he turned his back, making his way lamely toward the river and the Sanctuary.

I jolted as Sparrow appeared beside me out of nowhere, silent and somber. Her eyes dropped to her husband's lifeless body, but her face remained expressionless, empty.

"I am so sorry," I mumbled, tears rolling down my cheeks.

Her expression was a mask, thick enough to conceal any emotion, with no sign that she heard me, as if I wasn't even there. A tear trickled down from her hollow eye, stopping on her small chin before falling onto the blood-soaked grass.

"You fought well, my love. I shall join you soon, but there is one more demon to be slain."

Her bead-like eyes were now on the prince's back, and for a brief moment, rage flickered in them, more fiery than the flames of the Burning Hells and brighter than the marble palace of the High Heavens. Then, calm returned, and all traces of hatred vanished from her demeanor, replaced by a steely resolve.

The Sparrow flew in the pursuit of the Lion, her speed far surpassing that of Darion, especially with both of his feet being lacerated. It was only a matter of time before she would catch him, before all the souls he had taken would finally be avenged. But even with him dead, Wolf would not return… nothing could bring him back.

I wanted to see that; to see him dying. It was the only time I could remember when I wished for such a thing, the only time when it felt right.

I sprinted in Sparrow's wake, unable to bear the sight of the deceased Daesho any longer.

Darion said he stood before one of the First Gods too. He was a *shikori* too, then. The thought almost made me stagger—that meant he also had a strong mind. He disappeared into the thick layer of trees that flanked the river, limping with great urgency for the Sanctuary. But what awaited him there? Ashin would likely take his life with the steel sword even without magic. Oh, if only Wolf had used the ether to end Darion's life.

The air grew colder as I stopped on the sandy bank of the river, nearly slipping into the sand while scanning my surroundings for any sign of Sparrow and Darion. The sound of the flowing water was loud now, drowning out the faint whispers of the forest, its howling echoing in the dimming light like a bad omen. The penumbra cast by the few remaining rays of the sinking sun made the shadows impenetrable—dark thresholds I was reluctant to cross.

I noticed two pairs of footprints descending into the water, so I rolled up my pants to my ankles and cautiously stepped in, cursing as the water seeped into my low boots. Taking small, careful strides, I navigated the slippery stones beneath my feet. Thankfully, the water wasn't too deep, making the river relatively easy to cross. Emerging on the other side, I continued to follow the wet imprints left by their feet on the stony terrain, until I once again stepped onto the grassy bank and soon found myself back among the ancient trees.

It wasn't long before I spotted them—two shadows dancing in the shade. Sparrow's movements were soft and elegant, like silk brushing against skin, while Darion's were weary and stumbling, like a blind troll. The ground beneath their feet was even, flanked by tall stone walls rising vertically behind them like silent watchers—witnesses to the execution to come—stretching several meters to the left and right.

A cry of pain escaped Darion's lips as Sparrow's katana pierced his belly. She withdrew, giving him a chance to regain his stance. Something unfamiliar gleamed in her eyes, and a wicked smile, twisting into grotesque grimaces with every breath, made my blood run cold. She had lost her mind.

"*Kill him quickly,*" I silently prayed, watching she lunge at him again, cold steel gleaming like flames in their hands.

But she didn't. She didn't!

She attacked relentlessly. Her swords lashed at his body like whips—too quick for him to deflect, too precise for him to dodge. Darion stumbled backward, enduring each cut with choking moans of pain.

"*The battle is over. Kill him. Please just kill him!*"

With a trembling hand, Darion raised his sword in a futile attempt to defend himself, but Sparrow's katana struck like a viper, slashing his pinky and ring finger, forcing him to drop the weapon. He didn't flinch, only watched with a hint of sadness as the sword slipped from his grasp. Staggering back, he nearly lost his balance, his back hitting the stony wall, his legs trembling beneath him as if he carried mountains upon his shoulders.

In the back of my mind, I kept whispering, "*Kill him, please! This is torture! This is wrong!*" but I voiced none of it.

Covered in blood, Darion grinned—a smile devoid of empathy, tinged with sadism, not reflected in his teary eyes.

"I'm sorry... for your husband," he uttered.

"*Kill him quickly,*" I prayed silently.

Sparrow let out a cry, her fury evident as she tossed both swords aside with a flicker of hatred. In their place, she drew Merwin's silver dagger, intent on watching the life drain from Darion's eyes up close.

I shook with fear, sensing she was making a huge mistake—even so severely wounded, he was taller, broader, and stronger. I wanted to yell at her, to tell her to stop, but my lips stayed sealed shut.

She charged at him, driving the blade toward his neck, but he reacted with thunderous speed, stopping the attack with his left hand. The silver dagger pierced his palm and emerged from the other side, stopping just shy of his heart, while his right hand closed around her neck. He slowly overpowered her despite the wounds he had endured, and with a powerful spin, he slammed her body against the rock.

Only once.

I could hear the crack of her neck even from that distance. After that terrible sound, all strength left her body, and her eyes became vacant. Her lifeless form slid down, coming to rest in a seated position, chin on her chest, feet stretched out in front of her.

His gaze locked onto mine. "Your turn," he whispered.

For a moment, I felt like a helpless little girl, powerless against that dying man and the malice surrounding him. But the moment passed, and fury filled my heart.

"This ends now!" I howled, immersing myself in the Great River and gathering all the stones I could find around me. They all began to hover, from small pebbles to boulders, surrounding me in a swirling vortex of earth and stone. "I'll crush your head like a snake," I growled through clenched teeth.

He sank down beside her, his back resting against the cliffside.

They both died, murdered by him. Now I stood alone, lost in the depths of the forest, deep within the mountains, with little hope of ever seeing civilization again. Their farm, their dream... all gone. And he, the creature who smirked mockingly through bloody teeth, was responsible for it all. That monster. That demon.

I was determined to pummel him over and over, stone after stone, until he finally met his end. I could have left him there, already bleeding from a thousand cuts, but I chose not to. There was no way he could cling to life much longer, but I wanted to be the one to kill him.

"You don't deserve to breath this air…" I whispered when I got close enough.

I took one more step before striking.

A cry of terror escaped me as the ether's embrace vanished abruptly, leaving me powerless. I had stepped into the Sanctuary! Not only that, but all the stones hovering around fell, a large one striking the back of my shoulder and pushing me down onto my knees, before him. I attempted to jump back, but his fingers were already entwined in my hair.

He rose to his knees too, shaking, then pulled me onto my belly, pinning me down with his own weight. With half of my face pressed into the ground and him standing on top of me, I could see the shape of his shadow spreading over the ground, his right hand reaching for the silver dagger still lodged in his left. With a muffled scream, he pulled it out, and warm droplets of blood seeped through the thin material of my tunic, dripping onto my back from his hand.

I closed my eyes, bracing myself for the inevitable blow, wondering how much it would hurt. He was already too badly injured, having lost too much blood for a swift, clean strike, so I prepared myself to be stabbed repeatedly before succumbing to death's embrace. But his bloodied hand pressed hard against my head, pulling it up by the hair and forcing me to stare at Sparrow.

"Look at her!" he yelled in anger. "You did this! All of you!"

Warm blood now trickled down my forehead, the result of his bloody hand that was holding me, which was missing two fingers.

"And why?" he whispered in my ear. I was shaking and sobbing underneath him, the grip of fear rendering me unable to speak. "Why!?" he yelled with such force that the birds nestled in the trees around us tuck flight. "What did I ever do to you? What did I ever do to them? Why wouldn't you just leave me alone?!"

He was crying too. "I wanted nothing," he whispered then. "Just to be left alone. Just to live with her."

"I'm sorry," I cried amid sobs. "Please, let me live, and I swear I won't ever return. I promise I'll tell everyone you are dead!"

"I am dead, Saya."

"Then… can I live?"

We were both crying.

"You damn woman. Why did you have to return?"

I clenched my teeth as the cold silver was placed on my nape. "Please don't! Please, I beg you, please!"

He raised the dagger. I held my breath and closed my eyes, forcing myself to think of something beautiful—anything. But there was nothing, as if his evil had drained all beauty from my mind.

He raged, tossing the dagger aside, then got off me, leaning against the cliff wall near Sparrow's body.

I dared not rise—not yet, at least—until I heard him say, "I am such a weak idiot." I got up on my knees, hugged myself tightly, and trembled. "A sparrow piercing my left hand," he laughed, bringing his bloodied hand to his face. "Maybe that's why I dreamed of you," he said then, his voice weak. "Because you were supposed to be the last face I would see before I die. It... could be."

"Maybe," I barely voiced. There was no point in lying to him that everything would be fine; he was dying, possibly in his final moments, and he knew it. He had dealt so much death, he surely recognized it.

"Do you know your way back?" he asked.

I shook my head from side to side.

"You will find your way, you seem smart."

"I'm not... what do I do? How do I get back? Don't die yet, please."

"Aella," he said so softly that I wondered if it was all in my head. After a final, loud breath, he became motionless, his head drooping onto his chest.

The silence grew heavy, as did the solitude I felt. I even felt sorry—though I knew I shouldn't—not for him. He had amassed so much evil chakar through his countless crimes that this was surely the result of his own actions.

"I'm sorry," I said to Ashin, who was lying shoulder to shoulder with him, almost in the same position. Looking at him, I whispered, "I'm glad you suffered."

I had to go. Night would fall soon, and I had no idea what to do next. I wanted to bury her and Wolf, but I needed to return to our camp to grab the shovel first. With the darkness deepening, I wasn't sure I would remember the way. I felt numb.

Before I could even begin the walk back, a shadow fell in front of me, likely having jumped from somewhere on the towering stone wall behind, which loomed twice as tall as Darion. The shadow executed a quick pirouette, a steel tip landing beneath my chin. A spear. I swallowed hard, staring at the burnt face of the young woman.

"*Hashar har!*" she barked at me as I took a step back.

"I don't understand," I cried.

"Hurry, you damn grass chopper!" she yelled after noticing Darion.

Then I saw him. A nartingal, much like Aella, running with great haste along the naturally grown wall. His eyes gleamed like two ember beads, and atop his head, protruding from beneath his blue hair, there were four horns. He knelt in great hurry, placing his palm on Darion's chest. For a moment, I wondered what he was doing, but soon I heard the prince taking a deep breath.

Darion opened his eyes, glancing around for a few seconds, then slumped to one side, resting in Sparrow's lap.

"One heartbeat away from dying," said the nartingal with a weary voice.

"The Fair Lady will be pleased."

Darion was sleeping now, the rhythmic movement of his chest indicating a peaceful slumber, and all his wounds appeared as if they were old scars. Even the severed fingers grew back. The nartingal had healed him. He picked up Darion's sword from the ground, then untied the sheath of the dagger from Ashin and secured it to the prince's belt, placing the silver knife back inside.

With Darion in his arms, he turned to me, his face seemingly empty, while his amber eyes pierced into my soul. "We don't need her," the nartingal said to the woman with the burnt face. "Kill her."

"Please, no!" I yelled, almost attempting to grab her spear. Good thing I did not; she would have impaled me on the spot.

The woman spun her weapon, the wooden end striking my head so hard that I lost my balance.

"Why kill? Maybe the Fair Lady is hungry. Rise and move, and don't you ever think of running, girl, for I once outran a lion and pierced its throat with this very spear."

I did as she said, rubbing my head in the process and thinking that I surely was slower than a lion.

"My name is Saya," I told her, carefully making my way around, following the nartingal. That way, I was no longer just a nameless face, but a person, and maybe she would find it harder to take my life. It was always a good idea to befriend those trying to harm you.

"A great honor is bestowed upon you, Saya, for…"

"You will be eaten alive," the nartingal interrupted, his voice cold.

"What?" I shuddered.

"But not in my tree," he continued. "If Ezereen is hungry, she'd do well to eat outside and clean herself thoroughly before coming back in, or I will keep her at the door like a dog—like a disobedient Eshari."

"I won't tolerate any disrespect toward the Fair Lady!" the woman growled.

"Where in the world does she keep finding you?" the nartingal wondered aloud.

"Are you asking where I am from?"

The nartingal pursed his lips and remained silent. Despite Darion's larger size, he seemed to be carrying him without much difficulty.

"What did he mean by 'eaten alive?'" I whispered to the girl.

"What do you think I meant?" retorted the nartingal.

I was doing my best to keep the tears out of my eyes, but how could I, when I was about to be eaten alive? The light was dim when we reached his house—which was the giant stump of a tree—and the air grew so cold. Perhaps that was why I was shaking.

We descended among the roots of that tree, using some stairs that at first were concealed by shadows. I expected to find some gross dirt hole filled with dead animals and water, but there were no such things. The room was circular. The ground beneath our feet was a lush carpet of grass, and the walls, like ancient tapestries, bore intricate patterns of roots adorned with white, luminous flowers. Their soft glow bathed the room in a soothing radiance. In the heart of this subterranean room stood a massive rectangular table, its single leg sprouting directly from the earth. Around it, chairs resembling delicate nutshells hung suspended from the ceiling by roots. The air hummed with an otherworldly energy, and I wondered what secrets this ancient place held.

An old man with short, grey hair, clad in worn steel armor, leaned against the wall. His breastplate bore the scars of countless battles, each dent reflecting the light streaming from the white flowers.

Beside him stood a young woman, her long hair was as black as a starless night sky, flowing loosely against her back. She wore a simple white dress that draped around her like moonlight, its hem gently brushing against the floor. Her skin was so pale, nearly snow-white, appearing devoid of blood—a striking contrast to her crimson eyes. They didn't sparkle like Yermoleth's; instead, they seemed glassy, akin to a wolf's gaze caught in the blaze of torches.

"Ezerekai?" asked the red-eyed woman.

"Alive," responded the nartingal, taking Darion through a gap that opened in the wall before my eyes. He came alone not long after.

"And she?" asked the woman, her eyes falling on me.

"For you, my Fair Lady," responded the girl with half of her face burned.

"But not here. Take her out if you're famished," warned the child of night.

I took a step back as she approached, but the other young woman grasped me from behind and held me still, forcing my hands against my back. She was much stronger than me, and without access to magic, I was defenseless. The Fair Lady stopped, her body almost melding with mine. I strained to pull my head away from her.

Her warm breath softly brushed my neck. Then, a sharp pain—a muffled scream escaped me. I kicked out with my leg, but she remained unmoved, and soon the woman with the burnt face released me, stepping back. I attempted to push the Fair Lady away, but she seized both my hands, pinning them to my sides with surprising force in her skinny arms.

My eyes darted to the nartingal, silently pleading for help, but he watched the entire scene with disgust. There wasn't even a shred of mercy for me.

The Fair Lady withdrew her head, her pale skin now streaked with blood—my blood. I felt dizzy, shaking uncontrollably.

"Please spare me," I whispered to her, but like Yermoleth, she showed no empathy for my suffering.

She stepped back, and the old man swiftly approached with a handkerchief, which she used to clean her face. Her dress remained immaculate.

She left with uncertainty; desire still evident in her expression. Spinning on her heels, the hem of her dress swayed with her movement as she turned away, her breath coming in heavy gasps. I deeply feared she would turn back to bite me again. "This is enough for now," she whispered. "Thank you, my child, but I shall feast more in Romir.

"What to do with her?" asked the burned woman.

"Close her somewhere until he awakens. She wanted to take his life and is only right for him to decide."

I trembled, tears streaming down my face as I felt the warm blood trickle from my neck. I was pushed towards the wall as the roots retracted, revealing a small room, then was forced to sit on a hanging bed, its vines restraining me.

The indifferent stare of the burnt-faced girl was the last thing I saw before the doorframe was covered, plunging me into darkness.

Tempest of Hatred

Excerpt from Elena's journal, dated the twenty first day of the seventh month, Iureia, in the year six hundred twenty-three after the Conversion:

... Larion scuffed a spiteful laugh, but his lips remained shut. It was not long since he finally awakened, after seven days of continuous sleep. Radagrim, freshly arrived in the royal room, opened his mouth with a plash, then, at a closer inspection of my red-furious face, decided to hold the words for himself. Ser Roderick, the new captain of the city guard, stood motionless, clad in heavy armor of red, green, and white, the colors of the Grayfang house.

"Do you understand why I had to do this, at least?" I asked.

"There will be an investigation," responded my betrothed, pulling the blanket higher with a shudder. "Some will be removed from the palace guard, but I don't want any man to be executed. By the High Heavens! Did you really have to arrest Captain Dohert?"

"No more incompetents in positions of power, Larion! An armed man burst into the Great Hall, walked among dozens of guards, and shot the King. Tell me this doesn't smell like treason to you."

He sighed, turning his head to Roderick. "I'll discuss it with Dohert after the fever passes. Until then, I want him to be released. Have we found out where Oswin came from?"

"Not yet, my King," responded Roderick. "We've managed to narrow down the circle to somewhere in the northeastern part of the city, thanks to witness reports. His mind seemed clouded, as he was heard uttering all kinds of nonsense about the end of the world, like a doomsayer."

"The end of the world?" frowned Larion.

"According to the testimonies, he seemed to suggest that the king himself would be the one to bring the apocalypse. He was likely tortured, perhaps even subjected to magic, but we can never know for sure."

My betrothed let out a restrained chuckle, his eyes fixated on the cloudless sky visible through the window. He was troubled. So was I. I remembered Oswin's trembling lips forming the words *'he must die'* right before pressing the arbalest's trigger. What had he witnessed, what had he endured to come to such a conclusion?

"Radagrim, any tidings about the wizards?" asked Larion.

He inquired about the wizards who were supposed to arrive from the Circle. They were expected to be here yesterday.

"Nothing yet, my King. They were probably delayed on the road, but I'm sure they'll be here soon."

"Good. Roderick, you are dismissed. So are you, master."

Roderick made a deep bow and reached the door in only a few strides, then left without question. However, Radagrim did not move.

"Forgive me, Your Majesty, but there is something deeply troubling me," said the wizard.

"Then speak," urged Larion with a gentle tone.

"That witch, Merideth, has healed you…"

I hissed at him. "For your own sake, master Radagrim, I hope there comes no 'but'," I warned.

"She shouldn't have been able to do that. No matter how hard you train, it just should not be possible. Only a healer could do that, but last known healer died centuries ago."

"What do you want me to do?" asked Larion.

"We need to keep a close eye on her. If she had been able to do that, she could be really dangerous."

"That is good," I interjected. "We need more dangerous allies nowadays."

"She saved me, Radagrim," said Larion. "I will be forever in her debt. Leave her be, please."

"As you command," responded Radagrim, displeased with the King's answer.

"Now, let me rest."

Radagrim bowed, then left the room with his back a little slouched, like a beaten dog. I felt an outburst of fury and for a mere second, I almost yelled for him to come back and explain why he thinks Merideth should be punished for saving Larion. My betrothed placed his hand on mine.

"You had taken my uncle prisoner," he stated firmly, the weight of accusation heavy in his voice. It wasn't a question.

"Too many things could have gone wrong if I would have just let him leave. He could..." I trailed off, my mind racing with possibilities.

"He is not our enemy, my love. Darion is. I'm sure Wolf and Sparrow are wrong. I'm sure Aella still lives, and I would bet my life she is to blame for what Oswin did and for what happened to you."

"Still, I feared..."

"You held him closed in his room for seven days. I would be really, really mad if not for that cursed fever. You could have started a rebellion..."

"Not with Alfric as my prisoner," I interjected firmly.

"Heavens, Elena! Leave it like that. I'll fix the mess as soon as I'm better. The maids have told me you didn't leave my side at all while I slept. Thank you for that!"

I lay next to him, holding him close, and rested my head upon his warm chest. For seven days, I remained by his side, summoning Merideth intermittently to attend to him. Jane also stood vigil with me, her presence being a comforting constant. At times, she even had a bed brought in, so we could converse through the night. This morning, after Larion awakened, she had returned to her own chamber.

I must have dozed off, because the next thing I remember is the wizard-apprentice Lars, knocking on the door with such force that both Larion and I jolted awake.

"You better have a damn good reason to pound on the door like that!" I yelled.

"Come in," Larion invited.

The apprentice came in and curtsied quickly in front of our bed. He looked pale.

"Forgive me, my King! The wizards sent by the Circle arrived not long ago, but they were attacked on the road."

My numbness and tiredness faded. I sat up straight, feeling almost choked by the gravity of the tidings he brought. Larion observed the wizard with furrowed brows, remaining seated on his bed.

"By whom?" I asked.

"A lone witch. She blocked the path of the carts and attacked them."

"Her eyes?" Larion inquired.

"She had them covered."

"The Black Queen!" roared my betrothed. "Has Radagrim contacted Wolf and Sparrow?"

"He tried to reach them multiple times through the pal'ether, but no one responded. It's the first time this has happened."

"They're most likely dead," Larion said, his voice hollow. He stood up, clenching his teeth. "Burning Hells!"

"Where are the wizards?" I asked.

"Only three survived," said Erik. "Master Kain is awaiting with Radagrim in the throne room. He is the only one that could stand on his own."

"But they were all battle-wizards. How could a single witch…" I trailed off, too astonished and terrified to continue.

"I don't know, Princess Elena. Should I invite them here?"

"We'll come to them," Larion said, struggling to rise.

I bit my lip, resisting the urge to contradict the King's order in an uncalled-for manner.

"My love, may I suggest something?" I asked. After he nodded, I continued, "Your fever has still not passed. Let's invite them here. Traversing the entire palace to reach the throne room may worsen your condition."

The King attempted to speak, but he was choked by a cough. He nodded instead. "Call them here," Larion commanded.

After he left, Larion shook his head, his eyes filled with disdain as they navigated to the corner of the room. "I am losing my mind…" he murmured, absent-mindedly.

"You have been through a lot."

"No. I've been losing my mind since forever. Since before experiencing much of anything," he muttered, narrowing his eyes and swallowing hard. Rising slowly, he limped towards his wardrobe. "My mother told me to keep it hidden, not to talk about it. She feared people would think I'm insane. It wasn't difficult to pretend nothing was happening back then, since it occurred so rarely. But now... Heavens."

When he turned from the closet, his eyes were full of tears.

"Don't try to face this alone," I urged, wanting to go to him, but he gestured for me to wait there. "Whatever is happening, I want to know," I continued, my voice firm.

His entire body tensed. His chin trembled as he mumbled in a hushed voice, "I hear whispers."

When I've seen the canvas of fear and fury painted over his face, my heart urged me forward, drawing me to him. I pressed a gentle kiss upon his warm lips, but his visage remained unchanged.

"The first time it happened," he continued, "I was at the Temple with Mother and Darion. I couldn't have been more than eight years old. I wanted to ask Mother if we could leave earlier when I heard it, barely above a breath, yet so clear as if someone had spoken directly inside my head. 'Larion,' that was all it said. Mother had to forcefully pull me out of the Temple that day, because I believed that my desire to leave before the service's end had displeased Azerad. A few months later, it happened again, this time while I was preparing to sleep. After the third time, I told Mother and Father. They laughed it away, saying that I had an imaginary friend, but when I kept crying and insisting that something was talking to me, they made me promise I'd keep my mouth shut and not tell anyone about it."

"Have you told this to…" I was about to say Doctor Jared or maybe a priest—I don't know which one would be better suited for such a task. "Anyone?" I finished the sentence.

"Only to you and my parents."

As I assisted him in donning a more fitting attire, his voice grew increasingly hollow with each spoken word.

"After I brought that accursed demon in Romir, the one that took my brother, it began anew. It wasn't long before your arrival. I was in the Temple with Darion, deep in prayer, when I heard it: 'awaken me.' For the first time, the words were different, no longer echoing my name. And it continued, incessantly. It's only worsening. Just days ago, you asked why I kept telling you to talk before we go to sleep. It's because the whispers won't stop, and your soothing voice calms my mind." He shuddered and goosebumps formed on his skin. "Sometimes, it speaks in tongues unknown to me, lacking any recognizable feature of a language, only eerie whistles and guttural growls. But still, I understand. By the Heavens, I fear I'm truly losing my mind."

After the last words were spoken, the silence that remained felt grim and heavy. When the knocks pierced through the stillness, signaling the arrival of our guests, we found solace in each other's embrace, clinging tightly as if to ward off the unseen horrors, whispering words of comfort to one another.

"Come in!" commenced Larion after taking a seat on one of the chairs, lined up by the table.

As the door creaked open, Merideth entered, her delicate golden eyebrows arching in surprise. "Forgive my intrusion, were you awaiting someone?" inquired she.

"Yes," responded Larion. "But please, since you are here, maybe you can hear what they have to say."

Merideth nodded in approval and came forward with an elegance so refined that the folds of her crimson dress scarcely stirred. She settled into the chair beside Larion, clasping her hands together and resting her chin upon them.

"How is the fever?" she asked Larion, looking at him out of the corner of her eye, while her face was turned to me.

"Better, I think. Thank you again for saving my life and for being there for Elena."

"Your demise would have been an immeasurable catastrophe for all of us."

"I wouldn't phrase it quite so dramatically, but I suppose some people would have been saddened," Larion mused.

Another knock shattered the moment, and this time it was Radagrim who entered, accompanied by a tall, bald man with dark skin adorned with mysterious glyphs tattooed across his muscular arms, left bare by the unbuttoned white jerkin he wore. Following closely behind was Erik, and then Lord Alfric who swiftly shut the door behind him.

Merideth's gaze immediately fixated upon the man of color, her emerald eyes drawn inexorably to the bloody bandage that covered his torso, stark against the backdrop of his unfastened jerkin. Her mouth fell slightly agape, her eyes widening in shock. For a fleeting moment, I almost anticipated tears welling in her eyes. After a few rapid blinks, her expression settled into its customary serenity, betraying no hint of the turmoil that had briefly crossed her features.

Radagrim and Erik made a subtle reverence, while the dark-skinned man slowly sank to his knees, bowing so deep that his forehead touched the ground. Rising, still on his knees, he spoke, his voice carrying a weight of tradition and respect. "This is required when standing before a king in Rahanda, my motherland."

"You don't have to do this here, I can see you are wounded," said Larion with concern.

"Then please, let a wounded man keep his customs," the man chuckled, though his laughter bore a sharpness, like the crack of a whip against old leather. He seemed around fifty.

"As you wish. You can take a seat. I am King Larion Grayfang, this beauty here is Elena Tarrygold of Frevia and our dear friend Merideth."

Radagrim settled across the table, his gaze filled with concern as it rested on Merideth's face. Erik, seated beside him, also looking at the golden-haired witch, though his gaze betrayed a different sentiment from mere concern. When she met his stare, his face flushed pink instantaneously.

The other man rose too and took a seat next to Radagrim, opposite me. "Kain," the man presented himself.

"When I asked you to come to my room, it was because I did not expect the wounds to be so grave," said

Larion. "Erik, for Heaven's sake, please make sure not to omit such details next time."

"I've had worse cuts and still lived. You seem quite unwell yourself, King Larion," remarked Kain.

"I narrowly survived an assassination attempt," responded the King. "Probably plotted by the same woman that attacked you. Aella, the Black Queen."

"I can take a look at your wound," interjected Merideth, looking at Kain. "I know my way around healing magic."

"The last time I heard that, someone peed on my wound," the man laughed.

"I'd be willing to take the risk in your stead for such a bad wound," said Merideth, causing both the man and Larion to burst into laughter at the same time.

"She healed a mortal arrow wound that pierced a lung," said Radagrim, making the smile dissipate from that man's lips.

"I would gladly accept your help, my lady," declared he. This time, his words lacked their usual buoyancy, tinged instead with a hint of something new, something I interpreted as caution.

Merideth later confided in me that Kain had accepted her help only to verify if the waves of ether she would draw would resemble those made by the witch who had attacked them on the way. However, they were distinctly different. She explained to me that their fear was understandable, as her unique proficiency in healing spells was unusual among wizards. They assumed that if someone could heal such a wound, she must surely be a powerful ether-wielder.

"Incredible," exclaimed the man after unraveling his bindings, staring amazed at the place where the wound had been.

"I feel I could fall asleep any moment now," giggled Merideth, blinking rapidly. "Such waves are very demanding."

"You are incredibly skilled in your craft, my lady. The Circle would welcome you with open arms should you ever consider joining us. I'm confident the Council would even consider promoting you to the rank of master upon your acceptance."

"I politely decline."

"May I ask why?" Kain insisted.

"No, you may not."

Kain inclined his head, then looked again at his healed wound. "Could you take a look at our friends as well?" he asked. "They're in an even worse state than I was."

"I could, but not anytime soon. I'm still exhausted from healing the king, and now I'm completely depleted. I won't be able to assist in that capacity in the near future, and by the time I'm able to, I doubt it will still be necessary."

The man exchanged a quick glance with Radagrim, then his black eyes drafted to Larion. "Very well, then. I shall proceed with the chain of events that transpired on the previous night."

Larion adjusted to a more comfortable position at the table, while Merideth rested her forehead in her palm, eyes closed.

"As Romir appeared on the horizon, the carts that carried us stopped abruptly. I was in the first one and could clearly see a woman standing in the middle of the road. Her hair and face were obscured by a triangle-shaped hood, and a horned, golden mask, but I could sense her connection to the Great River. Her magical signature was unmistakable. Even my cousin Fyria sensed her and laughed. 'I*f she's planning to rob someone, she's picked the wrong targets,*' she said. I drew in the ether around me and conjured a fireball, hoping she would turn back upon realizing she had to face wizards. And not just any wizards."

The man flinched, shifting his gaze from Merideth to me. With a deep inhalation, he uttered a prayer under his breath, the words barely audible, before gathering himself to continue.

"Then all the ether vanished. Only small and feeble traces remained, floating in the air. That woman, that... thing, devoured all the magic. All the ether around us perished. It goes without saying that this should not be possible. Not even all ten of us, using powerful artifacts, could have achieved something similar. The ether began to flow back into the void she created, but before we could even utilize what was left, she attacked. She summoned a tempest of fire; a whirlwind that spun and burned everything in its path: grass, wood, flesh. We attempted to raise shields around us and flee into the forest, but only three of us managed to escape. The demon chased us for a while, but eventually gave up, assuming we would succumb to our wounds. Which nearly happened. Our luck came in the form of a fisherman who rode to Romir and brought help as soon as he discovered us."

"Her eyes?" Larion inquired.

"I couldn't see them, obscured by the corner of her hood," came the reply.

"Are you certain her horns were part of the mask and not her own?" queried my betrothed.

"Yes."

"How can you be certain? You mentioned it was nighttime."

"I am, my King."

"My King, forgive me, but I think the Black Queen may not be to blame." The one that said the last words was Erik. "I was there, in the Night of the Blood Moon and however strange this may sound, I haven't seen her sip from the ether at all. I haven't even seen any magical signature around her."

"Are you implying that she doesn't use the Great River for magic?" Kain asked.

"No, forgive me, it's just..."

"Boy," the wizard interrupted. "I wasn't scolding you before, but now I am. Speak your mind without fear."

"Yes, Master Kain. She didn't seem to have used the Great River. I was with her from the moment of her arrest. I was there during her torture to confess her alleged crime, throughout the trial, and even during the massacre. She never took a sip from the Great River, I can assure you of that. And it's impossible to hold the ether in for an entire day, especially considering the beatings she endured. Furthermore, she managed to snap the suppression bindings around her wrists while still shackled."

"That shouldn't be possible," Kain scowled.

"I was there too," Larion interjected. "And I distinctly recall witnessing the chain of her handcuffs shatter."

"Perhaps there was another ether-wielder concealed nearby," said Kain. "Or perhaps... perhaps the runes were incorrectly inscribed on the bracelets. There is only one source of magic."

"The runes were accurate," Radagrim affirmed. "They were retrieved, and I personally verified them not long ago, entertaining the same notion you have now."

"But it's entirely plausible that another witch was present," Larion suggested. "I recall a witness report from a noble who followed the crowd to the execution site. He observed from a distance, but recalled seeing a redheaded woman, loosing an arrow into the mist before departing. Perhaps she was an ally of Aella."

"Maybe..." Erik began, but I slammed both hands onto the table, drawing all gazes towards me.

"We're veering off topic here. A murderous witch has single-handedly bested ten wizards who were supposed to be trained in battle magic, and she's still out there, free. At this very moment, it matters less who she is—whether she's the Black Queen returned from death or someone entirely new—and more about how we fight her. She's already killed seven wizards, and having a solid defense is our best plan of action right now."

"You're right, my love," Larion conceded, visibly exhausted.

"The Circle has been informed, and we're currently on high alert. More wizards will join us. This will be the largest action our organization has ever undertaken," Radagrim explained.

"We are in direct war with that woman, and we should hold back nothing," I declared.

"Good," Larion responded, blinking rapidly.

"I think you should rest now," I suggested, gently placing my hand on his warm forearm.

Larion shoved my hand aside, then rose, slowly walking at the window. Merideth followed closely. "Radagrim, please inform the new captain of the guards, whoever he may be, that I want the palace to be brimming with archers and arbalests," he said. "Leave no corner unguarded. Lord Alfric, could you please summon all the lords to the Great Hall tomorrow morning? If my fever does not pass, you will be my regent."

Alfric's eyes lingered on my face for a moment before nodding in acknowledgment. Except for Merideth, they all departed. She checked on Larion, then returned to the window, gazing into the distance.

"Curse you, storm," I heard her whisper, barely above a thought, as she watched the ominous black shapes of the clouds looming in the distance.

"A storm is coming," I remarked, stopping beside her.

"And it's going to hit us full force," she added, lost in contemplation.

I was certain that despite what Larion believed, Aella was not to blame. Not this time. In this accursed city, a far greater evil lurked.

Only bad things will follow; of this, I'm sure.

The Way Ahead

Aella leaned her back against the dead trunk of a tree, slowly raising her head to peer through the gray branches of the silent, lifeless forest. The moon, resembling a round shield perfectly sliced in half, cast scant light, but Aella watched it nonetheless, letting out a gasp. She was in her human form now, the large cloak from Yermoleth draped around her like a blanket.

"Everything is dead here," remarked Arya, collapsing next to Aella.

"Except you," Aella smiled.

"How much longer until we leave this cursed forest?" Arya asked with frustration.

"Last time when I journeyed to Rhal'Ellieh, it was with Erik Grayfang's army, and we took a direct path through the fields, not through these swamps and forests. If I were to guess, I'd say seven more days."

"I could transform, and we could fly across it."

"Too dangerous," Aella responded. "The Enemy's eyes are everywhere. They wouldn't miss a dragon flying so close to the city."

"We're not even close to it. It'll take one week, Aella, maybe two. I could take us there in one night," Arya insisted.

"I said no. Do you remember the plan?"

Arya nodded reluctantly.

"Tell me," Aella pressed.

The drakar rolled her eyes, clearly annoyed by Aella's repeated questioning. "We sneak in. I take the key and fly away with it. You'll sip from the Great River and unleash destruction upon the enemies before they get the chance to follow me," Arya recited, irritation evident in her voice.

"No," I whispered, kneeling beside her. She planned to sacrifice herself to release her sisters. High Heavens, I must stop that.

I reached out my hand toward her cheek, but the fingers passed right through it as if I was made of gas. Her shining eyes met mine for a brief moment before returning to the sky.

"I need to leave," I said to her with great difficulty, knowing she couldn't hear or see me. It was as if I was looking at a memory. "I think I may still be alive; I think Yermoleth healed me. I need to... reach Rhal'Ellieh before you do. I am so tired."

I gazed at her one last time, attempting to plant a kiss on her forehead, but my lips passed right through. I couldn't touch her. Reaching out, I grasped a knife that materialized from thin air. Though I'd never done this before, the process felt instinctive. It seemed I was growing more adept at dream walking. Slowly, I pressed the knife's tip into my palm until the pain jolted me awake.

I was right. I was in Yermoleth's home, under the Yerdrasil. Alive yet again. Under the scarce light of the white flowers covering the walls, I could see a small red dot on my palm, next to a big scar crossing almost perpendicular over the scar made by the shield handle. That big scar was probably made by Sparrow. That woman fought like a demon; I had never witnessed such skill and fluency in combat. I couldn't help but smile, recalling the teachings of Master Anduin, my sword trainer from Romir. If only she had kept her mind clear, she could have easily killed me.

I rose, my numb body protesting with every movement. Stumbling towards the wall, I watched as the roots retracted, clearing a path before me. "I need to find

Yermoleth," I whispered to myself, stepping through the doorway.

"You are finally awake," remarked a woman seated at the head of the table, leafing through a book. "Aisha Fire-Kissed, go bring the nartingal."

Another young girl, whom I had missed at first, rose and turned to leave. She carried a short spear in her right hand and a long-bladed knife scabbarded at her back. There was one more man in the room, clad in worn-out steel armor.

"I am Darion," I presented myself, feeling for my sword that wasn't there.

"We have already meet," the woman said, "but I did not tell you my name. I am Ezereen."

"Strange. I don't remember seeing you before, and I have a very good memory for faces."

Then I noticed her eyes—glassy red. It was impossible to miss the visible outline of a tattoo through the neckline of her white dress, positioned right between her small, round breasts. She was the dhampir who caught me when I fell.

I stiffly turned my head to the armored old man, but he remained immobile, like a statue. His eyes bore down heavily on me, his steel-clad arm resting on the head of a mace poised next to his sword.

The woman giggled, her laughter flowing like a gentle breeze through the room. "I have a feeling that you remember me now," she said, clearly amused by my tense body.

"Thank you for saving my life."

"You are most welcome, but please, try not to squander it. One of my men perished in that forest, a wizard; consumed by the flames from the black dragon your lover is likely pursuing."

So that was the corpse Aella found and assumed to be mine. I fixed my gaze upon the old man in worn armor. "Are you also a dhampir?"

No response. It was almost like he had no life behind those eyes.

"He is not," replied Ezereen.

"How did you arrive here so swiftly from Shartat? I assume you flew, but what about the ones accompanying you?"

"Galarr and Aisha weren't anywhere near Shartat with me. My warriors and I were on the opposite side of Redat, where we parted ways with a plan to regroup in Derahia. We were tracking something far more perilous than that dragon. However, our intelligence was flawed, and our target has been hiding in Frevia for quite some time; now it's in Romir."

"What precisely are you pursuing?" I asked, feeling my stomach twisting with concern, because I already knew the answer.

"Her name is Aveloth. The last of the Immortals still active."

I was almost certain. I couldn't shake off Yermoleth's words. He said that Aveloth may still be alive and that she is constantly pursued by a tamed screamer. A screamer was just another name for a dhampir.

"Big prey. I hope you succeed." As that dream where I've seen the blonde woman, along with Queen Lenore and Aethelred came back in my mind, I said, "I am pretty sure your informants are right this time."

Our conversation was interrupted by the sound of retracting roots. Yermoleth entered, his bare feet barely making a sound as they brushed against the grassy rug, with Aisha following closely behind. The young woman, her face marked by burns, appeared to be one of the

Arkals—desert people residing in the vast expanse of sand that served as a barrier between Verdavir and the rest of the continent.

The nartingal halted, turning his head towards the armored warrior, then exhaled sharply, his feral ears slowly lowering.

"The sun is sleeping now; you may soon take your leave," he mumbled. "The hatred you bring into this tree is undesired and unnecessary."

"Hatred is what we hunt; the Demon of Hatred herself," Ezereen replied in a sweet tone. "You know her story, don't you? Of course you do. Just like me, you collect tales of old. Unlike me, you do it for the sake of knowledge, not revenge or anything else—anything interesting. 'Hers is the Hatred.' I have faced that hatred many times, and I will either extinguish it or be extinguished by it."

He sighed, clearing his throat. "I know the story of Avelanora. I feel your heart and you seem to be following in her tracks. What was I expecting? It is in your nature, after all. Zarya may have freed you from the influence of your creators, but your nature would never change. The unfavorable surroundings are forcing me, however, to approve this ungodly alliance for the sake of the Creation."

She smirked. "This is not the first ungodly alliance you're making, is it?"

Another set of roots retracted somewhere on my left, revealing a new dark room from where Saya emerged with small steps and eyes widened in fear. I couldn't hide my astonishment, as I was more than certain she either fled or met her end somewhere in the mountains. The left side of her neck was red with dried blood.

"Pick a seat," Yermoleth urged her. "We must decide your fate, along with our course of action."

She nodded and approached, briefly glancing at the book Ezereen was holding. The dhampir closed it with a snap and placed it on the table, pushing it towards her. She snatched it with a sudden movement, then stepped back, her head swiveling from side to side as she alternated her gaze between me and Ezereen. Perhaps she was counting the seats, because she chose one three seats away from me and four from her. It seemed she feared her the most.

I turned to the dhampir lady, recalling the words she said before Saya came.

"If you kill Aveloth, wouldn't she just return if the First Gods will be unleashed again."

Saya flinched, her eyes falling gravely on me. It seems she gained some knowledge since the Battle Near Blackstone, for back then she did not know what the First Gods were.

"When, not if," corrected Ezereen. She rose from her chair, slowly bending her back and gripping the hem of her dress. With a steady pull, she revealed her right leg, exposing it up to almost her buttock. There, above her knee, was a dagger sheathed in a black sheath, secured to her thigh with two leather belts. "She won't return if I kill her with this."

Yermoleth turned to me. "That is…"

"Ameterium dagger," I finished, almost laughing at his confused expression. I remembered Arya mentioning that Yermoleth was supposed to give me one of my own, but for some reason he did not.

"I have one for you," said Yermoleth.

"I know that," I said blankly. "But there is something I don't know. Are we allies?"

He frowned, while Ezereen smiled, placing both hands on the table and leaning forward to better observe Yermoleth's expression.

"I saved your life," he said.

"I wonder why. You sent me to Saherdrakar knowing that the dragons could sense my blood and yet, you decided not to warn me. So, what is it, nartingal, are you friend or foe?"

He pondered for a few moments. Behind his back, Aisha slowly lowered the iron tip of her spear, aiming it at his back. I noticed she was seeking confirmation from Ezereen. I shook my head at the dhampir, shooting a warning gaze meant to convey that if Aisha attacked Yermoleth, I would have to intervene. Not because he was my friend—I barely cared if he lived or died—but because I needed his help.

"It was a misjudgment on my side, forgive me," came his excuse.

"Fine."

He moved a few more steps, seating himself at the opposite end of the table, lost in thought. I considered him a weak man, always prattling on about his feelings and the beauty of nature, subsisting solely on grass. It was difficult to see someone like him as a threat. But the truth was, he was ridiculously powerful. If Ezereen had given the order, Aisha would have been dead, followed soon by the old man, and ultimately the dhampir. Despite his frail appearance, he was a seasoned warrior with over seven thousand years of experience honing his senses. Unfortunately, his love for Khyalis made it difficult for him to pick a side.

Aisha remained standing close to him. I prayed to keep her spear to herself, for I was not looking forward to face the man in steel armor, and even less a dhampir.

"I need your help," I told him.

"I can only provide guidance. You are trying to reach Rhal'Ellieh, is that right?"

I nodded. "I hoped you could accompany me."

"I cannot. I am required…"

"Spare me!" I snapped at him. "Damn your reasons, I don't give a rotten apple about them. If you cannot, don't waste my time with meaningless excuses and better give me a map, or some instructions!"

"I will give you a guide and, as you demanded, instructions."

His voice was maddeningly slow, pronouncing every word with such leisure as if I had all eternity to wait for him to finish the sentence.

"What about you?" I asked Ezereen. "Could you spare some of your fighters?"

"They all will receive the last kiss when I decide it is time. But if by spare you meant to send them with you, then I cannot."

I sighed and remained silent.

"You can take the witch with you," suggested Yermoleth.

When I turned to Saya, she was pale, swallowing hard as our eyes met. Her fingers trembled as she clutched the book she had taken from Ezereen to her chest.

"For what?" I asked hurriedly. "Spare food?"

Saya gasped in terror, tears welling up in her eyes. Unbeknownst to me, Aisha had brought her there as food for Ezereen, and the blood on her neck was from the dhampir's bite. Now, the poor girl likely believed we were a cult of cannibals.

"You may need spare food for later," joked Yermoleth. "Or you may need some bait to lure away the creatures that lurks in the lands you'll have to traverse."

She was trembling.

"She will stab me in my sleep," I said.

Yermoleth raised his shoulders in a shrug. "Then, Ezereen, you may do whatever you please with her," he said with indifference.

"I don't even know how to hold a knife," she burst out with pleading eyes. "Please take me with you!"

I hesitated. Ezereen's red eyes were already piercing Saya's neck like a rapier, while Saya's brown eyes seemed to pierce my soul. She looked at me like a caged animal, imploring me not to leave her in the dhampir's grasp.

"It's not my problem," I said to Ezereen. "You can do whatever you want with her; I don't care."

Saya closed her eyes tightly as Ezereen shrugged.

"Not in my home," cautioned Yermoleth. "Ask your servants to take her out if you're hungry."

Seeing the witch struggle to maintain her composure as she awaited her fate, something shifted within me. Despite my initial decision, I found myself wavering.

The dhampir opened her mouth to reply, but I cut her off. "Burning Hells! Fine, damn it, fine!" I observed the handcuffs lying on the table, adorned with suppressive runes. They were likely procured by Yermoleth from Saya's belongings, or from the assassins. "But you will wear these," I growled, sliding the handcuffs across the table towards her.

She nodded spasmodically, her hands trembling as she hastily clasped the iron bracelets around her wrists. Then, extending her arm towards me, she displayed the securely fastened cuffs, confirming their restraint. I could understand her palpable fear as she had to choose between to travel with the man that killed her masters, rumored to be the most feared assassins of the Circle, and facing death on the spot.

"Before hurrying to join me, hear first where we are heading, for you may choose death instead. I take it you have already heard about the First Gods, haven't you?"

She approved in silence.

"Good. I hope you know enough to make a choice, because we are heading towards one of their cities, to steal a key from a corrupted dragon."

Her reaction was minimal, her expression shifting imperceptibly from a faint scowl. I could barely believe my own words, and I harbored no expectations for her to do so.

"And you need to hurry. Aella left alone, am I right?" asked the nartingal. This time, Saya shuddered, for she believed Aella to be dead.

"With Arya. She thought I was killed by Beithir, because she saw the burnt body of your wizard and assumed it was mine."

"Unfortunate," commented Ezereen.

"Can I get there before she?"

"It depends on how far she is already," said Yermoleth.

"Around ten days to reach the city," silently hoping the question of my knowledge would remain unasked. I felt like time was a luxury I couldn't afford to squander. "They didn't want to fly directly there out of fear that the enemy would spot them and mount a defense."

"Smart," Yermoleth said. "Then you may get there just in time. There is a shortcut, one that, instead of waving around the mountains, cuts directly underneath them, emerging on the other side."

"What is the catch?" I asked.

"The catch?"

"It sounds too good; there must be a catch."

"It is far more dangerous than if you take the longer route, that is for sure. You may be burned, crushed, eaten alive, get forever lost in the darkness; and this only if you are lucky enough."

I started to laugh, and he offered a brief smile.

"Are you lucky Saya?" I asked. She shook her head with a faint movement. "Me neither. So, we don't have to worry about that. Tell me, what awaits down there."

The door to the outside opened, and a large bird flew in, resting in the middle of the table. A peregrine falcon, I noticed quickly.

"This will be your guide. He will lead you to the entrance in the tunnels and await you on the other side. If you arrive at the door during the day, wait there until nightfall. Don't try to burst your way in; the inhabitants would not be happy. They will come to check on you after the sun sets, maybe even try to scare you away. Tell them that I sent you and that you require passage."

"These inhabitants…" I started.

"Trolls."

"Great!" I sarcastically exclaimed.

"These are the remnants of those who declined the Gift. Possibly the last of their species, as I am of mine."

I glanced at the falcon again, noting how it seemed to study me with its sharp, black eyes. As I extended my hand, the bird gave a graceful flick of its wings, effortlessly hopping to land atop Saya's head. She let out a startled cry, instinctively ducking, but didn't make any move to shoo the bird away.

"How should we call it" I asked.

"*Him*," corrected Yermoleth. "His name is unpronounceable for our throats and tongues, but he responds to Verti." I rose from the table. "I packed your backpacks with supplies," added Yermoleth.

"Backpacks?" I queried. "Were you aware I would be taking her with me?"

"I made an educated guess."

"Based on what?"

No response came. With a subtle tilt of his head, he gestured towards the satchels resting against the wall, their surfaces obscured by tangled roots. Positioned nearby were the Heart of Dawn, Merwin's silver dagger, my bow and arrows, and another knife sheathed in black, reminiscent to the one carried by Ezereen—the ameterium blade.

"That dagger?" I asked.

"It is bound to an ancient prophecy. That will be the weapon that will… pierce Khyalis's heart, and you must be the one to wield it."

"Even if I don't believe in your prophecies, I won't say no to a weapon. But is it wise to give it to me, now that I'm ready to embark on a suicidal quest?"

He pondered, his orange eyes flickering. "I have my reasons."

"*Your* reasons?" Ezereen asked with a wide smile, stretching out the word '*your*' as if savoring it.

"Yes."

I asked, "What would those reasons be?"

"Private, for now. But you will find out when the time is right."

"The time is never right," I whispered.

I gestured for Saya to come and grab her backpack, because the time has come for our departure. She complied, but moved with extreme caution, wary of the falcon's sharp talons perched upon her head. I had to carefully untie the straps of her backpack and then secure them around her arms, as her hands were bound together with the handcuffs adorned with suppression runes.

That damn falcon remained unfazed. Despite my attempts to shoo it away, it remained steadfast as a tree. However, it finally flew away as we reached outside, allowing the witch to relax her tensed posture. It appeared to wait for us nearby, perched on a shadow-covered branch.

That night was exceptionally cold. I recall the distant howls of wolves echoing through the air, followed by the gentle hoot of an owl.

"Can we first burry my masters?" asked Saya.

"No," I responded.

"Please, they would have done the same for you. They had profound respect for the deceased," she insisted with a fear-filled voice.

"They should have had respect for the living. Now, let's move!"

Her breath caught in a staggered gasp. I did not like that I had to take her with me, but I took pity on her. Releasing her was not an option; her knowledge of my existence was a risk I couldn't take, especially after the near-fatal consequences of her previous escape. Thus, the only viable path was to bring her along… or to kill her. Perhaps that decision, like so many others I had made throughout my life, wasn't truly mine at all, but was driven by the destiny I was meant to fulfill, by the fate that held me captive.

"I will bury them," promised Yermoleth. "I won't leave unburied bodies to rot on my mountain, don't worry."

"Thank you."

Ezereen and her companions were there too, watching the glow of the crescent moon filter through the pine trees.

"Do you feel it?" she asked.

I listened for a few seconds before replying, "I feel nothing."

"It's the nature," Yermoleth interjected. "It feels different. The air seems rotted and heavy, the wind carries a sense of something new. New for this age, however, for it is ancient by nature. Even the moonlight seems sick. There may not be much time remaining."

"*Time remaining for what?*" I wanted to ask, but I feared I already knew the answer. For the Last Sunset to come.

Ezereen nodded with gravity, then turned at me. "Then we'd better begin our journeys. Let the hunt begin. Safe travels, Darion!"

"Good hunting!" I responded.

I could still feel Yermoleth's gaze on us long after we departed. Ezereen and her companions headed south, while Saya and I followed Verti's lead along the northern paths.

The Flame-Stone received from the blue dragon proved to be a valuable gift, for we walked many hours with our path illuminated by it. The clans didn't venture near the Demon's Fang, so there was no need to worry about the light attracting them.

Saya remained completely silent. She asked nothing, although her face told me she had many questions. It didn't bother me. A part of me was glad that she was there, for I desired silence, not solitude. Sometimes, silence can be a medicine, as solitude can be a poison.

We stopped a few hours before dawn. That morning was chilly too; I can remember that well because Saya was completely covered in her cloak, like a caterpillar in its cocoon, with Verti resting on her head.

"Why does *he* keep landing on my head?" she asked under her breath.

I shrugged. I almost considered that her hay of brown curly hair was the reason, but never voiced that to her. Probably it was vaguely reminiscent of its nest. If I would see something that looked to some extent as a house, of course I will sleep there rather than in the forest.

She stood a short distance from me, her back pressed against a tree. Morning would soon arrive, and we needed to resume our journey. Time was not on my side. I had to remain vigilant around Saya, sleeping with one eye open. The key to her handcuffs was tucked away in my inner pocket, and I feared that given the chance, she might attempt to kill me and take it.

Before reaching Bragovik, I had a vision of Aella and me standing atop a black pyramid that towered above the clouds—most likely Rhal'Ellieh. When I shared the vision with Aella, she assured me, saying we needn't worry, as we would never end up in such a place. No one with a sane mind would.

I stifled a laugh at the mere memory.
Who could afford sanity in such times?

THE END OF THE SECOND BOOK

Closing notes:

Weary traveler, I'm glad to see that you have reached the end of this part, but rest assured, the journey ahead is far from over. For now, you may rest, but don't get too comfortable in your warm bed, for adventure still beckons.

With this, the second part of **The Song of the Last Sunset** concludes. The third part of this story is already in progress, as is the first book from **The Dawn of the Immortals**, a prequel to the current series.

Thank you for being here. Until next time, stay safe!

From

The Song of the Last Sunset

series

Now available:

The Black Queen

The Mountain of Dragons

Coming next:

Daughters of the Night

War of the Lions

…and others

Made in the USA
Columbia, SC
29 October 2024

43658118R00305